Legacy of the Jedi

SECRETS OF THE JEDI

Legacy of the Jedi

SECRETS OF THE JEDI

JUDE WATSON

SCHOLASTIC INC.

New York   Toronto   London   Auckland   Sydney
Mexico City   New Delhi   Hong Kong   Buenos Aires

www.starwars.com
www.scholastic.com

No part of this publication may be reproduced, stored in a retrieval system, or transmitted in any form or by any means, electronic, mechanical, photocopying, recording, or otherwise, without written permission of the publisher. For information regarding permission, write to Scholastic Inc., Attention: Permissions Department, 557 Broadway, New York, NY 10012.

Legacy of the Jedi, ISBN 0-439-53666-9, Copyright © 2003 Lucasfilm Ltd. & ™.
Secrets of the Jedi, ISBN 0-439-53667-7, Copyright © 2005 Lucasfilm Ltd. & ™.
"The Last One Standing" Copyright © 2006 Lucasfilm Ltd. & ™.

All Rights Reserved. Used Under Authorization. Published by Scholastic Inc. SCHOLASTIC and associated logos are trademarks and/or registered trademarks of Scholastic Inc.

12 11 10 9 8 7 6 5 4 3 2 1   6 7 8 9 10/0

0-439-85146-7

Printed in the U.S.A.
First printing, May 2006

Contents

Legacy of the Jedi

SECRETS OF THE JEDI

Legacy of the Jedi

JUDE WATSON

The corridor was empty. The two thirteen-year-old boys paused outside the closed door. There were locks at the Jedi Temple, but they were rarely used. There was no need. There was nothing to hide. Nothing was forbidden. The Jedi's code of honor gave each individual the challenge and privilege of walking the Jedi path. It was assumed that the discipline needed for this would also prevail in one's private life.

So to enter another Jedi's room without an invitation would not violate a rule. Not one that needed to be spoken or written, at least. Yet Dooku knew it was wrong. It wasn't *terribly* wrong. But it was wrong.

"Come on," Lorian said. "No one will find out."

Dooku glanced at his friend. Lorian's face was eager. A dusting of freckles scattered across his blunt nose like a dense constellation of stars. His eyes were warm, lit with mischief, a dark piney green with amber lights, like a forest shot with sunlight. Lorian had been suggesting schemes since they were seven, and he'd talked Dooku into exploring the garbage tunnels. The experience had left Dooku with a reeking tunic and a healthy respect for sanitation practices.

"Besides, he's your Master," Lorian said. "He wouldn't mind."

It was true that Thame Cerulian was Dooku's Master. The renowned Jedi Knight had chosen him last week. Dooku had just turned thirteen, and he was relieved that he wouldn't have to wait any longer to become a Padawan Learner. Yet he had not had time to get to know Thame at all. Thame was in the Outer Rim completing one last mission before taking on a Padawan. Dooku was proud to have been chosen by such a legend.

The question was, could he live up to that legend?

Dooku had to. Getting a peek into Thame's personal quarters might give him a head start.

He nodded at Lorian and accessed the door. It slid open silently. He stepped inside. If he expected a clue to his new Master's inner character, he was disappointed. The sleep couch was narrow, pushed against one wall. A gray coverlet was folded neatly at the bottom. A data-screen sat on a bare table. No laserprints or holograms hung on the wall. No personal items were on the desk or the small table beside the sleep couch. There was a glass carafe with a small glass stopper. The transparent vessel and the gray blanket were the only signs that someone actually inhabited the room.

"Wait," Lorian said. "I found something."

He slid his hands along a seam in the wall that was

almost invisible. He pressed a recessed button and the wall slid back to reveal shelves over the desk. They were filled with holobooks.

Dooku bent to examine the titles. Thame, he knew, was a historian, an expert in Jedi history. He had never seen most of these titles before. Galactic history, biographies, the natural sciences of different atmospheres and planetary systems. It was an impressive library.

Lorian dismissed them with a glance. "You'd think he'd have had enough of studies after Temple training. I can't wait to get out into the galaxy and do things."

Dooku reached for a holobook with no title or author. He flipped it open and scanned a page.

Meditation beforehand is necessary in order to ready the mind. Some suffer from nausea or dizziness at first viewing. But primarily one must prepare for the effect of the dark side upon the mind, especially the young or weak. Nightmares and dark visions can result, lasting years. . . .

"This is a manual about the Sith Holocron," Dooku said, his voice a whisper now. He handled the holobook carefully.

"The Sith Holocron? But no one can view it," Lorian said.

"That's not so. Jedi Masters are allowed. Not many are interested. Most Jedi Knights think the Sith are extinct and will never return. Except for my Master." Dooku gazed at the book. His stomach twisted, as though he'd gazed upon the Sith Holocron itself. "He believes there will come a time when the Jedi will have to fight the Sith again."

"Does this manual tell you how to access the Holocron?" Lorian asked, interested now.

Dooku flipped through it, his heart beating. "Yes. It gives warnings and instructions."

"This is so galactic," Lorian murmured. "With the help of this handbook, we could access the Sith Holocron ourselves!" He looked at Dooku, his eyes shining. "We'd be the first Jedi Padawans to do it!"

"We can't!" Dooku said, shocked at the suggestion.

"Why not?" Lorian asked.

"Because it's forbidden. Because it's dangerous. Because we don't know enough. Because of a million reasons, all of them good ones."

"But no one would know," Lorian said. "You could do it, Dooku. You have a better Force connection than any Padawan. Everyone knows that. And with the help of the holobook, you'd succeed."

Dooku shook his head. He put the holobook back on the shelf.

"It would be amazing," Lorian said. "You could find out Sith secrets. If you really knew the dark side, you'd be a better Jedi Knight. Yoda says that we can't fight evil without understanding it."

"Yoda never said that."

"Well, it sounds like something he'd say," Lorian protested. "And it's true. Isn't that what Temple training is all about? All we do is study so we can be prepared. How can we prepare to meet evil if we don't understand it?"

That was the trouble with Lorian, Dooku thought. He had a way of putting things that made sense, even when he was asking you to break the rules.

He looked over at the holobook again. It *was* tempting. And Lorian had put his finger on Dooku's secret wish — to be the best Padawan ever. He wanted to impress his new Master. Could the Sith Holocron be the key to his wish?

"We'll only take a quick look," Lorian said. "Just think, Dooku. The Jedi are the most powerful group in the galaxy. We could be the best of the best."

"A true Jedi does not think in terms of power," Dooku said disapprovingly. "We are peacekeepers."

"Peacekeepers need power, just like everybody else," Lorian pointed out. "If they don't have it, who will listen?"

Lorian was right, even though he wasn't expressing himself in what would be considered a true Jedi way. The Jedi *did* have power. Jedi did not use that word, but it fit. Lorian knew that, and he wasn't afraid to say it. Jedi were renowned throughout the galaxy. They weren't feared, but they were respected. They were asked by governments, by Senators, for their help. If that wasn't power, what was?

The best of the best. Wasn't that what he wanted?

"Thame is a great Knight," Lorian continued. "I'd think you'd want to be worthy of him. If I had a Master, I'd prepare as much as I could before we left the Temple. I wouldn't want to disappoint him."

"I won't disappoint him if I do my best," Dooku said. "That is all I can do."

Lorian threw himself back on Thame's sleep couch with a groan. "Now *you* sound like Yoda."

"Don't sit there!" Dooku hissed, but Lorian ignored him.

Lorian stared at the ceiling. "No one has chosen me."

Dooku held his breath. Here it was, the big thing between them. He had been chosen by a Jedi Knight, and Lorian had not. Dooku had been one of the first to be chosen. Every day afterward, the two boys had waited for a Jedi Knight to choose Lorian. They knew that many had watched him, and some had considered him seriously. Yet each time, the Knight had chosen someone else. Neither Dooku nor Lorian knew why. Dooku had always been ahead of Lorian in battle skills and Force connection, but Lorian was just as brilliant in his studies and commitment. It was unthinkable that Lorian would not be chosen eventually.

"It will happen," Dooku said. "Patience exists to be tested."

Lorian flipped over on his side and gave Dooku a flat stare. "Right."

Dooku wished he could take back his words. They were so . . . correct. They were something a Jedi Master might say, not a best friend. But the truth was that he didn't know what to say. The period of waiting was hard, but everything would turn out all right.

Lorian coiled his body into a ball and then shot off the bed. "Okay, make a decision. Do we access the Sith Holocron or not?"

Dooku reached over to straighten the wrinkles Lorian had made on his new Master's bed. Thame was everything he'd hoped to get as a Master. He couldn't jeopardize that. Not even for his best friend.

"Not," he said. "We'd get in serious trouble if we got caught."

"You never worried about getting caught before," Lorian said.

That's because I never had so much to lose. But Dooku couldn't say that. If he did, it would only point out that Lorian didn't have a Master.

Dooku felt Lorian's eyes on his back as he bent to smooth the coverlet at the end of Thame's sleep couch.

"If you could do it without the risk of getting caught, you would do it," Lorian said. "So the fact that it's wrong isn't really the reason you won't. Maybe you're not the true Jedi you think you are."

He sauntered out the door. "Just wanted you to know that I noticed."

Now that Dooku was through with his official Temple training, he was allowed to structure his days himself. Although he was expected to continue to study and devote himself to battle training and physical discipline, it was also expected that he would allot the time for activities he enjoyed. In the brief period between a Padawan's last official classes and becoming an apprentice, the Jedi Masters indulged their students and gave them freedom to roam.

Dooku woke early. His conversation with Lorian the day before still troubled him. He decided to head to the Room of the Thousand Fountains to stroll among the greenery and let the music of the water calm his mind. It felt luxurious to be able to decide how to spend his time. He knew such days would be over soon, and he intended to enjoy every second of them. He wouldn't allow a small disagreement with his friend to ruin them, either.

He stepped out into the hallway and immediately noticed a change. Dooku sometimes wasn't sure whether the Force or his intuition was working — he wasn't that experienced yet. But he knew that the atmosphere in the

Temple had changed. There was a humming current underneath the calm, an agitation he could pick up easily.

Ahead of him, a few students stood in a cluster. Dooku approached them. He recognized Hran Beling, a fellow student his age. Hran was a Vicon, a small species only one meter tall.

He didn't have to ask the students what they were discussing. Hran looked up at him, his long nose twitching. "Have you heard the news? The Sith Holocron has been stolen!"

Dooku was naturally pale, but he felt his blood drain from his face, and he was sure he looked as white as a medic's gown. "What? How?"

"No one knows how," Hran said. "There could be an intruder at the Temple."

One of the younger students lowered his voice to a whisper. "What if it's a Sith?"

Hran's eyes twinkled. "Yes, what if it is?" he asked solemnly. "He could be walking the halls. He could be anywhere. What if he's behind you right now?" Hran gasped and pointed behind the young student, who jumped in alarm, his Padawan braid flying.

The others burst into nervous laughter. Dooku didn't join them. His heart thumping, he turned away.

There had been no intruder. He was sure of it.

Dooku hurried to Lorian's quarters. The privacy light was on over Lorian's door, but he accessed it anyway. The door was locked.

Dooku pressed his mouth against the seam of the door. "Let me in, Lorian."

There was no answer.

"Let me in or I'll go straight to the Jedi Council room," Dooku threatened.

He heard the smooth click as the lock disengaged, and the door slid open. The room was dark, the shade drawn against the rising sun. He stepped inside and the door hissed shut behind him. All was dark except for the hologram of *Caravan,* a model star cruiser Lorian had designed. It traveled the room in an endless loop.

Lorian sat in a corner, as if he were trying to press himself against the wall hard enough to melt inside it. His hands dangled between his knees, and Dooku saw that they were shaking.

"You took it."

"I didn't mean to," Lorian said. "I just wanted to look at it."

"Where is it?"

Lorian pointed to the far corner with his chin. "Do you feel it?" he whispered. "I feel so sick. . . ."

"Why did you take it?" Dooku asked sharply, his gaunt features making him look older than his years. Sweat broke out on his forehead. He could feel the dark power of the Holocron. He didn't want to look at it. Just knowing it was behind him in a dark corner was enough to make him feel shaky.

"I was in the archives. I had it in my hands. Someone

was coming. I put it underneath my cloak. Then I ran." Lorian shuddered. "I was going to take it back, but I can't . . . I can't touch it again, Dooku. I didn't expect it to be like this."

"How did you expect it to be?" Dooku asked angrily. "A pleasant walk in the woods?"

"I have to bring it back," Lorian said. "I need your help."

Dooku looked at him in disbelief. "I told you I didn't want anything to do with this."

"But you have to help me!" Lorian cried. "You're my best friend!"

"You got yourself into this," Dooku said. "Just stick it under your cloak again and bring it back."

"I can't do it alone, Dooku," Lorian said.

Dooku's gaze rested on Lorian's shaking hands. He didn't doubt that Lorian wouldn't be able to do it.

"Please, Dooku," Lorian begged.

Dooku didn't get a chance to answer. The door suddenly hissed open. Oppo Rancisis, Jedi Master and revered member of the Jedi Council, stood in the doorway.

"Are you ill, Lorian?" he asked kindly. "Some of the Masters noticed that you . . ." His voice trailed off. Dooku felt the atmosphere in the room change, as though gravity had increased. He felt it pressing against him.

Oppo Rancisis stared at them. "I sense a tremor in the Force," he said.

They could not speak.

His keen gaze swept the room. Suddenly he turned

and strode to the corner and picked up the Holocron. He placed it carefully in the deep pocket of his robe.

Then he turned and regarded the two boys.

Lorian pressed himself back against the wall and pushed himself to a standing position.

"It was Dooku's idea," he said.

CHAPTER 3

Dooku was too shocked to say a word.

"The Council will want to see you both," Oppo Rancisis said sternly.

"But I didn't —" Dooku began.

Oppo Rancisis held up a hand. "Whatever you have to say will be said before the Council. The truth will be spoken there." He turned and walked out.

"Dooku, listen —" Lorian started.

Rage filled Dooku. He couldn't even meet his friend's gaze.

He ran blindly down the hall. He didn't know where he was going. He had so many sanctuaries in the Temple — a favorite bench, a spot by a window, a rock by the lake — but he could not imagine any of those places offering him sanctuary now. His heart was so full of black anger and bitterness that he felt he was choking.

His best friend had betrayed him. Throughout the years at the Temple, he could always depend on Lorian. They had shared jokes and secrets. They had competed and helped each other. They had quarreled and made up.

The fact that this person could betray him shocked him so deeply he felt sick.

He didn't know how he passed the day. Somehow the news got out that the two had been caught. Students sent him sidelong looks and hurried by him. Jedi Knights who did not know him studied him as they passed in the hall. Dooku longed to go to Yoda and explain everything, but he knew that Yoda would only repeat what Oppo Rancisis had said. He had to suffer through the days until the Jedi Council found the time to speak to them.

Dooku did not have the appetite or the nerve to face the others in the dining hall for the evening meal. He stayed in his room. When at last the hallways glowed with the cool blue light that meant the Temple was settling down to sleep, he felt relief. At least for the next hours he wouldn't be under scrutiny.

He couldn't wait to be called before the Council. He couldn't wait to tell the truth. He knew the Masters would believe him and not Lorian. A Jedi Master was adept at discerning truth. Lorian would not get away with his lie, and Dooku would have justice.

He turned out the light and lay on his sleep couch, his heart burning. He imagined how clearly he would speak. He would tell the truth — all of it. He would tell them how Lorian tried to tempt him. He would tell them how he refused him, and how Lorian had pressed him. It was with great satisfaction that Dooku imagined Lorian's punishment. A reprimand would surely not go far enough. Lorian could even get expelled from the Jedi Order.

His door hissed open. He hadn't locked it. Dooku never locked his door. He'd never needed to, until now.

Lorian slipped into the dark room. Dooku said nothing, hoping his contempt would fill the space better than words.

Lorian sat on the floor, a few meters away from the sleep couch.

"I had a reason for saying what I did," he said.

"I'm not interested in your reasons."

"You don't understand anything," Lorian burst out. "Everything comes so easily to you. You never think about other people, about how they suffer. You just kept telling me I shouldn't worry about getting chosen. Why shouldn't I worry? Time is running out! It's so easy for you to say. You were picked right away."

"So you're blaming me for that?" Dooku hissed. "Is that why you lied to Oppo Rancisis?"

"No," Lorian said. "And I don't blame you for anything except not trying to understand how I feel. We're supposed to be best friends, and you never, ever really tried. All you think about is your own pleasure in your success."

"Get out of my room," Dooku said.

Instead, Lorian stretched out on the floor. His voice lowered. "Can't you understand, Dooku? I'm in trouble. I need your help. I know I was wrong. I shouldn't have taken the Holocron. But I was desperate. I thought if only I had an edge, if only I could know something that no one else knows. . . . Can't you understand why I would want that?"

"No," Dooku said. But he did.

"Now if the Council finds out I did it, I could be kicked out of the Jedi."

"You're exaggerating, as usual," Dooku said scathingly. But hadn't he been thinking the same thing?

"Everything is at stake for me," Lorian said. "But you've already been chosen by the great Thame Cerulian. Not only that, Master Yoda has taken a personal interest in you. The Council has watched you, too. They know you have an extraordinary Force connection. They'll forgive you. Especially since your Master is interested in the Sith. You could say you just wanted to do some research."

Lorian's voice floated up in the darkness, ragged with desperation. "I panicked when Oppo Rancisis came in. I saw my future, and it scared me. I could get kicked out, and where would I go, what would I do?"

"You should have thought of that before you stole the Sith Holocron."

"I know I shouldn't ask such a big thing, but who else can I ask but my best friend? Because no matter what, you're still my best friend." Lorian paused. For a moment, all Dooku could hear was their breathing. "Will you cover for me?"

Dooku wanted to burst out with a savage "No!" But he couldn't. He didn't know if Lorian could get kicked out of the order — he didn't think so. But it served Lorian right to have to worry about it.

Punishment would be severe for him, especially since he'd tried to lie and cover up. But Lorian was right — Dooku was a favorite of the Jedi Masters. He knew how he could tell the story so that he would just get a lecture, most likely. He would let them think it was a hunger for knowledge, a desire to impress his new Master. They would believe that.

Dooku didn't know what to say. He wasn't prepared to lie, but he couldn't say no to his friend. So he said nothing, and, after a long while, the two friends fell asleep.

CHAPTER 4

Dooku woke before dawn. Lying in the dark, he listened to the silence and knew that Lorian had left sometime during the night. He lay on his back, feeling the weight of the air on his body as though his friend was sitting on his chest.

Reluctant to rise, he stared at the walls, watching the darkness slowly silver into gray, until he could see the outlines of his furniture. The light on his bedside table began to glow softly and increase in intensity, his signal to wake up. Then a holographic calendar appeared and glowed in the air overhead. Usually the day calendar had been filled with appointments and classes. Lately he had liked looking at its blankness. Soon he would fill it up with missions.

He stared at it, thinking of his future. It was secure. Was Lorian right? Had he been smug about that and failed to appreciate his friend's distress?

He stared at the calendar for long minutes, thinking of this, before it registered on his brain that the entire day had been blocked out. Dooku sat up. The urban search exercise! It was today! Not only that, he saw that he and Lorian had been summoned before the Jedi Council following the search.

The exercise was designed more for competitive fun than for serious training. The older students, the ones who had either been chosen as apprentices or who had finished their formal Temple training, were invited to sign up. They were divided into two teams, and had to track one another through a segment of Coruscant near the Temple. They had to use stealth, cunning, and surveillance techniques. Dooku and Lorian had signed up the week before.

Dooku swung his legs over the bed. Would he and Lorian still be allowed to participate?

He dressed hurriedly and grabbed his training lightsaber. He walked out into the hallway and saw Yoda ahead. Yoda nodded a greeting.

"Heading to the tracking exercise, are you?" Yoda asked.

"I—I don't know if I am permitted . . ." Dooku stammered.

Yoda cocked his head at him. "A commitment you made. A Padawan you are. And thus the answer you find is . . ."

"I'm going," Dooku said. He hurried off. He had just enough time to grab some fruit for the morning meal before the students assembled outside on the landing platform. He wondered if Lorian would have the nerve to show up.

Lorian stood at the edge of the small crowd on the exterior platform. He was clearly uncomfortable and avoided standing too near or too far away. He wore his hood low so that it shaded his eyes. Dooku stood at the edge of the group, opposite from Lorian. No one paid attention to them. Whatever the gossip had been, it had died down, and the students now only thought of the contest ahead.

The cool morning air flushed their cheeks and the wind whipped their robes around them as they chattered in excited voices. Dooku felt the combined Force from the group, energetic, unfocused, but strong.

For a moment he stood outside himself. It was something that happened to him from time to time. Suddenly he would feel removed, as though he floated above his classmates.

How young we all are, he thought, amused. *Someday I will look back on this and wish for such simple things as a learning exercise on a cool morning.*

It made him feel better for a moment. Someday his problem with Lorian wouldn't matter. It would be a blip, a moment of static, something lost in a sea of missions in a remarkable career.

Then Yoda and Oppo Rancisis emerged from the interior of the Temple. His gaze rested on Dooku only briefly, but it brought Dooku back to reality with a bump. His mood suddenly soured as he thought of the Jedi Council he would have to face.

The students quieted as Yoda approached. He stood in the middle of the group, nodding greetings at the familiar faces. He'd known them all since they were babies and had trained them all when they were younglings.

"In an exercise know you do that every year the oldest students participate," he said. "Urban tracking, this year's will be. That this is a test remember you must. Yet graded you will not be. Take it seriously but lightly you must. Attempt to win you will; if you lose, enjoy it you may."

The students smiled at Yoda's contradictions and fiddled with their training lightsabers. Everyone was anxious to begin.

"And now, the rules," Oppo said. "You will be divided into two teams of ten. In a moment, your team color will flash on your datapad. Each team will have a different starting point. The goal of each team is to successfully bring a muja fruit from one of the fruitsellers in the All Planets Market back to the Temple by sunset. Team members can be eliminated only by one light touch with a lightsaber."

The students smiled. They knew that no matter how easy it sounded, the actual exercise would turn out to be much harder.

"You must keep to the segment mapped out on your datapads. To cross the line is to be disqualified. Do you understand this?"

The students nodded, trying to conceal their anticipation. They all knew the rules.

Yoda nodded, letting them know that their attempts to hide their impatience hadn't fooled him a bit. "Perhaps wait you should until the sun is higher. . . ." he began, his eyes twinkling.

"No, please, Master Yoda!" the students chorused the words together.

"Ah, then teams you will become. Look on your data-pads, you must."

The students reached for the palm-sized datapads on their utility belts. Dooku's screen glowed blue.

"Blue and gold, the team colors are," Yoda said. "And the captains are these: Dooku for blue, Lorian for gold. Waiting, the Jedi Masters are, to take you to your starting points."

Startled, Dooku looked first at Yoda, then at Lorian, whose blank face showed how deeply surprised he was. Why had they been chosen as captains? Maybe yesterday morning they would have been chosen. Yesterday morning, when they were not suspected of stealing a Sith Holocron. Yesterday morning, when they were still Padawans in good standing.

Dooku gripped his datapad, still reeling by Yoda's words. He had not yet completely figured out Jedi logic, that was certain.

"Hey, Dooku, wake up!" Hran Beling grinned at him as he tugged on the sleeve of his tunic. "Is it a little early for you?"

"Jedi Master Reesa Doliq is waiting," Galinda Norsh said briskly. "Let's get started."

Dooku noticed that the Gold Team members were

all scrambling to board a transport. He hurried behind the other Blue Team members to get aboard their own transport. Reesa Doliq smiled at the students as they crammed in.

"Room for everyone," she said. "Don't worry, I'll have you at the starting point in no time. In the meantime, you can start on your strategy."

The two transports lifted off. Dooku found that every Blue Team member was staring at him, waiting for him to begin. He was the leader, after all.

He cleared his throat and looked down at his datapad. The map of the area they would be operating in flashed onscreen. Dooku was familiar with much of it. It consisted of the Senate buildings, several grand boulevards that he knew quite well, and the All Planets Market, which was held in a large plaza near the Senate complex. As a promising student of diplomacy, he had signed up for special tutorials in Senate procedure, so he'd had plenty of opportunities to explore the Senate grounds.

Quickly Dooku scanned the map, trying to locate streets and alleys and space lanes. Everyone had to be coordinated and a strategy must be devised. They should spread out and each student should get a muja fruit. That would increase the odds of their win.

But why? Dooku thought suddenly. It was just what Lorian would expect him to do, so why should he do it?

"Our starting coordinate is Nova level," Galinda said. "That's good. There are many alleys there to hide in. And the gravsleds and truck transports will be unloading supplies for the market. We can use them for cover." She looked over Dooku's shoulder at the map.

Hran Beling nodded. "We can pick the fastest among us to pick up the fruit."

"They'll probably be staking out the fruit stands," Galinda said. "We have to get there first."

"Maybe not," Dooku muttered, his head bent over the map.

"Do you have a better idea?" Hran asked.

Dooku didn't answer. He was thinking. What would Lorian expect him to do?

He would expect me to race to get a muja fruit first. He would expect me to send three Padawans to retrieve the fruit, and guard them with the rest. If they all didn't make it, I'd send back two.

He looked at the map again.

"Do you have a plan or, what?" Galinda asked impatiently.

Dooku looked up at last. "Yes," he said. "We're not going after the muja fruit at all."

They looked at him skeptically. Dooku only smiled. He would bend them to his will. He would make them see his strategy. Because he knew one thing on this day: He had to win.

CHAPTER 5

"Why expose ourselves to get the fruit at the start?" Dooku asked them. "Why not let the Gold Team try for the fruit, and pick them off one by one? We might lose a few team members, but not as many as they will. When you are intent on getting something, you take more chances. Then, when no Gold Team members are left, we can simply stroll to the market, pick a fruit, and head back to the Temple. Simple."

"Sure, if we're able to pick them all off," Galinda said. "What if one of them gets through and makes it back to the Temple?"

"That is not an acceptable outcome," Dooku said. His coolness made the others exchange glances. Dooku had learned early that in order to inspire confidence he should not admit doubt.

Galinda was still skeptical. "But where can we set up surveillance? There's not much cover in the market. We need good sight lines."

"I have a plan for that, too," Dooku said.

Dooku stood as the transport landed. He noticed that

Master Doliq was watching him curiously. He tucked his datapad into his belt. "Follow me," he told the others.

He jumped off the ramp and led the way through the twisting streets to the Senate complex. He walked so purposefully that no one asked him where they were going.

When he arrived at the complex he led the others onto a turbolift and descended to the lower sub-offices. He had a foolproof strategy. It just depended on his powers of persuasion and how much a friend of his was willing to bend the rules. He was learning that sometimes it was better to come at things sideways, especially when his opponent assumed he would come at them head-on. Persuasion and deception could work better than battles.

Dooku turned to the others as he reached a door. "Wait here. I'll just be a minute."

He accessed the door and walked in. A tall, spindly creature with waving antennae and bright yellow eyes sat at a datascreen. He looked up and saw Dooku, then pretended to tremble.

"Dooku! Oh, no! Have you come to show me up again?"

"Not at all, Eero." Dooku smiled. His first meeting with the young Senatorial aide Eero Iridian had cemented their friendship, but not in the usual way. Dooku had been attending a seminar on the political history of the Correllian system. Eero had read a paper he'd written on the subject, and Dooku had raised a hand to correct a number of points he felt were inaccurate. Eero had bristled at the newcomer, but a quick search of the archives had revealed that Dooku had been right.

Eero had been hoping to impress both his father, a Senator, and his boss. Instead, he'd been publicly embarrassed. Yet after the seminar he'd come up to Dooku and asked if the student would be interested in joining his study group. He'd been annoyed at Dooku, but he wanted to learn from him, too. Dooku had joined the group for a time, and he and Eero had become friends. Eero's father was powerful and Eero longed to follow in his footsteps. Dooku admired how hard he studied and the fact that he took the job of a Senatorial aide so seriously.

Of course that was not why he had come to see him today.

"I need a favor," Dooku said.

"Anything I have is yours," Eero declared.

"I need your code card to the C level transport hallway," Dooku said.

"Except that," Eero said.

Dooku said nothing. He just waited.

Eero fiddled with a flexible antennae. "Okay, why?"

"A Padawan exercise," Dooku said. "I need the element of surprise, and that passage overlooks the All Planets Market. There's also an exit with a turbolift straight down to market level. We can use it as a base."

"But it's restricted to Senate personnel."

"That's why I need your access card," Dooku said patiently. Eero's fault as a scholar, he recalled, was that he had trouble putting different facts together to reach a conclusion. He noted the reluctance on Eero's face. Maybe he should offer a favor as an exchange. This was the Senate, after all.

"I'll help you with that Tolfranian brief that's giving you so much trouble," Dooku offered.

Eero looked torn. "I could use the help. But I could get in trouble with Senate security if I give you the code card. It could go on my record. On the other hand, this brief is really important to my boss. . . ." Eero began to fiddle furiously with both antennae now, twirling them around his fingers until they sprang loose in coils. "Okay," he finally said in a rush of breath. He tossed the code card to Dooku.

"I'll have it back to you by this evening," Dooku said, hurrying out.

Now I have you, Lorian. You won't beat me.

The plan worked perfectly . . . for a while. Dooku and the team had a perfect view of the muja fruitseller from a window in a storage area. They could clearly see the bustling market and the fact that Lorian and the Gold Team members had set up several stakeout areas. They were waiting for Dooku to strike. Dooku knew that Lorian believed the Blue Team would make an aggressive first move. It was usually how Dooku began a lightsaber battle. But a trademark move could betray you. It was better to mix up tactics. Lorian had no idea that he, too, had a trademark move. When he began to lose a battle, he made a deliberately wide pass to the left, then spun around to his opponent's rear. This gave him precious seconds to catch his breath and compose his mind.

Dooku sent out his group in pairs. They communicated by comlink. From their perch above they were able to track the evasive procedures the other team employed. It was easy to direct their team members below. With a slight touch of the lightsaber, one after another, Gold Team members went down. Each hit was recorded on everyone's datapad.

They were winning. Lorian's team had managed to hit only one Blue Team member, and they'd taken out five of his.

Then Lorian must have figured out what they were doing.

Suddenly Dooku saw two Gold team members running toward the turbolift. Unable to access it, they began to use their cable launchers to scale the glass tube. They would find a way in. That left three Gold members. If Dooku were Lorian, he would try to ambush them at an exit.

Or Lorian would go for the muja fruit while he was running from him.

No, Dooku thought. *Lorian knows the Senate well. He will think he can catch me here.*

Just in case, Dooku barked into his comlink at his two team members in the market. "Guard that fruitseller. We have to abandon the surveillance post." He turned to the remaining six members of his team. "Let's get out of here."

The team members raced out of the storage unit. There was only one other way down — through the turbolift that connected to the Senate main halls. Dooku thought rapidly as the turbolift sank downward. Lorian had also attended seminars in the Senate. Lorian knew the building even better than Dooku. Lorian loved poking around in places he shouldn't. If he didn't know before that this turbolift led to only two exits, he had no doubt made it his business to know. It would have been easy to access a Senate map and find out.

Dooku reached out and pressed the button to stop the turbolift. "We're not getting out," he told the others. "We're going up."

He leaped up and balanced on the handrail. He accessed the escape hatch at the top and climbed up. Above his head was a door leading to a Senate level. A training lightsaber did not have the power of a true lightsaber, but it could most likely get through the metal door over his head.

He worked his lightsaber along the seam of the door. "Galinda, Hran, I need some help," he called down as he worked.

The two Padawans squirmed up through the opening. They got out their lightsabers to help him. Within minutes they had peeled back the metal just enough for them to squeeze through.

They crawled through the opening. Dooku saw an orientation kiosk and hurriedly accessed the Senate map. He found the fastest route to an exit.

"We have about three to five minutes before Lorian figures out that we're not coming out of that turbolift and we're no longer in hallway C," Dooku said. "That's enough time to buy some muja fruit, I think."

Stained and dirty now from the turbolift tunnel, the rest of the team grinned as they tucked their lightsabers into their utility belts. Winning was so close now they could taste it.

They ran down the hallway toward the exit. They burst into the open air and ran in the direction of the market. The sun was high overhead now, but clouds were beginning to gather. Shade and shadow dappled them as they dodged shoppers and carts and made their way toward the fruitsellers.

Suddenly Dooku wished they had formed a plan before they'd charged into the market. They were all running full-tilt, all of them hoping to be the first to buy a muja fruit and get it back safely to the Temple. He had lost his focus because the end was so near.

His datascreen flashed. His other two Blue Team members, the ones in the market, had been hit. Lorian hadn't set up an ambush in the Senate after all.

"They're in the market!" Dooku yelled. "Split up!"

A blur of red, then green came to Dooku out of the corner of his eye. He stopped so quickly he almost fell backward into a display of children's toys. Members of the Gold Team were charging at his team, their lightsabers held discreetly at their sides, but ready to strike. He saw Hran get tapped and he turned away, a disgusted look on his face. Galinda held a muja fruit in her hands as Lorian suddenly appeared from behind an awning. His lightsaber whirled gracefully and came down with the slightest touch on the back of her shoulder. Galinda winced. Lorian smiled, plucked the muja out of her hand, and tucked it into his tunic.

Now each team had five members left. It was a tie. Dooku had lost his lead.

Lorian threw a glance at Dooku through the crowd. Dooku saw a playful challenge in his friend's gaze. Fury coursed through him. He didn't feel playful.

This isn't a game, he thought. *Not for me.*

Dooku leaped over the display of toys. He snaked around a couple with a baby in a repulsorlift carrier. He dived under a table, rolled, and came up behind a Gold Team member. He struck him lightly between the shoulder blades. He didn't stay to notice his reaction, but moved on, striking another team member from behind, then moving in to engage in battle with another. He dodged the whirling lightsaber and kicked at a jar of syrup on display. It smashed on the floor, the Jedi student slipped, and Dooku claimed another hit. He did not pause but ran full-tilt toward another Gold Team member who was racing toward the fruitseller. Dooku accessed the Force and leaped. Usually his control wasn't the best for this maneuver — he still had much to learn — but he surprised himself with perfect execution. He landed in front of the student and simply tapped his shoulder.

Breathing hard, Dooku glanced at his datapad. Lorian's strike had been successful. Every one of his team members had been hit. But he had managed to take out the rest of Lorian's team. That made them even. Except for the fact that Lorian had a muja fruit.

No time to get the fruit. If he got Lorian, he'd get the muja. He'd make it to the Temple and deposit it politely right into the hands of Master Yoda.

The Padawans had all trudged off, some in pairs or groups, to make their way back to the Temple. They were not allowed to help their captains. Lorian had disappeared into the crowd.

Think, Dooku. Don't act until you think. Dooku called on the Force to help him. At first he saw only beings and goods in the market. He concentrated, waiting until his brain registered the familiar. A certain tilt of the head. A step. An angle of the chin. Some movement so tiny that his senses would pick it up in a sea of information that he couldn't process. But the Force could.

The Force surged. Everything fell away, and he saw Lorian. Cleverly he had reversed his cloak so that the darker underside was out. Dooku set off after him. He would not make the same mistake again. He would wait for his moment.

He stayed well behind Lorian. He didn't think Lorian knew he was on his trail. Lorian headed out of the market and turned down an alley that Dooku wasn't familiar with. Leave it to Lorian to find all the back ways in Coruscant. Dooku faded back, careful to stay out of sight. It was afternoon now, and the sun had dropped behind heavy cloud cover. It was almost as dark as evening, and the glow-lights were on their lowest setting.

The alley twisted back behind the market and made a sharp left turn, now snaking along the back entrances of a variety of shops and restaurants. The odor of garbage was strong. Dooku put his cloak over his nose. He had a fastidious nature. He liked cleanliness and order.

To Dooku's surprise, the Temple suddenly loomed ahead. They were much closer than he'd thought. His heartbeat raced. Lorian was in sight of winning! He couldn't let that happen. He had to strike now.

Gathering the Force, Dooku leaped. He landed on a soft heap of garbage, which gave him plenty of spring. *Garbage is good for something, after all,* he thought as the momentum sent him skyward. He flew over Lorian's head and landed in front of him, lightsaber activated. He did not wait to absorb the shock of his landing but used the bounce for his charge.

Lorian had less than a second to adjust, but his reflexes were excellent, a source of envy among the other students. He leaped backward, reaching for his lightsaber and tilting his move so that Dooku's first strike whistled through the air.

"So you found me," he said. He seemed delighted, not dismayed. Their friendship had been built on competition. It had always been fun. But Lorian's reaction only enraged Dooku. He resented Lorian's ease, his assumption that they would always be friends, no matter what. That's what made Lorian push the boundary of their friendship. He pushed too hard. Then he expected Dooku to take it.

There was a flash of surprise on Lorian's face when he noted the coldness in Dooku's gaze. He stumbled backward as Dooku came at him furiously, his lightsaber a blur of color and motion.

Lorian recovered almost instantly. He counterattacked in a series of aggressive moves while Dooku was forced on the defensive.

The two friends knew each other's moves so well by now. Again and again Dooku tried to surprise Lorian, but he was checked every time. Frustration built in him, clouding his mind. He knew he had to find his calm center in order to win, but he couldn't. He had lost his battle mind.

They fought down the length of the alley, using the garbage bins as cover and occasionally as weapons, pushing the bins toward each other in order to gain a precious moment or two to take a breath.

Time stopped. Dooku was lost in the battle, lost in his own sweat and his own need to win. They were both tired now. Lorian's face was bright red with effort, and his hair was wet. Every so often they both had to stop, exhausted, and lean over to catch their breaths. Then one of them would recover more quickly and launch himself at the other. Their grunts and cries echoed down the alleyway.

Time may have stopped, but the sun still moved. Long shadows snaked down the alley floor. It was past time for them to return to the Temple. By the rules, they had both already lost.

"Come on, Dooku," Lorian said. "It's over."

Dooku took several ragged breaths. Spots had formed in front of his eyes, a sign that he was seriously exhausted. He felt dizzy. He reached for the Force. It was elusive. Instead of flowing through him, he could barely feel it trickle. But it was enough to send a small spurt of strength through his limbs.

"Not yet," he said, attacking Lorian.

Lorian was at the end of the alley now. He had only a few steps before his back would be against the wall. Dooku knew he could finish him there.

But Lorian suddenly turned, leaving his back exposed for a split second, and ran at the wall. He used a basic Padawan exercise, but Dooku was surprised he still had the strength. He ran up the wall, then flipped over Dooku's head. As soon as he landed, he leaped again, this time on a pile of garbage. From there he gained the roof overhead.

Dooku found the strength he was looking for. He followed Lorian's path, launching onto the garbage and then to the roof so quickly and gracefully it seemed one long, continuous movement.

The breeze had sharpened and quickened, and it gave them fresh energy. Dooku flew toward Lorian, putting extra strength into his moves, his footwork sure despite the uneven material of the roof.

"You hate me, don't you?" Lorian grunted, parrying a thrust. "Just because I finally asked something of you."

"Something it wasn't fair of you to ask."

"That is what friendship is."

"Not my definition."

"Yes, your definition is that someone gives and you take. Someone admires you and you accept that admiration." Lorian was breathing hard now. "Someone you can use."

"You have always resented me," Dooku said. "Now I know how much."

He drove forward. Lorian's words filled with him anger. He knew he was only supposed to touch Lorian to win, but that inability to reach him, to even graze his skin, had built up the frustration to a boiling point. His body felt hot.

Lorian made a half-turn to the left and swung out in a wide arc.

I have him now. He knows he's losing. It was Lorian's trademark move.

Dooku already knew Lorian would spring to his rear. If

Lorian hadn't been so tired, he wouldn't have tried it. Instead of moving to the left, Dooku moved back two steps. When Lorian came at him, he was ready. He brought his lightsaber down on Lorian's shoulder, right where his tunic had torn along the seam.

Lorian cried out and stumbled back. He looked at Dooku with disbelief. It had been a true blow, designed to hurt.

"You gravel maggot," he said. He sprang at Dooku.

Now they fought without regard for rules of engagement. They fought hard, using every trick. They used their feet and fists as well as their lightsabers. They kicked at each other and struck out blindly as they moved by. Dooku had never fought like this. In a part of his mind he knew that this style of fighting brought him nothing, that it was sloppy and unfocused and would turn them both into losers, but he couldn't stop.

"Enough."

The word was spoken quietly but it cut through the sound of their battle. They stopped. Yoda had appeared on the roof. They hadn't noticed him. They hadn't noticed that their battle had brought them within sight of the Temple windows, either.

Yoda walked over to Lorian. Dooku saw now that the lightsaber blow had left a deep bruise on Lorian's bare arm. It looked terrible, the center a deep red with a blue-black bruise surrounding it. Lorian had a cut on his cheek and one hand was bleeding.

"To the med clinic go you must, Lorian," Yoda said. "Dooku, to your quarters. Send for you both we will."

Lorian's gaze rested on the ground. He lifted his head. His eyes met Dooku's. In that moment everything formed into a hard knot of certainty in Dooku's heart. They were enemies now.

6

Dooku stood before the Jedi Council. He did not know if Lorian had come before him or would be appearing after. He only knew one thing: It was time to tell the truth. He described how Lorian had wanted them to take the Sith Holocron, and later, how Lorian had asked him to lie for him.

"And were you prepared to lie for him?" Oppo Rancisis asked.

Dooku took a moment before answering. He wanted to lie and say that he had never considered Lorian's request, yet he knew the Jedi Masters could see through him like water. He wasn't as powerful as they were, not yet.

"I was not prepared to lie, no," Dooku said. "I thought about it. Lorian was my friend."

"No longer your friend, is he?" Yoda asked.

This he could answer without getting mired in doubt and hesitation. The truth was clear. "No. He is no longer my friend."

"Clear to us is this as well," Yoda said. "A training lightsaber is not meant to wound, yet wound Lorian you did."

"I did not mean to," Dooku said. "I was angry and my control was not the best. My best friend had betrayed me."

"Lost control you did," Yoda said. "And too old for excuses you are."

Dooku nodded and looked down. He had expected this rebuke, but he had not expected it to sting so badly. He had never disappointed Yoda before.

"Tension between you there was, controlled the anger should have been," Yoda went on. "Used the exercise for feelings you should have let go in other ways you did. Meditation. Discussion."

"Physical exercise," Tor Difusal broke in. "A conference with a Jedi Master. You know the outlets available to you. Yet you chose not to use them."

Dooku saw that he had been tricked. He had no doubt now that he and Lorian had been made team captains deliberately. The Jedi Council had wanted to pit them against each other to see how deep the tensions ran.

"Tricked you were not," Yoda said, as if he'd read Dooku's thoughts. "Given an opportunity you were. Not alone are you, Dooku. To ask for help is no shame."

"I know that." He had been told it enough times.

"Know this you do, but practice it you must," Yoda said sharply. "Conquer your pride, you must. Your flaw, it is."

"I will, Master Yoda." Dooku almost sighed aloud. Would he never get away from lessons?

"Go you may," Yoda said.

"Your decision?"

"You will hear of it," Tor Difusal said.

There was nothing to do but bow and leave. Dooku

heard the door slip shut silently behind him. Only a few words had been spoken, but he felt as though he had emerged from a battle.

The Jedi Council did not make them wait long. Dooku received a reprimand for excessive aggression during the exercise. Lorian was expelled from the Jedi Order, not for stealing the Sith Holocron, but for lying and implicating his friend.

Dooku felt relief course through him. He hadn't felt in danger of being expelled, but the affair could have had worse complications. Thame Cerulian could have dropped him as an apprentice. That had been his worst fear.

He took the turbolift up to the landing platform. It had always been one of his favorite places. He and Lorian had sneaked in here as younglings, hiding in a corner and naming all the starships. They'd imagined the day when they'd be the Jedi Knights striding through, hoisting themselves up into their cockpits and zooming off into the atmosphere.

He strolled down the aisle as the mechanic droids buzzed over the ships, doing routine maintenance. Now the time that he would be leaving was approaching. Thame was returning in three days. He could be off on a mission within a week.

He saw ahead that the exit door to the exterior platform was open. Someone must be leaving or arriving.

He walked out. The clouds had gone and the night was crystal clear. The stars hung close and glittered so hard and bright it felt as though they could cut pieces in the sky.

He wasn't alone. Lorian stood on the platform, looking out over Coruscant.

"You've heard," he said.

"I'm sorry," Dooku said.

"Are you?" Lorian asked the question softly. "I hear no sorrow in your voice."

"I am sorry," Dooku said, "but you have to admit that you got yourself into this mess."

Lorian turned. His eyes glittered like the stars above, and Dooku realized there were tears in them. "A mess? Is that what you call it? How typical of you. Nothing touches you, Dooku. My life is *over*. I'm never going to be a Jedi! Can you imagine how that feels?"

"Why do you keep asking me to feel what you feel?" Dooku burst out. "I can't do that. I'm not you!"

"No, you're not me. But I know you better than anyone. I've seen more of what's inside you than anyone." Lorian took a step toward him. "I've seen your heart, and I know how empty it is. I've seen your anger, and I know how deep it is. I've seen your ambition, and I know how ruthless it is. And all of that will ultimately destroy you."

"You don't know what you're talking about," Dooku said. "You wanted me to lie to protect you. Do you think you're better than me?"

"No, that was never what it was about," Lorian said. "It was about friendship."

"That's exactly what it was about! You've always been jealous of me! That's why you wanted to destroy me. Instead," Dooku said, "you've destroyed yourself."

Lorian shook his head. He walked past Dooku, back toward the darkness of the hangar. "I know one thing," he said, his voice trailing behind him, but clear and even. "I will never be a Jedi, it's true. But neither will you. You will never never be a great Jedi Master."

Lorian and his words were swallowed up by the darkness. Dooku's cheeks burned despite the coolness of the air. Words crowded in his throat, threatening to break free. Then he decided he would let Lorian have the last word. Why not? He had the career. Lorian had nothing.

Lorian had been wrong. Dooku's heart hadn't been empty. He had loved his friend.

But he had changed. Lorian had betrayed him. He would never believe in friendship again. If his heart was now empty of love, so be it. The Jedi did not believe in attachments. He would fill his heart with nobility and passion and commitment. He *would* become a great Jedi Master.

Dooku looked up at a sky that glittered with stars and hummed with planets. So much to see, so much to do. So many beings to fight and to fight for. And yet he would take away from his time at the Temple one lesson, the most important one of all: In the midst of a galaxy crowded with life-forms, he was alone.

Dooku was blindfolded and playing with a seeker when he felt a presence enter the room. He knew it was Yoda. He could feel the way the Force gathered in the room. He continued to play with the seeker, swinging his lightsaber so the wind batted it gently, teasing it. He circled, listening and moving, knowing he could slice the seeker in two whenever he wanted.

Yoda had not spoken to him since Lorian had left the Temple. Dooku passed the time waiting for Thame to return, performing classic Jedi training exercises, wanting to impress the Council with his commitment.

"Of your ability, sure you are," Yoda said mildly. "Yet between sureness and pride, a small step it is."

Dooku stopped for a moment. He had wanted to impress Yoda, not provoke a rebuke. The seeker buzzed around his head like an angry insect.

"Fitting it is that blindfolded you are," Yoda continued. "Pride it is that blinds you. Your flaw, pride is. Great are your gifts, Dooku. Mindful of the talents you do not possess as well as the ones you do you must be."

Dooku heard only the slightest whisper of the fabric of

Yoda's robe as the Jedi Master retreated. The Force drained from the room.

Dooku was not used to criticism. He was the gifted one. He was the one the teachers always pointed to as an example. He hated to be corrected. Coolly, he struck out with his lightsaber and severed the seeker in two.

Thirteen Years Later

Dooku and Qui-Gon Jinn

7

Over the years, Dooku had thought of Yoda's words often. They were more a legacy than a lesson, for they were with him still.

He thought of them, but he did not accept them. He had not yet encountered a situation where his pride was his downfall. He did not think of it as pride, anyway. It was assurance. Assurance of his abilities merely grew with each mission, as it should. Yoda had mistaken sureness for pride, which is exactly what he had warned Dooku not to do.

And if it was pride for Dooku to think of himself as wiser than Yoda in this instance, Dooku wasn't concerned. Yoda was not always right. Dooku was not as great a Jedi as Yoda — not yet. But he would be one day. If he could not believe that, what was he working for?

Dooku had learned much from Thame Cerulian. Now he was a Master with an apprentice. Qui-Gon Jinn had been the most promising of the Padawans, and Dooku had maneuvered to get him the first time he saw him in lightsaber training, at ten years old. Dooku knew that a Master would be judged by the prowess of his Padawan, and he wanted the best of the best. When Yoda had given his approval of the match, Dooku had been satisfied. Another step had been taken toward his goal — to surpass Yoda as the greatest Jedi ever.

Luxury did not impress Dooku, but he did appreciate elegance. Senator Blix Annon had a beautiful starship, gleaming outside and all luxury within. In addition, the Senator had spared no expense in defensive systems. The starship's armor was triple-plated, with energy and particle shields, and front and rear laser cannons. It was a little large for Dooku's taste, but it was impressive.

He could tell that Qui-Gon was dazzled by the plush seating, the brushed durasteel facings on the instrument panels, and the silky, soft bedding in the quarters. Qui-Gon was only sixteen and what he'd seen of the galaxy so far had not shown him the luxurious side of life. Their missions lately had been on dreary planets or isolated outposts in the Outer Rim.

Dooku had been glad when they had been summoned back to Coruscant, although under normal circumstances he would consider this mission beneath him. He was simply an escort, a mission any Jedi could do. Lately there had been a series of kidnappings of Senators while they traveled between their homeworlds and Coruscant. The Senators and sometimes their families were held for enormous ransoms, which were always paid. No one knew the identity of the space pirate, and efforts to catch him had been unsuccessful. Dooku wasn't surprised. Senate security did well with protecting the Senators within the Senate building, but when it came to a galaxy-wide search, they were hopeless.

Blix Annon was an important Senator who had done many favors for the Jedi, and when he requested their presence, the Jedi Council had not only agreed, but had asked Dooku if he would take the assignment. A little weary of bad food and bleak surroundings, Dooku had considered a short flight on a luxurious cruiser not such a bad idea, with the additional benefit that it would give Qui-Gon an inside look at a Senator's entourage.

Senators never traveled alone. Blix Annon felt the need to travel with a speechwriter, a secretary, a chef, a hairdresser for the elaborate style he wore, and an aide whose sole function seemed to be to hover at his elbow, waiting to approve of whatever he said. That aide turned out to be Eero Iridian, Dooku's old friend.

When Dooku had arrived at the Senate landing pad, he had been as surprised to see his friend as Eero was to see him. They had done favors for each other over the years, but after Eero had lost the election for Senator of his homeworld for the second time, he had dropped out of public life. Dooku had lost track of him. Now he had turned up as an aide to one of the most important politicians in the Senate.

Dooku sat and stretched out his long legs. It had been

good to see Eero again, good to remember the boy he had been. They had talked about those years, about how mystifying the various rules of the Senate had been (admitting, with a laugh, that many were still mystifying). Then they'd talked about the dreams they'd had. Dooku had achieved his — he was a Jedi Knight, traveling throughout the galaxy. Despite his heritage, Eero had never achieved his dream of becoming a Senator. By the time his father retired, the old Senator had run through the family fortune. Eero had contacts but no wealth, and wealth was what won elections.

Now Eero dropped into the seat next to him with a sigh. "I've just been talking with your apprentice. Well, he didn't talk much, but I did. He's a good listener, that young man. I probably said more than I'd meant to about my Senate experiences."

Dooku nodded. He had noted this ability of Qui-Gon's. Beings told him things, and then were surprised that they had said so much. This could be good or bad, depending. Good if you were in the market for information. Bad if you were looking for peace and quiet on a journey and a scruffy space pilot was telling Qui-Gon his life story.

"He will be a great Jedi Knight," Dooku said. He had no doubt of that. Qui-Gon was quick to learn and very strong in the living Force. Dooku never had to tell him anything twice. If he could get rid of Qui-Gon's rather irritating tendency to befriend every scoundrel and vagabond they came across, the boy would be a perfect Padawan.

"I showed him the safe room," Eero said. "He was very impressed."

"It impressed me, too," Dooku said. The safe room was an additional security measure. In the event they were boarded, the Senator could retreat there. The door was blast-proof — the only way to break it down would be to use enough explosives to destroy the ship itself.

"I just hope we never have to use it," Eero said, his eyes scanning the expanse of space outside the window.

"I'm sure you will not, but we're prepared for anything," Dooku said.

Eero gave him a nervous look. "The ship is impregnable. That's what the security experts told us."

"No ship is impregnable," Dooku corrected. "That's why the Jedi are aboard."

He saw Qui-Gon hover in the doorway and waved him in.

"Do you need me, Master?" Qui-Gon asked respectfully.

Dooku gave his apprentice a small smile. "Yes. I need you to enjoy the trip. Mind the present moment, Padawan. We have a chance to rest and relax. We do not know when it will come again."

Qui-Gon nodded and seated himself a short distance away. He did not stretch out as Dooku was doing, but he did look a bit more relaxed as he glanced out the window. Dooku always admired his apprentice's manner. Even at sixteen, Qui-Gon had a quiet grace. Qui-Gon also had a quality of reserve that Dooku should also have admired. Yet somehow he found it frustrating not to know what his own apprentice was thinking most of the time.

"Allow me to make up a tray for us," Eero said, rising. "We have some excellent pastries. The Senator's chef —" Eero stopped abruptly as a sharp buzz came from the pilot's instruments. "What's that?"

"Nothing to be alarmed about," Dooku said, glancing over. "The pilot has the warning system activated. A ship is within our airspace, that's all." Despite his words, he kept an eye on the instruments, noting that Qui-Gon was doing so as well.

"A small cruiser," the pilot said aloud. "Everything seems normal . . . except . . ."

"Except?" Dooku leaned forward.

"There's no airspeed. The ship is dead in space."

Alarmed, Eero looked at Dooku. "Is it a trick? It could be the pirate!"

"Let's not jump to conclusions, old friend," Dooku said. "Ships break down all the time. See if you can raise them on the comm unit," he told the pilot.

But before the pilot had a chance, a frightened voice came over the speaker. "Somebody help me, please!" a girl's voice cried. "Our ship has been attacked!"

"Well now," Dooku said, his voice unruffled as he smoothly rose to stand behind the pilot. "It appears our relaxation time is over."

The pilot looked over at Dooku. "Answer it," Dooku said, smoothly coming up behind him. "But don't identify yourself."

"We acknowledge your transmission," the pilot said. "What is your situation?"

In answer, sobs came over the air. "I . . . I didn't think anyone would hear me. . . ."

The pilot looked up at Dooku again. "This sounds genuine."

Dooku nodded. It did sound genuine. But that didn't mean it was.

The pilot's tone was gentler now. "Tell us what happened so we can help you."

The intake of breath was so shaky they heard it clearly. "We were attacked — a space pirate. Our ship was under heavy fire. The pilot is dead. My father . . ." A sob shuddered, and then they could almost hear the child's effort to control herself. "They were taking him away. But he fought back, and they killed him."

"Identify yourself, please," the pilot said.

"I am Joli Ti Eddawan, daughter of Senator Galim

Eddawan of Tyan." The voice quavered. "The ship is failing. The warning system lights are all blinking. What should I do?"

"Who else is aboard?"

"They are all dead." The voice was small.

"That attack missed us by hours," Eero said.

"Do you know the planet Tyan?" Dooku asked.

Eero nodded. "It's a Mid-Rim planet, I think. Part of the Vvan system. I don't know the Senators there."

"Can you check on the whereabouts of Senator Eddawan?" Dooku asked. "We need to stall," he told the pilot.

"But the systems are failing —"

Dooku turned to Eero. "Now," he said, as Eero hesitated. "Go!"

Eero hurried toward the onboard computer suite. He sat down and his fingers flew over the keys.

"Hello?" the child's voice called. "I think maybe the oxygen is failing. It's in the red level. It's getting hard for me to breathe."

"Master Dooku!" the pilot exclaimed. "What should I do?"

"The order is the same," Dooku said calmly. "Stall."

"But she's suffocating!"

"Talk to her," Dooku said. "Tell her we are getting ready to save the ship."

"Joli, hang on. We are putting together a plan," the pilot said kindly. "Take very slow breaths. Lie down."

They only heard rasping breathing. "All right," Joli said. "I'm so tired. . . ."

"Oxygen deprivation," Qui-Gon murmured.

Dooku felt a spurt of annoyance. He didn't need Qui-Gon to give him a diagnosis. "Eero, do you have anything?" he called.

"Not yet! Hold on."

"Stars and planets, Master Dooku, we have to do something!" the pilot cried. "That child could die while you wait for information!"

Qui-Gon looked pale. He bit his lip, as if to prevent himself from speaking. Dooku felt very calm.

"I've got it," Eero said. "Senator Galim Eddawan of Tyan. He does have a daughter named Joli. And he was scheduled to arrive at the port station Alpha Nonce yesterday. He never arrived."

"Slowly approach the ship," Dooku told the pilot, who let out a held breath. "Keep your flank away from the center of the ship."

"It's just a small cruiser," the pilot said. "A ship like that might have some small arms, but nothing that can penetrate our shields."

"Do as I say," Dooku snapped.

"Joli? We're coming to get you," the pilot told the child.

Her voice was a mere whisper. "Good."

"Master?" Qui-Gon's voice was low. "Do you think the distress call is authentic?"

"I do not know, Padawan," Dooku said. "What do you think?"

"I feel that child is in great danger," Qui-Gon said.

Dooku raised an eyebrow at him. "I did not ask you what you felt, but what you thought." The Jedi insistence on feelings was all well and good, but Dooku preferred analysis.

"I think we should proceed carefully. We cannot ignore a distress signal," Qui-Gon said.

"Better." Dooku turned to the pilot. "Engage laser cannon tracking. Be prepared to fire."

The pilot set the controls. The silver ship dipped closer gracefully, as if initiating the first movement of a dance. The other ship sat, eerily motionless.

"Stay out of range of laser cannons," Dooku said.

"But if we don't get closer, we can't send the shuttle to board," the pilot said.

"Just do it." In another moment, Dooku would take the controls himself. He trusted the pilot's abilities more than his judgment, and he wanted to remain free to move in case the worst happened. In Dooku's experience, it often did.

Suddenly, the dead ship roared to life. It veered to the right in a burst of speed. At the same time, panels slid back on the underside of the cockpit.

"Turbolasers!" Dooku shouted. "Reverse engines!"

"Turbolasers?" the pilot asked, stunned. "That ship is too small to have that kind of firepower."

Dooku lunged forward and grabbed the controls. He

reversed the engines himself. The ship shuddered and the engines screamed in protest as they struggled to reverse at high velocity. The ship responded, zooming back out of range.

"A lesson for you, Padawan," Dooku said as the pilot took the controls again and the first turbolaser fire erupted. "Never trust anything."

The ship shook from the percussive effect of the fire, but they were out of range. Senator Blix Annon rushed into the cockpit. "What's going on?"

"We came to the aid of a distress signal," Eero said, hanging onto the back of a chair while the craft dipped and surged in evasive action. "Apparently it was a ruse."

"Apparently!" the plump Senator roared. "What are we doing answering distress calls? Who authorized this?"

"I did," Dooku said. "You put the Jedi in charge when you asked for us to escort you, Senator."

The Senator disturbed his carefully arranged hair by raking his fingers through it angrily. "I did not authorize rescue missions!" The ship lurched, and he almost fell. He snapped at the pilot, "Stop this ridiculous maneuvering. Our particle shields will protect us."

"We'll have to lower the particle shield in order to fire the laser cannons," Dooku said.

"I'm aware of that," the Senator snapped, beginning to look nervous. "Eero?"

"We also have an energy shield, to protect against turbolaser fire," Eero reassured him.

"Of course," the Senator said. "I'm aware of that, too."

"There is a difference between a particle shield and an energy field, which I'm sure you know," Dooku said as a blast shook the ship. "The energy shield will not protect against laser cannons. And we can't operate both shields simultaneously. That means that we'll have to alternate as we attack."

"Stop telling me things I know and do them," the Senator ordered. It was obvious to Dooku that despite his words, Senator Annon had no idea how his defensive and offensive systems worked. There really was no reason why he should, except that he had most likely paid a fortune for them.

Laser cannons fired as the ship bore down on them. The pilot sent them into a steep dive, and the cannonfire missed them by meters.

"They can outmaneuver us," the pilot said to Dooku. "Their ship is smaller and faster."

As if to punctuate his words, suddenly a blast hit the ship, nearly throwing them to the floor.

"What was that?" the Senator screamed.

"Direct hit," the pilot said tersely. "Another one like that and we could be in trouble."

"What are you talking about? We have a triple-armored hull! It can't be penetrated."

"Well, it has," the pilot said.

"This kind of firepower is usually reserved for capital ships," Dooku said. "The attacking craft must be custom-fitted with scaled-down versions."

Suddenly the pilot leaned over and began to frantically hit the controls. "The energy shield is malfunctioning!"

Qui-Gon's eyes flickered at his Master. This would make the difference, they knew.

"Then we'd better go on the offensive," Dooku said calmly.

"Senator, I should escort you to the safe room," Eero repeated. "Now."

The Senator looked pale. His hand fluttered and clutched at his chest. "I hardly think that's necessary —"

A blast suddenly shook the bridge, sending them flying. Dooku held on to the console and managed to stay upright, but the Senator and Eero skidded across the floor. Qui-Gon fell but anchored himself by grabbing the base of the co-pilot's seat.

Already the attacking ship was zooming to the left, ready to inflict another blow. It was nimble, darting closer and retreating, coming at them from all angles, making a tough target. The Senator's ship by contrast was now a lumbering beast. Dooku could see a plume of smoke coming from its underbelly. The intense heat was causing the armor to peel off the ship's surface in strips of gleaming metal.

"We've lost one of our laser cannons," the co-pilot reported.

"You'd better get to that safe room, Senator," Dooku said as another blast shook the ship.

The Senator didn't argue this time. Eero and Senator Annon left, staggering as they moved.

"Have you noticed something unusual, Qui-Gon?" Dooku asked his apprentice.

Qui-Gon nodded. "The ship is firing whenever we drop the particle shield in order to fire our weapons. That would take incredible reflexes on the part of whoever has the controls. Even an onboard computer couldn't obtain that kind of speed and accuracy. I've never seen anything like it."

Dooku nodded. "Neither have I."

"They've blasted the loading dock bay doors!" the pilot shouted. "They're going to get on board!"

Dooku and Qui-Gon raced down the halls of the ship. When they arrived at the docking bay, the pirate ship had already landed. War droids were rolling down the ramp. It took less than a second for the droids to pinpoint their targets. Blaster fire tore up the ground in front of them and they heard it ping off the walls of the docking bay.

Dooku admired how Qui-Gon did not flinch or hesitate, but kept moving in the same fluid, graceful manner. Qui-Gon had so little of the awkwardness of adolescence. He moved swiftly and easily, his arm swinging with the motion of his lightsaber as he parried the blaster fire.

"If we can prevent the pirates from disembarking, we've got them," Dooku said as they moved. "They might decide the prize isn't worth the effort."

Suddenly the droids ejected smoke grenades from their flanks. Thick, acrid clouds rolled toward them, stinging their eyes. They kept on advancing, their eyes streaming tears.

Then a voice echoed through the thick smoke. "Please . . ."

It was the girl's voice again. "Stop — please don't

shoot. I'm here. I'm standing on the ramp. They made me. Please!" Her begging voice was full of tears and terror.

Qui-Gon stopped.

"Keep fighting!" Dooku snapped. "Don't listen!"

But Qui-Gon ran ahead and was swallowed up by the smoke. The fool was going to try to save the girl.

Angrily, Dooku rushed after him, straight into the worst of the cloud. He felt that the voice was a ruse. It had been from the start. Yet Qui-Gon's respect for the living Force would not allow for doubt. If he thought there was a chance that a child was in trouble, he wouldn't hesitate. *Curse him and his empathy,* Dooku thought, coughing from the smoke.

He took out the droids as he moved, hearing them before he saw them. The smoke thinned. He could see now that droids littered the ground. He stepped over them. Qui-Gon stood on the ramp, alone. Dooku raced up to join him and together they rushed the ship.

It was empty. Dooku strode over to the ship console. A recording rod was resting on the pilot's chair. He activated it.

"Help me, please."

Dooku shut it off.

"I'm sorry, Master." Qui-Gon looked stunned, as if he couldn't believe someone would use a child in jeopardy to get what they wanted.

"Let's go." Dooku vaulted over the pilot's seat and raced down the ramp, hearing Qui-Gon follow behind him.

Something about the situation nagged at Dooku. In the middle of a mission, he never lost his focus, or his faith that he would prevail. Why did he suddenly feel that failure was breathing on his neck as closely and persistently as Qui-Gon's footsteps behind him?

Dooku felt his heart fall when he saw that the safe room door was open. The pirate had worked extraordinarily fast. The gleaming durasteel facing was still glowing red from the blast that had blown it open.

Inside, Eero lay unconscious. His skin was blackened. Qui-Gon bent over him and began to feel for vitals.

"Not now," Dooku said. He turned and raced back out the door, down another corridor that led to the docking bay. Qui-Gon caught up to him with long strides. The ship lurched, and emergency sirens were now wailing continuously. The systems were failing.

They raced back to the loading dock. As they entered, they were just in time to see Senator Blix Annon, his hands bound with laser cuffs, being pushed inside the craft. The pirate was tall and lean, dressed in full-body armor and a plastoid helmet that concealed his face. He turned, even though they'd made no sound.

Accessing the Force, Dooku leaped. He landed on the ramp, lightsaber raised. He felt Qui-Gon land behind him. Blaster fire had already peppered the air, zinging past his ears, close and rapid. The pirate had excellent aim. Dooku had to keep the lightsaber moving in order to deflect the shots, advancing all the while. He had no doubt that he would win this battle. The pirate's eyes gleamed, the green of his iris so intense that Dooku could read it from behind the gray tint of his visor.

A dark green, shot with glints the color of flames . . . Dooku's mind lurched.

The pirate made a half turn to the left and swung out in a wide arc.

Dooku moved in an instinct so old it was automatic. He stepped away to avoid a blow that did not come.

Lorian.

Did he hear a chuckle from underneath the helmet? Dooku wasn't sure. But Lorian took advantage of that split second of hesitation, as he always had been able to, and jumped backward into the ship. The ramp closed rapidly, spilling Dooku onto the floor. He landed next to Qui-Gon and together they watched the ship roar out of the bay doors.

I will not think of this now, Dooku told himself. *If I think of Lorian, I will lose control.*

The ship was dying. Eero could be dead. The first thing to do was check on him. They ran back to the safe room, where he was struggling to rise.

"Lay back," Qui-Gon said gently. He folded a cloak and placed it beneath Eero's head.

Eero's eyes fluttered. "The Senator?"

"Gone," Dooku said.

"We have to go after them," Eero said, trying to get to his feet.

"We have more immediate problems," Dooku said. "The ship is falling apart. And you don't look so well yourself."

"I'm fine," Eero said. He stood quickly, then immediately crashed to the floor.

"Obviously," Dooku said dryly. "We'll send someone for you. In the meantime, I have a feeling the pilot needs our help."

They could feel the cruiser shudder and list to one side as they ran to the cockpit. The pilot was feverishly flipping switches. "I've got the maintenance droid working on the electrical systems, but the sublight is going."

"Where's the nearest port?" Dooku asked, striding to stand behind the pilot's seat.

"I'll check," Qui-Gon offered, moving to the onboard computer. In only a few seconds, he called out, "Voltare spaceport." He read out the coordinates. "Master, I can try to work on the sublight mainframe control."

"Do it." Dooku had no patience for the details of technology. He had already recognized that his apprentice was better at repairs than he.

"What can I do?" the pilot asked, his eyes darting nervously to the controls.

"Just keep us flying," Dooku said.

Qui-Gon released a control panel in the floor and jumped down to work on the system controls. "I think I can fuse it," he called. "If we don't push the engines, we might be able to make it."

"Push them? I'll baby them," the pilot muttered.

Qui-Gon vaulted out of the chamber and switched places with the co-pilot. "I'll keep my eye on the warning lights. You just fly," he told the pilot.

With the white-knuckled pilot gripping the controls and the steady presence of Qui-Gon in the co-pilot's chair, the ship finally limped into the Voltare spaceport.

Eero was rushed to the med clinic. The other passengers and the pilot headed for the spaceport cantina.

Dooku and Qui-Gon sat in the cockpit. Qui-Gon kept a respectful silence, realizing that his Master needed time to think.

At last, Dooku had a chance to consider what he knew.

Lorian. How could he fall so low? Once a bright Padawan, now a space pirate, preying on Senators he had once been trained to protect.

Lorian still had Force abilities, which explained the split-second timing of his laser cannon attack. It wasn't as though Dooku could have guessed, but he should have been more alert.

Enough. Jedi did not waste time on what they should have done.

What now? A momentary flame of fury burst in Dooku as he thought of his old friend on his ship, laughing at how he'd outmaneuvered him.

He controlled it. Anger was a waste of time. Action was what he needed.

Because Lorian could not win.

"We should contact the Jedi Council," Qui-Gon said.

Of course they should contact the Council. That was standard procedure. But if they contacted the Council, Dooku would have to tell them that he had no doubt that Lorian Nod was now a space pirate, and had kidnapped Senator Blix Annon right under his nose. That was something that Dooku could not do.

The Council didn't have to know yet, anyway. What

would they do? Merely tell him to proceed. They wouldn't send another Jedi team at this stage. They would trust that Dooku and Qui-Gon could handle it.

"Master?"

"Yes, Padawan," Dooku said. "We will contact the Jedi Council. All in good time." What he needed to do was find the Senator before anyone knew he was missing. "But it would be better to contact them when we know where we are going. When it comes to a kidnapping, speed is the most important factor. We are in a position to find the Senator. We must act quickly."

Dooku remembered from the data file that the pirate usually waited twenty-four hours before releasing his ransom demands.

His comlink signaled, and he saw that Yoda was trying to contact him. He placed the comlink back in his utility belt. "We should maintain comlink silence from now on," he told Qui-Gon. "All of our energies need to be focused on our search."

Qui-Gon nodded, his face showing nothing of what he felt. If he thought it was odd to maintain comlink silence, he wouldn't utter a word or even twitch an eyebrow.

"What's our first step, Master?" he asked. "Until we get a ransom demand, we don't have a place to start."

"There is always a place to start. Go over the battle in your mind, Qui-Gon. If you examine every detail, you will find at least one clue to follow. Try to remember anything that seemed out of order or doesn't make sense."

Dooku waited, watching his Padawan. Qui-Gon's gaze was remote. He could tell that his Padawan was looking out at the busy spaceport without seeing it. He was reliving the battle. Dooku already knew what his first step would be. But telling Qui-Gon would not help his Padawan learn. Qui-Gon had an excellent mind. He could analyze data rapidly and organize it to reach a conclusion.

Dooku had to wait less than a minute.

"The energy shield failed," Qui-Gon said. "And the armor plating peeled off. If the Senator really used the best security outfitters, that doesn't seem likely. The cannon fire wasn't prolonged enough to explain it."

"Good," Dooku approved.

"There must be serious flaws in the ship's armor and shields," Qui-Gon went on. "And they were able to blast through the safe room doors using conventional explosive devices."

"And what does that tell you?"

"That the Senator was lying to us, or has been cheated."

"And was the pirate lucky, or smart?"

It took Qui-Gon less than a moment to understand. "The pirate worked so fast that he had to be aware of the ship's vulnerabilities."

"Perhaps. Let's look over the data file again." Dooku reached into his travel pack and extracted the slender holofile. He accessed it and leafed through the reports of previous kidnappings. Qui-Gon read over his shoulder.

"There's a pattern," he said. "The pilots report malfunctions in security, or failures they can't explain."

"Nothing catastrophic enough to raise suspicions," Dooku noted. "First of all, the pilots and security officers are too interested in covering up their own failures. And second of all, everyone is focusing on the kidnapping, not how it occurred."

Dooku knew something else, something he would not share with his Padawan. Lorian took calculated risks. He did not like surprises. It made sense that he would somehow find a way to attack a ship that he already knew had a flawed security system.

"With all this information, what would your first step be?" he asked Qui-Gon.

"Find out where the ship was outfitted with its security devices," Qui-Gon said promptly. "Go there and investigate whether there is a connection. It will be difficult without the space pirate's identity, but maybe we'll turn up something." Qui-Gon hesitated. "There is something else. . . . I don't know how to say this."

"Just say it, Padawan."

"Something I am picking up from you," Qui-Gon said. "Anger? Something out of proportion to what happened."

There was that irritating living Force connection again. "You are mistaken, my young apprentice," Dooku snapped. "Let us focus on the matter at hand."

"Yes, Master."

Dooku would tell Qui-Gon eventually, but not yet. If

Qui-Gon knew that a former Padawan was involved, he would wonder why they weren't contacting the Temple immediately. Dooku wanted Lorian in custody before the Council found out the details. When Dooku's name was spoken throughout the Temple, it would be in the name of glory, not humiliation.

Pale and weak, Eero's head shake was surprisingly vigorous. "That's impossible," he said. "I myself arranged the security upgrades. I chose the most renowned company for vessel security — Kontag. I have an extensive file on them, I did my research. If you could get me my travel bag —" Eero pointed to a bag resting near his clothes.

Dooku handed it to him and he extracted a holofile. "Here. Just look. They are experts."

Dooku flipped through the file. It was a promotional piece that Kontag gave to prospective customers. He saw long lists of clients, and he recognized the names. Descriptions of highly technical systems, images of the factory floor. It was impressive. He himself had heard of Kontag. They were justly renowned for their excellent security systems and were often linked to the Techno Union. He couldn't imagine that there could be sabotage at one of their plants.

Nevertheless, if something looked wrong, it had to be wrong.

"Qui-Gon, see if you can look up the histories of the

ships that were attacked," he told his Padawan. "They should be in the file."

Qui-Gon accessed their data holofile and quickly flipped through it. "They were all serviced by Kontag," he said, looking up at Dooku.

"There has to be a connection," Dooku said.

Dooku stepped away from Eero's bedside and used his comlink to contact Kontag headquarters. But after questioning a number of officials, he got nowhere. He shut his comlink in disgust.

"All security information is confidential. I'm not surprised. That's how a company dealing in security has to operate."

"If they won't tell us what we need to know, what can we do?" Qui-Gon asked.

Dooku rose smoothly. "They will tell us what we need to know. But they will not know they are doing it."

CHAPTER **11**

It was not far to the planet Pirin in the Locris sector, where the Kontag headquarters and factories were, yet even the few hours it took to get there were too many for Dooku. He had learned long ago how to conceal impatience, but he had not learned how to eliminate it.

Dooku had time to think on the way to the factory and decided that it would do them no good to demand anything. In his experience, a little subterfuge always worked better than direct confrontation.

"Do we have a plan, Master?" Qui-Gon asked, breaking the long silence.

"Follow my lead," Dooku said. "We will pose as prospective clients. The main thing we need to do is get a look at the factory floor. If there is sabotage, perhaps we can pick up something."

Dooku strode into the company offices. A recording rod flashed a holographic worker, a pretty young female. "Welcome to Kontag," the image said in a musical voice. "Please state your business and make yourself comfortable in our custom-designed seating that can be retrofitted into any cloud car."

Dooku introduced himself and Qui-Gon and said that the Jedi were interested in a large-scale project to upgrade their security devices on spacecraft. Almost instantly, a salesperson materialized from an inner office.

"I am Sasana," she said. "We're so pleased that the Jedi have thought of Kontag for their needs. We thought your order preferred to handle security internally."

"We are considering other options," Dooku said.

Sasana nodded. "Always wise. Let me show you what kind of top-notch security Kontag can provide." She handed Dooku a file identical to the one that Eero had showed them.

Dooku pretended to look through it and handed it to Qui-Gon. "Interesting. Can you show us the factory?"

Sasana's smile slipped. "That is an . . . unusual request."

Dooku's smile took the place of hers. "A deal breaker, I'm afraid. The Jedi are very particular."

He could see that the visions of a big contract were dancing in front of Sasana's eyes. "Of course," she said finally. "This way."

Sasana tried to control the pacing and thoroughness of the tour, but Dooku knew that once he got inside the factory he would see whatever he wished. They strolled down the aisles while droids flew or walked by. Panels were examined, sensor suites were worked on, and the hum of machinery made it difficult to talk. The tour ended at a prototype of a state-of-the-art speeder.

Dooku had seen enough. He told Sasana that they would be in touch and left.

As soon as they were outside, he looked at his Padawan. "Impressions?"

"Something isn't right," Qui-Gon said.

"Why is that?" Dooku asked.

"There is evidence both of prosperity and decline," Qui-Gon said. "The offices are luxurious, but there were empty work spaces, as though staff had been dismissed. The list of clients includes jobs in progress. Yet from the activity I saw, the amount of droids and material, they couldn't possibly be serving that number. And there were areas on the factory floor that indicated that machinery had once been there and had been removed."

"Excellent," Dooku said. "Conclusion?"

Qui-Gon hesitated. "They are concealing something, of that I have no doubt. But I don't know what it is."

"If the client base is correct, the work *is* being done somewhere. Just not at this factory," Dooku said. "What I see is a once-wealthy company who fell on hard times and has turned to a cheaper factory to do the work they once did. The factory here is a sham. It is not where the real work is being done."

"How can we discover the real factory?" Qui-Gon asked.

Dooku removed a sensor suite from underneath his cloak. "I think this might tell us something. Sensor suites always have a factory mark buried in their software. I took the liberty of removing it from the prototype." He drew out his datapad and inserted the suite, then tracked the information streaming across the screen. He pressed a few buttons. After only a moment, he smiled. "The Von-Alai factory planet," he said.

Von-Alai had once been a cold planet covered with snow and ice. Its inhabitants were adept at foraging a living from the icy wastes. With the introduction of factories and toxic refuse, the climate had warmed, and periodic floods devastated the countryside. Instead of halting growth, more and more factories were built, and worker housing was built on raised platforms. The owners of the factories held political power, so the decision was made to adapt to the changing climate instead of limiting toxic outflow. As a result, the native plants died, floods were common, and a once-beautiful, silvery planet was now a soggy wasteland. The air was thick and tasted metallic. Pristine snow no longer fell, only a cold rain tainted by toxins.

Qui-Gon stood on the landing platform, breathing the yellow air, silently taking in the wasted planet. "What a terrible destiny," he said. "The Alains have lost their planet."

"Beings choose their own fate," Dooku said. "They could have fought for their planet, but their indifference and their greed made them passive. There was no war here, my young apprentice. Merely beings who did not choose to fight the power that ruled them."

"Perhaps they tried and failed," Qui-Gon said quietly.

"Then they are also weak, which is worse," Dooku said dismissively. "Come."

This time, Dooku thought it better not to announce their approach. He simply walked through the factory gates. There was no security.

They entered a clamorous production facility. Grease stained the floor and accumulated in puddles. The ceiling was low and the air was dense and hot. Row after row of various workstations unfolded down the long space. Battered droids wielded servodrivers and airpumps. The workers looked half-starved and unhealthy, and Dooku saw that most of them were quite young.

"They are using children," Qui-Gon said, shocked. "Under these conditions! This violates galactic laws."

"There are many such places, unfortunately," Dooku said.

"We must do something!" Qui-Gon said, his gaze anguished as it roamed the factory. "They look as though they are ill and starving."

"Keep your focus on the mission, my young apprentice," Dooku said sharply. "We cannot save everyone in the galaxy."

"But Master —"

"Qui-Gon." Dooku only had to say his Padawan's name as a warning. Qui-Gon's mouth snapped shut.

A plump human male, his sparse hair matted with sweat and grease, came running toward them. "Excuse me, who are you? Never mind, you're trespassing, so leave."

Dooku did not move.

"Excuse me, you're not moving," the man said with a frown. "Do you want me to call security?"

"Please do," Dooku said. "Perhaps we can discuss the number of galactic laws you are breaking."

The man stepped back. "You're not Senate inspectors, are you?"

"We need information," Dooku said.

"Well, you've come to the wrong place," the man replied.

Dooku looked around the factory pleasantly. "You are busy, I see."

The man nodded warily.

"It most likely would not please your superiors if the factory was shut down under your watch."

"You have the authority to do that?"

Dooku shrugged. "Child labor. Dangerous conditions. I see grease pools on the floor, toxic compounds left open to the air. . . . There are a dozen violations I can see without even turning my head."

"What do you want? Money? We pay our bribes, but I have an emergency stash."

"As I said, merely information. Who owns the factory?" Dooku asked.

"I just send in reports. I don't know anything —"

"Who do you send reports to?" Dooku was getting impatient. He fixed his gaze on the manager.

"A company . . . I send them to a company. . . . The name of it is Caravan."

Caravan. The name of the holographic cruiser Lorian had designed. He had gone to sleep dreaming of the places he would travel in it.

That was all Dooku needed to know. He reflected on how smart and simple the scheme was. Behind the screen of a company, Lorian cut corners on security, then exploited his knowledge of a ship's vulnerability in order to attack it.

He heard a rustle behind him and turned to see Eero threading his way through the machinery toward them.

"Great. Another inspector," the manager muttered.

"I had to come," Eero said. "I followed you here — onto the transport and now to this facility. I can't bear to hear that the firm I hired to protect Senator Annon ended up being the reason he was kidnapped. I've got to help you catch the pirate and free the Senator. It's the only way."

Eero was sweaty and pale. "You look as though you need to lie down," Dooku said. Clearly, his old friend had gone to great lengths to follow them. Dooku admired his tenacity — and was suspicious of it as well.

Eero shook his head. "I've found a factory worker here who is willing to talk," he said. "He says the pirate makes regular visits here. He might know where his hideout is."

The manager had faded back, anxious to disappear.

"Let's talk to the worker," Dooku said.

He and Qui-Gon followed Eero through the aisles. No one looked at them as they walked. No doubt the workers had been punished for lagging behind, because they worked doggedly, without raising their heads.

Eero stopped suddenly and looked around. "Where did he go? He was right here." Craning his neck, he took a few steps and disappeared around a large bank of machines.

Dooku felt the rush of the Force as it warned him. He reached for his lightsaber. Qui-Gon was only a fraction of a second behind him.

Colicoid Eradicator droids wheeled around a corner and headed for them, blasters at the ready. Dooku held his lightsaber aloft.

"Master." Qui-Gon's voice was urgent. "We can't fight them. Look around."

Dooku surveyed the area around them. Child workers were everywhere here, no doubt because their smaller fingers were useful for work on sensors. If the Jedi engaged the Eradicators in battle, the blaster fire would spray the workers. They would have nowhere to hide.

Still, Dooku did not drop his lightsaber. He had no doubt that Lorian had arranged this. He knew that Jedi would not fight if it meant endangering innocent lives — especially children's lives. He would force Dooku to surrender. But he would never surrender to Lorian!

"Master." There was steel in Qui-Gon's voice. His light-saber was already deactivated and at his side.

Dooku deactivated his lightsaber. He felt helpless rage take him over as the droids took them into custody. In his heart, he vowed revenge.

CHAPTER **12**

Gray swirled before his eyes. Shadows that moved, that hurt as they moved, exploding inside his brain like pulses from a hot laser. Dooku tried to reach out and could not. He flexed and felt pressure at his wrists and ankles.

His vision cleared, and the shadows resolved themselves into objects. A table. A chair. He saw that his wrists and ankles were encircled by stun cuffs.

He breathed slowly, accepting the pain in his head and telling his body that it was time to heal. He called on the Force to help him, and he felt the pain ease its grip.

They had been taken by the droids, and a paralyzing agent had been introduced through a small syringe. With a painful glance down at his utility belt, he saw that his lightsaber was gone.

Qui-Gon was beside him. They were lying on a cold stone floor, the laser cuffs binding them to durasteel hoops embedded in the stone. Qui-Gon groaned and opened his eyes. His breath came out in a hiss.

"Breathe," Dooku said. "The pain will ease in a moment."

He watched as his Padawan closed his eyes again and took slow, heavy breaths. Color returned to his face. He opened his eyes. "Do you know where we are?"

"No idea." They could have been unconscious for hours and transported off Von-Alai. It didn't matter. Because Dooku had not contacted the Temple, no one had known they were on Von-Alai. There was no way to track them.

Lorian would not beat him. He vowed that it would not happen. Things didn't look good — he was bound and imprisoned at the moment — but Dooku would find his opportunity and he would use it.

"Perhaps Eero will find us," Qui-Gon said. "Or tell the Temple where we are."

"Eero is part of this," Dooku said. "He set us up."

"But he is your friend," Qui-Gon said. "And he was hurt in the invasion."

"So it seemed. Injuries can be faked. Eero was a good actor, nothing more. I was foolish not to think of it before. This should be a lesson to you, Padawan. Have as many friends as you want, but do not trust them. Believe me, I know what I am speaking of. The person who has imprisoned us was once in training with me."

"He is a Jedi?" Qui-Gon asked, shocked.

"No. He went through training but was dismissed. Never mind why. We were friends once. I am beginning to suspect that he might hold some kind of grudge against me. So there is more going on here than you know."

"You mean you knew he was the space pirate?" Qui-Gon said no more but the words hung in the air. *And you did not tell me?*

"I recognized him as he left Senator Annon's ship."

"And you think Eero is in league with him?"

"I suspect so. Betrayal is part of life, Qui-Gon, and we can't always see it coming."

Qui-Gon strained against the energy cuffs.

"That won't do anything but exhaust you," Dooku told him. "You must accept that sometimes you are in situations over which you have no control. Accept the situation and wait for your opportunity. Besides, we are farther along than we were before."

"In what way?"

"We were looking for the space pirate, and now we have found him. We'll get taken to him eventually. He won't be able to resist gloating — he never could. When we find him, we will wait for our opening, and we will not make mistakes."

Dooku closed his eyes. He did not like to feel anger and humiliation roiling inside him. He needed inner calm. He never acted out of anger.

Long minutes passed. He felt his heartbeat slow. Then he heard the swish of the doors opening.

"Old friend," Lorian said.

At the sound of his voice, rage spurted up in him again. He did not open his eyes until he had controlled it.

"I realized some time ago, Lorian, that we were never friends," Dooku said evenly.

Lorian had grown into a handsome man. He was all lean muscle. His thick gold hair was cropped short, throwing into relief the bold lines of his face and his green eyes. "You haven't changed," he said, then smiled. "Yet it's good to see you, even though it's unfortunate for me. If a Jedi had to be tracking me, I would've hoped for anyone but you. You knew me too well. Once."

"Yes," Dooku said. "I knew how you would lie and cheat to get your way."

"What is so bad about what I've done?" Lorian asked. "It was hard being in the galaxy all alone, trying to make my way. All I knew was the Temple. Did that ever occur to you, Dooku? We were raised in a bubble, and then everything I knew was taken away from me. I was forced out into the galaxy, a young boy with no Master to guide me."

"The Jedi hardly set you adrift," Dooku said. "They arranged a position for you in the Agricultural Corps."

Lorian snorted. "Tending hybrid plants on a Mid-Rim planet? Would you be satisfied with that life, after all the training we went through?"

"I had no reason to have to accept it," Dooku said. "I did not violate the Jedi Order. You did. You seem to forget that."

"I was young and made a mistake." Lorian's face hardened. "I paid dearly for it. Was I supposed to turn into a farmer? I was trained as a Jedi! So instead I went into business for myself."

"As a space pirate."

"Just temporarily. I started out kidnapping criminals, but that got risky. You'd be surprised how reluctant gangs can be to come up with the ransom. So I looked to Senators next. The only problem was, they had the best security. But what if their security wasn't as good as they thought it was? When I heard Kontag was sliding into bankruptcy, it gave me the idea. So I bought this factory and offered Kontag a deal."

"A factory that employs children." Qui-Gon's voice was flat. His gaze told Lorian that he held him in contempt.

Lorian strolled toward Qui-Gon, his face alight with curiosity. "So this is your apprentice, Dooku? Qui-Gon Jinn? Yes, I can see you in him. He is as sure of his own rightness as you are. What would you have me do, young Padawan? Fire the child workers? Many of them support families. Parents who are injured or too sick to work, or parents who have abandoned them so they are support-ing their brothers and sisters. Would you have them starve?"

"I would find a better way," Qui-Gon said.

"Ah, he is unshakable. Well, I'll tell you this, young Jedi. I am planning to phase out the child labor. Improve conditions. But do you know what that takes? Money. The Jedi don't deal with credits. They don't speak of them. But the rest of us have to eat, you know."

"You are full of justifications," Qui-Gon said.

"They make the planets turn," Lorian said with a shrug. Qui-Gon's words did not sting. "Have you been to the Senate lately? It runs on justifications. I am not evil, Qui-Gon Jinn. I know this for certain. I've seen the face of true evil," Lorian said, his voice dropping. "And I have known the terror of it. So don't be too quick to judge me."

"True evil?" Dooku asked. Could Lorian mean the Sith?

Lorian turned back to him. "Yes, Dooku, I did access the Sith Holocron. I was curious. And what I saw chilled my blood and haunted my days for a long time. It haunts me still. And yet it is comforting somehow. Once you've seen true evil, you can be sure that you will never be able to fall that low."

"Don't be so sure," Dooku said. "You're a kidnapper. A criminal. How can you justify that?"

Lorian shrugged, smiling. "I need the money?"

Dooku snorted.

"Look, so what if I kidnap a few corrupt Senators for a couple of weeks? Some of them even enjoy the attention. Nobody gets hurt."

"What about us?" Dooku asked.

"I'm not going to kill you, if that's what you're wondering," Lorian said. "I'm just going to hold you until the last job is done. I'm ready to retire anyway. I'd like to return to my homeworld and start a legitimate business. I still owe some credits to Eero for setting up the whole security thing, but I have enough for myself."

"So Eero was in on your scheme from the beginning."

"Pretty much. We ran into each other on Coruscant. He was upset about his lack of a career. He was positive he'd be a Senator by now, but he didn't have enough money to really run an election. So he agreed to use his contacts in the Senate to recommend Kontag. Then once the kidnappings began, more and more Senators lined up for extra security. It was a truly brilliant plan." Lorian sighed. "Too bad it all has to end."

The doors suddenly slid open, and Eero ran toward Lorian. "Now you've done it!" he cried. Dooku could now see that outside the room was some kind of office. Laying on a console were two lightsabers.

"Calm down, Eero," Lorian said irritably. "There's no need to shout at me."

"Yes, there is!" Eero said. "The Senator is dead!"

"Dead?" Lorian looked confused. "How? He's being held in comfortable surroundings. I even sent in pastries, for galaxy's sake."

"He had a heart attack. He died instantly."

"Ah. This isn't good," Lorian said.

"No, I'd say so," Dooku said. "It's murder."

"Exactly!" Eero said. "How did you talk me into this! We'll be tried for murder!"

"Only if they catch us," Lorian said.

"I just got into this for the credits," Eero said fretfully. "I'm a politician, not a murderer!"

"Yes, this certainly changes things," Dooku said

smoothly. Eero was just as afraid of getting caught as an adult as he'd been as a young man. "You've killed a Senator. The full might of the Senate security force will come down on you. Not to mention the Jedi. They are already looking for us. This will certainly give them a reason to hurry."

"We have to get out of here!" Eero said shrilly to Lorian.

"Calm down!" Lorian barked. "Can't you see what he's doing? Shut up and let me think!"

"Don't give me orders!" Eero suddenly drew out a vibroblade. "I'm sick of it. You've bungled everything!"

"You fool!" Lorian hissed. "Put that away!"

But it was too late. Dooku summoned the Force. The vibroblade flew from Eero's unsteady hand and landed on the energy cuffs binding Dooku's wrists. The blade cut through the cuffs easily. With split-second timing, Dooku slipped out his hand before the vibroblade could injure him. He felt only a slight burn of heat.

Within seconds, he had released the other cuff and the ones binding his ankles.

Eero took one look at him and bolted out the door. Dooku reached out a hand and his lightsaber flew from the room next door into his palm.

When he turned, lightsaber activated, Lorian had Eero's vibroblade and a blaster in his hand. Dooku smiled. This time it was not a game.

Lorian backed up toward the door. Dooku saw that he meant to escape. He would try to avoid the battle if he could. Dooku leaped, blocking his exit. Lorian would not leave this room alive.

He had never forgotten Lorian, and he had never forgiven him. It was not in Dooku's nature to forgive or to forget.

"You betrayed me once, and now you've tried to make a fool of me," Dooku said.

"So glad to see you haven't changed," Lorian said, giving his vibroblade a twirl. "Can I point out again that the galaxy doesn't revolve around you, Dooku? The kidnapping wasn't personal. I didn't know you were on that ship." He grinned. "But I have to admit, I enjoyed winning."

The light mockery that danced in Lorian's eyes inflamed Dooku. The old resentment balled up in his chest, the choking rage he had felt as a boy. Now it joined the fury of a man. Dooku felt it surge, and he didn't fight it.

He was older now, and wiser. Anger no longer had the power to make him sloppy. It made him more precise.

"Talk all you want. You will never leave this room," he said with such icy control that the smile faded from Lorian's eyes.

"Let's not be so dramatic," Lorian said uneasily.

"Master give me my lightsaber!" Qui-Gon called.

The words only buzzed faintly, as if they came from a long distance away. Dooku did not need his Padawan. Qui-Gon would only get in his way. He needed to finish this alone.

Lorian had seen his intent in his eyes. Between them

now was the knowledge that Dooku would not allow him to surrender. He fired the blaster. Dooku deflected the fire easily. There was no way that Lorian could win this battle. Dooku could see the desperation in his eyes, the sweat forming on his brow. He enjoyed seeing it.

Lorian kept up a steady barrage of fire while he swung the vibroblade, using the same Jedi training he had absorbed so long ago. Dooku kept advancing. He knew perfectly well where Lorian was headed — to Qui-Gon's lightsaber. Dooku decided to speed up the process. He lunged forward and with an almost casual swipe severed the vibroblade in two. Then he whirled and kicked the blaster out of Lorian's hand.

Lorian sprang and fumbled for Qui-Gon's lightsaber. Dooku allowed him to pick it up. He had no reason to fear.

Qui-Gon cried out, but Dooku didn't hear what he said. All his focus was on Lorian now.

"Go ahead, attack me," Dooku said, holding his light-saber at his side, letting it dangle casually. "Show me how much you've forgotten."

Lorian activated the lightsaber. Even in the midst of a battle Lorian could not win, Dooku could see the pleasure the former Jedi took in holding a lightsaber again.

He leaped at Dooku. The first strike was easily deflected. Without his connection to the Force, Lorian could not handle the weapon as he once had. Dooku enjoyed this humiliation the most. He parried Lorian's attacks, barely moving.

"Pity," Dooku said. "You were a worthy opponent once."

Now a flare of anger lit Lorian's gaze. He suddenly shifted his feet, moved unexpectedly, and came close to landing a blow.

Dooku decided it was time to stop playing with him. It was time to show him what fear was. Time to show him who the winner was.

He moved forward in perfect form, gathering the Force and molding it to his desires. His lightsaber danced. Lorian managed to evade one strike and parry the next, but it cost him. He stumbled with the effort.

"Master!"

Qui-Gon's voice cut through the heart of Dooku's concentration with the same annoying buzz.

"Master. Stop."

Qui-Gon did not shout this time. Yet his tone penetrated Dooku's concentration better than his cry had. Dooku looked over. Bound and helpless, Qui-Gon looked back.

That gaze. Dooku almost groaned aloud. He saw integrity and truth there, and he could not hide from it. He saw himself through Qui-Gon's eyes, and he could not do it. His Padawan had revealed to him what he should have known already. He could not go down this road.

He deactivated his lightsaber. Lorian took a deep, shuddering breath.

"It's over," Dooku said.

CHAPTER 13

Dooku handed over Lorian and Eero to Coruscant security. He didn't speak much with Qui-Gon on the journey back. Dooku knew that there were things that needed to be said, but he wasn't sure what they were. He knew that Qui-Gon had saved him from something, and he was grateful. Yet he did not want to admit that he had come so close to violating the Jedi code he was so proud of upholding.

They walked past the rows of cruisers in the Temple landing area, the place where he had said good-bye to Lorian so long ago, for what he thought was forever.

"So what did you learn from the mission, Padawan?" he asked Qui-Gon.

"Many things," Qui-Gon answered neutrally.

"Name the most important one, then."

"That you will withhold facts from me that I need to know."

Dooku drew in a sharp breath. He did not appreciate a rebuke from his apprentice. This natural assurance of Qui-Gon's could get out of hand. What Qui-Gon needed was a little more fear of his displeasure.

"That is my decision," he answered severely. "It is not for you to question your Master."

"I am not questioning you, Master. I am answering you." Qui-Gon's gaze was steady.

Angrily, Dooku walked a few more steps. "I will tell you the lesson you should have learned." He stopped outside the landing bay doors. "Betrayal should never take you by surprise. It will come from friends and enemies alike."

He left his Padawan and walked down toward the great hall. He drank in the sounds and sights of the Temple. He was glad to be back among the Jedi. Seeing Lorian again had disturbed him greatly.

He found himself in front of the Jedi archives. Now he knew why he had felt driven here. What Lorian had left him with was envy, and he realized why.

Lorian had accessed the Sith Holocron. He had looked upon it. Maybe he had even gleaned some secrets from it.

And he wasn't even a Jedi!

Dooku had put it out of his mind for so many years, and now it had all returned — the same hunger, the same irresistible urge to know the Sith. Was it fair that a non-Jedi had glimpsed the Holocron's secrets, and Dooku, one of the greatest Jedi Knights, had not?

Dooku stood for a moment outside the archives, drinking in the silence, thinking about what lay within. Now no one could challenge his right to see it. He deserved to know, he told himself. *He deserved to see it.*

The massive doors opened, and Dooku strode in.

Dooku and Qui-Gon's final mission together had lasted two years. It had been difficult and filled with dangers. They had worked together as never before, their battle minds in perfect rhythm. They had succeeded. They returned to the Temple, weary, leaner, and older.

Dooku had not spoken of the future. Qui-Gon would now undergo the trials. They both knew he was ready. Qui-Gon waited for some parting words on the long journey home, but none came.

They passed from the landing platform into the great hallway of the Temple. Almost immediately, Qui-Gon saw a familiar form ahead and his heart lifted. Tahl had come to welcome him.

They had not seen each other in years. They walked toward each other, and they clasped each other's shoulders in their old greeting. Qui-Gon searched Tahl's striped green-and-gold eyes, needing to see that she was well and in good spirits. She nodded to let him know this was so.

"You're tired," she said.

"It was a long mission," he admitted.

He could feel Dooku waiting impatiently behind him.

They were scheduled to go straight to the Jedi Council for their report. Tahl, too, felt his Master's irritation. She nodded a quick good-bye and mouthed "later."

Qui-Gon turned back and walked in step with Dooku.

"I see your old friendship has not died, even after all these years," Dooku said.

"I trust Tahl with my life," Qui-Gon said.

Dooku was silent for the entire length of the long hallway.

"You have been an excellent Padawan, Qui-Gon," he said at last. "I could not ask for a better one. I will tell the Council this as you face the trials. But I will not tell them this: You have a flaw. This in itself is not a bad thing. Each of us has one. It is bad when we don't see it. Yet what is far worse is to see your flaw and to think it is not a flaw at all." Dooku stopped. "Perhaps it is my fault that I was never able to teach you my most important lesson."

Qui-Gon looked at his Master. The long, elegant nose, the dark hooded eyes, the pale skin. It was a face he knew intimately, but he also knew, and had known for some time, that it was a face he did not love. At first this had bothered him — until he realized he did not need to love his Master, merely learn from him. He was grateful to have a Master so strong in the Force. He had learned much.

"Your flaw is your need for connection to the living Force. Qui-Gon, the galaxy is crowded with beings. The Jedi Order is here to support you. Nevertheless you must carry the following knowledge in your heart," Dooku said. "You are always alone, and betrayal is inevitable."

Thirty-two Years Later

Qui-Gon Jinn and
Obi-Wan Kenobi

Qui-Gon was the Master now, and he still remembered the lesson. It was the only one Dooku had given him that he had not heeded. Qui-Gon had come to believe that beings were more complicated than such a simple formula. And he had come to see that to live without friendship or trust was to inhabit a galaxy he did not want to live in.

Yet hadn't events in his own life proved his Master right?

Qui-Gon felt the hardness of the bench underneath him. He and Obi-Wan Kenobi were on a space cruiser crowded with beings. His eyes were closed. Obi-Wan was beside him, no doubt thinking that Qui-Gon was sleeping. Behind his closed lids, Qui-Gon imagined he could feel the speed of the ship vaulting through the stars. Every kilometer that passed in a flash carried him forward into an uncertain future.

Betrayal should never take you by surprise.

But it did. Every time.

His first apprentice, who he had nurtured, had betrayed him. Xanatos had turned to the dark side, had invaded the Temple itself, had tried to kill Yoda. Now Xanatos was dead. He had chosen death rather than surrender, stepping off firm ground into a toxic pool on his homeworld of Telos. Qui-Gon had leaped to prevent him even as his heart knew he was too late. He had seen the man Xanatos fall, blue eyes blazing with hatred, but at the same time, he had seen the boy he had once known, blue eyes full of eagerness, full of promise. It had cut him, made him grieve. Months had passed since the incident, and Qui-Gon felt the memory as fresh as if it had happened yesterday. Had his former apprentice failed his training? Or had Qui-Gon been the one to fail?

His second Padawan, whom he also loved, had also betrayed him. Obi-Wan sat beside him now, but Qui-Gon did not feel the old harmony between them. Obi-Wan had left the Jedi Order in order to devote himself to a cause on a planet they had tried to save. Qui-Gon still remembered standing on the rocky ground of Melida/Daan, seeing something in the eyes of his apprentice he had never seen before. Defiance. Obi-Wan would not listen to Qui-Gon's order to leave. He had remained.

Obi-Wan had come to see that he had been wrong. He had done everything he could to rebuild what they'd had between them. They had begun on a long road. Trust was the goal.

Tahl's disapproving frown rose in his mind. *You are always so dramatic, Qui-Gon. Obi-Wan is a boy who made a mistake. Do not hold him responsible for your failure with Xanatos.*

Was that what he was doing?

Time, you need, Yoda had advised. *That is all.*

Qui-Gon accepted that. But how much time was appropriate? When would he know? And would Obi-Wan sense his struggle and come to resent him for his stubborn heart?

Your flaw is your need for connection to the living Force.

Qui-Gon saw the truth of this. He had not completely discounted what Dooku had to say. In his daily life he tried to keep that connection in balance with his Jedi path. No attachments. He did not see this as a conflict. He saw it as a great truth — that he could love, but have no wish to possess. That he could trust, but not resent those who let him down.

Lately, that last one had been tricky.

"We're stopping for fuel," Obi-Wan said, breaking into his thoughts. They were returning from a routine training mission, and their pace was not rushed. "I'm sorry to interrupt you, Master, but do you wish to disembark? We'll be here for several hours."

Qui-Gon opened his eyes. "Where are we?"

"A planet called Junction 5. Do you know it?"

Qui-Gon shook his head. "Let's disembark," he decided. "It will do us good to stretch our legs. And I bet you could use some decent food."

"I'm fine," Obi-Wan said, bending for his pack.

Qui-Gon frowned. There it was. Once Obi-Wan would

have agreed, would have grinned at him and said, "How did you guess?" Now Obi-Wan was intent on being a "correct" Padawan. He would not admit that the days of gray, tasteless food and protein pellets were dismaying.

Maybe it wasn't a case of forgiveness at all, Qui-Gon thought as they joined the line to disembark. Maybe it was a case of missing what he'd had. He had his correct Padawan back. Now he missed the imperfect boy.

The planet of Junction 5 seemed to be a pleasant world. The capital city of Rion was built around a wide blue river. Obi-Wan and Qui-Gon took a turbolift down from the landing platform to the wide boulevard that was one of Rion's main thoroughfares.

"Every visitor must register with the local security force," Obi-Wan said, reading off a pass they had been given. "That's unusual."

"Some societies are tightly controlled," Qui-Gon said. "As the galaxy becomes more fragmented, beings are more afraid of outsiders."

They strolled down the boulevard, glad to feel the sun on their faces. But Qui-Gon had not gone more than a few steps when he felt that something was amiss.

"There is fear here," Obi-Wan said.

"Yes," Qui-Gon said. "We have an hour or so. Let's find out why." He reached for his comlink. Since Tahl had been blinded in a battle on Melida/Daan, she had made her base at the Temple and was available for research. She rarely had to access the Jedi archives; her knowledge of galactic politics was immense.

"Are you busy?" Qui-Gon asked.

Tahl's dry voice came clearly through the comlink. "Of course not, Qui-Gon. I am sitting here waiting for you to contact me so that I'll have something to do."

His smile was in his voice as he answered, "We have a stopover on the planet Junction 5. The Force is disturbed here. Can you give us an idea why?"

"We have been monitoring the situation," Tahl said. "The planet has not asked for Senate or Jedi help, but we are prepared for it. For many years Junction 5 has maintained a rivalry with its moon, Delaluna. Several years ago Junction 5 discovered that Delaluna was developing a large-scale destructive weapon, capable of wiping out cities with one blow. The citizens of Junction 5 call it the Annihilator. They live in a state of constant fear that it will be used one day."

"Have they tried to negotiate a treaty?" Qui-Gon asked.

"The problem is that Delaluna denies the existence of the weapon," Tahl said. "Talks between the two governments are stalled. Because of this great fear that has gripped the population, there are rumors of double agents and spies trying to undermine the government to prepare for a Delaluna invasion."

"Are they planning an invasion?"

"They say not. But we don't know. In the meantime,

because of the imminent threat, the government of Junction 5 has instituted a crackdown. With the help of a security force called the Guardians, they have infiltrated every aspect of the citizens' lives. Nothing they do goes unrecorded by the government. All computer use, all comm use, is monitored. At first the citizens voluntarily gave up their privacy in the face of the great threat. But I'm afraid the Guardians have abused their power over the years. Now they really run the government. Citizens are arrested and held without trial, just for speaking out against the government. The prisons are full. The citizens live in fear. Their economy is failing, and there is even more unrest. As a result —"

"The Guardians have cracked down harder," Qui-Gon said wearily. It was a familiar scenario.

"So be careful," Tahl warned. "They don't like outsiders. You'll be watched, too. If it's a stopover, treat it that way."

"I plan to," Qui-Gon said.

"Qui-Gon? Our connection must be breaking up. I thought I heard you agree with me," Tahl said.

"Don't get used to it," Qui-Gon replied, breaking the connection. He didn't know what he'd do without Tahl. That was a connection he trusted absolutely. *No matter what Dooku told me.*

"Should we go and register now?" Obi-Wan asked.

"Let's eat first," Qui-Gon suggested. As long as they were here, he might as well gather information in case a

Jedi presence was needed at a future time. It would be easier for now if the Guardians didn't know he was here.

Besides, he never liked being told what to do.

He filled in Obi-Wan on his conversation with Tahl as they walked to the closest cantina. There weren't many selections, but Qui-Gon was able to buy some vegetable turnovers for them, along with a drink made from a native herb. As they ate, they listened to the conversations around them. The citizens spoke in hushed tones, as though they were afraid of being overheard and reported.

Qui-Gon and Obi-Wan were able to screen out background noise with the help of the Force, concentrating on a conversation at a table behind them.

"The rumor started yesterday," a soft voice said. "It could be true, or they could be covering up her death. Jaren is desperate."

"He must be careful."

"He is past that. I am afraid for them."

"She has risked everything."

"She was always willing to do that."

The voices lowered further, as if they suspected someone was trying to overhear.

"Can't we do something to help here?" Obi-Wan asked, just as quiet as everyone else.

"Our transport is scheduled to depart in less than two hours," Qui-Gon said. "No one has asked for our help. We can't solve the problems of every world in the galaxy." Even while talking and eating, Qui-Gon's gaze had continually swept the cantina. He was not particularly surprised when a security officer in a gray uniform entered and walked straight over.

"Passes, please."

"I'm afraid we don't have any," Qui-Gon said.

"All visitors are required to register at the Registry Office."

"We thought we'd eat first. Of course we'll head over that way once we're done."

"Not possible. Please follow."

The officer waited politely. Qui-Gon considered resisting, then rejected it. He wasn't on this world to make trouble, merely to observe. He stood and motioned for Obi-Wan to do the same.

They followed the officer back down the boulevard and down a side street. A large, gray building sat behind an energy wall. It was built of blocks of stone and looked like a prison.

The officer led them past the energy wall and into the building lobby. There was a small office with a sign reading REGISTRATION ONLY. The officer ushered them inside, clearly intending to make sure they followed through.

"Visitors to register," the officer said.

Qui-Gon walked forward and gave their names to a clerk. The clerk's fingers faltered when he gave their homeworld as the Jedi Temple, Coruscant.

"One moment," the clerk said, her eyes downcast.

It took more than a moment — almost ten minutes —

but the clerk finally slid two cards across the counter. "Carry these with you at all times. You are scheduled to depart in one hour, fifty-three minutes."

They walked back into the hall, their footsteps loud on the polished stone. A voice stopped them.

"It is always a pleasure to welcome Jedi to our world."

Qui-Gon felt it before he even turned, the sureness that he had heard that voice before.

The person greeting them was tall, with close-cropped blond hair that was now threaded with gray. His body was still muscular, still strong. Qui-Gon did not even need a second to remember him.

It was Lorian Nod.

Qui-Gon did not think that Lorian Nod showing up was a coincidence. The clerk must have alerted him to their presence, which was why it had taken a bit too long to obtain their identity cards.

Nod was dressed in the same gray security uniform as the officer, but with a variety of colored ribbons woven through the material on the shoulders, indicating a high rank.

It was obvious that he remembered Qui-Gon. His gaze traveled over him, and Qui-Gon remembered the way Lorian had made everything, even a life-and-death struggle, seem like a huge joke played on all of them. He had been puzzled by that as a Padawan. Now he recognized it as the defense of a man who had lost the only thing that had mattered to him, once long ago, and would never get that pain out of his heart.

"You are surprised to see me," Lorian said. "Junction 5 is my homeworld."

"I am surprised to see you out of prison," Qui-Gon said dryly.

Lorian waved a hand. "Yes, well, I was a model prisoner. I ended up helping the Coruscant security force with a number of problems they were having inside the prison, and they were grateful."

"You mean you were an informer," Qui-Gon said.

Lorian cocked his head and smiled at the Jedi. "You haven't forgiven me for what I did to your Master."

"Forgiveness is not mine to give," Qui-Gon said.

"And how is Master Dooku?" Lorian said.

"I hear he is well," Qui-Gon said. He was not in touch with his old Master. He had not expected to be. Their relationship had not been based on friendship. It had been one of teacher and student. It was natural that they should not be in each other's lives.

It would be different with Obi-Wan, Qui-Gon thought. He saw ahead to the days when Obi-Wan would be a Jedi Knight, and he would like to be part of that.

"I see that you work for the Guardians," Qui-Gon said.

"I *am* the Guardians," Lorian replied. "The old security force was helpless in the face of the great threat, so I proposed a new force. The leader of Junction 5 asked me to be the head of it."

Qui-Gon was surprised. A former criminal was head of planetary security?

"You see, I am completely rehabilitated. So, what are you doing on Junction 5?" Lorian asked, smoothly changing the subject.

"A stopover," Qui-Gon said.

"And this is your Padawan?"

"Obi-Wan Kenobi, Lorian Nod," Qui-Gon said.

"Did you know I was once a Padawan as well?" Lorian asked Obi-Wan, who shook his head. "I left the Order."

Obi-Wan could not conceal the surprise on his face. Qui-Gon could read him like a datascreen. Someone else had left the Order? So he was not alone. And then the apprehension came as Obi-Wan realized — *if I had left, is this what I would have become?*

"At first I thought it a terrible punishment, but now I see it was meant to be," Lorian continued. "Well, this has been delightful, but I have duties to perform. Enjoy your journey. I suggest you be on time for your transport. Security here must be very tight, to protect us. If you over-stay your pass, there could be some trouble for you."

Qui-Gon knew they were being threatened. "Jedi are used to trouble," he said.

Lorian gave him a keen glance. "I have a brilliant idea. Because of my old ties to the Jedi, I will help you. I'll provide you with escorts to make sure you arrive at the transport on time. The streets of Rion can be confusing to the traveler."

"That is not necessary," Qui-Gon said.

"Now, now, don't thank me," Lorian said firmly. "It is done."

The two security officers followed behind the Jedi as they made their way back to the landing platform.

"Lorian Nod seemed pretty insistent that we leave," Obi-Wan said.

"I never like being shown to the exit," Qui-Gon replied.

Obi-Wan caught his meaning and grinned. "Should we lose them?"

"In a minute. Do you notice something, Padawan? Since we arrived, more and more security officers are out on the streets. Somehow I doubt this has anything to do with us."

"Do you think there is an alert?" Obi-Wan asked.

Qui-Gon turned to the officers behind them. "Rion is a beautiful city."

"Yes, we are proud of our homeworld," one of them said stiffly.

"The citizens seem happy."

"They know they inhabit the best planet in the galaxy," he said.

"Tell me," Qui-Gon went on pleasantly, "it appears you have much crime in your capital city."

The officer stiffened. "There is no crime in Rion."

"Then why do I see so many security officers?" Qui-Gon asked.

"Extraordinary circumstances," he answered, frowning. "There is an Outstanding Threat to Order. An enemy of the state has escaped from prison. Cilia Dil is very dangerous. The security officers are looking for her."

"I see," said Qui-Gon. "What was her crime?"

"I have told you enough," the officer snapped. "Hurry

or you'll miss your transport. If that happens, you'll be arrested."

"You arrest people for being late?" Qui-Gon asked mildly.

"Don't be ridiculous. For overstaying your pass."

Ahead, a large utility vehicle was unloading cargo from a repulsorlift platform. Traffic backed up behind the large vehicle, and pedestrians were stepping into the street in order to get by. Qui-Gon indicated the mess ahead to Obi-Wan with just a shift of his eyes. Obi-Wan didn't nod or show any sign, but Qui-Gon knew that his apprentice was ready.

As they came up toward the vehicle, Qui-Gon used the Force to disturb a precariously stacked column of boxes. The produce spilled over into the street while the workers shouted and cursed.

The pedestrians stepped on the produce, mashing it into the pavement and making the workers shout at them angrily. Qui-Gon and Obi-Wan leaped. The Force propelled them over the mess, the citizens, and the workers, leaving the security officers behind.

They hit the street and ran, dodging between pedestrians who quickly jumped out of the way. They turned onto a smaller, quiet street, then another and another. Soon Qui-Gon was sure they had lost their pursuers.

"Now what?" Obi-Wan asked.

"I say we find Cilia Dil," Qui-Gon said. "It's likely she would have many interesting things to tell us."

"But the entire army of the Guardians are looking for her," Obi-Wan said. "How can we find her?"

"Good point, my young apprentice," Qui-Gon said. "In such cases, it becomes more reasonable to create a situation where *she* finds *us*."

It didn't take them long to find out more about Cilia Dil. Although no one would speak to them directly, afraid they were spies, conversations were easily overheard, and everyone was talking about the escaped rebel. Qui-Gon was not surprised to discover that the conversation they'd overheard that morning had been about Cilia, and that Jaren was her husband.

He lived in the middle of the city, in a large building with many apartments. The Jedi paused, pretending to look in a store window at the end of the block.

"There is surveillance on the roof," Obi-Wan said. "But they are only watching the front door. We can come from behind, go down the alley, and find a side window."

"That is exactly what they want you to do," Qui-Gon said. "Look again."

It took only a moment for Obi-Wan to scan the area again. He looked crestfallen, as if he'd deeply disappointed Qui-Gon. "I saw a flash in a window next door overlooking the alley. Electro-binoculars. They are watching the alley, too. I'm sorry, Master."

It wasn't like Obi-Wan to apologize for a wrong call. He

had always absorbed Qui-Gon's small lessons without comment. Then he never made the mistake again.

How can I give him back his confidence? Qui-Gon wondered.

"What do you propose?" Obi-Wan asked.

"Do you have any ideas?" Qui-Gon asked, prodding gently.

But Obi-Wan wouldn't venture another plan. His lips pressed together, and he shook his head. He was afraid to disappoint him again, Qui-Gon saw.

Qui-Gon buried his sigh in an exhaltation of breath as he glanced up at the sky. "It's late. The end of a working day. I say we seek our advantage in routine."

"Workers and families will be coming home," Obi-Wan said.

"So let's see what develops," Qui-Gon agreed.

At first it was just a trickle of passersby, but within minutes the street was crowded with people on their way home. Repulsorlift transports jammed with workers paused to open their doors and more beings spilled out on the walkways.

Qui-Gon and Obi-Wan loitered outside a shop near Jaren Dil's building. They didn't have to wait long. Soon a mother and a group of children came down the street. The mother carried a sack of food and various other bags as her children ran around her legs, shrieking with joy at being released from school. They paused for a moment at the entrance ramp outside the building. One of the small children, daydreaming, almost got swept up in the sea of people on the sidewalk. Qui-Gon quickly moved forward and picked him up. He joined the group at the ramp. Obi-Wan quickly followed.

"Tyler," the mother scolded. "How naughty." She reached for the boy while she fumbled for her entrance card. Obi-Wan lifted several sacks from her arms to help.

"Allow me to carry him," Qui-Gon said, making a face at the boy. "We've made friends."

The mother thanked him gratefully while inserting her entrance card. Obi-Wan juggled the bags and put a hand on another boy's shoulder. To an observer, it would appear that the Jedi were simply two other members of the family.

They helped the mother to her door and said good-bye to the children. There was no turbolift, and they had to climb the stairs to the top floor. Qui-Gon knocked politely on the door, which was opened by a tall man with sad eyes.

"Are you Jaren Dil?" Qui-Gon asked.

He nodded warily.

"We have come about your wife," Qui-Gon said.

Jaren Dil blocked the doorway. Despite the fact that he was almost a meter shorter than Qui-Gon and so thin he was almost gaunt, he did not seem intimidated. "I know nothing about my wife's escape."

"We wish to help," Qui-Gon said.

A twisted smile touched Jaren's lips, then disappeared.

"You would be surprised," he said softly, "how often we have heard those words. They always say they wish to help."

"We are Jedi," Qui-Gon said, showing the hilt of his lightsaber. "Not Guardians."

"I know you are not Guardians," Jaren said. "But I don't know who you are, or who your friends are. I am expecting to be arrested at any moment. My crime is being married to Cilia Dil and not betraying her."

"I would like you to get a message to her," Qui-Gon said.

"I have not seen Cilia since she was arrested. She was allowed no visitors. I don't know where —"

Qui-Gon interrupted. "Tell her the Jedi want to help." Qui-Gon reached for Jaren's comlink, hooked onto his belt. He entered his code. "I have given you a way to contact me. We will meet her anywhere she wants."

Jaren said nothing. They walked away, down the stairs. They did not hear the door close until they were out of sight.

"He didn't trust us," Obi-Wan said.

"He would be foolish if he did. He is used to betrayal."

"So why do you think she'll contact us?" Obi-Wan asked.

"Because in desperate times, the desperate seek out those who offer help. The fact that we are Jedi is on our side. They will discuss it. Then she will contact us."

"You seem sure of it," Obi-Wan said. "How do you know?"

"They have no one else to turn to," Qui-Gon said.

It was lucky for them that a full-scale hunt was on for Cilia, so catching the Jedi was not a high priority. That was why the guards around Jaren's house did not notice as they left. Qui-Gon and Obi-Wan walked the streets, reluctant to sit in a café or even on a bench in a park. They needed to be mobile in case they were spotted. Security officers patrolled, but they were able to avoid being stopped.

Dusk fell like a purple curtain. The shadows lengthened and turned deep blue. With the cover of darkness, they felt a bit more secure. Qui-Gon was beginning to wonder if he was wrong, and Cilia would not contact them. Then, the comlink signaled.

"What is it that you think you can do for me?" a female voice asked.

"Whatever it is you need," Qui-Gon answered.

There was a short silence. "I'm going to hold you to that."

Qui-Gon marveled that Cilia could sound humorous after escaping from a notorious prison. "Tell me where and when we can meet you."

Cilia named a small pedestrian bridge that crossed the river and the hour of midnight. Qui-Gon and Obi-Wan had passed the bridge several times that day in their looping journey around the city. They were tired later that night as they walked there and stood at the edge, out of reach of the glowlights. The city was silent. Most of the citizens were home. They heard only the soft lapping of the river against the stones of the bridge.

Yet Qui-Gon felt that Cilia was near, close enough to hear them.

"You may as well trust us," he said out loud.

A reply came from underneath the bridge. "It's a little early in our relationship."

Qui-Gon realized that Cilia must be in a small boat, but he did not bend over to look.

"Well, you've come to meet us," Qui-Gon said. "I'll take that as a sign."

A dark shape suddenly vaulted out from underneath the bridge and landed close to them. Cilia was dressed in a waterproof suit, and her short hair was slicked back behind her ears. She was tiny and slender. The bones of her wrists looked as delicate as a bird's. The slash of her cheekbones created hollows in her face. Her eyes were the dark blue of a river. Underneath them were dark circles, marks of her suffering.

"Why do you want to help me?" she asked.

"Lorian Nod was once a Jedi in training," Qui-Gon said. "He has created trouble for this world. Let's say the Jedi owe the people of Junction 5 their support."

"He was training to be a Jedi? That could explain things. He seems to know things . . . things he couldn't know, even by surveillance." Cilia pushed away a lock of hair that had fallen onto her forehead. "I have a plan. Some Jedi help would be welcome. It's dangerous, though."

"I would expect so," Qui-Gon said.

"I've put together a team to travel to Delaluna," Cilia said. "Our idea is to break into the Ministry of Defense and Offense in order to steal the plans of the Annihilator. We can't rely on our government to take action — obviously they are paralyzed with fear — and they are afraid action will lead to reaction. Yet if we get the plans, perhaps we can discover a way to defend ourselves from the weapon. And if the citizens again feel free, the repressive government will have no reason to exist, and we can refashion a more just society."

"*Dangerous* is putting it mildly," Qui-Gon said. "I'd add difficult and foolhardy to that."

Cilia put one foot on the railing, ready to vault back down into the river.

"Count us in," Qui-Gon said.

They spent the night in Cilia's hiding place, a safe house on the outskirts of the city. Cilia disappeared into an inner room, and Obi-Wan and Qui-Gon were left to share floor space in a small, bare room painted a surprising pink. They laid out their sleeprolls and settled down on the hard floor.

"Master," Obi-Wan murmured, "should we contact the Council?"

"Why?" Qui-Gon asked.

"Well, we're about to break into another planet's government building and steal state secrets," Obi-Wan said. "Master Windu can get touchy about things like that."

"Precisely why we shouldn't bother him. I'll speak to the Council after the mission is over. Don't worry, Obi-Wan. The Council doesn't have to know every move we make, nor do they want to. You worry too much."

"You don't know what I'm thinking all the time," Obi-Wan growled.

"Not all the time," Qui-Gon said. "But at this moment I do."

"What am I thinking, then?"

"You are thinking about that turnover at the cantina and wishing you'd had time to finish it."

Obi-Wan groaned and turned his face into his sleep-roll. "I'm too hungry to argue. I'm going to sleep."

Qui-Gon smiled into the darkness. Obi-Wan's breathing grew steady, and soon he had dropped off into sleep.

Qui-Gon rolled himself tighter in his blanket and stared at the ceiling. Flakes of paint had peeled off the surface, revealing a dark undercoat somewhere between brown and green. He had forged his own path apart from Dooku, but there were some lessons he had kept. A certain independence from the Council made things easier on a mission. Afterward was another story. Obi-Wan was right. The Council would not be happy they had joined Cilia's raid.

Qui-Gon was impressed by the organization of the resistance. Cilia had arranged transport for the team and had even obtained worker identification tags from the Defense and Offense Ministry of Delaluna.

"You must have been planning this for some time," Qui-Gon said.

Cilia nodded as she climbed into the transport. "I planned it from prison. I was tired of peaceful protest. We need to strike one blow — and win."

"How did you communicate with your group?" Qui-Gon asked. "Your husband said you had no visitors in prison."

"The resistance has many friends," Cilia said, setting

the coordinates. "There was a guard at the Guardian prison who smuggled in messages. He had joined the Guardians and became disillusioned. He said there were others like him. That's why I have hope."

The transport lifted off and streaked toward the moon of Delaluna. The journey wasn't long, and soon they had exited the craft at the landing platform outside the capital city of Levan.

Cilia had kept the group small. In addition to the Jedi, there was a security expert named Stephin and a weapons specialist named Aeran.

Their passes worked, which eliminated one of Qui-Gon's worries. The ministry was a bustling workplace, and they didn't attract any attention as they walked through the halls.

Cilia had memorized the layout. She led them onto a turbolift and down a long hallway into a separate wing of the building.

"I got the layout from a friend," she told Qui-Gon. "There are also those on Delaluna who don't like this situation. She passed along the blueprints to Stephin."

They reached the Weapons Development wing. Cilia stopped. She swiped her identification card, but the doors did not open.

"Stephin?"

"It's supposed to be card entry only," Stephin said, stepping forward.

Qui-Gon had taken in the situation in a glance. "It's now retinal and daily code."

"Daily code?" Stephin shook his head. "We're sunk. I can crack it but it would take hours. Plus I don't have a mainframe on me."

Qui-Gon admired Cilia's coolness. She did not show her exasperation. Her skin seemed to tighten over the sharp cheekbones. "We're here," she said. "I'm not leaving without those plans. We have to find another way."

"We don't necessarily have to get into the secure wing ourselves," Qui-Gon said. "Not if we can get in through a computer."

Cilia looked at him, interested. "How?"

"We need to go to the only one who has access to all files and documents in the system," Qui-Gon answered.

"The director," Cilia supplied. "Of course. I don't know what kind of security he has, though."

"Let's find out." Qui-Gon indicated that Cilia lead the way.

They returned to the main wing of the Ministry. The director's office was behind a frosted panel. An assistant sat behind a desk. Beyond him was another door.

"No doubt the assistant has a panic button if we try to force our way in," Stephin said. "And we have no way of knowing if the director is in his office or not."

They walked on, anxious to avoid attention. At the end of the hallway, Cilia frowned. "We have to get both of them out of that office. We need a diversion."

"I think we can supply that," Qui-Gon said, beckoning to Obi-Wan.

They turned off from the others. Ahead, down a side hallway, Qui-Gon had already seen what he was looking for — the office for Internal Security.

"What are we doing?" Obi-Wan murmured.

"You are a new employee," Qui-Gon told him. "Just be as confusing as possible and leave the rest to me."

What Qui-Gon had found was that security officers in corporations or government offices were all basically the same in one respect. They were all afraid of being dismissed.

He strode in and scanned the room. Security screens lined two walls, and the tech equipment panel was as big as the room. Just as he'd hoped, there was only one technician there. A burly man rose from where he was idly playing a one-handed game of sabaac.

"Thought I'd walk him over," Qui-Gon said, indicating Obi-Wan. "Your new employee. Clearance from the top."

"Whoa, hang on, slick," the burly man said. "Just who do you think you are?"

"Security consultant from Constant Industries," Qui-Gon said. "I guess the director didn't tell you I was hired."

The burly man looked a little uncertain. "Credentials?"

Qui-Gon flashed his identification badge. "Look it up on the computer. Or call the director's office."

"I'm a secured weapons surveillance expert," Obi-Wan explained. "Trained at the tech institute? I'm supposed to monitor the in-house systems and coordinate the armed-response team."

"Wait a second. I'm the head of in-house systems," the burly man said.

Obi-Wan shrugged and looked at Qui-Gon.

"Not anymore, I guess," Qui-Gon said. "Let's take a look at what you've got here."

"Now, wait a second," the man said. "You can't come in here and —"

"Right, right, you're absolutely right. The security drill is coming up. We're supposed to monitor that closely."

"We're not scheduled for a security drill."

"You'd better check that," Obi-Wan said. "There was a test system override and a cross-tech flareup with a monitor glitch that fried the subsystem. Let me show you." He leaned over the panel.

"You can't touch that!"

"Wait a second. You didn't set the security drill?" Qui-Gon took out his comlink. "I'd better notify the director."

"Wait, wait."

"I can take over," Obi-Wan said.

"I'll do it!" the man said, roughly pushing Obi-Wan aside. He made several keystrokes, and an alarm sounded.

"Security drill," a voice announced. "Please go to your stations."

"Come on," Qui-Gon said to Obi-Wan. "We'd better monitor the procedure. It's bound to be sloppy."

"But wait!" the burly man called. "What are your names?"

Crowds of beings had spilled out into the hallways. Obviously used to security drills, they continued to chat as they moved slowly down the halls to the exits. Obi-Wan and Qui-Gon threaded through the crowd.

Cilia was watching for them anxiously. "I'm assuming you did that," she said.

"Yes. We'd better move forward or we'll look suspicious. Has anyone come out of the director's office?"

"Not yet."

"There they are," Obi-Wan said quietly.

The door to the director's office opened, and several people filed out and headed for the exit.

"Come on, let's go," Qui-Gon said.

They left the stream of people and quickly slipped into the room.

"I'd guess you have about three minutes or less," Qui-Gon told Stephin.

Stephin didn't take the time to reply, but immediately entered the director's office and accessed his computer. He clicked keys quickly.

"Can you crack it?" Cilia asked.

"Hang on." Stephin's fingers flew. Qui-Gon was fairly adept at cracking computer security, but even he couldn't begin to follow Stephin's code.

"I'm into his personal files," Stephin said. "Nothing out

of the ordinary . . . whoa! Hold that transmission. I found the Annihilator file." He clicked a few keys. "This is strange. You'd think there'd be a number of files, but there's only one." A holofile appeared. "It's subtitled Misinformation," he said. "Odd, don't you think?"

Cilia and Qui-Gon bent in front of Stephin to read the file while Aeran peered over their heads. Obi-Wan stood lookout.

Qui-Gon and Cilia's eyes met. "Do you think it's true?" she whispered.

"I think so," Qui-Gon said. "It's incredible, but it makes sense."

"I don't believe this," Aeran said slowly.

"What?" Stephin asked impatiently. Their heads were blocking the file.

"You know that awesome weapon capable of wiping out our entire civilization?" Cilia asked. "It doesn't exist. There is no Annihilator."

"What? How can that be?" Stephin exclaimed.

"This is a record of correspondence between the director and the ruler of Delaluna," Cilia explained as she scanned the file. "The Ministry Director has tracked a rumor that Delaluna has developed a fearsome weapon. He admits this is untrue, but suggests they take advantage of the rumor."

"Why quash it?" Qui-Gon said. "It will help them with security if planets think they are too strong to attack."

"They know that Junction 5 once looked at them and thought of colonization," Aeran filled in. "So why should they let their enemy know they are vulnerable?"

Cilia jackknifed erect, her dark eyes blazing. "Do you see what this means? If there's no weapon, there's no need for the Guardians to exist! We won't have to fight them, they'll simply disband!"

Qui-Gon was about to speak, but Obi-Wan signaled him.

"Guard droids approaching," he said. "Someone must know we're here."

"We must escape," Qui-Gon told the others. "If we are captured here, the news might never get out."

Cilia reached for her blaster. "We're ready."

The droids on Delaluna were small, airborne, and quick, equipped with paralyzing darts and blasters. Qui-Gon did not recognize the model, but within seconds he had estimated velocity, path, and blaster range.

He needed to protect the group. Cilia and Aeran were adept and fast, but Stephin was obviously not trained with weapons. Still, Qui-Gon also had to make sure they had proof that the Annihilator didn't exist.

Obi-Wan must have had the same thought. He deflected blaster fire from the droids and leaped in front of Qui-Gon as three droids headed for him. Qui-Gon reached over and hit "copy" on the computer console. FILE COPIED flashed on screen. He reached out to extract the disk just as two droids headed toward him, flanking him on either side.

Obi-Wan moved before Qui-Gon could react. He jumped in the midst of the heavy attack, his lightsaber a constant arc of movement as he deflected the barrage of blaster fire. Qui-Gon grabbed the disk and tucked it into his utility belt, then gave a backhanded sweep with his lightsaber that cut a droid in two and sent it crashing in a battered heap of twisted metal and fused circuits.

Stephin had taken refuge behind a desk and emerged to spray blaster fire in a random pattern that only occasionally hit an airborne droid. Cilia and Aeran worked back- to-back, covering each other as they moved toward the door, trusting the Jedi to take care of the bulk of the droids.

Obi-Wan launched himself over a desk, striking out at one droid with a carefully aimed kick that sent it crashing against the wall, splitting it into pieces. At the same time he swiped through another. Qui-Gon took out two droids with one swift stroke and moved to get Stephin as Cilia and Aeran took out two new droids buzzing through the doorway.

"There they are!" the security officer shouted, pointing at Obi-Wan and Qui-Gon.

"Time to go, Padawan," Qui-Gon said. He pushed Stephin in front of him, turning to deflect a new spray of blaster fire from behind.

Obi-Wan moved to take out a droid and landed in the doorway, lightsaber slashing. The security officer stepped back, unwilling to engage. He expected the droids to do his fighting for him.

With a Force push, Qui-Gon sent the officer flying. The man slumped on the floor, dazed and unwilling to get up.

"There's an emergency exit this way," Cilia said, jerking her chin toward a side corridor. "It should be open, since we're in the middle of a drill."

Workers were beginning to stream back into the building. They took advantage of the confusion by separating and melting into the crowd. Qui-Gon and Obi-Wan followed Cilia as her slight figure weaved through the crowd, heading purposefully toward the exit.

They stepped out. The sky had darkened and was threatening a hard rain. A few drops pattered against the building.

Ahead in the dark sky Qui-Gon saw a light. It was moving fast, traveling far beneath the clouds.

"Security vehicle," he said tersely. "We'd better get to our ship."

Because of the rain, many pedestrians had moved to the sheltered walkways that hugged the buildings and shops. A large canopy overhead blocked out the downpour as it began. Qui-Gon and the others hurried along this path.

The overhang protected him from the ship above. The crowds acted as further camouflage. Their ship wasn't far. They climbed inside and Cilia started up the engines. They shot into the dark sky, streaking toward Junction 5.

Cilia let out a whoop of triumph. "We did it. We did it!"

Stephin shook his head. "I still can't believe there is no Annihilator."

"This is all we need to end this reign of terror," Cilia said. "We can go straight to Minister Ciran Ern and tell him that the Annihilator is a hoax. He'll disband the Guardians."

"We can free our citizens from fear and terror," Aeran said. "It is almost too much to believe."

"I suggest that before you do anything, you ask a most important question," Qui-Gon said. "Rumors don't arise out of the air. If the Annihilator is a fabrication, who made it up?"

The others paused.

"Does it matter who made it up?" Aeran asked.

"I'm afraid it matters very much," Qui-Gon said softly. "Let me ask another question. When did Lorian Nod come to power?"

"Eight years ago," Cilia answered.

"And the memos dated back —"

Cilia's face changed. The happy flush drained away, and she grew pale. "Nine years," she said.

"And who benefited the most from the Annihilator?"

Cilia's face hardened. "The Guardians. They seized control." She looked at him shrewdly. "So you think Lorian Nod created the rumor."

Qui-Gon nodded. "I do. It is a bloodless grab for power. Create something the population fears enough, and they will hand over control to whoever appears with a solution."

"Yes, at first Lorian appeared to be our protector," Aeran said.

"Ciran Ern is said to be a puppet of Lorian Nod's," Cilia said.

"What makes you think that he would allow the truth to get out?" Qui-Gon asked. "He has much to fear from Lorian, and Lorian will certainly find out. I guarantee that you will be denounced as crazy or as a spy, and be thrown into prison again."

"So what can we do?" Stephin asked.

"You must bypass the rulers and tell the people," Qui-Gon said.

"Impossible," Aeran said. "The Guardians control all communications."

"That is what makes it possible," Qui-Gon replied after a moment's pause. "We must get control of that system. We must discover how it works and where it is."

"I already know how it works," Stephin said. "I was part of the original design team. The central control is within the Guardians compound. It's impossible to break in."

Cilia nodded. "The Guardian compound is way out of my league. The security is flawless."

"No security is flawless," Qui-Gon said. "I can guarantee one way to get inside."

The others looked at him. Obi-Wan smiled. He already knew the answer.

"We must get arrested," Qui-Gon said.

18

With Guardians swarming all over the city, it was not hard for Cilia, Stephin, Qui-Gon, and Obi-Wan to get arrested. They were all wanted. Aeran had no outstanding warrant, but as a weapons specialist, her skills were no longer needed. Promising to alert the resistance to be on the lookout for a big announcement, she left them.

Qui-Gon suggested that in order to conserve time, they simply do what Lorian expected them to do. Cilia pretended to try to see her husband. She and Stephin tried to sneak into Jaren's apartment by going over rooftops. Within moments they were surrounded by undercover Guardians. As Jaren watched, white-faced, his wife was once again led away to prison.

Once they were sure that Cilia and Stephin had been captured, Qui-Gon and Obi-Wan headed to the part of the city known to be a meeting ground for the resistance. They were picked up almost immediately.

Qui-Gon and Obi-Wan were led to the Guardian compound, where they were ushered into a holding cell. Cilia and Stephin were already there.

"Guardian Nod will be informed of your capture after

the planet-wide address," the officer said, engaging the security lock. The durasteel door clanged shut.

"What planet-wide address?" Obi-Wan asked Cilia and Stephin.

"Nod gives them from time to time," Cilia said. "It usually has to do with some new alert about the Annihilator that requires stricter security measures. Now we know what a fake that is."

"How is the address broadcast?" Qui-Gon asked.

"It goes out simultaneously on all data and vid screens all over the planet," Stephin explained. "There's a studio right here in the Guardian compound."

"Could you patch into the feed with this?" Qui-Gon asked, holding up the disk that contained the information they'd seen on Delaluna.

Stephin nodded. "Absolutely. But we'd have to get out of here and into a secure area. All the studio feed lines run though the central information console."

"Speaking of which, how *are* we going to get out of here?" Cilia asked.

"That won't be hard," Qui-Gon said, pulling aside his tunic and revealing his lightsaber.

"But weren't you searched?" Stephin asked.

"We have ways of diverting attention," Obi-Wan told them. He and Qui-Gon had used the Force to distract the guards from their lightsabers during the search.

The Jedi ignited their lightsabers and sank them into the durasteel door. The metal melted and peeled back, glowing orange, and they stepped through the hole. The corridor was empty, but they could see by a blinking light that a silent alarm had been tripped.

Qui-Gon looked back at the gaping hole. "You lose the element of surprise, but it's a quick escape."

"We'll have to move fast," Cilia said.

They ran down the corridor. Cilia and Stephin both knew the complex well, and they led them through a maze of back hallways to the central computer station. It was empty, but a high-security lock was on the door. Through the glass, they could see a row of vidscreens. Lorian Nod had already begun his address.

"How long will it take you to bypass the circuits and patch through into the feed?" Qui-Gon asked.

"Hard to say," Stephin answered. "Three minutes. Maybe four."

"The alarm will go off as soon as we break in," Qui-Gon said. "They'll be able to pinpoint our location then. Just do the best you can. We'll take care of whatever comes along."

Cilia and Stephin nodded to tell them they were ready. Qui-Gon and Obi-Wan used their lightsabers to break through the door. Immediately, a red light began to pulse. As they walked through the doorway, another indicator light began to blink.

Now they could hear Lorian Nod's voice. ". . . And it is with great reluctance that I stand before you now. Yet even with bad news we can gain comfort from the fact that we are strong and able to protect ourselves from the great threat. . . ."

Stephin hurried to the console. His fingers began to fly. Qui-Gon gave him the disk and turned to face the doorway, lightsaber at the ready.

It took only seconds before the droids came. Qui-Gon had no doubt that they would be followed by armed guards. Obi-Wan sprang forward, his lightsaber flashing. They moved in the same rhythm, ready to cover each other, knowing when the other would go on the offense. It was a flow Qui-Gon remembered, when he knew what his apprentice would do before Obi-Wan did it. The Force surged around them, gathering so that it felt like heat and light, making every move easy.

Within seconds, battered and smoking droids littered the floor.

"Stars and galaxies," Cilia breathed. She had not had time to draw her own blaster.

"Three more minutes," Stephin muttered.

". . . We are tracking a group of spies who are planning to undermine our society, striking at our security itself. Thanks to the Guardians, we will be safe from them and their plans. . . ."

"I'm entering the disk codes now," Stephin said.

"The information will come onscreen," Cilia said. "But will the citizens believe it?"

"Leave on the audio feed," Obi-Wan told Stephin.

Obi-Wan spoke the words crisply, like an order. He did

not glance at Qui-Gon. He was totally focused on the moment, on the problem at hand.

Qui-Gon felt a surge of satisfaction. It was as though Obi-Wan had taken a step on a journey back to him.

Puzzled, Stephin nodded.

Qui-Gon heard the sound of boots thudding in the hallway. "Take no lives," he told Obi-Wan. If they could accomplish this without loss of life, it would be a good day.

". . . that a new blast potential of the Annihilator has been discovered . . ."

The security officers thundered in, blasters pinging, electrojabbers swinging.

"Stay behind us!" Qui-Gon shouted to Cilia, who now was ready to fight and had stepped forward.

The blaster fire was furious. Qui-Gon jumped and twisted, trying to be everywhere at once. Obi-Wan moved to protect Stephin. The guards were well trained for battle. They kept constantly on the move, using sophisticated flanking maneuvers. Qui-Gon realized that Lorian's Temple training had come in handy.

Still, the security officers were not Jedi. Qui-Gon and Obi-Wan could keep them at bay. He heard more boots thundering down the hallway and the distinctive whirr of oncoming droids.

Yes, they could keep the attackers at bay, but if more and more arrived, how long would it be before blaster fire got through?

Qui-Gon could see that the same thought had occurred

to Obi-Wan. His Padawan did not flag, but a renewed burst of energy sent him in a spinning arc. He deflected blaster fire at the same time he destroyed two oncoming droids with a well-placed kick.

Then the moment Qui-Gon was waiting for occurred.

The image of Lorian Nod fuzzed and broke into shattered pieces. A memo flashed onscreen.

Stephin had been able to keep the audio feed open. The voice of Lorian Nod boomed out.

"What is that? What is happening? Get that off the screen!"

MISINFORMATION REGARDING "ANNIHILATOR"

The memo title could be read clearly. More information streamed across the stream as the holofile unfolded.

WE KNOW NOT HOW OR WHY THIS RUMOR BEGAN . . .

"Get that off the screen!" Lorian shouted. "Don't you see what it is, you fools? It's a lie!"

The focus of the security officers wavered. Qui-Gon saw their eyes drift to the screen. They tried to keep fighting and keep track of what was flashing.

Another voice came through the feed. "This says that there is no Annihilator!"

It must have been another officer in the studio who had blurted it out.

"It's a trick," Lorian said. "Spies . . ."

"It's an official document from Delaluna," another voice said. "Look at the code seal."

The officers had all stopped fighting. They stared at

the screen in disbelief. Whoever was programming the droids had stopped. They stopped in midair.

"Let's go," Qui-Gon said to Obi-Wan.

They raced out into the corridor. Following directions Stephin had given them, they ran to the studio and burst through the door.

Lorian's face was dark with rage. "You are under arrest, Jedi!"

"I believe you are mistaken," Qui-Gon said calmly. "We are arresting *you*."

"That arrest can only be ordered by the president himself!" Lorian snapped. "Guards! Take these Jedi away."

A guard across the room lowered his comlink slowly. "The arrest order has come through," he said. "I am to detain you, Lorian Nod, by order of Minister Ciran Ern."

The color slowly drained from Lorian's face. He tried to smile, but it looked as though it cost him a great deal of effort.

Looking at Qui-Gon and Obi-Wan, he shrugged. "How strange life is," he said. "The galaxy is so immense, but I can't get away from the Jedi. They have destroyed my life once again."

19

Lorian Nod was in prison, awaiting trial. Cilia was no longer an underground hero, but a public one, able to walk the streets with her husband. The Guardians had fallen into disarray and the minister had promised to disband them.

It was time for the Jedi to leave.

Qui-Gon waited at the landing platform with Obi-Wan. He remembered arriving on this planet while worrying about what was to come with his apprentice. It was true that he missed that pure trust, that lack of shadows between them. He had seen the flaws in Obi-Wan, and the flaws in himself. He had seen where their flaws could rub up against each other and create fissures in their relations, cracking them open like a groundquake could split the very core of a planet.

Yet there was something to be gained from that, Qui-Gon thought. Now their relationship could truly begin, for they had seen the worst of it and they had both decided that what they wanted, the most important thing, was to go on. There had been no betrayal. Qui-Gon knew Dooku was wrong — he was not alone.

"The idea to leave the audio feed open was a good one," he told Obi-Wan. "Lorian was trapped by his denials."

"I thought he might say something incriminating," Obi-Wan said.

"You ordered Stephin to do it," Qui-Gon said. "You did not check with me. You did not even look at me."

"I am sorry, Master —"

"It was the right thing to do."

Qui-Gon saw the flash of pleasure in Obi-Wan's eyes.

He is no longer afraid of displeasing me, Qui-Gon thought. *Good.*

"Shall we board?" Qui-Gon asked.

"Of course, Master." Obi-Wan paused and looked longingly at a food court. "But can we eat first?" He grinned. "I'm still thinking about that turnover."

Qui-Gon laughed. Yes, his Padawan was back. And the boy was back, too. Now they could begin again.

He had not known the Jedi cruiser to Naboo was taking him on what would turn out to be his final mission with Qui-Gon. Yet they both had understood that the time was coming when Qui-Gon would recommend him for the trials. Obi-Wan knew he was ready, but he was not yet prepared to leave his Master. He was anxious to be independent, but he was reluctant to come out from the protection of his alliance with Qui-Gon. It was not apprehension that kept him there, but loyalty. Friendship. Love.

They had spoken more on that trip than they had ever spoken before. Qui-Gon had been in a rare talkative mood, and they had remembered old missions, old acquaintances. They had laughed over the exploits of Didi Oddo, the friend who was always in trouble. They had remembered the loyal brothers, Guerra and Paxxi, now heads of large families on their homeworld of Phindar. From time to time a shadow would cross Qui-Gon's face and Obi-Wan knew he was thinking of Tahl, who he had loved. Tahl had been killed during a mission to New Apsolon despite their intense efforts to find and save her.

The pilot dimmed the lights for sleep. Still Qui-Gon and

Obi-Wan did not move. They sat on their chairs, reluctant to move to the sleep area. A silence fell between them, as companionable as always. In the dark silence, Obi-Wan had asked the question that had been in his mind for months.

"Master, can you tell me something I am lacking? Something I cannot see that I need to work on?"

He could not see Qui-Gon's face clearly now. "Do you mean a flaw, Padawan?"

"Yes. You have told me that I worry too much, and I've tried to work on that."

"Ah. You mean you've worried about worrying too much?" Qui-Gon's voice was light. He was teasing him.

"I can be impatient with living beings, too. I know that. And sometimes, I'm a little too confident of my abilities, perhaps."

Now Qui-Gon's tone was serious. "These things are true, Obi-Wan, but they are not flaws. I have seen how hard you have worked. I've seen what you can accomplish."

"Then what is my flaw?" Obi-Wan asked.

There came a silence so long that Obi-Wan wondered if Qui-Gon had fallen asleep. Then his voice rose out of the darkness, soft and deep.

"You will be a great Jedi Knight, Obi-Wan Kenobi. I know that with every breath, with every beat of my heart. You will make me proud I was there at your beginnings. If you do have a flaw, perhaps it is simply this: You wish to please me too much."

Twenty-three Years Later

Obi-Wan Kenobi and
Anakin Skywalker

Obi-Wan had never understood the meaning of Qui-Gon's words. He had meant to ask him after the mission was over. He had puzzled over the words, forgotten them, remembered them again, pushed them away only to have them reappear in his mind.

And now, they haunted him.

The Clone Wars had begun. The galaxy had fractured and the Republic was threatening to split apart. They had discovered that the former Jedi, Count Dooku, was leading the Separatists. Many Jedi had lost their lives on Geonosis six months earlier. The tragedy of that battle infused the Temple, made every Jedi walk with a heavy step. Their vision had been clouded for so long. They realized this, yet their vision did not clear. It was as though a dark curtain was draped over the Temple.

And something had changed within Anakin Skywalker. Something that made Obi-Wan uneasy. And now a worry had been pushed to the forefront of his mind — had his love for Qui-Gon blinded him to the faults in Anakin for too long?

The uneasiness he felt about Anakin, the sense of dull dread that had the power to wake him up from a deep sleep, now had a partner: the conviction that it was too late to do anything about it.

His Master could not have foreseen all that had taken place. Yet he had placed a sure finger on the spot that was most vulnerable in Obi-Wan. Obi-Wan had opened his heart to Anakin because of Qui-Gon's belief that Anakin was the chosen one. Had he tried too hard? Had he overlooked what he should not have overlooked?

Love had never blinded Qui-Gon. But it has blinded me.

There was too great a distance between him and Anakin now, at a time when he needed to keep his Padawan even closer than before. Every instinct told him that Anakin had been profoundly changed while they were apart before the Battle of Geonosis. He knew that Anakin had been to Tatooine and he knew Anakin's mother was dead. He knew that a bond had grown between Anakin and the brilliant Senator Padmé Amidala.

He sensed that some of the change was for the better. Some not. It was as if Anakin had grown harder — and more secretive. One thing Obi-Wan saw clearly: Anakin had lost his boyishness. He was a man now.

Whatever the changes were, they did not bring Anakin peace. Obi-Wan sensed his Padawan's restlessness, his impatience. He saw that Anakin no longer felt the same sense of peace from the Temple. He always wanted to be moving. He always wanted to be somewhere else.

Obi-Wan stood in the doorway of the Map Room of the Temple, watching Anakin. This was a place Anakin came when his mind was restless. For some reason his Padawan found it calming to set dozens of holographic planets spinning while voices intoned their details: geography, language, government, customs. Out of the chaos, Anakin would distinguish one voice. Then he would trace another, then another, until he could clearly hear each voice amid the babble.

Anakin had grown quite adept at this game, Obi-Wan saw. Holograms whirled around his head like angry insects. The voices were a confusing blur to Obi-Wan. He couldn't imagine why someone would find peace during this. As he watched, Anakin lifted a finger and added another planet to the mix.

"Anakin."

Anakin did not turn. Most beings would. Instead he lifted a hand. One by one the planet holograms disappeared, the voices cut off until the last solitary voice was silenced. Obi-Wan noted that it had been intoning the precious metals of Naboo. Anakin stood and turned. Obi-Wan could see that Anakin was still not used to his new artificial hand. He hugged that arm a little closer to his body. The sight tore at Obi-Wan's heart.

"Master."

"Master Yoda has requested our presence."

"A mission?"

"I do not know."

Over the past weeks there had been much to do, too much to plan — too many battles. The Jedi Council held constant strategy sessions. It was necessary to carefully place the Jedi where they were most needed. Systems and planets were now vulnerable, and many were highly strategic. The Separatists were gaining new planets with a combination of coercion and force. Supreme Chancellor Palpatine pledged to help planets loyal to the Republic.

"You go to the Map Room when you are troubled by something," Obi-Wan said as they walked. "Do you want to talk about it?"

Anakin made a restless gesture. "What is the good of talking?"

"It can be very good," Obi-Wan said gently. "Anakin, I see that the past months have marked you. I am your Master. I am here to help you in any way I can."

He could see his Padawan only in profile, but Anakin's mouth tightened. "I have seen things I wish I had not seen. I did not think so many Jedi could die. I did not think a once-great Jedi Master could fall so far."

"Count Dooku's fall has troubled us all," Obi-Wan acknowledged. "Now we have a great and powerful enemy." His thoughts turned to his battle with Dooku. He had never met such power in battle before. He had never come up against something that had completely overpowered him. Even meeting the Sith Lord who had killed Qui-Gon had not been the same. If only Qui-Gon were alive, to give them insights into Dooku. Now Obi-Wan thought back and wondered why Qui-Gon had never spoken of his Master. He would never know that, either.

He would have liked more time to talk to Anakin, but they drew up in front of the reception chamber where Yoda had asked them to convene. Obi-Wan stepped forward to access the door but it slid open before he could. Yoda was always a step ahead of him.

Yet Yoda had a more significant surprise. He stood in the middle of the room with Lorian Nod. Lorian was older, his hair completely silver now. He wasn't as lean, but his body still looked strong. Dressed in a cloak of veda cloth, he looked more like a successful businessman than a soldier, but it was unmistakably Lorian Nod.

"What is he doing here?" Obi-Wan barked. He was seldom, if ever, rude. But lately he hadn't had the time to hide his feelings. Anakin was not the only one who had developed impatience.

"To help the Jedi, Lorian Nod has come," Yoda said.

"Really," Obi-Wan said, strolling in. "Are you offering to set up your own security force, Nod?"

Lorian bowed his head slightly, as if he had expected Obi-Wan's jibe and accepted it as his due. "I knew I would meet skepticism if I came here," he said. "All I can say is that I admit I have not operated within galactic laws during some periods of my life. Yet now, when things are so serious, I find that I must return to my beginnings. I wish to help the Jedi."

"And how do you think you can do that?" Obi-Wan asked.

Yoda blinked at Obi-Wan. It was just a blink. But it told him that his tone was not appreciated.

"Ruler of Junction 5, Lorian Nod is," he said.

Again, Obi-Wan was surprised. "How did you manage that? The last time I saw you, you were about to go to prison for a very long time."

"I did go to prison for a very long time," Lorian answered. "Then I got out."

"And you seized power," Obi-Wan said, disgusted.

"Obi-Wan." Yoda's voice had a quality Obi-Wan recognized, something he thought of as durasteel sheathed in ice.

Chastised like a youngling, Obi-Wan indicated that Lorian should go on.

"I was elected," Lorian said. "When I got out of prison, things had not changed much on Junction 5. Because Delaluna had allowed them to believe that they possessed the Annihilator, the great distrust between them had not diminished. The population still lived in a climate of fear. I suggested that I be an envoy to Delaluna and open talks between us. As the one who caused the worst of the trouble, I could be the one to stop it."

Obi-Wan crossed his arms, waiting.

"I would have failed," Lorian said, "if it wasn't for Samish Kash. He had recently been elected as ruler of

Delaluna. He, too, believed that the mistrust between two such close planets was harmful to them both. He believed that open trade and travel between Junction 5 and Delaluna would benefit everyone. So we sat down at a table and began to talk. We reached an agreement, and trade began. Borders were opened. We formed a partnership with the Bezim and Vicondor systems to build the Station 88 Spaceport. Both our worlds thrived and prospered. Because of the success of our plan, I was elected leader of Junction 5 three years later. I have ruled during a peaceful time. Our two little worlds were overlooked by the powers in the galaxy. In the Senate, we were one tiny voice among many. And now everything has changed."

"The systems of Junction 5 and Delaluna, found they are. Crucial to the success of the Separatists, they have become," Yoda said.

"The Station 88 Spaceport," Lorian Nod explained. "We are a gateway to the Mid-Rim systems."

Yoda lifted a hand, and a holographic map appeared. Junction 5 and Delaluna were illuminated. "If Junction 5 and Delaluna fall under Separatist control, fall Bezim and Vicondor will," he said. "Control they will a vast portion of the Mid-Rim systems."

"Count Dooku knows this very well," Lorian said. "He has contacted me. So far he has tried flattery and bribes to sway me to the Separatists, and I have lied and said I was leaning that way. Officially Samish Kash and I have not allied ourselves with either the Separatists or the Republic. I am not sure which way Kash is leaning, but I know that I have kept my own allegiances hidden. If Dooku knew I was loyal to the Republic, he could use force against my world — something I desperately wish to avoid. And I want to keep the Station 88 Spaceport as a strategic base for the Republic."

Obi-Wan nodded. He was interested now. He could see how important the tiny worlds of Junction 5 and Delaluna had become.

"Why not just declare your allegiance in the Senate?" Anakin asked. "They would send troops to protect you."

"Spread thin, the clone troops have become," Yoda said. "Our last option, that would be. A better way, Lorian has suggested."

"You may not be aware of this, Obi-Wan, but Dooku and I were friends during Temple training," Lorian said. "We had a falling out, but that was many years ago. I'm not sure if Dooku trusts me, but he needs me. It also makes sense to him that I would want to join the Separatists."

"It makes sense to me, too," Obi-Wan said. "Why don't you?"

"Because I have seen how making beings afraid or angry is the best way to make a power grab," Lorian said. "The Separatists have a point — the Senate has become a corrupt place where the needs of smaller systems go unheard. They have taken this resentment and used it as a screen for their own ends. Who are Dooku's main backers? That is where I look. The Commerce Guilds. The Trade Federation. The Corporate Alliance. The InterGalactic Bank Clan. What do they all have in common but wealth, and the desire for more power? This movement is a cover for greed." Lorian shook his head. "I am no longer able to access the Force as I did before. But I don't need the Force to show me that this road is a road to darkness."

Yoda bowed his head in agreement. Obi-Wan agreed as well. He just didn't like hearing this from Lorian Nod.

"Master Yoda, you had my first loyalty, and you have it still," Lorian said. "I have done things in my life that I know were wrong, but I am here to do right. I am here to serve the Jedi."

"What do you propose?" Obi-Wan asked. He wasn't interested in Lorian's avowals. He was only interested in what he would do.

"Dooku has called a meeting," Lorian said. "I have indicated to him that Samish Kash is leaning toward the Republic. He thinks he needs me to persuade or strong-arm Samish into the Separatist camp. Also at the meeting will be the rulers of Bezim and Vicondor. Dooku has proposed this as a friendly meeting at his villa on the world of Null."

"I've heard of this world," Obi-Wan said. "Dooku has its leader in his pocket. It was one of the first to join the Separatists."

"Although he proposed this as a neutral place to meet, obviously we are on his territory," Lorian agreed. "I have agreed to come, as have Samish Kash and the rulers of Vicondor and Bezim. We have a strong alliance among us. We have always acted as one. Dooku is hoping that I will help him convince the others to join the Separatists."

"And what do you propose?" Obi-Wan asked.

"I am not proposing anything except that I will attend this meeting as a spy, and hope to bring back useful information," Lorian said. "If the Jedi give me a specific task, I will perform it."

"Request we do that while we confer you wait here," Yoda said.

He accessed the door to an interior chamber. Obi-Wan and Anakin followed.

"I don't trust him," Obi-Wan said as soon as the doors closed behind them.

"Ask for your trust I do not," Yoda said. "Asking for your help I am. No matter his past, help us Lorian Nod can."

"He could have been sent here by Dooku," Obi-Wan said. "This could be a trick."

"Unlikely it is," Yoda said.

"Qui-Gon told me that Dooku and Lorian Nod were bitter enemies," Obi-Wan said. "Why would Dooku trust him now?"

"He said that Dooku didn't trust him," Anakin said. "But he needs him. Alliances are seldom based on trust, only need."

Yoda nodded. "Wise, your Padawan is. Think I do that best for this assignment, you are. If refuse you must, understand I will."

"What is it you wish us to do?"

"Travel to Null. This thread you must follow. Discover if Lorian is truthful. On this, the downfall of Dooku could depend."

CHAPTER 21

Null was a world of forests and mountains. It had no large cities, only small mountain villages, each so fiercely individualistic that attempts at alliances had always failed. There was a planet-wide government and a system of laws, but crimes tended to be solved among villagers according to an ancient tradition of fierce, swift retaliation that left no witnesses.

It was a perfect world for Dooku's hidden retreat. The villagers had a fierce sense of privacy and kept his comings and goings secret.

As Obi-Wan guided the small cruiser to the landing platform, he deliberately looped around the coordinates of Dooku's villa. Dooku had taken over the cliffside dwelling of a monarch who had reigned hundreds of standard years before. It had originally been built of stone, but Dooku had faced it in durasteel that was the exact gray of the mountain cliffs. The durasteel had been treated so that it did not gleam. It seemed to suck in light rather than reflect it. If Obi-Wan had not been looking for the villa, he would have missed it.

Obi-Wan guided the cruiser to the landing platform.

They stood, feeling a bit odd in their clothes. They were dressed as hunters, with thick short cloaks made of animal skins. Hunting was the only tourist trade that Null supported. The mountains were full of wild beasts prized for their skins, especially the wily laroon. They disembarked, feeling the cold wind against their faces like a slap.

"We're scheduled to rendezvous with Nod in the Spade Forest," Obi-Wan told Anakin as he paid a fee to an attendant droid to keep the cruiser at the platform. "We should avoid being seen with him, even though we're in disguise. We have time to check into the inn at the village."

Anakin nodded as he slung his pack over his shoulder. "Just don't make me shoot anything," he said.

Obi-Wan grinned. The small joke brought back the days when everything was easy between them.

They were below the tree line, so the path ran through a heavy forest. The mountains rose around them, stabbing the thin air with their snowy, jagged peaks. The landing platform had been built into the largest mountain, which rose into the clouds. It was under this mountain that the village crouched.

The thick trees cleared as they walked down the mountain and the roofs of the village appeared. The buildings were made of stone and wood and were only a few stories tall.

Narrow streets wound through the cluster of buildings. The villagers seemed to rely on a sturdy native animal, the bellock, for transportation. Obi-Wan saw only a few speeders parked in yards.

Then they turned a corner and saw a cluster of gleaming speeders in front of a tall stone building, and they knew they had found the inn. Obi-Wan and Anakin entered, keeping their hoods on. The interior lobby was scattered with seating areas made of plush materials. A fireplace twenty meters tall held a huge blazing fire that chased away the damp chill. Various beings sat around the fire, some consulting datapads, others drinking tea. By the look of their clothes, Obi-Wan guessed they were outsiders, most likely aides to the rulers of the four planets. In a dark corner a hunter sat, covered in skins, an awesome array of weapons at his feet. His bored gaze seemed to regard the sleek, sophisticated beings with contempt.

"He's got enough weapons to bring down a capital ship, let alone a laroon," Anakin remarked in a low voice.

Obi-Wan's gaze traveled up the fireplace. The wall was fashioned of jagged stones from the mountain, fitted together in intricate patterns. He could see no evidence of mortar or joinery, but each stone nestled against each other in what must have been perfect balance.

The innkeeper smiled as he greeted Obi-Wan and Anakin. He was obviously a native Null. They were tall humanoids, easily a meter taller than Obi-Wan and Anakin. The men wore heavy beards, which they braided, and both men and women dressed in animal skins and thigh-length boots. "I see you are admiring the stonework of the inn," he said. "It is a native art. One pull of the keystone and the whole wall comes tumbling down."

"And which is the keystone?" Obi-Wan asked.

"Ah, that is the maker's secret," the innkeeper said. He noted their traveling clothes and sacks. "Always glad to welcome our hunters to the inn," he said. "As you can see, we have important guests, very important guests. But we do not neglect our regular trade." He pushed the data register toward Obi-Wan.

"What's going on here?" Obi-Wan asked, bending forward to sign the register. "I didn't realize Null was now on the tourist track."

The innkeeper leaned closer. "A very high-level meeting, I believe. Don't know what it's about. But I expect more of these meetings in the future. So book early or you'll be out of luck!"

"We'll be sure to." Obi-Wan pushed the register back along with the credits to pay for a room.

A young woman sat in a small chair tucked against the wall. He had not noticed her before, and would not have noticed her if a flicker of recognition didn't jolt him. He could not place her, but he felt he knew her. She was slender, dressed in a dark green tunic the color of the leaves outside. A matching headwrap covered her hair. He had met thousands of beings all over the galaxy, and though his memory was excellent, it was hard to remember everyone. Or maybe she just reminded him of someone. . . .

He turned. "Anakin, do you recognize that woman in green, sitting against the wall?"

"What woman?" Anakin asked.

There was a flicker of green, and the door of the inn closed. Obi-Wan filed the woman away in his mind to investigate later. He didn't like it when something nagged at him.

The hunter warmed his hands at the fire, picked up his weapons, and rumbled to the door. The native Null workers rolled their eyes after he had passed, clearly considering him an overly armed amateur.

"Come on," Obi-Wan said. "Let's find our room. It's almost time to meet Lorian."

First they stowed their gear in their room, a small one tucked under the eaves of the roof. Obviously they were not among those "important guests" the innkeeper had mentioned.

They walked out into the village street and toward the path that led into the forest. Obi-Wan called up the prearranged coordinates on his datapad. They would meet not far from the village in a forest clearing that Lorian had already determined was secluded but not difficult to reach.

As they reached the edge of the village, they saw a villager running down the mountain path. The thud of his panicked footsteps came to them clearly.

"Sound the alarm!" he shouted. "There's been a murder! Samish Kash has been assassinated!"

22

Three blasts of a horn sounded as Obi-Wan and Anakin raced up the trail. They found Samish Kash lying a few meters off the main path. Villagers crowded around him, and a speeder arrived. Samish Kash was loaded onto it. Obi-Wan saw the blaster wound near his heart. He was a young man with curly dark hair, dressed in a plain tunic. As far as Obi-Wan could tell, he was unarmed.

Lorian Nod stood by, his face full of sorrow. He acknowledged the Jedi with a glance, then leaped aboard the speeder that held the body of Kash.

Obi-Wan saw the young woman in green turn away. Her shoulders were shaking. The hunter with the impressive arsenal put a hand underneath her elbow.

"An aide to Samish Kash," one of the villagers whispered. "She found his body."

Then we will most definitely need to talk to her, Obi-Wan thought. He watched the young woman and the hunter. Now his mind was clicking. They were arguing in a way that told him they were not strangers. Obi-Wan began to drift closer, hoping to overhear. But they kept moving away from the circle of villagers, the woman trying to get away from the hunter while still talking to him.

As she made an abrupt move to turn away, her hood fell back, and he saw that she had blond hair, braided tightly and coiled around her head. Then he caught a flash of wide blue eyes. The hunter spoke urgently in her ear.

"It's Floria and Dane," Obi-Wan said.

Anakin looked where Obi-Wan had indicated. "The brother and sister bounty hunters we met on Ragoon-6? How can you be sure? It was so long ago."

"Look carefully."

Anakin studied them. "You're right. What are bounty hunters doing here?"

"Exactly what I'd like to find out."

The two Jedi moved quickly through the crowd. Floria and Dane had now moved well away from the commotion.

"If you had done what you were supposed to —" Dane was saying.

"So you're saying it's my fault?" Floria's voice was choked with anger and tears. "You always —"

"You never —" Dane stopped talking as Obi-Wan and Anakin walked up.

"I must confess I never expected to see you again," Obi-Wan said.

Floria and Dane stared at them for a long moment.

"Black holes and novas, it's the Jedi," Dane said. Now Obi-Wan could see his blue eyes, so much like Floria's. "What are you two doing here?"

"Which is exactly what I want to know about you two," Obi-Wan said, steering them farther away from the others, and underneath the trees. "Who are you hunting? Are you involved in the death of Samish Kash?"

"No!" Dane exclaimed. "We're his bodyguards!"

"Obviously, you are doing an excellent job," Anakin said. Floria burst into tears.

"Bounty hunting was getting too dangerous," Dane said, handing his sister a cloth to wipe her tears. "There were so many of us out there that all honor was lost. Some were using truly cutthroat techniques."

"I've seen a few," Obi-Wan concurred.

"So we decided to become bodyguards. It's simpler. Samish Kash hired us a couple of months ago for protection. He didn't want the usual big goons or guard droids. He didn't want anyone to know. So Floria posed as an aide, and I just used disguises. Then this meeting was called. Samish told us to be especially careful. He's the glue that keeps the Station 88 Spaceport alliance together. Without him, it would fall apart. He's the one everyone trusts. So he thought if some group wanted to take over the spaceport, they'd go for him first." Dane looked distraught. "Then instead of staying in my sight, or Floria's, the way he promised, he disappeared. I followed, and . . ."

"You found him dead?"

"Lying there," Dane said. "Shot in the heart."

"And you saw nothing?"

"What does it matter?" Floria asked them. She had wiped her tears away and her face was pale. "He's dead."

Dane shook his head. "I was too late." He looked off into the trees. "I should have —" Dane stopped abruptly and squinted into the trees.

Without another word, Dane took off. He raced to his swoop hovering nearby in suspended mode. He leaped aboard and took off.

"Come on, Anakin," Obi-Wan said, spurting forward. "We'll have to follow on foot."

The trees were dense here, and Obi-Wan could see ahead that Dane was having trouble navigating between the trunks. He had to continually slow his speed. He was obviously chasing someone ahead of him on a swoop, which appeared and disappeared through the trees.

They gained on Dane, hurtling through the spaces between the trees. When they were meters away, Anakin leaped high to grab a tree branch. Using the momentum, he swung forward and dropped neatly on the back of Dane's swoop. The swoop lurched and careened toward a massive tree trunk. Dane let out a piercing yell. Calmly, Anakin stood on the back of the swoop and leaned forward to grab the controls. He steered away from the trunk, circled, and came back to Obi-Wan.

"He'll get away!" Dane cried.

"Who?" Obi-Wan asked.

"I don't know! But I think he killed Kash!" Dane cried

breathlessly. "I don't know where I know him from, but I know him. He's a bounty hunter."

"Mind if we take over?" Obi-Wan asked Dane.

He jumped off the swoop. "Be my guest. Just be careful with my swoop!" he yelled after them as Anakin sent the engines screaming to maximum.

Suddenly, Obi-Wan wished he were driving.

The suspect glanced back once and saw they were still following. He chose a difficult route through the trees. The narrow spaces were hard to get through, especially at high speeds. Anakin flipped the swoop, turning constantly to come at the openings at the best angle, never slackening speed. He crashed through leaves and branches. They were gaining, but Obi-Wan was positive he'd lose an arm or an ear in the process.

"Do you think you could slow down?" Obi-Wan yelled over the sound of cracking twigs and the screaming engines.

"And miss all the fun?" Anakin asked, executing a quick left turn, flipping the swoop, then flipping it back again. Obi-Wan tried to find his breath.

The ground was rising sharply. The suspect pushed his speed. He careened through two trees, lost control, and the swoop flipped over and scraped the side of the next tree, sending the swoop spinning wildly. The assassin leaped off a moment before the swoop crashed into a large tree. He hit the ground and ran.

"We've got him now," Anakin said, gunning the engine.

Obi-Wan caught a blur of large brown spots speckling the tree trunks as they zoomed fast. A *strange mold?* he wondered. The spots had hairs that waved in the air like legs. They were legs, he realized.

Spiders. About the size of a small rodent animal. Obi-Wan had read about them in his briefing notes on the journey to Null. They weren't poisonous, but one had to watch out for their —

"Anakin, watch out!"

Ahead the sunlight had just caught the silky threads of the giant web slung between the trees. The swoop hit it head-on. The web did not break. The reclumi species of spider had a web so strong it could stop a moving vehicle.

It did.

CHAPTER 23

The swoop boomeranged backward, crashed into the tree trunk behind them, then shot forward again, caught in the sticky web. The ropy tendrils clung to Obi-Wan's skin and hair and caught in his mouth. When he tried to pull the skin of the web off him, it stuck to his fingers.

"Aarrgh!" Anakin gave a strangled cry as he tried to pull the web off his face.

Obi-Wan managed to unsheathe his lightsaber and activate it. He cut a swath through the web, creating a hole. He dropped to the forest floor. Anakin landed next to him. Tendrils of the web still stuck to their skin, and they tried to get it off, but it stuck to them like a strong glue. The swoop hung above them while a spider with legs more than a meter long scuttled across a tree trunk to see what it had caught.

Meanwhile, the assassin had disappeared. They would have to track him.

They ran quickly through the trees, snaking through the forest. The assassin had doubled back. After tracking him for a kilometer, Obi-Wan suspected that he was heading back toward the village.

They came out on another path that veered downhill sharply. Through the trees they could occasionally see the rooftops of the village. The path ended at the outskirts of the village, near some outbuildings. A large stone building had a side parking area for speeders.

"Anakin, stop. There he is."

The assassin was moving from shadow to shadow across the street. They could see now that he was a human male, dressed in dark clothing and wearing a helmet with a brim that that shadowed his face.

Then Lorian Nod appeared from the back pathway to the mountain. He was walking quickly and didn't notice the Jedi.

"He's meeting Lorian," Anakin said.

Suddenly the street came alive with villagers. They surged forward, shouting in their native language and brandishing blasters and the native weapon, a sharp blade atop a thick wooden pole. The assassin melted back into the shadows.

The villagers rushed down the street. Lorian was lost in the midst of them. Suddenly, Obi-Wan saw that Floria and Dane were being herded near the front of the crowd. Their hands were bound in lasercuffs in front of them.

Dane caught sight of Obi-Wan. "They think we killed Samish!" he shouted. "Help us!"

Floria and Dane were carried along with the crowd. The villagers surged into the stone building like one giant moving beast. The street was suddenly empty. Lorian had vanished.

"Should we try to find him?" Anakin asked.

Obi-Wan sighed. "He's not going anywhere. And we'd better see what's happening with Floria and Dane."

They walked into the building. It was a basic prison, but the security wasn't sophisticated. The cell was a small room in a corner with a durasteel door and a basic security coded lock. There were no official guards, no datascreens, no evidence of record-keeping or comm devices. Obviously this was used as a holding cell until the villagers decided on their own brand of justice.

The locals sat around a massive wooden table, drinking tea and grog and arguing. Obi-Wan stepped forward.

"We would like to see our friends."

"They are our prisoners." This was growled from the largest villager who sat at the head of the table.

Obi-Wan dug into the bag at his side and threw the skin of a laroon on the table. They had brought skins and furs with them to cover their identities.

"We would like to see our friends," he repeated.

The fur of the laroon was inspected with knowing fingers. Then the villager nodded. He rose slowly, ambled to the lock, and keyed in the security code. The door slid open.

Dane was pacing in the cell. Floria sat quietly on the one chair provided. The door slid shut behind the Jedi.

"Thank the stars you are here. They are going to kill us," Dane said.

"Don't be so dramatic," Floria said. "You don't know that."

"Let me think. They just debated on whether to use

blasters or do it slowly by lowering us into a laroon den. What's your conclusion?" Dane asked fiercely.

"They can't just kill us without a trial," Floria said. Obi-Wan noted that she had regained the color in her cheeks. Floria had been a pretty girl. Now she was a beautiful woman.

"Of course they can! This is Null! They don't bother with trials here!" Dane cried.

"Floria, Dane, if you could stop arguing for a moment," Obi-Wan said, holding up a hand. "Do they have evidence against you?"

"I found the body, and Dane came up right after," Floria said.

"In other words, they don't need evidence," Dane said. "We're outlanders. We were in the vicinity. That's all they need to know." He slumped against the wall of the bare cell and drifted down until he was sitting on the floor.

"We will protect you from the villagers," Obi-Wan said. "But you must help us."

"You were Kash's bodyguards," Anakin said. "You must have a few likely suspects. Who would have hired that assassin?"

Floria shook her head. Dane shrugged.

"No one and everyone," Dane said. "He didn't have any particular enemies. He had brought prosperity and peace to his people. But with this Separatist thing, every-thing changes. It could have been Dooku himself. It could have been one of the other members of the alliance, Telamarch or Uziel, if they wanted to control the alliance."

"You didn't mention Lorian Nod," Anakin said.

"Him too, I guess." Dane looked gloomy. "I don't trust anybody."

"Not Lorian Nod," Floria spoke up. "They started the alliance together."

Obi-Wan crouched down near Dane. "Dane, you said the assassin looked familiar. You have to remember where you met him."

Dane buried his head in his hands. "Floria and I have been all over the galaxy. I've met so many beings. He's one in a line of awful ones. I really need to retire." He looked up. "Hey, how's my swoop, by the way? Is it safe?"

Obi-Wan and Anakin exchanged a glance.

"Well, it's definitely not going anywhere," Anakin said.

"We ran into a reclumi," Obi-Wan said.

"Web!" Dane shouted.

"Yes, a big one —"

"No, Web! That's his name! The assassin," Dane said. "I met him about two years ago. Robior Web. We had auditioned for the same job but he didn't get hired. The thing about him was, he got started as a security officer but the security force was disbanded on his planet so he found himself out of a job. He's got a reputation for taking on big jobs, assassinations, things like that. He used to be a Guardian on Junction 5."

Obi-Wan slowly rose.

"There is our connection to Lorian Nod," he said.

Promising to return, Obi-Wan and Anakin raced out of the prison and into the inn. They found Lorian in a secluded area of the lobby, deep in conference with the rulers of Bezim and Vicondor. Obi-Wan and Anakin hovered unseen, able to pick up some of their conversation.

"What is happening?" Yura Telamarch asked, his voice full of distress. The ruler of Bezim was a tall humanoid with a domed head and a grave manner. "Do you think Count Dooku is behind the murder of Kash?"

"I don't know, Yura," Lorian said. "They've arrested Samish's bodyguards. It could be an internal plot of Delaluna."

"We are not safe here," Glimmer Uziel, the ruler of Vicondor, said. She had a musical voice and pale gold skin. Four tiny tentacles waved delicately in the air, like fronds. "What if this is a trap? There are those among my aides who say that Count Dooku will not show up. He has lured us here to kill us all and take the space station by force."

"Without Samish, our alliance is weaker," Yura said. "No doubt the pressure will increase. What do you think, Lorian?"

"I think we trust Dooku for now," Lorian answered. He stood. "I suggest you get some rest. The meeting is scheduled to take place in an hour."

Reluctantly Yura and Glimmer rose and headed for the stairs. As soon as the rulers were out of sight, Obi-Wan and Anakin walked up to Lorian. "Trust Dooku?" Obi-Wan asked sardonically. "Good advice, Lorian."

"What did you expect me to say?" Lorian asked. "Dooku must not suspect that I am against him."

"Are you against him?" Obi-Wan asked. "Things have changed now that Samish Kash is dead. If someone wished to drive a wedge through the alliance, it has worked."

"Are you accusing me of killing Samish? He was my friend."

"So you say. Have you ever heard of Robior Web?" Obi-Wan asked.

Lorian frowned. "The name is familiar, but . . ."

"He was a Guardian."

"I could hardly be expected to remember every Guardian."

"He is now working as an assassin."

Lorian took several moments to reply. "He is on Null?"

"Yes. Dane recognized him."

Lorian nodded slowly. "You think this Web killed Kash, and I hired him to do it."

Obi-Wan said nothing.

"I did not," Lorian said. "And if you think about it for a

moment you will see that if someone wanted to smash the alliance, the way to do so would be to kill one member and pin the murder on another. It is no accident that the assassin is a former Guardian. Naturally you would suspect me."

"Naturally," Obi-Wan said.

"And that is exactly what Dooku would want Yura and Glimmer to do," Lorian continued. "This is how he works. He waits. He watches. He likes to undermine loyalties. He likes to fracture bonds. He likes to encourage betrayal."

All of this was true, but it didn't mean Lorian wasn't guilty. Just clever.

"There is more going on here than the Force can sense," Lorian said. "And more than your logic can decipher. There are feelings here, Obi-Wan. And among those feelings are mine for Samish. I did not do it."

"We have only your word for it, along with everything else," Obi-Wan said. "That is the problem."

"There is only one solution to the problem, then," Lorian said. "You must trust me."

"Can you give me any reason to do so?" Obi-Wan asked.

Lorian hesitated. "No. I cannot prove my honesty."

"Then we'll continue to suspect you," Anakin said.

"We come from the same place," Lorian said, looking at them both. "I was raised in the Temple. I fell away from its teachings for a time. Why? I was afraid. I was young and alone and I took a step forward, the only step I felt I could take. Then I took another, and another, and I ended up in a life I didn't recognize."

"These are excuses," Obi-Wan said. "Tell that to the people of Junction 5. Tell that to Cilia Dil."

"I harmed my people," Lorian admitted. "And I must say that Cilia is not one of my supporters. She can't forget what I was. I know all I have are excuses. When you live a life filled with wrong, what else do you have but excuses and blame?" He paused. "Do you believe in redemption, Obi-Wan?"

Obi-Wan had been asked the question, but it was Anakin who spoke up. "I do."

"I do, as well, young Anakin Skywalker," Lorian said. "It is what keeps me going. At the end of my life, I will do good. That's all I can tell you for now."

"Do you believe him?" Anakin asked as they walked outside the inn.

"I think he talks well," Obi-Wan said. "And I don't know what to believe. Not yet." Would Qui-Gon have known? He had always seemed to know who to trust.

"You are too hard on beings sometimes," Anakin said. "Mistakes are made. Things happen. That means that change can happen, too."

"The meaning of life *is* change," Obi-Wan said, startled at Anakin's characterization of him. The charge stung. He did not think he was hard on other beings. Perhaps that had been true once, but he had learned from Qui-Gon. "I didn't say I didn't believe Lorian. But I can't discount the rest of his life just because he tells me I should. If he is in league with Dooku, we should find out what they are planning. And if he is not in league with Dooku, we should still find out."

"So what's our next step?" Anakin asked.

"Do you have any suggestions?" Obi-Wan asked.

"I have a question," Anakin said. "If Robior Web was hired to kill Samish Kash, he has accomplished his objective. Why is he still on Null? Assassins seldom hang around after they finish an assignment."

"He was going to meet Lorian and give his report," Obi-Wan said.

"That could be true," Anakin said, "but usually that is done by comlink or dataport. Usually an assassin and his employer don't like to be seen together."

"So if he's still on Null, he could have another assignment to accomplish before the meeting," Obi-Wan said. "Maybe we should find him."

"Sure," Anakin said. "But how? It's a big mountain."

"Exactly," Obi-Wan said. "If I were Web, I'd want transport. His was destroyed. I'd need to do it without attracting any attention, so that lets out stealing one from a villager or an aide. But he knows where another one is —"

Anakin grinned and finished the sentence. "— just hanging around."

*　　*　　*

When they got to where Dane's speeder was hanging emeshed in the spiderweb, Robior Web was in the tree, trying to slice the web with his vibroblade. It was clear he had been trying for some time to release the swoop. His hands and tunic were covered with the sticky, ropy web. He had managed to free the back of the swoop, and it hung suspended from the handlebars, which were covered in the sticky goo. Below on the ground, a dead reclumi spider lay in pieces, a victim of the same vibroblade, no doubt when it tried to defend its web.

Robior Web consulted a chrono, then attacked the web even more fiercely. He succeeded only in winding a large tendril of the web around his arm. They could not hear his curses, but they could see his frustration.

"Time is running out," Obi-Wan murmured. "My guess is he has an appointment."

With one last savage thrust, Robior Web managed to cut loose a ropy tendril, but it flopped away, then smacked back against the body of the swoop. Now it was more enmeshed than ever.

With a strangled cry, the assassin dropped from the tree and hit the ground. He began to run.

Obi-Wan and Anakin followed. They had to keep well behind, but it was easy to track his progress through the forest. He was heading around the mountain but climbing steadily.

"I think he's heading for the landing platform," Obi-Wan said. "We'll be coming at it from above."

After a hard climb, they realized Obi-Wan was right. Robior Web climbed over a peak and disappeared below. Obi-Wan and Anakin waited a moment, then climbed behind him and peered over the edge. Web was moving down toward the landing platform below.

Suddenly the sun was blocked out overhead. They looked up. A large transport was hovering. Robior Web quickened his pace and almost slid down to the deserted landing platform.

Behind the large transport, a sleek interstellar sloop dropped down from the sky, a sail ship, like none other in the galaxy.

"Dooku has arrived," Obi-Wan said.

The solar sailer landed. The landing ramp slid down and the tall, elegant figure of Count Dooku emerged. Obi-Wan felt Anakin tense. Unconsciously, he touched the metal hand that had replaced the one Dooku had severed.

"So Dooku hired the assassin," Obi-Wan muttered as Robior Web skidded to a stop in front of Dooku, then bowed. "With or without Lorian, we don't know."

Distracted, he had not realized Anakin was rising until his Padawan was almost to his feet.

"Anakin what are you doing? Get down!"

"Let's get him now," Anakin said.

"Get down!" Obi-Wan insisted. To his relief, Anakin crouched down again. He faced him, his eyes full of fire and purpose.

"We have our chance to end it here," Anakin said. "Let's kill him. We can take him together. We won't make the same mistakes this time."

"Like being reckless and rushing him without a plan?" Obi-Wan asked pointedly. "It is what cost you your hand last time, and you are doing it again, Padawan."

"What are we waiting for?" Anakin asked. "We missed him at Raxus Prime, but we won't here. If we kill him, we kill the Separatist movement. What is one life against thousands? Maybe millions?"

"Anakin —"

"He killed our brothers and sisters on Geonosis," Anakin said bitterly. "Have you forgotten how they died?"

"I remember it every moment," Obi-Wan said. "But this is not the time. This is not the way."

"You don't know what I can do," Anakin said, and there was an ominous tone in his voice. "My connection to the Force is stronger than yours. I'm telling you I can do it! No matter what you say."

Obi-Wan was shocked. "You are still my apprentice," he said sharply. "I am your Master. You must obey."

The set of Anakin's mouth was sullen.

"Anakin, you must trust me," Obi-Wan said forcefully. "There will be another time to face Dooku. This is not the time."

Anakin looked at him. The sullen look was gone. His gaze was clear and cool. Obi-Wan could almost read contempt in it. But as the thought occurred to him, the look was gone. Had he really seen it?

"Look below," Obi-Wan said. "What do you think is in that transport? Super battle droids. We would be dead before we took two steps on that platform. They're being unloaded now."

Anakin looked down at the platform. Lines of droids clicked into formation as they rolled off the transport. Obi-Wan could see the way Anakin's mind focused on the immediate problem. He could almost feel Anakin's anger drain away.

But why had it been there in the first place? Obi-Wan had a feeling he had seen a flash of something much deeper than he'd ever known before.

"He is taking no chances," Obi-Wan guessed. "If things do not go his way at the meeting, he will use force."

Reluctantly, Anakin tore his gaze away. "We should warn them."

"Yes," Obi-Wan said. "But who? Any one of them could be secretly in league with Dooku. We must consider our next step carefully. We must figure out who to talk to first."

"I say we talk to Floria," Anakin said.

"Why Floria?" Obi-Wan asked, puzzled. He didn't know what Anakin was thinking. He rarely did, anymore. But at least he was glad they were talking.

"I sense she is not telling all she knows," Anakin said.

Obi-Wan thought back. He realized that he had picked

up something from Floria, too. But he had been too focused on Lorian to consider it.

Your mind must be everywhere at once, Padawan. The truth has many sides.

Yes, Qui-Gon.

"There is more going on here than the Force can sense," Anakin said, repeating Lorian's words. "*Feelings*, he said. What did he mean?"

"I don't know," Obi-Wan said.

"That is why we must talk to Floria," Anakin said. He rose to his feet in one quick movement and began to run. Obi-Wan had to put on a burst of speed to catch up.

"Do you remember," Anakin said, "how upset she was when the body of Samish Kash was found?"

"She had failed in her mission to protect him," Obi-Wan said.

"I think the loss was more personal," Anakin said. "And later she called him 'Samish.' Dane always calls him 'Kash.' I think she's in love with him."

"How is that relevant to our mission?"

Anakin shot him a sidelong look. Amazing that they were running hard down a mountain, and Anakin could still have the energy for a healthy dose of scorn.

"Love is always relevant, Master," he said.

CHAPTER 25

Another bribe got them access to the cell.

"Take your time," the villager said, waving a hand as the door slid open. "We've decided to kill them at dawn."

The rest of the villagers roared and pounded the table. They had been drinking grog for some time now. The door slid shut, drowning out their laughter.

"Did you hear that?" Dane hissed at Floria.

"She's not afraid," Anakin said. "Why is that, Floria?"

"I am not panicking like my brother, it's true," Floria said.

"And you are no longer grieving," Anakin said. "Why is that?"

Floria turned her extraordinary sky-blue eyes on Anakin. They looked at each other for a long moment.

"You love him," Anakin said.

"Of course she loves me," Dane said. "I'm her brother."

Another long silence. Anakin waited her out. Obi-Wan kept very still.

"I love Samish," Floria admitted. Her chin lifted and her eyes flashed, as though to say the words out loud had given her great pleasure.

"You love who?" Dane shouted.

"And he is still alive," Anakin said.

Floria nodded.

"What?" Dane cried, leaping in front of Floria. "You love Samish Kash, and he's still alive?"

"Dane, stop. He was shot, but he survived," Floria said. "He decided to let everyone think he was dead after the attempt on his life. He wanted to find out who had put a price on his head and why. The alliance is very important to him, and he doesn't trust Dooku."

"He was our employer!" Dane said. "We worked for him. You were his bodyguard. You went against all professional standards —"

"Be quiet," Anakin ordered, turning on Dane. "Floria couldn't help her feelings."

"You can always help your feelings," Dane said. "Feelings *need* help. Otherwise they get completely out of control!"

Obi-Wan ignored Dane. "When we first saw you, you thought Samish Kash was dead." At Floria's nod, he continued. "How did you find out he was alive?"

"You let me think I was going to be executed!" Dane cried, as a fresh wave of indignation swept over him.

"Lorian told me," Floria said. "He had brought Kash to the clinic. He, too, had thought he was dead. Kash revived on the med table. Lorian bribed the doctor and he and Samish came up with the plan. The first thing Samish asked Lorian to do was tell me. Right after that, we were arrested."

"Did you ever think of mentioning that the person we supposedly killed wasn't dead?" Dane asked.

"I couldn't say anything. Not until the meeting," Floria said. "If Dooku has a plan, it will take place there. Lorian and Samish decided that Samish should show up at the meeting. If Dooku had arranged his assassination, it might be enough to foil his plans."

"So Lorian told the truth," Obi-Wan said. "He didn't hire the assassin. He could have gotten off the hook by telling us Samish was alive, and he didn't."

"He had sworn to keep the secret," Floria said. "Samish always said Lorian had come both early and late to honor. I wasn't sure what he meant."

"I think I do." Obi-Wan looked at Anakin. "They are walking into a trap," he said.

A trap he could have prevented. He could have told Lorian about the battle droids, and he had not. Angry with himself, Obi-Wan piloted the speeder up the mountain toward Dooku's villa at maximum speed. It had only taken a little truth, a little persuasion, and two glowing lightsabers to get the villagers to release their prisoners. As soon as they heard that Samish Kash was alive and that the two hunters were actually Jedi, they even turned over several speeders for their use.

Obi-Wan and Anakin had each taken a speeder. Floria and Dane insisted on coming with them. Despite everything, Dane considered Samish Kash his responsibility to protect. Floria just wanted to be with him, "whatever happens."

The villa rose above them, as gray and forbidding as the stone mountain. The meeting was about to begin. Obi-Wan saw the security gate ahead. The speeder had light armor mounted on the hull. He opened fire and blasted his way through the gate. Immediately a durasteel shield began to descend over the wide double doors of the front entrance. It would no doubt prove impenetrable to explosives.

Before Obi-Wan could react, Anakin gunned his speeder, blasting his weaponry at the double doors beyond the descending shield. In an amazing display of skill, he cut the power, flipping his speeder up at the same time and leaping off. The speeder skidded to a stop, its armored hull pointing up toward the swiftly descending shield.

The shield came down on the speeder. Metal shrieked and groaned, slowing the descent of the shield. Anakin ducked under the moving shield and leaped through the hole he had blasted through the double doors. He disappeared into the darkness of the villa.

This had all taken only seconds. Obi-Wan had already leaped off his speeder and was running toward the durasteel shield, now slowly crushing the speeder underneath it. There was just enough room for Obi-Wan to duck underneath and inside. Floria and Dane followed, rolling under the door as it goaned downward and shut with a crash, the speeder now part pancake, part mangled transport.

Anakin was waiting in the darkness of the hallway. The ceiling was so high it was lost in the gloom above. Together they ran down the grand hall, looking into the large rooms as they passed. They heard voices ahead.

Obi-Wan slipped into a circular room that had been built in the center of the villa. There was no ceiling, only the roof above. Narrow windows were cut into the stone high above and let in a faint light. One entire wall was made up of an enormous fireplace, big enough for a Null to stand erect in. A large circular stone table sat in the center of the room, but it was dwarfed by the soaring space. Dooku stood at one end. Samish stood at the opposite side of the table, facing him. Yura, Glimmer, and Lorian looked small and defenseless. The table was so large that there was an expanse of space between each of them.

Obi-Wan guessed that Dooku had sensed his presence. He felt the dark side in the room, how it surged and grew. Anakin came and stood next to him, and Floria and Dane followed, staying against the wall in the shadows so that they would not be seen.

"I believe you tried to assassinate me so you could smash the alliance," Samish was saying.

"So much emotion, so little logic," Dooku said. "Let us be calm. Station 88 Spaceport is a vital strategic link. This is something that must be decided carefully. You have not even heard what my organization is willing to give to you for the rights to the spaceport. I am sure your partners would want to hear. Do you deny them that right?"

Samish looked uncertain. "Yes, we should at least hear him out," Yura said.

Anakin stirred. Obi-Wan put a hand on his arm. If they moved, Dooku was capable of anything. And he had seen Robior Web standing against the wall, almost lost in the shadows. He had no doubt that Samish Kash was in danger, and most likely all of the other rulers in the alliance, as well.

Samish turned to the others. "Why should we listen? Everything he is about to tell us will be lies."

Dooku turned to Lorian. "We haven't heard from you, old friend. Tell Samish what you have decided."

Lorian stood. "I support Samish Kash. And I support the Republic."

Dooku gripped the edge of the table. It was clear that a great surge of rage had overtaken him. He controlled it. His dark eyes seemed to suck in the light around the table and devour it.

He leaned over the table. "So you betray me again. I assure you, it is for the last time, Lorian."

"Yes," Lorian said. "I am certain of that."

"Vicondor must stand with Delaluna and Junction 5, my friends Samish and Lorian," Glimmer said. "The alliance will support the Republic."

Dooku looked over into the shadows and acknowledged the Jedi for the first time. "So you support a corrupt government?" he thundered. "Have you forgotten the battle of Geonosis, how they crushed a small planet with an invading army? They are ruthless. They hide in the shadows. Look!"

The rulers turned and saw the Jedi. Lorian appeared very glad to see them. "That is one way of looking at it," he said. "But it is not the truth."

"I stand with the decision of the alliance," Yura said.

"It appears the negotiation is over," Dooku said. He had controlled his anger and spoke now in a mild tone. "How unfortunate. I suppose I could try to persuade you. But as I grow older, I have found that I have so little . . . patience for such things."

The door behind Obi-Wan, Anakin, Floria, and Dane slid shut. They heard the security locks snap. Shutters slid down over the windows and the room was thrown into deep shadow.

Then hidden doors in the walls of the circular room slid open and at least a dozen super battle droids marched in.

Obi-Wan saw it all happen in a frozen moment. There was Dooku. There were the droids. There was Robior Web, the capable assassin.

Yura, Glimmer, and Kash were not fighters, but politicians. Floria and Dane could handle themselves, but not against such firepower. There were too many beings to protect. And it was clear that Dooku meant to murder them all. The room was a trap. It was a tomb.

He remembered the arena at Geonosis, the arrival of the gunships, the battle, the slaughter.

In that frozen moment the thought blazed, white-hot and searing: *I cannot bear one more death.* It was illogical — he knew in his heart that he would have to bear many more — but not today.

Not today.

Dooku stepped back from the table. Anakin charged, putting himself between the approaching droids and the politicians. Fire erupted from the super battle droids at the same time. Yura and Glimmer both sensibly dropped to the floor.

No one had expected Floria to move so fast.

She streaked across the space as Obi-Wan was moving to deflect the blaster fire of the droids. She would come between Dooku and Anakin, a dangerous place to be.

Single-minded, intent, Anakin increased his speed. Obi-Wan saw him move from light to shadow, shadow to light. He felt the Force in the room like a pulse, like a heartbeat, like a rolling wave.

"Anakin, Floria!" he shouted.

Anakin shuddered with the effort of stopping his relentless charge. He altered his path to scoop up Floria, tucked her under his arm, and kept his lightsaber moving, deflecting the blaster fire of the droids. He deposited Floria next to Samish Kash, so lightly and gently in the midst of his soaring leap that not even a hair of Floria's coiled braids was disturbed.

Obi-Wan saw the relief on the face of Samish Kash. Anakin had been right about Floria's love. Now Obi-Wan saw the same love on Samish's face. He would not allow these two to die.

He caught the surging Force from Anakin and embraced it, doubling it, making it grow. The droids re-converged on the rulers. Obviously they were programmed to target them. Anakin leaped again, and Obi-Wan met him in mid-air. They swept the room in a glance. There were only seconds to decide on a strategy.

Dooku was leaving. They saw his cloak flicker as he moved toward the wall, toward the one door that still stood open.

Lorian saw Dooku moving and ran toward him.

Yura and Glimmer had no weapons. They sat, back-to-back behind a massive chair for protection that was being rapidly decimated by the droid blasts. The expression on their faces told Obi-Wan that they were waiting for death and would meet it bravely.

Floria handed one blaster to Samish and had the other in her hand. While Samish and Dane tried to protect her, she shot a droid repeatedly with unerring accuracy. It flamed out and fell heavily on the table.

Robior Web took aim at Samish.

Obi-Wan landed, then jumped again, somersaulting in midair and landing against Web's chest with both feet. The assassin flew back and hit a chunk of stone protruding from the wall. He lay still.

Obi-Wan had time to register the chunk of stone with only a flash of his consciousness, but something about it was important. He was busy deflecting blaster fire as it pinged past him toward Yura and Glimmer.

Anakin had managed to herd the group together in one corner of the room so that they would be easier to protect. With a swipe of his lightsaber, he hewed off a chunk of the stone table, then pushed the others behind it for protection.

They could only last so long, Obi-Wan thought desperately. They could not win against these droids.

The chunk of stone — why did it keep rising in his mind?

The keystone. One pull of the keystone and the whole wall comes tumbling down.

Obi-Wan raced back to Anakin. They spoke while they protected the others, deflecting fire. Samish, Dane, and Floria popped out to fire at the droids, then dived for cover again.

"Glimmer has been hit in the leg," Anakin said. "Lorian went after Dooku. We have to help him. We have to get out of here."

"The keystone in the fireplace," Obi-Wan said. "If we herd the others to the opposite end of the room quickly, then pull the keystone, it would knock out most of the droids."

Anakin's eyes traveled over the fireplace wall even as his lightsaber whirled.

"Finding it, of course, is the problem," Obi-Wan said.

He felt Anakin gather in the Force then, feeling it shimmer from the stones and the wood and the living beings, feeling it grow . . . Anakin focused on the wall.

Obi-Wan saw one stone midway up the wall ease out a fraction. He heard a rumble.

"Move!" he shouted, leaping toward the others. He picked up Glimmer, pushed Yura, yelled in Samish's ear, "Go to the doorway!"

They moved, ran, scrambled, as the wall began to move and the rumbling and scraping filled the air. Then the rocks shot forward, tumbling in a lethal avalanche, spewing dust and debris far taller than any person. The rocks and part of the ceiling tumbled on the droids, sending them careening into walls, the floor, and one another.

Obi-Wan and Anakin pushed the others down and tried to cover them with their bodies as the wall collapsed. The dust and smoke bit into their lungs and stung their eyes. They could taste the mountain in their mouths.

But they were all alive.

Three droids were still standing. Obi-Wan and Anakin ran, covered in dust, and brought them down.

Then they faced the pile of rubble. Behind it was the doorway where Count Dooku had disappeared and where Lorian had followed. It would take some time to get out of the collapsed chamber.

"May the Force be with him," Obi-Wan said.

CHAPTER 26

Lorian had not felt the Force in many years. When he reached out and felt it move, it startled him, as if he'd burned his hand.

But within seconds, it all rushed back, and he knew he could depend on it.

Dooku was ahead of him in the narrow passageway, running toward an airspeeder. Dooku must have known very well that Lorian was behind him, but he didn't bother to turn and engage him. Lorian was sure that Dooku was taking no more notice of him than he would a fly.

He had no time to think of strategy. He knew Dooku was vastly more powerful. Why was he doing this? he thought as he ran. Why? It was a death wish, a fool's errand, and he had never courted death or been a fool.

All the wrongs of his life, all the mistakes, all the unforgivable deeds, all the pain he had caused, all the lives he had broken, they were all here in this dark corridor. They would choke him, they would lay him flat, but the Force had touched him just when he needed it, bringing a memory of a childhood when he knew what was right and wanted to do it.

He had a blaster, but he knew its puny power would mean nothing to Dooku. Within seconds it would be wrenched from his grasp and fly across the corridor.

So why use it? Why use any weapon when Dooku could swat it away like a fly?

Lorian had not stopped running while he thought. What did he have that Dooku did not have? What did he know about Dooku that no one else knew? What did he know about him as a boy that would not have changed? Did he have a flaw?

Pride. He was vain. He liked to be admired.

That wasn't much to go on.

Then Lorian noticed the airspeeder at the end of the corridor, ahead of Dooku. He was familiar with the model. It was a Mobquet twin turbojet with a boosted max airspeed. Mobquet Industries were known for their swoop bikes, not their speeders. Dooku's transport was a good choice for quick getaways, with its boosted airspeed and high maneuverability. But possibly, just possibly, Dooku did not know this: The Mobquet speeder had a flaw. The data cables that connected the frontal controls to the cabin were mounted behind a thin panel on the underside of the body. It would take Lorian about six seconds to find that panel and fuse those cables with a barrage from his blaster.

All he needed was six seconds.

He called ahead, his voice echoing. "You've done well for yourself, Dooku. But did you ever realize that you couldn't have done it without me?"

Dooku stopped and turned, as Lorian had known he would.

"Excuse me, old friend?"

"The Sith Holocron. You accessed it, didn't you? Sometime later. You could never stand it if I knew something you didn't."

"Why shouldn't I have accessed it?" Dooku asked.

Lorian kept moving forward. "Of course you had the right. Yet you never would have had the courage if I hadn't done it first."

Dooku laughed. "You are unbelievable. Don't you realize how tempted I am to kill you? And now you're provoking me. You certainly live dangerously, Lorian."

Lorian had circled around Dooku and stood near the speeder. Dooku was not afraid of him; he would allow him to come as close as he wanted. Lorian leaned against the speeder, crossing his leg as though he had all the time in the world to chat. "I realize now that I was wrong when I asked you to cover for me about the Holocron."

"An apology at this late date? I'm overwhelmed."

"I should have taken the responsibility myself. I wouldn't have been kicked out of the Jedi Order. I see that now. But now I wonder . . . why did I think I would?" Underneath the cover of his cloak, Lorian's fingers searched for the panel.

"I find revisiting the past so tedious," Dooku said. "If you'll excuse me —"

He put one foot on the speeder, ready to leap inside.

"Could it be that you encouraged my fears? Looking back, I find that strange. I would not have done that to you. I would not have fed your fears, but tried to allay them." His fingers slid across a seam. He had found the panel.

Dooku's eyes flared. Lorian brought out the blaster and put the barrel against the panel.

The dark side surged in a shocking display of power, and Lorian found himself flung like a child's doll in the air. He slammed against the wall and then hit the floor, dazed. Somehow, he held on to his blaster.

Dooku saw it, of course. "That was your clumsy attempt at a diversion, I suppose," he said, drawing his lightsaber with the curved hilt. "I think I've shown enough mercy. Let us end now what should have ended then."

He had one last chance. One only. He could blast the panel and prevent Dooku from taking off. Obi-Wan and Anakin would have to do the rest. If he failed, he would die. If he succeeded, he would also die. He had no doubt about that.

Lorian reached out to the Force to help him. He needed it here, at the last. He felt it grow, and he saw Dooku's eyebrows rise.

"So you haven't lost it completely," he said. "Too bad it isn't enough."

He moved toward Lorian. Lorian remembered his footwork. The attack would come to his left. At the last moment, he rolled to the right, and Dooku's lightsaber hit rock and sliced through it. Expecting an easy blow, Dooku turned a second too late, and Lorian had already begun to run. He knew Dooku expected him to turn and try to get behind him. He would not expect him to run to the speeder.

He had the blaster aimed and ready, but he knew he would get only one shot, and it had to be a good one. It had to be dead solid perfect —

Behind him was a whisper. That was all he heard. He looked down and saw the lightsaber and he thought, how odd, Dooku is behind me, why is the lightsaber in front of me? Then he realized he had been pierced through.

He fired the blaster, but the shot went wild. He went down.

I have failed, he thought. *I have failed.*

Dooku stood over him. He saw the dark eyes like hollow caves. He did not want this to be his last sight. He had lived so long with hate, he could not die with it in his vision. So with a great effort, he turned his head. He saw the rocks of the corridor, the stones both smooth and jagged, and noticed for the first time that they weren't gray, but were veined with silver and black and red and a blue the color of stars. . . .

The thought pierced him with the same sure pain as the lightsaber had: *What else have I missed?*

Too late to find out now.

He drew the Force around him like a blanket, and with an explosion of color lighting his vision, he smiled and let go of his life.

CHAPTER 27

Anakin sat on the cold ground, watching the streaks of orange cut through the gray. The sun was rising.

"It is time to go," Obi-Wan said.

Anakin rose. He was tired after having moved the hundreds of large stones that had barred their exit.

"I've brought Lorian's body aboard," Obi-Wan said. He stood next to Anakin, facing the rising sun. "We will take him back to the Temple."

They had found him in the corridor with a blaster nearby, his eyes open and, oddly, a faint smile on his face. There was evidence of a struggle in the disturbance in the dirt. Blaster fire had marked the rocks. They could see the acceleration blast marks from a speeder. Dooku had escaped.

"Lorian went up against impossible odds," Obi-Wan said. "He was never more a Jedi than at the last."

"So redemption is possible," Anakin said.

"Of course it is," Obi-Wan said. "As long as there is breath, there is hope. If not, what are we fighting for?"

"I wish I didn't feel that I had failed," Anakin said. "Dooku escaped. The Station 88 Spaceport is saved for the Republic, but for how long? What is to stop Dooku from trying to kill them again?"

"We are," Obi-Wan said.

"There is such darkness ahead," Anakin said. He stopped outside the cruiser and looked up at the stars. They were fading in the growing light. "I can feel it. It weighs on me."

You worry too much. Qui-Gon had told Obi-Wan this, more than once. Was that his legacy to Anakin? He had tried to give him so much more.

"You didn't fail here, Anakin," Obi-Wan said. "Our mission was to ensure that the spaceport didn't fall to the Separatists, and to gather information. We succeeded. Dooku's villa contains valuable data."

"A small victory," Anakin said with a curl of his lip. "Can we win a war that way?"

He had not reached him. Anakin had wanted to end the Clone Wars here. He had wanted to destroy Count Dooku. His ambition would always be greater than every mission. Obi-Wan saw that clearly, and it pierced him. He had taught Anakin everything, and Anakin had learned much — but had he missed the most important things?

I have failed, Qui-Gon. I have failed.

They walked up the landing ramp. Anakin slid behind the controls. Obi-Wan sat at the computer to enter the coordinates for their journey back. On the surface, everything was as it had always been.

Soon they would be ending their journey together.

They both knew it. He had never had to bid good-bye to Qui-Gon as a Master. He was still Qui-Gon's Padawan when he died. Maybe that was the reason he felt so close to him still.

He did not know if Qui-Gon would have left him with words of wisdom, with a direction to follow. Now he had no way of knowing what else he could give Anakin. He had given him everything he could. It wasn't enough.

Sadness filled Obi-Wan as they blasted into the upper atmosphere. He loved Anakin Skywalker, but he did not truly know him. The most important things he had to teach he had not taught. He would have to let him go, knowing that. He would have to let him go.

SECRETS OF THE JEDI

1

Qui-Gon Jinn couldn't sleep. Every night he spent some time trying, but in the end he decided to walk off the need for rest.

He didn't understand it. As a Jedi, he was used to sleeping anywhere, in all sorts of conditions. He had slept in cargo holds and spaceport hangars and on a pile of droid parts. He had slept four hours in the middle of a field during a driving rainstorm. When he needed sleep, he told his mind to empty and his body to unwind, and they obeyed.

But in the past, he'd never had to deal with his heart.

He had done the forbidden. He had fallen in love with another Jedi Knight. He had pledged himself to her. And she had died. He was paying a price he was glad to pay, because those few days of loving and of knowing he was loved were worth it. But how to put his heart back together? Tahl had changed him. She had made him whole, and she had broken him with her death. Qui-Gon could not figure out how to reassemble.

So he didn't sleep. He and his Padawan, Obi-Wan

Kenobi, had been at the Jedi Temple for weeks now. Yoda had called them back for what they'd expected to be a briefing for a mission, but there had been no mission. "Need your Padawan does days of reflection," Yoda had said. "Important they are as days of action."

There had been much action lately. Mission after mission. The Senate was fractured, torn apart by special interests, by warring clans and alliances.

There seemed to be plenty Qui-Gon and Obi-Wan could be doing, but Qui-Gon did not want to cross Yoda, so they stayed. But the weeks at the Temple only made Qui-Gon's sleeplessness worse. He walked the empty halls at night. The glow lamps were powered down to a soft blue, making it a restful time to stroll. It seemed that every hall, every room, held a memory of Tahl, but he didn't court those memories. He tried to allow his grief to be his companion, not his master. He opened his mind and simply walked.

He found himself, at the end of a long night, back near his quarters. Qui-Gon hesitated. He was not ready to return to his small room and stare at the walls.

"Glad I am to find you awake." Yoda scuttled forward, leaning on his gimer stick.

He blinked at Qui-Gon. "And why, my friend, does sleep not find you?"

Qui-Gon did not want to discuss his heart with Yoda. He loved the Jedi Master, but he did not want to confide in him. He had never told Yoda of his feelings for Tahl, and there was no need for Yoda to know how close Qui-Gon had come to violating the rules of the Jedi Order. So instead of the full truth, he said, "I find peace from walking."

"See I do many things in you," Yoda said. "Peace is not one of them."

Qui-Gon didn't answer. He didn't shrug, or turn away, or drop his eyes. He knew Yoda would read the unspoken message. *I am not ready to talk about this.*

"Need a mission now, you do," Yoda said.

Qui-Gon nodded. "And you have one for me. It's about time."

Behind him he heard soft footsteps. The smell of rich tea came to his nostrils — his favorite, a blend from the leaves of a *sapir* plant, green and fragrant.

It must be near dawn, then. Obi-Wan had taken to brewing him tea and bringing it to his quarters in the early morning. Qui-Gon had gently tried to discourage him; he didn't want his Padawan to wait on him. But Obi-Wan, in his own stubborn way, kept showing up. Qui-Gon was both irritated and touched by this. Obi-Wan didn't know the details. But he was eighteen now, old enough to make a good guess as to what had happened on Apsolon between his Master and Tahl. He could sense the depths of Qui-Gon's sorrow, and he felt he had to do something to help, no matter how small.

Qui-Gon could feel him hesitating now, back behind a pillar. He did not want to interrupt his Master's conversation with Yoda.

"Step forward you may, Obi-Wan," Yoda said. "Concerns you, this does."

Obi-Wan came out of the shadows. Yoda took in everything in a glance — the small teapot on the tray, the steaming mug, the expression of concern in Obi-Wan's eyes.

His gaze returned to Qui-Gon. In that gaze Qui-Gon read the truth. Yoda knew of his nighttime walks. Yoda knew of the tea Obi-Wan brought every morning. And perhaps he even knew about Tahl. How could Qui-Gon have forgotten that there was so little that Yoda did not know?

Yoda had not called them back in order to give Obi-Wan a chance to reflect. He had called them back for Qui-Gon's sake.

"Not ready I am to let you go," Yoda said. "Yet let you go, I must."

CHAPTER 2

It all started with a young boy who liked to build things.

Talesan Fry was ten years old. He had long ago become bored with school. He much preferred to be home, in his room, working with devices he had built himself. At the age of eight, he had set up a communication system in his home that used voice activation to track his movements.

At the age of nine, he had discovered how to get around it by giving the system a false reading so that his mother was never exactly sure where he was or what he was doing. Now, at the age of ten, he had moved on to spying on his neighbors. Perhaps it was a normal pursuit for a young boy, but in this case, Taly made a special effort to spy on neighbors who went to great lengths not to be overheard.

Breaking into the main comm channels on his home-world of Cirrus was too easy. What Taly liked to do was lurk. He would break into the secure channels, past the security gates, opening one after the other with a few tweaks and clicks on his system. He never heard anything very interesting. Politicians. Security officers. Corporate vice presidents. Nobody with anything worth saying, in his opinion. Still, he kept lurking, because he liked to do what was forbidden.

And then one day he heard something interesting. At first, it wasn't enough to even raise his head from the sleep couch, where he was listlessly flying a model of a Gion speeder by remote. He heard a quick exchange, a communication about a job coming up.

"Negative," someone said. "Concussive missiles attract too much attention in close quarters."

"Wouldn't hurt to have them. I don't care what our employer says. He's not doing the job, we are. No blood on his hands. I want to be able to blast my way out if I have to."

Slowly, Taly raised his head.

"If it comes to that, you'll have half the galactic security force on your tail. It's got to be in and out, quiet and quick."

"You think bagging the leader of —"

"No names." The voice was curt. Taly now had his ear against the transmitter. He had activated a recording rod.

His eyes widened as he listened. He could pick out five distinct voices and it didn't take him long to realize they were bounty hunters. Five bounty hunters working together? Taly didn't know much about bounty hunters, but he knew enough to be sure an alliance was highly unusual.

He knew he had stumbled onto something big. They were talking about a rendezvous on some planet, about an assassination. They had already picked the date, and it was only fourteen standard days away. This was something he could not keep to himself. Something — and this was worst of all — he would have to tell his parents about.

An hour later, after he'd worked up the courage, he brought them the recording rod. His parents were too alarmed to punish him. They contacted Cirrus security, who notified galactic security on Coruscant. Eventually the story of a boy who had information on a major assassination plot made its way to the Senate Investigating Commission on Crime Syndication, Dissemination, and Proliferation in the Core and Mid-Rim Systems. The commission had been deadlocked for two months on the question of whether the scope of their investigation should include the Outer Rim.

Taly's news hit them like an electrojabber, prodding them into an action they had been reluctant to take. They called on him to be their star witness.

By the time this request had made it back to the Fry family on Cirrus, news of Taly's recording had reached enough security officials, Senators, and Senatorial aides that it might as well have been broadcast on the HoloNet.

It didn't take long after that for a corrupt official to find the right person eager to bribe. Within two days, Talesan Fry was marked for death by the very bounty hunters he had overheard.

Taly's parents knew enough to realize that their boy had landed in the middle of a great deal of trouble. They decided to keep the recording rod and bring it themselves to Coruscant. They would let Taly testify in secret, and that would be the end of it.

The night before they were to leave, they were attacked at midnight. The raid failed only because of the attacker's arrogance. The bounty hunters did not pause to consider that a young boy capable of infiltrating their secure communications system would also be capable of fashioning a security system in his own home that could confound them.

Taly and his parents escaped in an airspeeder that took off from their roof as the lights and alarms sounded. The bounty hunter, working alone because the five had decided that only one was needed, found the recording device. He used a concussion missile to destroy the house. He used double the firepower he needed. He was annoyed.

Now Taly and his parents were in hiding, afraid to move, afraid to trust. The Senate commission realized they had bungled this job and asked the Jedi for help. In a galaxy where no one trusted anyone, most still trusted the

Jedi. Taly's parents would allow them to escort the family to Coruscant.

The planet Cirrus was known for its golden seas and its lovely cities. The Jedi landed at the spaceport of the capital city of Ciran. The city folded around a vast bay that served to bounce the light, turning the sky pale yellow. Two orange suns blazed overhead. The combination of the golden light and the bright suns had a stunning effect, as though the very air was too bright to see.

Humans were native to Cirrus, but the streets were thronged with many species. The city was built on two levels, with businesses below and residences above. Lift tubes and ramps were stationed at regular intervals. Ciran was a city that tried to control its air traffic by making walking pleasant and easy for its citizens. Large awnings — pieces of strong, flexible fabric — stretched across the walkways, providing shade and eliminating some of the glare. They rippled like colorful flags and cast shadows like rainbows.

"We must take care that we aren't followed," Qui-Gon said as they took the tube down from the spaceport to the business level. "The bounty hunters will no doubt expect the Senate to send some sort of security to pick up Talesan. They'll be watching, hoping we lead them to the Frys."

"I don't pick up anything," Adi Gallia said. "Siri?"

Obi-Wan hadn't seen Siri Tachi with her Master in years. He noted a new sense of respect when Adi turned to her Padawan. For the first time since they'd boarded the ship together at the Temple, Obi-Wan really looked at his friend. Siri was taller, certainly, but she also carried herself differently. There was less aggression in her stance. She had grown comfortable with herself. Her own beauty had once thoroughly annoyed Siri, but now Obi-Wan saw that she was more comfortable with it. She did not try as hard to hide it; she simply didn't care.

Siri hesitated before answering, as if she wanted to be sure. "Nothing."

"Good. Siri has an extraordinary sensitivity to Force warnings," Adi told Qui-Gon. "She's gotten us out of quite a few tight spots."

"Well, I might sense the danger, but Adi gets us out of it," Siri amended, flashing her Master a grin.

"Just to be sure, let's walk a bit before we head for the Frys," Qui-Gon said.

Taly and his parents had kept moving since their home had been destroyed. They had chosen to hide in the densely populated city, moving from hotel to hotel, from hired room to hired room, not wanting to put friends in danger. The Jedi had received the coordinates of their current hideout just as they landed. The Frys were expecting them.

They had taken refuge in an inn that catered to short-term residents, beings who traveled to Cirrus frequently on business. The inn did not advertise and was known only among the network of business travelers. It had no sign outside, just an anonymous door. Taly's father had known about it through his contacts.

The Jedi waited in an alley a few steps away, just to make certain they were not followed. When they were sure, they went to the door and pressed the button alongside a security monitor.

"Key in your code number," a voice from the monitor requested.

"We don't have one," Qui-Gon said. "We're looking —"

"Full up." The monitor blinked off.

Qui-Gon pressed the button again. "We are expected by one of your guests," he said quickly, trying not to sound annoyed.

"Name?"

"Yanto." It was the name the Fry family was hiding under.

"One moment."

It was more than a moment, but the door slid open. The Jedi slipped inside. A heavy gray curtain was immediately in front of them. They pushed it aside and found themselves in a small circular hall. A round desk sat in the center of the space. The young man sitting behind it wore an expression of great boredom. He had long fair hair that he wore loose over his shoulders.

"They aren't in," he said. "I checked."

"We'd like to wait in their room," Qui-Gon said.

The young man shrugged.

Adi spoke crisply. "They left word that we could enter, didn't they?"

The clerk looked down at his datascreen. "I guess so."

"Then let us up." Adi's voice rang with authority.

The young man pushed a key card across the table. "Suite 2344. Have a ball."

The Jedi stepped into the turbolift. It rose swiftly to the top floor. They found the room. Qui-Gon knocked, and when there was no answer, he inserted the key card. A series of numbers flashed, and the door slid open.

The room was modest. Two sleep couches were in an alcove, and a desk stood against a wall. Vidscreens and datascreens were recessed in the wall. One window overlooked the street but was covered by a gray curtain.

Siri checked out the travel bags near the sleep couches. "Looks like it could be them," she said. "Basic necessities are still here."

"So we wait," Adi said.

Qui-Gon went to the window and slid the curtain back a slight bit. He looked out onto the street. Obi-Wan watched his face.

"He let us up too easily," Qui-Gon said.

"We were expected," Adi said.

"He didn't ask our names."

"He didn't seem to care much about security," Obi-Wan said.

"Yes, he seemed to advertise his indifference," Qui-Gon murmured, his eyes darting around the room.

Siri bent over to examine the items more closely. She fingered a few items thrown on the end of the sleep couch. Suddenly, she straightened.

"Something's wrong," she said.

Qui-Gon turned, his gaze sharp. "Tell us."

"They aren't coming back." Siri indicated the items at her feet. "I sense it. These items are camouflage. There should be something personal here, and there isn't."

"Their house was destroyed," Adi said. "They might not have any personal items left." She said this not as a challenge, but as an observation, trying to focus Siri's thinking.

"That could be true," Siri said. "But still. They have been here for three days, they said. There should be evidence that they have been living here. A crumb of food. A loose thread. A stain on the clothes. A wrinkle. A scent. Something."

"And the clerk . . ." Qui-Gon said, but he didn't finish his thought.

"If they felt they had been traced here . . ." Siri said.

Obi-Wan looked at the others. He had felt nothing, no surge of the dark side. He had only felt the normal uneasiness of being in a strange place, knowing that who they were looking for was being hunted. He felt a flash of envy of Siri, who seemed tuned into Qui-Gon's thoughts.

Just then, Siri looked up. Her hand flew to her lightsaber hilt.

Qui-Gon was already moving, streaking to one side of the door. "The clerk. He's coming," he said, just as the door slid open and blaster fire pinged through the air.

The being who burst through the door bore little resemblance to the bored clerk. Now he wore black armorweave body armor. A holster for a blaster rifle and vibroblade crisscrossed his back, and wrist rockets were strapped to his forearms. His long fair hair streamed behind him as he rolled into the room like a droideka, surprising the Jedi by the unusual angle of attack.

He rolled a Merr-Sonn fragmentation grenade into the center of the room. It exploded immediately, sending shrapnel in all directions. He rolled to a stop, crouching behind a lightweight shield.

Qui-Gon felt the air shimmer with the blast, and the shrapnel exploded around him. He leaped in front of Obi-Wan and Siri to protect them. It was hard for even a Jedi Master to deflect grenade shrapnel. It was fast, unpredictable, random. It took all of Qui-Gon and Adi's concentration to block it. The shrapnel was flung back from their lightsabers and slammed into the walls and floors. A few deadly missiles thudded into the bounty hunter's shield, but they bounced off.

Qui-Gon saw the flash of surprise on the bounty hunter's face at the sight of lightsabers. No doubt he'd been expecting a standard Senate security force, not a Jedi team. He fired off two wrist rockets in rapid succession, then backtracked, rolling out through the door again.

On his exit, he tossed another grenade inside the room. Qui-Gon leaped forward and turned it into a hunk of smoking metal before it exploded. He kept his eyes on the bounty hunter. He had paused for an instant outside the door. A flash of something lit the bounty hunter's eyes, and he turned around and fled.

Qui-Gon raced out as the bounty hunter blasted a hole through the hall window with his wrist rocket, then flew through the shattered panes. Qui-Gon saw a liquid cable line arc out.

He reached the window and looked down. He could just see the silver cable slithering back down through the air. The bounty hunter had landed on the pedestrian walkway below. Within seconds he had been swallowed up by the crowd, disappearing underneath one of the colorful awnings.

Adi stood next to him. "He was waiting for them. Figured he would take us out in the meantime."

"At least we know one thing," Obi-Wan said. "He doesn't know where they are."

"I'm not so sure about that," Qui-Gon murmured.

He strode back to the hallway outside the blasted door. He stood where the clerk had stood. A flash of surprise had lit his eyes, a revelation, and then smugness and purpose. All of this Qui-Gon had seen.

The bounty hunter, once disguised as the clerk, knew where they had gone.

There was so little time. The bounty hunter was already on his way. But Qui-Gon didn't let himself think of that. He slowly considered each object he could see from this vantage point.

Floor. Corner of a window. Corner of vidscreen. A pillow on the sleep couch. The edge of a pack.

Nothing.

Qui-Gon looked at the door itself. Then the keypad that they'd used to enter.

"The keycode," he said. "I know hotels like this. The occupant chooses a code that is easy to remember. The code is entered into security and on the individual cards. The occupant can either use the card or key in the number to get inside the room."

Adi nodded.

Qui-Gon lifted a hand, and the door card flew from where he'd left it on the sill and into his hand. He swiped the card and noted the number sequence that flashed.

"The code here is 2N533," Qui-Gon said. "The city of Ciran is shaped like a five-pointed star. There are five districts, and coordinates and addresses reflect that. Every address starts with the district number. 'N' could mean north."

"You think the key code is the address where they are staying?" Adi asked.

"That's taking a chance," Siri said. "Wouldn't they be afraid the bounty hunter would figure it out?"

"They didn't know he was here. They just knew he was close. But they had to leave us a hint."

"Besides," Obi-Wan said, "he wasn't sure they were gone for good. He was waiting for them to return."

As he spoke, he was already accessing the map of Ciran on his datapad. "2N533," he said. "Without a street name, I'll have to cross-check . . . wait . . ." He looked up. "District 2, 533 North Ascin Street. That's the only 533 address that's in the second district and has a north designation. It's got to be it."

"The bounty hunter has a head start," Adi said. "We can't afford to make a mistake."

"He is on foot," Qui-Gon said. "So are we. So we must be faster."

4

They ran through the streets, never hesitating, never stopping. Their Jedi training helped them. Obi-Wan was able to memorize the map in seconds. Siri was able to point out shortcuts. Qui-Gon and Adi used the Force to find the easiest way through the crowd.

They saw no sign of the bounty hunter. When they got to the address, Qui-Gon and Adi stopped to study the façade. It was a building of gray stone, appearing identical to the other residences surrounding it.

Qui-Gon crossed the street and stood in front of the door. He raised his hand to push the indicator bell on the intercom.

He felt it before it came. A window flipped open overhead and a large vibroblade swung down. He felt the whistle of the wind against his back as he jumped. Another second and it would have gone through his head.

Obi-Wan sprang forward to help his Master, and Adi and Siri began to move around him, trying to see in the windows by the door.

"There appear to be" — Adi started as darts flew out of a concealed panel — "booby traps."

"Enough of this," Qui-Gon muttered. "There isn't time."

He unsheathed his lightsaber and cut a hole in the door.

An oily, slick substance rolled out and covered the floor, splashing on Qui-Gon. He looked down at his soiled boots.

Blaster fire suddenly pinged from the lift tube. Qui-Gon swung his lightsaber to deflect it, not moving an inch.

"We're Jedi!" he thundered. "Stop this! There's no time!"

The blaster fire stopped.

The door of the lift tube was cracked slightly, the seam open just enough to give someone hiding a narrow view into the room. It opened a few more centimeters.

A boy poked his head out. His hair was red and stuck up in tufts all over his head. His eyes were a vivid green. His narrow, pointed nose twitched. Next to him were a man and woman. They each held blasters, but slowly lowered them as they saw Qui-Gon's lightsaber.

"We didn't know," the woman said.

Qui-Gon sheathed his lightsaber. "We understand."

"I am Nelia Fry. This is my husband, Grove. And this is Taly."

The boy pointed to the floor. "If you move, you'll slip. That's synthetic oil mixed with soap. My own recipe."

"I won't slip," Qui-Gon said, just as he took a step and slipped sideways. He regained his balance, slipped again, and slid into the lift tube door. His hands slapped against it and his aggrieved face was now centimeters from Talesan's.

"Sorry?" Taly offered.

Adi Force-leaped over the slippery mess and landed next to Qui-Gon. "We have to leave immediately. A bounty hunter is on your trail. He has this address."

The family exchanged worried glances. "No matter where we go, he finds us," Grove Fry said.

"We have an exit plan," Nelia said. "We have swoop bikes on the roof."

The Jedi hurried the family aboard the lift tube and it took them swiftly up to the roof.

There were three swoops, fully fueled. "We'll have to double up," Qui-Gon said. "Talesan, ride with me."

"Call me Taly," the boy said. "I have a feeling we're going to hang around together for awhile."

"If you two can fit on this swoop, my Padawan can take the pilot seat," Qui-Gon told Nelia and Grove. "We left our ship near the landing platform, in a secure location."

Just then a transmitter on Grove's belt blinked rapidly. "Someone else has entered the building," he said worriedly. "Taly rigged up a silent alarm."

"He's here," Siri said quietly.

"It's going to take him a few minutes to search," Qui-Gon said. "Let's go."

Grove and Nelia exchanged a glance. "We're not coming with you."

"What do you mean?" Qui-Gon asked.

"Dad? Mom?" Taly's voice suddenly sounded very young.

Nelia crouched to look into her son's eyes. "Dad and I think you'll be safer without us. He is too close. If we wait and leave a few seconds after you, he might follow us instead. We can lead him away from you. Give you time to get far from here."

"This isn't necessary," Adi said crisply. "We can protect you."

"We mean no disrespect," Grove said. "We trust the Jedi. But we also want every chance for our son."

"You must come with us," Qui-Gon argued. "To stay is too great a risk."

Grove's eyes filled with steely determination.

"That is for us to decide, not you," he said. "We have talked about this at length; we know what we have to do. Nothing you can say will convince us. And you cannot force us. If we can do any small thing to save our son, we will. You have a better chance without us, especially if we create a distraction. That is our decision."

"We'll find our way to Coruscant," Nelia told Taly. "We'll find you."

Taly had gone very still.

Nelia straightened quickly. Her eyes were wet with tears. "Take care of our son," she whispered. She put her arms around Taly and held him against her. Grove came behind her and the three of them rocked together. Then the parents broke away.

"No," Taly said. "Mom! Dad! Don't do this! I can protect us!"

The sight of their young son made the parents' faces crumple with love and pain.

"You can do so much," Grove said. "You can't do this."

Over Taly's head, Nelia turned her stricken eyes on Qui-Gon. "There's no time. Go. Please. Take him." Her voice ended in a sob.

Siri put her hand on Taly's shoulder. "Come on, Taly." She led him to Qui-Gon's swoop.

"Are you sure I cannot convince you to join us? Or two of us can stay with you."

"Go," Grove said. "Now."

Qui-Gon rested his strong gaze on Nelia. "I will protect him."

She nodded but did not speak. Tears streaked her face.

The Jedi felt the surge in the dark side of the Force. A warning. He was close.

"Hold on to me, Taly," Qui-Gon said kindly. "We will be traveling very fast."

They took off, keeping their acceleration low so as not to make noise. Then Qui-Gon quickly dipped down into a lower space lane so that they would not be visible from the building. Taly's parents disappeared from sight.

He felt the boy behind him, holding onto his tunic. He felt the cloth dampen with the boy's tears.

5

They made a clean getaway in the Republic cruiser. The city of Ciran retreated to a small yellow spot in a wide landscape. Then Cirrus became a yellowish round shape surrounded by clouds. In another few minutes, they were zooming through stars.

Adi piloted the ship. Qui-Gon set a course for Coruscant. Obi-Wan sat, watching Siri and Taly.

Siri did not speak. She moved about the cabin, close to Taly. She placed a small thermal blanket on his knees. Moments later she gave him something to eat and drink. Taly did not touch them. He held the blanket around his small body and stared at the ground.

Finally Siri came and sat beside him. She leaned forward and spoke to him gently. Obi-Wan could not hear her words but he saw by her posture how careful she was trying to be. He saw, gradually, how Taly's neck muscles relaxed, how his fingers no longer clutched the blanket with the same desperate grip.

Siri slipped something out of her utility belt. Obi-Wan recognized the warming crystal Siri always carried, deep blue with a star in the center. She handed it to Taly and he closed his fist around it, smiling at how it warmed his hand.

Siri drew her legs up underneath her and sat next to Taly, not too close, but not too far away.

Was this the Siri he knew? Hardly. Obi-Wan hadn't known she possessed such delicacy. Siri was never delicate. She said what she meant and she felt a great impatience for those who did not. She didn't like emotional reactions, she hated delays, she never waited on anyone or expected to be waited on. She liked to do everything herself.

These were the things he knew about her. But he did not know this. He hadn't realized she knew exactly what to do for a wounded child.

Suddenly Qui-Gon leaned over the nav console. "Unidentified cruiser coming up fast."

"I'll increase speed." Adi pushed the controls.

"He's speeding up," Qui-Gon said.

"You think it's our bounty hunter?"

"I have no doubt. And by the looks of that cruiser, he might be able to outmaneuver us. It's a SoroSuub light freighter."

Adi's mouth set grimly. "Nobody outmaneuvers me."

Qui-Gon gave a wry smile. "I didn't mean to suggest it. Deflector shields down." The Republic cruiser was an agile craft, but it was built to ferry diplomats and serve as a base for high-level meetings. Adi was an excellent pilot, but she would not be able to hold out against a heavily armed SoroSuub for very long.

By the posture of her shoulders, he knew exactly when she admitted this to herself. "Find us a safe port nearby, just in case."

Qui-Gon began to search the star chart on the nav computer. "We're close to Quadrant Seven," he said.

"I know," Adi said. "But what about a planet?"

"The planet's name *is* Quadrant Seven," Qui-Gon explained. "It's not in the Republic — it doesn't have a Senator and it's not particularly friendly to outlanders, but it doesn't forbid them, either." Qui-Gon entered the coordinates into the nav computer.

Adi pushed the ship to a faster speed. Obi-Wan and Siri got up and moved into the cockpit.

Taly followed. He leaned in close to the nav screen, sending a bluish light onto his features. "He's going to catch us," he said.

Qui-Gon met Adi's gaze. They both knew the boy was right.

Laser cannonfire thundered around the ship, rocking it. Taly gripped the console.

Adi kept the ship moving. She could not maneuver the way she would like, but she was able to swerve to avoid the next barrage. It boomed harmlessly in space.

"This is how he works," Taly said. "He uses everything. He never stops. He has blasters and grenades and missiles and . . . everything. I beat him, and that made him mad, because I'm just a kid. He won't let me go this time."

Qui-Gon looked at Taly. He had put the battle in terms of a young boy, but it made sense. Qui-Gon felt it, too, through his connection to the Living Force. This bounty hunter went beyond determination. This was a grudge.

"What should we do?" Adi asked. Her voice was perfectly calm despite the cannonfire that shook the ship. But Qui-Gon knew the situation must be dire, because Adi never asked him what to do.

Suddenly, a large blow rocked the ship.

"We've lost the horizontal stabilizer," Adi said. "It's affected the hyperdrive."

"We must send off the salon pod," Qui-Gon said. "He might think we escaped on it."

"But why would he fall for it?" Taly asked.

"Because then we're going to crash this ship," Qui-Gon said.

6

"Maybe you'd better fill me in on this one," Adi said drily. "After all, I'm the pilot."

"This ship has a double-reinforced cargo hold," Qui-Gon said. "The work was done in order to protect a shipment of vertex on its last mission. So if we were hit there, it would cause minimal damage. We could make it look worse. We could trick him into thinking the ship was failing. Then we eject the salon pod. He knows that salon pods on these cruisers are capable of long space flights." Qui-Gon leveled his gaze at Adi. "Can you do it?"

She would know what he was asking. Adi could be high-handed at times. She could be dismissive of other ideas than her own. But they had worked together often enough to be able to put their minds in sync when they needed to.

"Yes."

Qui-Gon turned. "Obi-Wan, Siri, Taly, get all the soft material you can and bring them to the cockpit. Flotation devices, roll-up sleep couches, bedding, pillows, cushions. Fast."

Obi-Wan, Siri, and Taly dashed out of the cockpit. The Republic cruiser was built as a diplomatic ship. There were plenty of cabins to raid. Within minutes, the cockpit had filled up with soft bedding. Qui-Gon directed the three to place it around the walls and hard surfaces as carefully as they could.

"We're going to have take a missile blow," he told the others. "Brace yourself."

Adi maneuvered the ship so that the blow would fall on the cargo hold. It would take perfect timing and a lot of guesswork. She had to make the bounty hunter think that he had outmaneuvered them and struck the death blow.

The ship screamed through space, twisting like a corkscrew. The Force filled the cabin as Adi concentrated, beads of perspiration on her high forehead. They saw the flash as the laser cannon boomed. They had less than a split-second to prepare.

The blast shook the ship and blew them like durasheets through the cabin. They bounced off the cushions and mattresses. Qui-Gon felt helpless as his wrist slammed against the edge of the console. He pulled in the Force to give him stability and balance. Adi crawled to the pilot chair.

"I didn't expect to do quite this good a job," she muttered, gripping the controls.

"Jettison some smoke," Qui-Gon said.

Adi put the ship into a death spiral. She released the salon pod. They were close to a planet now, twisting down toward it.

Qui-Gon had his eyes on the radar. "He's not chasing the pod. Not yet."

Adi looked at him worriedly. "He's waiting for us to flame out or crash."

Qui-Gon nodded. "So let's crash."

Adi gripped the controls. Siri strapped Taly down and belted down cushions around him. She and Obi-Wan covered themselves as best they could.

The ship was screaming now, belching smoke. But Adi still had control. She mimicked a dying ship, narrowing the circles until Qui-Gon had to close his eyes against the dizziness he felt. He opened them once to see the surface of the planet looming. He closed them again quickly.

"Here we go!" Adi shouted.

He never knew how she did it. The grace and precision of it were amazing. She was able to pull up slightly at the last minute, enough for the ship to shudder into a modified crash landing instead of slamming into the planet's surface. But from the upper atmosphere, it would look like a crash. She jettisoned the fuel early so that it sent up a fireball. The smoke would cover their escape.

Qui-Gon took out his lightsaber and cut a hole through the wall. Obi-Wan joined him, then Siri and Adi. Taly stood back, his eyes huge with shock.

Qui-Gon picked up Taly and jumped out the hole after the others. They took shelter behind some rocks as the ship exploded.

"Now what?" Siri asked.

"Let's start with the basics," Qui-Gon said. "I'd say we need to locate new transportation."

Taly still wore an expression of shock. "Don't you Jedi take a minute to recover?"

"He took off after the pod, but we should still take precautions," Adi said. "I think Taly should remain in hiding with Siri and Obi-Wan. We don't want to leave a trail. We know there is more than one bounty hunter involved."

"Good point," Qui-Gon said.

They walked toward town. The road was dusty and deserted, winding through a rocky canyon. Halfway there, Adi suddenly stopped. She leaned over and pressed her hand against the ground.

"There's water close to here," she said. "Follow me."

She took off through the rocks. They followed, Taly sometimes slipping and helped by Siri. Adi led them up a stony ridge and then down again. The air smelled fresher. Around a large boulder was a small, bubbling spring.

"A water source if you need it," she said. She glanced around. "There are caves around us. I can feel them."

She walked to a cleft in the rocks. Qui-Gon never would have noticed it. He would have thought it was a shadow. Adi melted inside and they saw only her hand beckon them.

It was a cave, small and snug. Although the sand was cool and damp, farther into the cave it was dry.

"A perfect hiding place," Adi said. "Invisible from the

air. Easy to exit and close to town." She slipped off her survival pack. "We'll be back for you as soon as we locate transport. You'll be comfortable here."

Siri looked around the cave dubiously. "If you say so."

Qui-Gon couldn't help smiling at Siri. "We'll return soon," he promised.

Qui-Gon and Adi left the cave and continued on the road to the city of Settlement 5. The city had no outskirts. It simply rose in the middle of a convergence of roads. There seemed to be no green spaces, no culture centers or amusements, just businesses and homes, all built on a grid of streets and lanes.

The city was more like an overgrown village than a sophisticated center. Qui-Gon and Adi walked through the streets, their hoods up, trying to blend in. It wasn't hard. They were taller than the average Quadrant Seven, but that wasn't a problem. All the Quadrant Sevens wore practical and neutral-colored robes, just as the Jedi did. Most of them walked with their hoods over their faces. Qui-Gon felt anonymous in the crowd, and he soon realized why.

"They're *all* trying to blend in," he murmured to Adi. "Even if they recognize us as outlanders, they won't show it."

Usually in a main city of a world in the Core or Mid-Rim, there were plenty of opportunities to buy or rent speeders, and often dealers in spaceworthy cruisers clustered around the landing platforms of the city. But there was a strange absence of such dealers on this planet. It took Adi and

Qui-Gon some time to find a seller of speeders tucked away down a narrow lane off a secondary road.

A laserboard outside discreetly flashed specials. "Nothing spaceworthy," Qui-Gon said. "But no doubt he can tell us where to purchase a ship."

They walked inside. The dwellers of Quadrant Seven were humanoid, with small, pointed ears and short, whiskery antennae that gave the appearance of bristly hair but were finely attuned to disturbances in the air. The dealer turned, his antennae quivering.

He didn't ask them what they wanted, or if he could help them. He just stood, waiting for them to speak.

"We're looking for a space cruiser," Qui-Gon said.

"I don't sell that here," the dealer said.

"We thought you could tell us where in Settlement Five we could purchase one."

"Nowhere. There's no call for selling of space cruisers. Quadrants don't like to travel out of their own atmosphere."

"But surely," Qui-Gon said patiently, "there is a way to get off planet."

"Well, of course there is."

Adi kept her tone even. "Maybe you could tell us what that is."

"Wait for the freighter. It comes once a month."

Qui-Gon felt his heart fall. "Once a month?"

The dealer seemed to feel that he had no need to elaborate.

"Can you tell us when it will stop again?" Adi asked.

The dealer consulted a calendar on his datapad. "Ah, that would be market day."

"And market day is . . ."

"In five standard days time."

Qui-Gon took out his comlink. "Can you tell us where on Quadrant Seven we could find a space cruiser? We could contact them and —"

"Ah, that would be Settlement Twenty-three. That's where you'd be able to bargain for a ship. But you can't contact them by comlink. There's a BlocNet on Quadrant Seven. Comlinks are licensed. Ordinary citizens aren't allowed to carry them, just emergency personnel. Your comlink won't work here."

"But why outlaw comlinks?" Adi asked.

"Don't believe in 'em. Comlinks make distances shorter. And when distances get shorter, problems get bigger. We like to slow things down on Quadrant Seven. Which reminds me, you need a permit to send a HoloNet message off planet. It will be monitored and archived, too."

"And who has access to the archives?" Adi asked.

"Everyone. Makes beings nicer if they know they can't send out messages that aren't public."

Adi and Qui-Gon stared at each other in frustration. That meant if they sent a message to the Temple, everyone would be able to see it. The bounty hunters could trace them.

"Can we buy a speeder to travel to Settlement Twenty-three?" Qui-Gon asked.

"Sure. But you have to apply for a permit. All outlanders do."

"How long will it take to get a permit?"

"Hard to say. Could be a week."

Adi was becoming used to the dealer's way of talking. "Or . . . ?

"Could be a month. Hard to say."

"This is ridiculous," Adi muttered. "What a way to run a planet."

"We haven't had a war in five hundred and seventy-three years," the dealer said. "Don't have toxic pools or chemical air. Everybody pretty much gets along. That doesn't sound too ridiculous, does it?"

Adi just sighed.

"If I were you, I'd wait for the freighter. Quadrant Seven is a nice place to visit. Of course we don't have much in the way of hotels or cafés. And we don't go in for amusements the way they do in other places. There's not much to do. But still."

"Look, we don't have time to wait," Qui-Gon said. "Can't you find a way to help us?"

"Nope." The dealer's face was still blandly polite. He would be friendly, but not help them. That much was clear.

They walked out of the shop.

"Looks like we're waiting for the freighter," Adi said.

"We'll just have to lay low. We could send a coded communication to the Temple. . . ."

"But why risk it?" Adi completed the sentence. "If by some chance the bounty hunter searches the planet, that's the first place he'd investigate. Even a coded message would stand out."

"We can canvass the area, look to see if anyone owns a ship and try to buy it," Qui-Gon said.

Adi nodded. "It doesn't appear that Quadrant Sevens travel, but we might get lucky."

"It's only five days," Qui-Gon said. "The assassination will take place in a week. This can all work, if nothing else goes wrong."

He felt the dark side surge as a warning just as Adi pulled him back from walking out into the watery sunlight. The bounty hunter was striding by on the street, his pale eyes flicking into the shadows.

"Something else just went wrong," Adi said.

CHAPTER 7

"Let's follow him," Adi murmured. "Better to know where he is — and perhaps we'll learn something."

Qui-Gon nodded. They melted into the crowd in the street. It was rare that a being knew when he was being followed by a Jedi. They were able to use the Force to direct objects to move into their path if someone turned to look behind them. They were able to move before their prey could track their steps. After a short time, the Jedi were able to so absorb their quarry's way of moving that they could predict it and easily avoid discovery.

The bounty hunter was good. He was careful. Yet he was no match for them. Adi and Qui-Gon followed him easily as he walked to the opposite edge of Settlement 5 and then struck out across the hills and rocks.

This area was even more rugged than where they'd left Obi-Wan and Siri. They trailed him through a series of small, deep canyons. The boulders offered plenty of hiding places. At last he slipped into a narrow opening and disappeared. Qui-Gon and Adi carefully moved forward. Positioning themselves behind an outcropping, they peered into the opening.

It led to a canyon that was just a cleft in the landscape. They recognized the bounty hunter's light freighter. Next to it was a slightly larger ship. Together they took up nearly the entire width of the canyon.

The bounty hunter disappeared into the larger ship. The ramp was down, and Qui-Gon and Adi slowly made their way there. With a glance at each other, they agreed to try to observe what was going on. It was worth the risk.

They crept up the ramp and slipped inside the ship. They heard raised voices coming from the cockpit.

Good, Qui-Gon thought. If a group was arguing, they would be too distracted to stay alert.

Tall and graceful, Adi moved ahead of him down the hall, her boots soundless on the polished floor. She beckoned to him. She had found a vent at eye level, in a storage room right off the cockpit. Qui-Gon could see quite clearly into the next room.

His heart fell. There were five bounty hunters in the cockpit, including the one chasing them. Among them was one he recognized — Gorm the Dissolver. He was a formidable presence, dwarfing the others in his plated armor and helmet. Created by Arkanian Renegades, he was half-bio, half-droid. His bio parts were made up of six different aliens. His droid components allowed him to be a nearly invincible killing machine. Gorm's tracking skill was legendary and his merciless attacks were spoken of in whispers in spaceports throughout the galaxy.

All of these bounty hunters in one place, for one assassination? Qui-Gon wondered again who the target could be.

"We've only got a week," one of the bounty hunters said. It was a humanoid woman, small and compact, dressed in a leather tunic and leggings. Her fair hair was twisted in many braids that fell to her shoulders. She appeared to be completely ordinary, if you didn't notice the firepower strapped to her waist, her wrist gauntlets with an array of weapons systems, or the armored kneepads she wore. By the look of her armor, Qui-Gon guessed she was a Mandalorian, or at least that she had somehow procured some of the warrior army's famous weaponry. "You shouldn't have blasted that escape pod, Magus," she went on. "Now we don't know for sure if you got the kid."

The bounty hunter who had chased them on Cirrus turned slowly and rested his steely gaze on the female.

"Don't give me that black-hole look, Magus," she said. "You know I'm right. We need proof that the kid has been neutralized. If he's still alive, he could compromise the mission. I don't mind pulling this off, but I don't want anybody to know I was involved. Those Senatorial committees can get touchy about political assassinations."

"We're only a week away from our hits," another bounty hunter said. He was a tall creature with green-tinged skin and a cranial horn on top of his head. "I for one don't relish the thought of assassinating a world leader if security is waiting for me. And we've got twenty targets. That's twenty times the security."

Qui-Gon and Adi exchanged a glance. *Twenty* planetary leaders?

"I told you, they won't have their regular security," Magus said.

"We still have no way of knowing how much this kid knows and who he's alerted," the female bounty hunter continued.

"You promised they wouldn't be expecting us, that we'd have the element of surprise," the third bounty hunter said to Magus. He wore a greasy cloak and his leggings were thick with grime. Tufts of wiry hair stood out on his head like horns. On his grimy face gills flapped open and closed with his breathing. He looked like a large, unkempt fish. A name floated into Qui-Gon's head. *Raptor.* This could be the bounty hunter he'd been hearing about, the one who was willing to take any job, no matter how dangerous or cruel. "That's one reason we agreed. Well — that and the fee. But if security gets tipped off, I'm heading back to the Core and picking up another job. What does our employer say?"

Magus rose slowly. If he was bothered by the dissension in the others, it wasn't apparent. "Our employer leaves the details to me. As you should."

"We did that," the being with the cranial horn said. "And now we don't know if the kid is dead or not. We don't know if he blabbed yet or not. We don't know if he's on his way to the Senate to testify."

"I heard you the first time, Pilot," Magus said, the anger now clear in his tone.

"Really? Because it doesn't seem like you're listening," the female said irritably.

"Lunasa is right," Raptor said. "You've got a problem listening to any voice but your own."

Magus slammed a vibroblade down on the table. "Enough whining!" he exploded. With the exception of Gorm, the bounty hunters all looked unnerved. "I said I would take care of the boy. First we need to complete the preparations we discussed. There's still much to be done, and we're wasting time here."

Without waiting for agreement, Magus simply strode off. Qui-Gon and Adi had to scurry back along the corridor to avoid him. He strode down the ramp and headed for his own ship.

"Who elected him king, I'd like to know," Lunasa muttered.

"He recruited us," Pilot said. "But the employer talks to me, too. I can go to him anytime." A bragging note had entered his voice.

"Whoa, and that makes you *so* special," Raptor said.

"I'm keeping track of what Magus does," Pilot said huffily. "That's all I'm saying."

"Shut up." Gorm spoke for the first time. "Let's go."

It took them a moment, no doubt because they didn't want to appear to follow anyone's orders, but the bounty hunters began to make preparations for departure. Pilot headed for the controls. Lunasa worked on the nav computer. The one Qui-Gon suspected of being Raptor shrugged and took off down the corridor, presumably to his own cabin. Qui-Gon and Adi ducked into a storage room.

"Twenty leaders? It's much bigger than we thought," Adi said. "We have to find out who they're targeting."

"And *why*," Qui-Gon added. "If we find the why, we can discover who hired them." He thought quickly. "We should stay aboard."

"But Taly —"

"Obi-Wan and Siri can protect him. They are well hidden. We can return for them. There's no way off the planet for five days. Magus knows that as well — that's why he's leaving. No doubt he plans to return, but we can be back by then."

Adi frowned. "I don't like leaving the three of them."

"Uncovering the plot will help Taly more than our presence," Qui-Gon said. "I don't like leaving them, either. But I feel Obi-Wan and Siri can handle this."

Adi nodded slowly. "Agreed."

"Once we're out of the Quadrant Seven atmosphere, we can send them a message," Qui-Gon said. "Incoming messages aren't recorded. It's a risk to leave, but . . ."

". . . we have to take it," Adi said.

They felt the thrust of the engines. The ship lifted into the air.

"Hey!" they heard Lunasa call. "Magus is staying!"

"He never tells us what he's doing," Pilot said.

"I guess he's going for the kid after all," Lunasa said.

Adi and Qui-Gon glanced at each other. The ship was already climbing to the upper atmosphere. It was too late to get off.

CHAPTER 8

"They should have been back by now."

Siri kept her voice low, but Taly seemed off in another world. He sat at the entrance to the cave, his arms around his knees. Occasionally he would dip his head down and stare at the ground.

"I know." Obi-Wan wanted to argue with her, but he didn't have a good feeling about the length of time Qui-Gon and Adi had been gone.

"I should go look for them."

"They told us to stay here."

Siri shook her head impatiently. "Obi-Wan, in all my years of knowing you, I can't tell you how many times you've told me what I *should* be doing."

"Well, somebody has to," Obi-Wan said with a grin.

But Siri didn't crack a smile. "They could be in trouble."

"Or they could be negotiating for a starship. Or they could be contacting the Temple. Or they could be on their way back. They could be doing a thousand things. None of which are our concern. Our concern is Taly. They told us both to protect him. So here we stay."

Siri's jaw set stubbornly. She stared stonily out into the landscape.

Taly suddenly rose and came back to stand with them. "I have a proposition for you," he said.

Obi-Wan wanted to smile. There was something so touching about Taly. Here was this slender, small boy who seemed ready to take on the world. Sometimes the lost look in his eyes made him look like a child. Yet sometimes he talked like an adult. Obi-Wan had no idea how much of Taly's confidence was bravery and how much was bravado. All he knew was that he admired him.

"Let's hear it," Siri said.

"I want you to let me go," Taly said.

"Let you go?" Obi-Wan repeated, incredulous.

Taly nodded. "I've been thinking about it. My uncle is a subplanetary engineer on the planet Qexis. It's a high-security planet with only one spaceport. It's in the Outer Rim. Nobody really knows about it except tech-heads. It's a total research planet. He'd hide me for as long as it takes. And you could tell my parents where I'm heading and they could meet me there. I could make my way there."

"You could make your way there?" Obi-Wan tried unsuccessfully to keep his voice from rising.

Taly looked at Siri. "Does he always repeat what people say?"

Siri nodded. "Yeah."

"Taly, there's no way we're going to let you go," Obi-Wan said. "That's preposterous. What makes you think you could get to the Outer Rim by yourself? You're just a kid!"

"Nobody notices a kid," Taly said. "I can do it, I know I can. It's just a question of getting from Point A to Point B. The bounty hunters think I'm dead."

"You don't know that for sure. We tricked one of them. We don't know if it worked. That's why we're still in hiding."

"That's what gives me a head start," Taly said. "Look, you know as well as I do that if I testify to those Senators, I'm dead."

"That's not true," Obi-Wan said, shocked. "They'll protect you."

"You trust the Senate?" Taly gave a bark of a laugh. "And you call *me* a kid?"

Obi-Wan shook his head. He wasn't going to argue with Taly. He shot Siri an exasperated look, but to his surprise, Siri was looking at Taly thoughtfully.

"You know it's true," Taly said, turning to Siri. "They won't care about me once I testify. Sure, they'll give me new ID docs. But they won't protect me or my parents, not really. But if I don't testify, maybe the bounty hunters will leave me alone."

"Taly, they won't leave you alone," Obi-Wan said gently. "I'm sorry to say it. But you'll always be a risk to them."

"Not after they do the assassination," Taly argued. "Then they won't care. Or even if they care, they're not going to chase me for long. I'm not worth it. I can disappear." He turned back to Siri. "Okay, I'll make a deal with you. You can escort me to Qexis. Then leave me there. Pretend I escaped. You can save my life. You can save my parents. You *can*."

"Taly, I'm sorry," Obi-Wan said.

"Siri?" Taly looked at her beseechingly.

Siri spoke through dry lips. "I'm sorry, too."

Taly stomped off to the front of the cave, a kid again. Obi-Wan looked at Siri.

"I could have used a little support," he said.

"What if he's right?" Siri asked.

"What if he's *right*?"

Siri rolled her eyes. "There you go again."

"There I . . . Siri, you can't be serious. You can't think that we could possibly let Taly go."

"No, of course not. But we *could* take him to Qexis. It *would* be a good place to hide. And the Senate *won't* protect him. Not the way they should. They just want what they want. Once he testifies, they won't care about him. He's not wrong, Obi-Wan."

"Sometimes I just don't understand you."

"I know."

"We can't defy the Senate. We can't defy the Jedi Council."

"We can. We just don't choose to. There are more options in life, Obi-Wan, than you seem able to imagine."

Siri's words stung. It was almost as though she felt sorry for him.

"Do I need to tell Qui-Gon and Adi about this?" Obi-Wan hated the way he sounded. Priggish. Pompous.

Siri turned her cool gaze on him, the color of an impossibly blue sea with hidden depths for the unwary. "If you like. Don't worry. I'll deliver Taly into the hands of the Senate. I'll do my duty. I always do."

Then she retreated from him, even though she stayed still and unmoving at his side.

The comlink message was full of static.

". . . trail of bounty hunters. . . . Stay where you are until we return . . ." Qui-Gon's voice was steady, but the transmission crackled. "A bounty hunter is on Quadrant Seven. Magus. Stay hidden. If we don't return . . ."

"Qui-Gon?"

"Freighter . . . landing platform . . . in five days time, midday. No other transport available —" The transmission cut out.

"Did you get all that?" Siri asked.

"Stay hidden for five days. If they don't return, take the freighter off planet. And a bounty hunter is still looking for Taly."

"Magus." Siri looked over at where Taly was sleeping. "So he knows Taly is alive."

"Or suspects."

She did not say what he knew she wanted to say. Without their Masters, it would be easy to go to Qexis. They could take Taly away from this.

But those were not their orders. And they would do their duty.

Siri didn't speak much. There was a tension between them now that Obi-Wan didn't understand. They had argued many times during their friendship. Why did this one make him feel so strained?

He hadn't realized before how much her steady friendship meant to him. She might mock him and annoy him, but he'd always known she respected him.

Now he wasn't sure.

The days passed slowly. The cave seemed smaller with each segment of passing time. Obi-Wan felt himself grow more silent with every passing hour. He felt himself tense whenever Siri brushed past. He felt like a fool, like a rule-following, dull, stupid apprentice who didn't dare to risk. He never felt like that when Siri wasn't around.

The tension between them grew, and he didn't understand it. Obi-Wan couldn't wait to get out of the cave.

They did what Jedi do when forced to remain in one place. They kept themselves limber with exercises. They meditated. They did not think of the future, only the present moment.

One would stand guard while the other went down to the spring for water. They saw no one and heard nothing. Every hour, they expected Qui-Gon and Adi to contact them. They both felt a responsibility to keep the atmosphere light. They didn't want to worry Taly.

For his part, Taly crunched on protein pellets and slept fitfully. He stopped eating much. Obi-Wan began to worry about him. He and Siri slept in shifts so that one of them would always be awake. He didn't think it impossible that Taly would try to slip away. He saw how Siri's eyes grew dark with worry when she looked at him.

"We just have to hang on," he said to her.

She was scratching patterns in the dirt floor of the cave with a stick. She didn't look up. "One of us should do some reconnaissance," she said. "We don't know what the road is like to Settlement Five, or how many kilometers it is."

"We have the coordinates and a map on our datapad."

"A map is not the territory. You've told me that yourself."

Yes, he had. It was a saying of Qui-Gon's. *Study the map, but do not trust it. A map is not the territory. Until your boots are on it, do not trust the ground.*

"Yes, that's true. But the settlement isn't far, and the road is well marked. I think we risk more by scouting it out. If our Masters thought we needed to do it, they would have told us. They've traveled the road."

Siri looked up. "Orders for the Jedi are not meant to be

literal. Padawans should use their own judgment. That is a Jedi rule, too."

"If situations change," Obi-Wan said. "Ours is the same." He hated this. He hated spouting Jedi rules to Siri as though he was a Master and she was a Padawan. He knew how much she hated it, too. But she pushed him to a place where he had to.

That night at the evening meal, Obi-Wan watched as Taly pushed his protein pellets away. "I want real food."

"We only have two more days to wait," Obi-Wan told him. "There will be food on the freighter. Until then you must take nourishment. You must be strong, Taly. You have a long way to go, and it would be illogical to weaken yourself now."

He watched as Taly took another protein pellet and nodded as he swallowed it.

"That's better."

The moon rose, and they rolled themselves into their thermal blankets. Obi-Wan heard Taly's breathing slow and deepen.

In a few minutes he heard a noise. Siri crawled over to his side. She held out a palm full of protein pellets. "I found these behind a rock."

Obi-Wan frowned. "They must be Taly's. I don't understand. Why won't he eat?"

Siri tossed the pellets toward the rear of the cave. "Because these taste like rocks with a frosting of sand, that's why. We're used to them. He's not. He's just a kid, Obi-Wan."

"He's a very smart kid who knows how much trouble he's in," Obi-Wan said. "We're leaving in two days. Why would he starve himself?"

"Because he's scared and he misses his parents and everything's out of his control," Siri said impatiently. "Because beings don't always behave *logically*. This is the Living Force. It's unpredictable."

"I hate unpredictability," Obi-Wan said.

Siri smiled. "I know."

"So what should we do?"

"Are you asking me? That's a first," Siri teased.

"Yes, I'm asking you."

"I don't know. Let me think about it. I'll take the first watch."

Siri crawled to the entrance to the cave and positioned herself against the curve of the wall. He watched her curl into the wall as if it were the most comfortable of cushions. The moon was so big that night that he could see her profile illuminated, the crystal clarity of her eyes, the gleam of her hair. She managed to look both alert and perfectly comfortable.

For the first time in days, Obi-Wan slept deeply.

When he awoke, Siri was gone.

Dawn was still at least an hour away. It was cold in the cave. Obi-Wan wrapped his thermal blanket around his shoulders and sat at the cave opening. Even if he had wanted to search for Siri, he wouldn't leave Taly.

The light was shifting to purple when Siri reappeared, running soundlessly toward the cave, never making a wrong step even on the stony ground. When she caught sight of Obi-Wan she slowed. He saw her shoulders rise slightly, as if bracing herself for his attack.

She crouched down in front of him and removed a small sack from her tunic. "I got food for Taly," she said. "A muja muffin, some bread, some fruit."

"But I'm carrying all the credits," Obi-Wan said.

"I traded for them," Siri said. "My warming crystal. I sold it to a vendor who was opening up his shop early."

She looked embarrassed. She had sacrificed her most prized possession for a boy she hardly knew. It was a gesture full of sentiment. In the past, Obi-Wan would have thought it unlike her. Now, he knew better.

"Go ahead," she said. "Yell at me."

He didn't say anything. He'd always admired Siri for her fierceness. He had never known how strong her connection to the Living Force was. She always seemed to hold herself above other beings. Now he saw that her brusqueness was a kind of distance she kept, but even so, she was watching. Feeling.

"He'll like these," Obi-Wan said. "It was a good idea. You can go to sleep now. I'll keep watch."

"I can't sleep," Siri said gruffly. "Mind if I sit for awhile?"

Obi-Wan moved over to make room. Siri sat next to him.

"It's cold," she said. "But it's going to be a nice day."

He threw the blanket over her shoulders so that it was covering them both. He felt her leg against his, her breath against his ear. Warmth spread through him. He saw the sun begin to touch the rocks outside.

"One more day," she said. "I hope Qui-Gon and Adi make it back in time."

"If they don't, we'll be okay," Obi-Wan said. "We can handle anything if we're together."

"I know." He felt the whisper against his skin. They sat together and watched the light come up.

Qui-Gon and Adi did not return, and they did not send another message. Obi-Wan and Siri began to pack up their survival kits. They would have to do this on their own.

"If the bounty hunter is still on Quadrant Seven, he'll be watching to see if we board," Siri said. "We'll have to sneak on somehow."

"Qui-Gon always says that when you're trying to sneak in someplace, go where the food is," Obi-Wan said. "They load it separately through cargo, and security is sometimes pretty loose. Let's try there first."

"Sounds like a plan," Siri said. "Ready, Taly?"

Taly shouldered his pack. Once again, Obi-Wan was struck by how resolute he could look. He had accepted Siri's gift of food gratefully and had tried to share. Obi-Wan and Siri had both taken a small piece of fruit but insisted he eat most of the fresh food. He had been more cheerful after that. It wasn't so much the food, Obi-Wan thought, as the caring that had improved his mood and given him hope. Siri had been so right. He had things to learn from her that went beyond a new fighting stance. He had things to learn about the heart. About giving.

"I'm ready," Taly said.

Siri put her hands on his shoulders and squatted so that she was eye-level with him. "Here's the most important thing, Taly. You have to do what we say. Your safety depends on it."

He nodded. "I will."

Obi-Wan could see that he meant it. Siri had won his trust.

They set off. Because it was market day, the road was

crowded with beings heading into Settlement 5. That was lucky. The crowds gave them plenty of cover.

The marketplace was set up around the landing platform, which was another lucky break. Stalls and vendors crowded the square where ramps and lift tubes led to the landing platform several stories above. Siri, Obi-Wan, and Taly blended in with the others in their plain robes and hoods. Siri and Obi-Wan kept their gazes constantly moving but they did not catch a glimpse of the bounty hunter. Nor did the Force give them a warning.

The freighter was docked and ready for loading. One passenger ramp was already down. It would be easy to board and search for seats, but Obi-Wan thought it best to wait until the last possible moment.

They saw metal bins being carried to the back ramp, fresh fruit and vegetables spilling over the top. Obi-Wan watched for several minutes as they milled through the crowd, pretending to study the wares set up in booths and spread out on tables.

The bins were carried by workers who plodded back and forth up the ramp. When they disappeared inside the freighter, they were usually gone for a minute or so. That would easily give Obi-Wan, Siri, and Taly a chance to pick up a bin and bring it aboard. If they timed it right, they could pull it off.

Obi-Wan nudged Siri. "There. They're loading the fresh

food. If we pick up a bin we could get aboard. Nobody is really watching."

Siri nodded. Then suddenly she paled. "He's here."

"Where?"

"I feel him." Siri's gaze raked the crowd. "There."

Obi-Wan looked where Siri's gaze was resting. Magus was across the square. He stood in a clever spot, right where the sun was in shadow, behind a bin of vegetables that were a popular item for shoppers. It would have been hard to pick him out if Siri hadn't felt his presence.

"It's all right," Obi-Wan said. "He's searching the crowd. Now's our chance."

Siri swallowed. She kept her head down. "He's standing with the vendor I bought the food from. He knows we're here, Obi-Wan!"

Obi-Wan looked again. He realized that vendor standing next to Magus was also watching the crowd. Magus was smart. While the vendor concentrated on the passenger ramp, his own flinty gaze roamed. Now Obi-Wan saw how the bounty hunter kept his eye on the cargo ramp as well as the food ramp. There were now less than a dozen bins to carry. Time was running out.

"What are we going to do?" Taly asked.

Obi-Wan knew it was hopeless. There was no way they could board without Magus spotting them. No matter how cleverly they tried. Yet staying on the planet wasn't a good idea. Sooner or later, Magus would find them. And it would probably be sooner.

The panic in Taly's eyes made Obi-Wan angry. They had to protect him. They had to get him to a place that was safe.

"If he's here, that means his ship is unguarded," Obi-Wan said.

A flash illuminated Siri's blue gaze. "You want to steal his ship?"

"The freighter is due to leave in five minutes. We've got to find it first."

"It will be close," Siri guessed.

"Come on."

They threaded through the crowd with a purpose now, but were careful to move with the flowing surge. Obi-Wan checked out the possibilities. It would make sense for Magus to keep the cruiser near. Usually there was a holding pen for star cruisers near landing platforms. He hadn't noticed one here, but there should be one somewhat close.

"There," Siri breathed.

Around a corner, down an alley, a clearly marked space. It was empty but for one cruiser, the light freighter they knew belonged to Magus. They hurried toward the durasteel gate.

There was no time to lose. Obi-Wan cut a hole in the gate with his lightsaber and they squeezed through.

He prowled around the outside of the ship. Siri did the same.

"There should be an exterior control panel for the ramp," he said.

"Here it is." Taly's voice came from underneath the ship. "Sometimes these SoroSuubs are refitted with foiling devices. I can cross the wires and tinker with the controls here. . . ."

"Taly, let me," Obi-Wan urged.

The ramp slid down. "No need." Taly slid out and jumped up, dusting off his hands, a huge grin on his face. "We're done."

They ran up the ramp. Obi-Wan slid into the pilot seat.

"Wait." Taly ducked underneath the control panel. "Let's make sure there's no locking device. I can bypass the access code."

"Are you sure?" Siri asked.

"Easy as cutting through air." Taly took a small servo-driver from his utility belt. "Standard security devices . . . Code deactivated . . . Remote tracking device cut . . . Okay. Let's go."

Obi-Wan fired up the engines. He kept the engine speed down until they were safely away from the city. Then he blasted into the upper atmosphere.

He grinned at Siri. They made it.

"Set the course for Coruscant."

"Course set."

Minutes passed. Siri watched the computer screen avidly. There was still a chance they could be followed.

"Setting hyperdrive," Obi-Wan said. He flicked the controls. Space rushed toward them in a shower of stars. They were free.

With a sigh of satisfaction, Taly leaned back in his seat.

"I bet I'm really starting to get on that guy's nerves," he said.

CHAPTER 11

The problem with eavesdropping, Qui-Gon thought, was that it required beings who liked one another enough to exchange information. He and Adi had hoped to overhear more of the bounty hunters' plans, but as soon as their argument was over and the ship blasted off, they all retreated to separate areas of the ship and did not speak. They passed one another in the corridors, they met in the galley scrounging for food, they bumped into one another at close quarters, but all Qui-Gon and Adi heard was an occasional grunt or grumble of, "Blast your stinking carcass, stay out of my way."

They had been on the ship for three days and had learned nothing. They didn't know their destination, and they didn't know the bounty hunters' targets. They had moved from hiding place to hiding place, from storage compartment to empty stateroom and back again, and at last found what they felt was safe refuge in the small escape pod compartment.

When night fell, the sound of snoring penetrated even the thick door on the compartment. Pilot slept across the hall.

"We've got to do something," Adi said. "We could be landing soon. Not to mention that I'm going to go out of my mind."

"Meditation not working?"

Adi cocked an eyebrow at him. "Very amusing, Qui-Gon. You forget that I am the Jedi without a sense of humor. We need a plan. Something logical."

Qui-Gon smiled. "Why don't we just sneak around some more and see what we can turn up?"

Adi regarded him gravely. "Sounds good."

"I have an idea," Qui-Gon continued. "Pilot said he's in touch with their employer. And that he's keeping records on Magus. Maybe he's kept things he shouldn't."

They listened to the snoring that thundered down the corridor.

"He does sound like a heavy sleeper," Adi said. "Let's go."

Together they crept into Pilot's cabin. He stirred but didn't wake, instead sighing and turning over on his sleep couch. One long arm flopped over the side, his knuckles grazing the floor.

Adi nudged Qui-Gon. Pilot had dislodged his pillow. Now his head was half-on, half-off, and they saw a small datapad underneath the pillow.

Slowly, Adi leaned over. She slid her hand toward the pillow.

Pilot grunted. Adi froze.

Slowly, bit by tiny bit, she moved her hand underneath

to grab the edge of the datapad. As if she had all the time in the world, she slid it out from underneath.

Pilot snuggled more deeply into the blankets.

Adi and Qui-Gon bent over the datapad. Quickly, they accessed its files. They were all in code. They accessed the last file used. It was correspondence between Pilot and someone whose name was also in code. But Pilot had made an additional notation and had not coded it.

20 targets. mtg day one set.

Pilot began to stir. He was waking this time. They saw him lift his arm. He began to pat underneath the pillow, eyes still closed, to reassure himself that the datapad was still there.

Adi moved noiselessly across the floor. She had to bend over him, only centimeters from his cheek, as she slid the datapad back in place. Wrinkling her nose, she jerked her chin toward the door. Time to go.

Moving slowly, she withdrew from the sleep couch. Suddenly, Pilot's hand shot out and grabbed her tunic.

"Where do you think you're going?" His eyes snapped open and confusion shot him to a sitting position. "And who are you?"

With a quick movement Adi dislodged herself from his grasp and kicked him in the chest, sending him back across the sleep couch with an *oof.*

She and Qui-Gon hurtled out the door, drawing their lightsabers. As they ran, an alarm began to clang. There must have been an alert button right near the sleep couch.

They heard pounding footsteps behind them. Lunasa must have slept half-dressed. She still wore a tunic and boots, but she was bare-legged and her hair was matted from sleep and stood out in dark wisps around her head. A small rocket whistled toward them and then blaster fire richocheted in the air. Qui-Gon sliced through the rocket while Adi deflected the blaster fire.

From the opposite side of the corridor, Gorm the Dissolver strode toward them, fire shooting from the blasters in both hands. Adi and Qui-Gon kept constantly circling. Pilot had advanced out from his stateroom and joined the melee.

"Any ideas?" Adi muttered to Qui-Gon as she twirled, deflecting fire. The corridor was filled with smoke.

"Seems like a good time to escape," Qui-Gon said. "How about the pod?"

An ominous *clacking* came to their ears. Droidekas suddenly rolled down the corridor, unfurling to their full, deadly length.

"The pod sounds good," Adi replied.

Qui-Gon and Adi moved grimly forward.

Qui-Gon moved to the left, trying to get Gorm between him and the droidekas. But the two had excellent homing devices and moved accordingly. Gorm kept on a steady pace, thumping forward, blasting with a repeating rifle.

Qui-Gon saw that he had to end this. Between the droidekas and the bounty hunters, he saw a danger of being wounded or captured.

He surged forward, cutting off the leg of a droideka

and almost getting clipped by blaster fire in the process. The droideka lost its center of balance and spun. Blaster fire peppered out in a random pattern, almost hitting Lunasa. She yelled and hit the ground, still firing at the Jedi. Raptor almost got in the way, and had to leap over Lunasa, placing himself between Gorm and the Jedi.

All this happened in just a few seconds.

Qui-Gon and Adi leaped through the door of the escape pod hatch. They accessed the door and tumbled inside. They could hear the bounty hunters pounding after them.

"The airlock!" Adi yelled.

Qui-Gon hit it. He quickly activated the prelaunch sequence. The door thudded with the impact of blaster bolts.

"Not a grenade, you idiot!" Lunasa shouted. "You could damage the —"

They never knew who the idiot had been, but the grenade exploded. At the same moment the escape pod shot out into space, rocking with the motion of the grenade blast. They heard shrapnel pepper the shell of the pod, but it did not damage any systems.

Qui-Gon took over the manual controls. He pushed the speed to maximum.

"That was close," Adi said.

They had escaped. But where were they headed?

With the ship in hyperspace, Obi-Wan and Siri were able to relax for the first time in days. Taly fell asleep curled up on a cushion in the cockpit. He was exhausted.

"At least the bounty hunter has a well-stocked galley," Siri said in a low voice. "When Taly wakes up he can have a decent meal."

"We should get some rest, too," Obi-Wan said.

Siri went over to sit next to him on the cushioned seat in the cockpit. She hugged herself for a minute, hands on her elbows in an uncharacteristically nervous gesture.

"Obi-Wan? I just want to say thanks."

"Thanks for what?" Obi-Wan asked.

"I could have put Magus on our tail by selling my crystal. He might not have known for sure we were alive. Or that we were close to Settlement Five."

"We don't know that."

"I feel it. And I shouldn't have done it. But thanks for not telling me that."

"I admire you for what you did," Obi-Wan said. "Taly needed to know that you'd take care of him. He was losing hope, and I didn't see it. You did. It would be logical for

Magus to go to Settlement Five to watch the boarding of the freighter. Even if he hadn't found the vendor, he would have been there."

Siri's gaze was warm and amused. "You're a terrible liar, Obi-Wan Kenobi. It's one reason I like you so much."

"Ah, so you like me," Obi-Wan said lightly. "I thought I'd lost your good opinion."

She leaned against him for a moment, nudging him, then swung away. "Don't worry so much."

Siri's smile was so free of tension that it transformed her face. It was almost as though he had a glimpse of another Siri, a Siri without the engine that drove her, the need to excel, the stubbornness, the discipline. There was a Siri inside that Siri, someone he didn't know very well at all.

Obi-Wan felt his cheeks heat up. He looked down at his hand, resting next to hers on the cushion. He knew the shape of her fingers, the texture of her skin almost as well as his own. He had to fight the urge to slip his hand over hers, wind his fingers around hers.

Obi-Wan stood quickly. He turned his head away to hide his flaming cheeks.

Siri stretched out on the cushioned bench. She grabbed a blanket and drew it over her. She closed her eyes. He could tell she wasn't sleeping. Had he hurt her feelings by getting up so abruptly?

Obi-Wan had never worried about things like that before with Siri. Why was he so conscious of it now? Why was he so conscious of her?

He didn't like the feeling. But he liked it, too. Thoroughly confused, Obi-Wan stamped over to stare with unseeing eyes at the nav computer and try not to look at his friend again.

A day later, they drew close to the coordinates for reversion. They were almost to Coruscant.

"By nightfall, we'll be sitting in the Temple," Obi-Wan said with satisfaction. He would be glad to be back. Glad to get Taly to safety. Glad to put this mission behind him.

Siri worked at the nav computer. "Coordinates set for reversion outside Coruscant airspace."

Obi-Wan began to flip switches. He frowned.

"Everything okay?"

"I'm getting a funny readout from one of the security system checks. I've never seen one like it before."

Obi-Wan went to the manual security scan. He ran through the readouts. Suddenly, he felt the blood drain from his face.

Taly drew closer behind him. Siri spun around in her chair. "What is it?"

Obi-Wan's throat felt tight. "It's an anti-thievery device. Magus did have a surprise for us. The ship is programmed to self-destruct upon reversion." He turned to Siri and Taly. "We can't get out of hyperspace without blowing up."

CHAPTER 13

Obi-Wan looked at Siri. "How much fuel do we have?"

Siri hesitated. She glanced at Taly.

"Say it," Taly said. "I need to know, too."

"Two hours. We barely had enough to get to Coruscant."

"Cancel reversion," Obi-Wan said. "We have to dismantle this device."

"Let me look," Taly said eagerly. Obi-Wan motioned him over and pointed to the schematic on the datascreen. "There are two places to try to dismantle it — at the switch, or at the source. The only problem is . . ."

"If you do something wrong, you destroy the ship," Taly said, nodding.

Siri leaned over the datascreen. When she turned to speak, her face was very close to Obi-Wan's. She quickly moved away. "These kinds of things aren't my strong suit," she said. "I don't know engines like you do, Obi-Wan."

Obi-Wan didn't know them that well, either, but he decided it was better not to say that. He, like any Jedi, could diagnose problems, even if the shipboard computer wasn't functioning. He knew how to bypass systems and tinker with a sublight engine. But this was way over his head.

"I can try to find the contact point for the device," he said. "If only we could contact the Temple and someone could talk me through it!"

But there was no comm service in hyperspace.

"We can send a distress signal to the Temple," Siri said. "We should at least do that, so they know we're in trouble."

Even if they can't help us. Obi-Wan knew exactly what Siri would not say.

She leaned over and sent the distress signal.

Taly was flipping through diagrams on the screen. "Let me study this schematic for awhile."

Taly leaned closer to concentrate. They watched as he studied diagrams and readouts. Then he turned around. "Uh, guys? Would you mind not hovering? It's not helping my concentration."

Obi-Wan crossed to another datascreen. He and Siri went over the same information as Taly.

"I don't know what to do," Obi-Wan confided to her. "I could go over this information a thousand times, and I don't think I could figure it out."

"You'll think of something," Siri said. "Or I will, or Taly will."

"We have two hours," Obi-Wan said.

*   *   *

Time seemed to creep, but suddenly, an hour had passed. Obi-Wan tried not to look at the chrono on the instrument panel, but the seconds ticked by in his head. Taly had his head in his hands.

"There's one thing we can try," Taly finally said. "Disrupt the reversion process during the last cycle and reverse it. Then go forward again, but this time, switch over to auxiliary power. "

"In other words, you'd activate the explosion, then cancel it, and hope it doesn't reactivate in time," Obi-Wan said.

"But we have no way of knowing how fast it will re-arm," Siri pointed out. "We could blow ourselves up."

"That's the danger," Taly conceded.

Obi-Wan and Siri exchanged a glance.

"At least Taly's plan gives us a chance," Obi-Wan said.

Taly balled up his hands into fists. "I should be able to figure this out! I should be able to dismantle it!"

Obi-Wan put his hand on his shoulder. "Taly, it's all right. It's very ingenious. Very detailed. None of us can dismantle it."

"Let's wait until the last possible minute, to be sure we can't come up with another idea. Then we can follow through," Siri proposed. "Agreed?"

"Agreed," Obi-Wan said.

Taly nodded, his face pale.

It was a gamble they could pay for with their lives, and they knew it.

* * *

They had nothing left to try.

Taly sat in the far side of the cockpit. He had accessed the holomap and was simply flicking through space quadrants, one after the other, staring at the light pulses that indicated planets and moons.

Siri had disappeared from the cockpit. She had been staring at the datascreen. She had climbed down into the engine bay. She had gone over operations manuals. She had not come up with anything. Obi-Wan knew she felt just as helpless as he did. They weren't used to feeling this way.

He went searching for her. She was curled up in the cargo hold, on the floor, wrapped in a blanket. Without a word she opened the blanket so Obi-Wan could slide next to her. It was cold. He was reminded of the early morning hours they spent in the cave, watching the sun come up.

"I think we've hit something we can't solve," Siri said. "That's not supposed to happen."

"Yoda would say that Jedi aren't infallible. We are only well prepared."

"Well prepared, we are," Siri said gently in Yoda-speak. "Infallible, we are not."

They laughed softly.

"When the moment comes, we'll be together," Obi-Wan said.

He put out his hand. Siri slipped hers into it. At her touch, something moved between them, a current that felt alive.

At last he felt what it was like to touch her. He realized that he'd been thinking about it for days. Maybe for years. She wound her fingers around his, strong but gentle, just as he knew she would. He could feel the ridge of callus on her palm from lightsaber training, but the skin on her fingers was soft. Softness and strength. He'd known he would feel that.

Something broke free inside him. He felt filled up with his feeling, even though he couldn't name it. He couldn't dare to name it. Yet it was suddenly more real than anything in his life. More real than the danger they were in. More real than the Jedi.

"Siri . . ."

Her voice was a whisper. "I feel it, too."

She turned her face to his. Her eyes were brimming with tears. She half-laughed, half-cried. "Isn't this funny? Isn't this the strangest thing?"

"No," Obi-Wan said. "This has always been there. I just never wanted to see it. Since that first time I spoke to you, when you were so angry at me for leaving the Jedi," Obi-Wan said. "You were eating a piece of fruit. You just kept chewing and staring at me, as though I didn't matter."

Siri laughed. "I remember. I was out to get you. I wanted to make you angry."

"You made me furious. You always knew how to do that."

"I know. And you were always so *right.* So *fair.* You made me furious, too. Lots of times."

"And then we became friends."

"Good friends."

"And now," Obi-Wan said, hardly daring to breathe, "what are we?"

"On a doomed ship," Siri said. "So I guess the question is, what would we have been?"

She tightened her grip on his hand. She leaned forward, and put her lips against his cheek. She didn't kiss him. She just rested there. In that instant Obi-Wan felt something: a connection that bound him to her, no matter what. Siri. He wanted to say her name out loud. He wanted to never move from this cold floor. He wanted to touch the ends of her shimmersilk hair and breathe in the scent that came off her skin.

"Whatever happens," she whispered against his cheek, her lips warm and soft, softer than he could ever imagine, "I'll remember this."

CHAPTER 14

Qui-Gon piloted the pod to the nearest landing available, a spaceport moon aptly named Haven. The bounty hunters tried a pursuit, but they weren't very determined and it was soon clear that they didn't regard the Jedi as much of a threat. They had somewhere to get to that was vastly more important. Bounty hunters were always concerned most with finishing the job and receiving their payments.

Qui-Gon and Adi sat at a table in a dingy café called The Landing Lights. They had tried to contact the Temple, but a meteor storm in the upper atmosphere at the spaceport had temporarily cut all HoloNet communication and grounded the ships. They had managed to procure a ship, a fast star cruiser with a pilot who would cheerfully do anything for the Jedi. It was fueled and ready to go. The only trouble was, they had no clue as to where they were going. If all had gone well, Obi-Wan and Siri had caught the freighter and were on their way to Coruscant with Taly. Their Padwans could even be waiting for them to be in touch.

"Well, we didn't learn much by boarding that ship," Adi said. "Was it worth it?"

"We acquired the tiniest bits of information," Qui-Gon said. "But with this last one, we might be able to put the puzzle together."

"M-T-G," Adi said. "A meeting."

"Exactly. So we can assume that all twenty targets will be present."

"Twenty planetary leaders at one meeting," Adi mused. "That could be any morning at the Senate. How can we possibly pin it down?"

"I don't think the meeting is at the Senate," Qui-Gon said. "Remember that Raptor said if he cancelled the mission, he'd head *back* to the Core? If the mission was on Coruscant, that wouldn't make sense." Qui-Gon glanced up at the display monitor overhead. "Interference is cleared. We can contact the Temple."

He reached for his comlink. "Let's find out what Jocasta Nu has to say." Qui-Gon quickly contacted her. Her crisp voice greeted him in seconds.

"Qui-Gon, it's about time you contacted the Temple." Jocasta Nu's tone never failed to make Qui-Gon feel like a disobedient student. "Are you aware that your Padawan has sent a distress signal from deep space?"

"No." Qui-Gon exchanged a worried glance with Adi. "From where?"

"It is not my job to interpret distress signals," Madame

Nu said huffily. "However, from what I understand, the signal was sent from hyperspace. We have been unable to track whatever ship it was sent from. It's not a registered ship."

"They aren't on the freighter," Qui-Gon said to Adi worriedly.

"Now, I suggest you tell me why you are contacting me."

"Adi Gallia and I are on the trail of a team of bounty hunters that are headed by a leader named Magus. They are set to assassinate twenty planetary leaders at a meeting."

"Twenty! That's rather ambitious."

"They are five very capable assassins. Do you have any background on Magus?"

"Magus . . . I know that name. One moment." Qui-Gon waited, knowing that Madame Nu was accessing her vast store of knowledge. All Jedi had access to the Archives, but Madame Nu had a gift for interpreting unrelated facts, as well as an unbelievable memory for names. Once she heard a name, she never forgot it. "Yes, Magus has done work for the Corporate Alliance in the past. Nothing illegal. But we suspect him of being a secret assassin. If you could confirm that, we could put him on the Galactic Apprehend List."

The Corporate Alliance! Of course. With the devious Passel Argente as Alliance Magistrate, the organization had changed from one that promoted good business relations to one that used trickery and intimidation to extend its power. But would they go so far as to back an assassination plot?

"I should be able to confirm that very soon. Now can you check on interplanetary meetings within the next five days?"

"Master Qui-Gon Jinn," Jocasta Nu said in her firmest voice, "are you aware how many interplanetary meetings there are every day in the galaxy? Hundreds, at least. Why, on Coruscant alone . . ."

"You can exclude Coruscant. And any planets in the Core. Let's start with any meeting that would concern the Corporate Alliance. And . . . my guess is it will take place in some sort of high-security location. Somewhere so safe that the leaders will forgo their usual security measures."

"All right, then. That helps. Somewhat." Qui-Gon could picture Madame Nu's thin-lipped frown. "Let's start with the treaty database . . . yes. Hmm. No, that wouldn't . . . perhaps . . . no. No, no, maybe? Let me try . . . wait . . . this is a possibility. Yes, yes, I think this is definitely a solid possibility. It's not an official meeting — not recorded, but we pick up things here and there. It's hard to keep a high-level meeting completely secret. Twenty planetary leaders, all heads of the largest worlds in their systems. They have various grievances against the Corporate Alliance and are considering a twenty-systemwide ban against conducting any business in the Alliance. They are trying to pressure Passel Argente, I imagine."

"He wouldn't like that," Qui-Gon said.

"No, indeed. He's a bully, and bullies can get nasty about such things. It would severely curtail the Alliance's power in a fairly large sector. Not to mention that it would send a message to other systems trying to resist Argente's strong-arm tactics that they can take action themselves. You see, the Senate has not been able to control these groups — like the Trade Association, and the Techno Union — we've been having a great deal of trouble with them lately —"

"Yes, I understand," Qui-Gon interrupted. He didn't have time for Madame Nu's summary of the bureaucratic problems of the Senate, no matter how insightful. "Where is the meeting to take place?"

"At a conference site on Rondai-Two. The Ulta Center — ultimate luxury, ultimate security. Do you need another Jedi team, Qui-Gon? I would be happy to pass along this information to Yoda, though it is not strictly within my purview to do so."

"I'll consult with Adi and be in touch. Thank you, Madame Nu."

Qui-Gon ended the conversation and turned to Adi. "Passel Argente. Even though he is a Senator, he is also a Koorivar and a leader of the Corporate Alliance, and his grudges against the Republic are plain to see. He's behind all this. He's not just a bully, he's cunning. He knows he has to stamp out resistance at the start. Has to hit it hard, to intimidate others who are thinking of crossing him. It's the way he operates."

"You don't know that for sure," Adi said.

"I feel it."

"Feelings are not proof and are inherently illogical," Adi said.

Qui-Gon turned to her. "Don't you feel it, too?"

After a slight pause, Adi inclined her head in her regal way. "I do."

While Qui-Gon was speaking, Adi had already located Rondai-2 on her datapad. Now she pushed the screen toward Qui-Gon.

"We're lucky. Two day's journey. We'll make it in time." Adi raised her troubled gaze to his. "But what about our Padawans?"

Qui-Gon looked out at the vastness of space, the clouds of stars. He felt the emptiness inside him, the yawning feeling he got when he knew Obi-Wan was in trouble and he could not get to him. For the shortest space of a moment, he thought of what it would be like to lose both Tahl and Obi-Wan, and the hugeness of that loss seemed to dwarf the vastness of what lay above him.

"There is nothing we can do. They'll have to take care of themselves."

CHAPTER 15

Taly suddenly burst into the cargo hold. "I remembered something."

Obi-Wan and Siri jumped up. "A way to fix the reversion?" Obi-Wan asked.

"No, no. I haven't figured that out. But I was just flipping through systems, and I saw this planet, Rondai-Two. You know when you feel a click in your head? I felt a click. I thought I heard the bounty hunter talking about a 'rendezvous' But he really said 'Rondai-Two.'"

"Are you sure?" Siri asked.

"I'm sure. He said 'on rendezvous,' which seemed weird, because nobody says 'on rendezvous.' He meant a planet."

"So that's where the mission is," Obi-Wan said. "But we can't get there." He started toward the cockpit. "We can do one thing. We can leave the information in the survivor box. If any part of the ship survives, the box might. And the information could get back to the Temple." He quickly accessed the box and entered the information into the datapad. "We need to put this in the escape pod."

Siri and Taly looked at him gravely. They might not survive, but they would have to hope that the information might.

"Now I just have to program the fact that the box has information," Obi-Wan said. "We just have to hope that whoever finds it will bring it to the Temple or the Senate. If it gets into the hands of pirates, it would be lost forever . . . and there's always space pirates lurking around the outskirts of Coruscant. . . ."

Obi-Wan's own words rang in his ears. "That's our answer," he said.

"What?" Taly asked.

"We can't reprogram in hyperspace. But we can send another distress signal. A general one this time, going out to all ships in the area of reversion. We would keep the signal open. That would allow whoever was tracking us to get a fix on us."

"Who is tracking us?"

"Nobody," Obi-Wan said. "Yet. But space pirates wait for distress signals. They like to prey on dying ships."

"I'm not getting this," Taly said.

Obi-Wan whirled around in his chair. "The ship will blow upon reversion. But what if we get *pulled out* of hyperspace against our will?"

"An interdiction field," Siri breathed. "If we go through one, we'll be pulled into realspace. But we'll also be sitting ducks," she pointed out. "The ship is almost out of power. If we're attacked, we won't be able to maneuver."

"At least we'll have a fighting chance," Obi-Wan said. "I'd rather meet space pirates than blow up."

Siri grinned. "Well, since you put it that way."

Taly swallowed. "If they capture me. . . ."

"We won't let that happen. We will fight to the death for you." Obi-Wan said. He thought for a moment. Taly looked scared and uncertain. But Obi-Wan knew one thing that would give him courage. He would treat him as an equal partner.

"You get a vote, Taly," he said. "If any of us says no, we won't do it. We'll keep with your original plan."

Taly bit his lip. "No, we have a better chance with your plan. Let's do it," he said in a rush. As he said it, he straightened. The color came back into his cheeks. "I'm ready."

Obi-Wan sent the distress signal and kept it on. Now events were out of their control. Obi-Wan tried not to watch the power drain. He tried not to think about what might happen. Siri came over to stand next to his chair. He stood and took his place beside her. They gripped each other's hands.

Taly moved to stand close to the windscreen, as though he could see what was ahead.

"Obi-Wan, no matter what happens," Siri murmured, "I want you to know —"

He looked into her eyes. "I already know."

The ship gave a violent shudder. They did not know if

it was the beginning of the breakdown, or if they were in the grip of the field.

"The interdiction field," Siri said as soon as she was sure. "It's sucking our power."

The ship groaned and shuddered. Stars seemed to wheel and crash as they entered realspace. The ship bumped and slammed against what felt like a wall. But it didn't explode.

The pirate ship was waiting.

Laser cannon boomed. Obi-Wan sprang forward to the controls. "I can't maneuver. We have no firepower. "

"They're going to board us," Siri said. "The escape pod?"

"They'll blast us right out of space," Obi-Wan said.

He stood. He drew his lightsaber. Siri drew hers. "Stand behind us, Taly," Obi-Wan said. "Just stay behind us. Don't try to fight."

They felt the shock of the landing craft hitting the loading bay. They heard the pounding of boots. Many, many boots. They heard the *clack clack clack* of droids. Obi-Wan glanced at Siri. He saw the same knowledge in her eyes. They didn't have to see them. They were too many.

They raced forward. Surprise was their only ally. They burst through the doors, into the thick of it — row after row of heavily armed pirates. They were a mangy group, all species, all sizes. What they had in common was weaponry and greed. Their faces were painted in bright colors, their belts hung with trophies from their many captures. He had never seen such a collection of fierce, ugly beings.

The corridor filled with smoke as small rocket fire ripped holes in the walls and thudded into the floors. Metal peeled back like durasheets.

Obi-Wan supposed that this was their warning shot, because the pirates didn't move.

A squat, powerful being walked forward. His thick black hair hung to his waist.

"What do we have here? Jedi? Ha! What luck! Do you know there's a bounty out for you?"

But he wasn't looking at Siri and Obi-Wan. He was looking at Taly.

Siri sprang forward. She was all energy, like a pulsating beam of light. The pirates fired, blasters and blaster rifles, rockets and darts. She flowed and struck and moved and rolled and leaped. Fire singed her tunic and did not slow her down. Obi-Wan felt sweat dampen his back as he struck again and again, knocking droids down, evading the pirate fire, and always, always, keeping himself between the attacking troops and Taly.

He was not tiring, not yet, but he could feel the hopelessness of the situation. Still, he had promised Taly not to surrender, and he would not.

And then, suddenly, over the thud of rockets and ping of blaster fire, he heard a scream.

"No! Take me!" Taly ran through the fire. Amazingly, he

was not hit. Coughing from the smoke, he yelled, "Take me, you cowards!"

"Taly, no!" Siri yelled.

"I can't let you die for me!" Taly called to them as a pirate swept him up and threw him back. The pirates roared as they tossed him like a toy, farther and farther back, to the end of the line. The last pirate holding Taly ran, while the others kept up a steady barrage at Siri and Obi-Wan.

Retreating, the pirates kept up the intense fire. Siri and Obi-Wan could not get to Taly. The pirates leaped onto the ship and took off into space with Taly, leaving Obi-Wan and Siri aboard a smoking, dying ship.

"We need a landing site, and fast," Siri said. Beads of sweat matted her hair. The expression in her eyes was ferocious as she gazed out at the galaxy, as if challenging it to dare to defy her. As if space itself was obliged to hold up the dying ship.

The power was draining so fast that soon it would hit all systems. Then they would be unable to choose a course or guide it to land. They could see smoke billowing out from the port side. The attacking ship had chosen their blast sites carefully, it was clear. The escape pod bay was a mass of molten metal. Another blast on the port side had taken out all the weapons, and the ship listed to the side, constantly in danger of spinning out of control.

"Refueling stop on a satellite," Obi-Wan called out. "There's a huge spaceport there, plenty of landing platforms. Ten minutes away. Can the ship hold on for ten minutes?"

Siri gritted her teeth. "This ship is going to do what I tell it to do."

Obi-Wan sat in the copilot seat, although there really wasn't anything else he could do but watch Siri battle with the controls. Keeping the ship on course took tiny adjust-ments and a constant eye on the readout systems.

"Adi crash-landed on purpose," Siri said. "But this is going to be different, Obi-Wan. I might not be able to con-trol what happens once we land."

He knew what she was telling him. They might not sur-vive the crash.

"I understand," he said. "I trust you."

She shot him a quick look that was so full of courage he could only marvel at how strong she was.

"Coming up on the spaceport," Obi-Wan said.

The spaceport was on the edge of a red nebulae. The color was deep and seemed to pulse. To Obi-Wan's eyes, it seemed an impossible sight, a blooming flower in space. They would have to fly into the heart of its beauty.

"Here we go," Siri muttered.

And then the spaceport loomed at them, coming impossibly fast.

"I can't slow it down," Siri said, panic in her voice.

At this speed, the craft would surely disintegrate on contact with the unforgiving ground. Obi-Wan no longer felt he was diving into a flower. All poetry left his soul, and he saw duracrete and metal, hard substances that would pulverize this ship like a plaything.

"Cut the power!" he shouted to Siri.

She looked at him wildly. "But I won't have control —"

"They'll be enough left in the hydraulics for a few sec-onds. It will be all over by then, anyway."

She reached over and cut the power. The ship stopped careening but it was now in free fall, and they could just make out beings below running to safety. Obi-Wan saw one tall figure shaking his fist at them before racing to get out of the way.

"Here we go!" Siri screamed, using the manual controls to steer the ship away from the other cruisers and one large freighter. She had just enough power left in the hydraulics to aim the ship toward the empty section of the platform and pull it up so that it wouldn't smash nose-first into the ground.

He had time for a flash of a look, that was all, and then the ship was down, starting to skid with a terrible jolt that sent metal screaming and smoke billowing. Obi-Wan felt his jaws snap together. His body lifted through the air. He grabbed at the edge of a console on the way down but his legs flew up again and his body slammed down, wrenching the console from his grasp. He hit the ceiling, then the floor. He had never felt so helpless. He didn't know his limbs could move in so many directions at once. Pain rocketed through him. He could feel the ship sliding on its belly, scraping against the duracrete platform. He smelled fire.

Siri. Siri. Her name was like a drumbeat inside him. Through the smoke, through his own flailing limbs, he searched for her.

Jedi could make time slow down. Did that mean his death and hers would take forever?

He saw the glint of her hair through the smoke. She was slumped on the floor.

No!

He fought his way to her as the ship burned and slid.

"Siri!"

He felt the pulse on her neck. It fluttered against his fingers.

He felt a surge of purpose. She was alive. He was alive. He would save them.

Somehow he managed to get out his lightsaber. With one arm around her, he dragged her across the floor of the cockpit. The ship was still skidding out of control across the ground, the friction heating the shell. The metal floor was already hot. Soon it would start to melt, to peel away. He willed his body. He reached out for the Force. This would take everything he had.

He half-crawled, half-slid across the floor. Siri began to stir. As soon as her eyes opened, she let him know by pushing him away. She never accepted help if she could do something herself. And she would will her body to obey.

He saw her wince as she reached for her lightsaber, but she joined him on the floor, crawling toward the wall of the spaceship. The ship was still out of control, but the crash had probably only been going on for three or four seconds.

He had time to do this. The ship would hold out. Obi-Wan activated his lightsaber and began to cut through the ship's wall. Siri joined him, sweat streaking through the grime on her face. It was so unbearably hot.

Coughing, they buried their lightsabers in the hot metal and it peeled back. Obi-Wan caught a glimpse of rushing sky and then he pushed Siri out, balancing on the toes of his boots. She reached a hand down for him and hauled him out with her amazing strength.

They balanced for a moment on the side of the sliding ship. They looked into each other's eyes. They gauged the speed and knew the jump would be hard. They called on the Force and leaped.

The Force helped them. They timed the leap high and wide so that they would be able to slow their descent. Still, the shock of the ground radiated up through their knees, and they rolled across the duracrete, putting as much distance between themselves and the ship as they could.

Ahead of them, the ship exploded.

They turned away from the blast, covering their heads. Molten metal rained down. Obi-Wan felt a piece sear his shoulder.

They slumped together, hardly daring to believe that they were still alive.

A tall being with arms almost to the ground came running. Obi-Wan recognized the being he'd seen shaking his fist at them. "What do you think you're doing?" the being yelled.

Siri and Obi-Wan stared at him.

"Surviving?" Siri said.

She giggled. Obi-Wan had never heard her giggle before. The relief flooded him. They were alive. They were alive. He began to laugh. They laughed and laughed, holding each other as they lay on the duracrete platform.

"Somebody's going to pay for this," the spaceport manager said, and they only laughed harder.

Obi-Wan waited for Siri in the hangar. They had separated in order to clean up. He had given the furious spaceport manager the registry number of the crashed ship, as well as Magus's name. Obi-Wan had no doubt that the spaceport manager would track him down somehow and demand payment for the damage.

Siri strode toward him, her hair wet and tucked behind her ears. "What now?" she asked as she came up.

"I found a pilot who will take us to Rondai-Two," Obi-Wan said. "She said that anybody who survived that crash deserves some help. It's a sublight cruiser. We leave in a few minutes. We could be landing by midday."

Siri nodded. "Nice to have some good news at last."

"We've got to get to Taly."

Siri's gaze clouded. "If he's still alive. Those pirates are going to turn him over to the bounty hunters for the reward."

"I feel that he's alive. We almost didn't make it ourselves."

"I know."

"But now that we have . . ."

Neither of them spoke for a moment. All around them, workers pushed through the hangar. But to Siri and Obi-Wan, it was as if no one else was there. They just looked at each other, remembering what they'd confessed on the ship. They tested it. Was it a result of circumstance, of being so close to death?

No. It was real. It was still between them.

"What do we do?" Siri asked. "What we feel . . . it's forbidden."

"But we can't just stop," Obi-Wan said. "We almost died. That could happen at any time, on any mission. I understand that. I accept it. But I won't accept going on without being together."

Siri swallowed. "What are you saying, Obi-Wan? We're Jedi. We can't be together. Attachment is not our way."

"Why?" Obi-Wan burst out. "It doesn't have to be that way. Rules can change. The Council can change the rules, they can find a way for us. We can still be Jedi and still . . . "

". . . love each other," Siri finished softly. "Let's name it. Let's not avoid saying what we know."

She reached out and touched his sleeve. "You know and I know that they won't change the rules for us. The Jedi Order doesn't work that way. The rules are there for reasons that go back thousands of years."

"All the more reason to change them," Obi-Wan said. "We could wait a few years, until we are Masters. Then we could be a team. We could go on missions together!"

Siri's eyes sparkled. "We would be such a great team." Then her gaze dimmed. "They won't allow it. And I won't let you leave the Jedi. I know what it cost you last time."

"I don't want to leave the Jedi. And I know you couldn't."

"It's everything to me," Siri said. "It's part of me. It's home." Her voice was soft. "But so are you."

"We'll just have to keep this secret." Even as he said it, Obi-Wan felt his heart fall. Keep a secret from Qui-Gon? Could he do that?

He's kept secrets from me.

But he was the Master. He had that right. Obi-Wan dismissed the thought. He knew it was born in the resentment he felt against anything that stood between him and what he wanted. It wasn't fair to blame Qui-Gon.

He could dismiss his resentment easily. What he could not dismiss was the awful feeling of concealing his heart from Qui-Gon.

"It would be hard."

Siri's gaze was cloudy. "It's the only way. Or else we decide we turn away from this."

Turn away? Obi-Wan couldn't bear it when her fingers dropped from his sleeve. In a matter of hours he had come to realize that Siri was as necessary to him as breathing. She was part of him. She was his heart and his lungs and part of what kept him standing.

He swallowed. "I can't turn away from this. I can't let you go."

Siri's eyes filled with tears, and that was the worst thing of all.

"We'll keep the secret, then? We'll see each other when we can, how we can."

Obi-Wan felt so dizzy. So full of relief at just being alive. So grateful that Siri was standing beside him. So full of joy that she loved him. But when he looked ahead, he saw deceit. Could he walk that path?

"We need to find Taly first," Siri said. "End the mission. Then we can decide what to do."

"Taly is the most important thing," Obi-Wan agreed.

Everything seemed against them, but strangely, he felt hopeful. They would find a way.

CHAPTER 17

The pilot left Adi and Qui-Gon off at the main spaceport on Rondai-2, telling them that the Jedi were "one amazing nova of a group." He'd be happy to help them out anytime.

It was close to dawn. The sky was still dark, but was beginning to gray. Qui-Gon and Adi lost no time in hurrying to the meeting site. Their two-day journey had given them plenty of time to plan. The Ulta Center was an exclusive conference site that had been built specifically to host high-level corporate and diplomatic meetings.

The center took up a large compound in the city of Dal. On the journey Qui-Gon and Adi had done their research. The center boasted top-level security for the most private of meetings and retreats. They had their own landing platform on the roof where guests could arrive in secret. No one was allowed inside unless he or she was a guest. It was necessary to reserve rooms months in advance, and guests from different groups did not ever see each other, as there were separate wings for each meeting. Every guest had to undergo a high-level security check. There was no way that Qui-Gon and Adi could simply stroll in.

"Any ideas?" Adi asked. "We have to get in so we can

figure out the plan of attack. We don't want to advertise the fact that we're Jedi. Better if the bounty hunters don't know we tailed them here."

Qui-Gon glanced around. "That café is just opening. It's a fine morning to sit outside."

Adi looked exasperated. "Surely we have better things to do." She scanned the area for a moment. "Oh, I see. We can conduct surveillance from there. Is that your purpose?"

"It is," Qui-Gon said. "And I'm thirsty."

Adi raised an eyebrow instead of smiling, but he was used to that.

They ordered a pot of Tarine tea and sat at a table outside. The chill in the air began to lessen as the sun began to rise. The Rondais began to emerge from their homes and go off to work. They walked past, some with purpose, some enjoying the morning. Several stopped in at the café. It seemed to be a popular morning spot. Qui-Gon was glad of the company. It would conceal them more effectively. Rondai-2 was a cosmopolitan world with many visitors. No one gave them a second glance.

Everything here was mild — the weather, which never dipped to freezing; the landscape, which had no high mountains, only rolling hills; and the tempo of the cities, which was busy, but not frenzied. Everything at the conference center had been designed to conceal its high security and make it blend in with its pleasant surroundings.

A security wall curved around the conference center. The entrance was staffed with two security guards. The wall was softened by fountains that flowed invisibly from the top and splashed down in a continuous, musical stream to a long pool that served as a moat around the curving structure. Colored lights that were concealed underwater presented a constantly changing array of soft blues and violets. In front of the pool, flowering shrubs massed in the same colors, shading to deep purple and navy.

The conference center behind the wall was built in a radial design, with wings that extended from a central lobby like outflung arms. It was faced in durasteel that had been buffed to a medium blue. In sunlight, Qui-Gon thought, it would blend with the sky. It was a building that tried to make itself as invisible as it could.

Airspeeders and air taxis floated by. The pace was beginning to quicken. Still, these were the early morning workers, the ones who went to work when the sky was still dark.

"Security traps in the wall," Adi murmured. "Motion sensors at the gate. Iris scans for guests. It won't be easy to launch an attack here."

"Which is why it will be here," Qui-Gon said. "They feel safe here. And why else would Argente hire five bounty hunters? He knows that he's asking the impossible."

"So," Adi said, "how will they make the impossible possible?"

"Each bounty hunter has different skills," Qui-Gon said. "Gorm is brute force. Lunasa is the impersonator. Raptor is the efficient killer. Pilot is the best at planning getaways."

"And Magus?"

"He's the mastermind. He comes up with the plan. If we can put the pieces together, we can figure it out before it happens."

"In other words," Adi said, "we have to be masterminds, too." Suddenly she gave him a sharp look. "You're waiting for something. What?"

Qui-Gon took a sip of tea. "In hotels such as this, they pride themselves on not using droids to clean rooms or deliver food. Not even protocol droids. They only use living beings. They say it gives the service a 'living touch.' That beings can anticipate needs and make you comfortable, do things that droids can't."

"So?"

Qui-Gon shrugged. "Rooms have to be cleaned." He swirled his teacup. "Did you notice how Lunasa looked on the ship during the battle?"

"I noticed the weaponry she pointed in my direction," Adi said. "Can you get to the point?"

"Her hair was different."

The familiar line of exasperation appeared between Adi's eyebrows. "I don't pay attention to hairdos, Qui-Gon."

"When we first saw her, she was fair-haired. She wore her hair in braids. During the battle, her hair was short and dark." Qui-Gon noted Adi's impatience but willed himself not to smile. Adi did not spend much time in tune with the Living Force. "Did you notice that the natives of Rondai-Two are all dark-haired?"

Adi pressed her lips together. She knew now that Qui-Gon was leading her somewhere. Adi did not like to be led.

"Ah, here come the service workers," Qui-Gon said.

Across the avenue an air bus pulled up. A group of Rondai natives got off. They wore trim black uniforms. They headed up toward the security office. The officer yawned and waved them in.

"No security check," Adi breathed.

"They come every day. Guards get bored. They cut corners. That's what makes every security system fallible." Qui-Gon took a gulp of tea. "See anyone you know?"

Adi drew in her breath sharply. "It's her. Lunasa. She's walking right in! Let's go!"

"Wait a moment. The others will be arriving. I have a feeling the attack will come this morning."

"Qui-Gon." Adi's voice was sharp. "That cloud car. Look."

Qui-Gon glanced to where Adi indicated. Pilot and Raptor were in a speeder, cruising by. Squeezed between them was Taly. The boy didn't see them. He stared straight ahead. It was clear that he was trying not to look as terrified as he felt.

"They've got Taly," Qui-Gon said. "So where are Obi-Wan and Siri?"

Adi shook her head, her dark eyes troubled.

"Why are they keeping him alive?" she asked.

"And for how long?" Qui-Gon wondered.

CHAPTER 18

Afraid of attracting suspicion, Qui-Gon and Adi left the café. They strolled down the street and doubled back, concealing themselves in the foyer of a building while office workers streamed past them.

"She will get the others in," Qui-Gon said. "Each of them — they've already planned it. Or else some of them are already inside. They've already been here for two days. We have no way of knowing."

"Except for Pilot and Raptor," Adi said. "And someone has to watch Taly, if they . . . if they don't kill him."

"If they were going to, they would have done so already. Pilot will watch Taly. He's responsible for the getaway. But Raptor still has to get inside. We know that for sure. He could be the last piece. When he gets in, the plan begins."

"We should notify security."

Qui-Gon shook his head. "Not yet. If the place goes on alert, it could hamper us from getting in. That is, if they even believe us. These bounty hunters are used to security officers. They'll mow them down in a flash. They won't be any help, and they'll lose their lives. I think we should do this ourselves."

Adi considered this. "Agreed." As much as Adi hated taking direction from someone else, she never let that interfere with her judgment.

She gazed over at the center, thinking. "The pool," she said. "We know that each suite of rooms has its own pool, too. They must be fed from a central source. And it must be substantial."

"Raptor," Qui-Gon said. "He has gills."

"Exactly what I was thinking."

Just then a large repulsorlift truck pulled onto the street, going fast. It veered out of its lane and crashed into a speeder bus. The driver waved his arms in frustration, blaming the speeder bus driver. They immediately picked out Pilot in disguise as the driver of the truck. The security guards in the entrance booth craned their necks.

"And there is the diversion," Qui-Gon said. "Come on."

They raced down the street and skirted the truck, not wanting to alert Pilot. Suddenly, they saw Raptor climb out of the flowering bushes and slip into the reflecting pool. He disappeared underwater.

Qui-Gon and Adi were only moments behind him. They donned their aquatabreathers as they ran and immediately slipped into the pool. The water was cold and surprisingly deep. They swam down quickly as the colors flashed, swimming through blue, then lavender. Adi nudged Qui-Gon. A shadow was moving, swimming quickly toward the wall. They followed.

The shadow disappeared. One moment he was there.

The next moment, gone. Qui-Gon swam forward, kicking his powerful legs. He came up against a blank wall.

Adi gestured at the bottom of the pool. Reflective surfaces had been set up and angled in different ways in order to deepen the effect of the colored lights. They had not seen Raptor's shadow. They had only seen his reflection. It had been impossible to tell the difference underneath the shimmering water. Qui-Gon wanted to groan aloud, but he didn't want to drop his breather.

Now they had lost a precious minute. They had to figure out the angles of reflection, and fast. The pool was too vast to search centimeter by centimeter. They didn't have the time. Adi kicked downward toward the reflectors. Qui Gon followed. He puzzled over the angles. Where was Obi-Wan when he needed him? This was exactly the type of thing that his apprentice was good at. Obi-Wan's brain was wired for logic.

But so was Adi's. She pointed and began to swim with a powerful stroke. Qui-Gon followed. Adi found an underwater conduit in a maze of smaller pipes. It was big enough to swim through. Qui-Gon saw her shadow on the wall in the same spot where Raptor had disappeared. She turned the lever and the sluice opened. She swam inside.

Qui-Gon followed. He could not use his arms to propel himself. The pipe was too small. He relied on kicking, following the movement of Adi's boots and the bubbles that streamed behind her.

The pipe spilled them out into another pool. The light

changed, and he knew the pool was partially open to the air. Adi began to swim toward the surface.

They surfaced silently. Across the pool and in front of a wide transparisteel door Raptor had already met up with Lunasa, Magus, and Gorm. All of the bounty hunters were heavily armed. Lunasa now had weapons strapped to her ankles and wrists. Gorm was wearing a weapons belt. A repeating blaster was strapped to Raptor's back. Magus wore an armorweave vest with various pockets and had two holsters strapped around his hips.

The four bounty hunters pushed through the door and split up. They still hadn't seen the Jedi, now running silently behind them. Magus headed for the roof, Lunasa down a corridor. Raptor took a second corridor and Gorm slipped through another door. Surprised, Qui-Gon and Adi stopped to consult for a moment.

"I'll take Lunasa," Adi said. Lunasa was still in sight, at the end of the corridor.

Qui-Gon had a split second to choose. Raptor. He was closest. The quicker they could take them down, the better.

There were only four. Five, if Pilot had somehow found a way inside. But Qui-Gon doubted that. He was betting that the huge truck outside was holding a cruiser in back that he could blast out and fly onto the roof. Taly, no doubt, was also in the back of the truck.

Four bounty hunters. Two for each Jedi. Not a problem. Qui-Gon told himself this, but he also knew that the Jedi were somewhat at a disadvantage. The bounty hunters had probably studied the structural plans of the conference center for weeks. If they'd done their job — and he had no doubt that they had — they would know every passageway, every utility turbolift, every duct.

And he also knew that time was against him. Even if one bounty hunter got through, he or she would be enough to wreak havoc.

Raptor saw Qui-Gon on his trail and veered off. He sent a blast of fire behind him, hoping to slow the Jedi down, but Qui-Gon did not ease his pace, deflecting the fire as he ran.

He followed Raptor into a vast space full of steaming pipes — the laundry. The heat and steam hit him. The clouds of vapor obscured his vision. He stopped, listening for footsteps. Only silence.

Then he heard the hiss of a rocket launcher. He was poised to move or deflect it if he could, but it hit at least a meter away.

Bad aim, he had time to think in a puzzled way, just before the pipe burst and scalding water spewed out in a violent flume.

Qui-Gon used the Force to leap and avoid the scorching water. Steam chased him as he landed meters away. Now he saw Raptor, saw his teeth flash in his grimy face as he grinned and released another rocket. As the rocket launched he charged forward toward Qui-Gon.

Qui-Gon ducked and rolled away from the rocket, which continued to chase him. Using the Force, he leaped over Raptor. Unable to track him, the rocket exploded into a large washing unit. Water sprayed out and hoses sprang from the machine like deadly snakes.

Qui-Gon backed up and collided with a bin of sheets that had been jarred from a conveyor belt. The folded sheets flew into the air like large, clumsy birds and then fell, an obstacle course of soft, downy fabric.

He saw that he had landed near a series of raised conveyor belts that ran high above his head. On the belts were large bins of linens, sheets, and towels. In a glance he saw that after being folded by droids, the sheets were loaded and sent to be dumped into bins. Then the bins continued on the conveyor belt to the exit, where wheels snapped down.

Raptor was inserting another rocket into the launcher on his wrist. Qui-Gon could see from this distance that it was a Merr-Sonn K21 — powerful enough to knock a swoop from the air and turn it into melted scrap. He saw the pinpoint of light that meant its laser homing system was activated. He had no doubt it was locked on him.

He directed the Force toward the bins. The conveyor belt moved faster. The bins smacked into each other and began to fall.

As Raptor shot the rocket, the bins crashed into it and the sheets wrapped around it, immediately interfering with its homing device. As Qui-Gon expected, the rocket slowed, momentarily hampered from target lockdown. At the same time, Raptor jumped forward in the same fashion he had moved when shooting off the other rockets. He plowed right into the sheet-wrapped rocket, which, misreading him as a target, exploded on impact. Qui-Gon turned away from the blast. Raptor was no longer a danger to anyone.

Qui-Gon now raced in the opposite direction, back toward the door through which he'd entered. He didn't want to get lost in the maze of corridors. He needed to backtrack.

He ran down the corridor and saw Adi racing toward him. "I've got Lunasa pinned down by security guards," she said. "No weapons on her. But I can't find the others. There's a security alert on, but it's silent. They don't want the guests upset."

"There'll be quite a few upset guests if we don't get Gorm and Magus," Qui-Gon pointed out. "We've got to comb this entire wing. Have you found out where the meeting is?"

"Down this way — the Constellation Suite. They're sending security there. They told me they'll handle this."

"Let's go," Qui-Gon said.

Their route took them past the place where Lunasa was supposed to be held. Four dead security guards lay on the ground.

"I shouldn't have left them," Adi said.

"You had to. Come on." Qui-Gon raced on. He was worried now. They could have used Obi-Wan and Siri in this situation. The bounty hunters were spread out. They wouldn't leave until they did their job. They would have to

314

come together eventually, but in the meantime, anyone who got in their way would be killed.

They found the Constellation Suite. A trio of guards stood outside the doors.

"Nobody gets in," the leader of them said. "And nobody gets out. We're in lockdown."

"They'll get in somehow," Qui-Gon said. "You have to let us examine the suite."

"We've got it covered," the guard repeated frostily.

"Listen," Adi said, "you've got four dead friends down the hall. You might want to allow us to help you."

"Something wrong with your hearing? We've got it — "

Suddenly, his eyes glazed, and he fell over. Qui-Gon bent over him and saw the dart in his neck. He twisted and saw that Adi was already running.

"Magus!" she told Qui-Gon.

The remaining guards looked resolute, holding their blasters forward but occasionally glancing down nervously at their fallen comrade. Trusting that they would not fire at him, Qui-Gon barreled through and used his lightsaber to create a hole in the locked door big enough for him to leap through.

Twenty planetary leaders sat at a large meeting table. Apprehension turned to panic when they saw Qui-Gon jump in, his lightsaber blazing.

"I'm here to help," he said.

Boots thudded against the window. Lunasa had used a liquid cable to rappel down. In the same quick movement she cut the transparisteel with one hand and tossed in a grenade with the other.

"Down!" Qui-Gon shouted.

The blast rocked the room. Qui-Gon pulled as many as he could with him under the table as debris rained down. One leader was wounded. Another lay still. Qui-Gon didn't wait for the dust to clear. He leaped for Lunasa, who was reaching for a repeating rifle on her back. He slammed into her, knocking her straight out the window. Both of them flew through the air, down ten stories, and landed with a splash in the pool.

Choking, Lunasa surfaced. She tried to swim away, but Qui-Gon caught her by the legs, flipped her over, and dragged her from the water. She lay gasping on the duracrete while security officers ran toward them.

"Don't let her move," Qui-Gon told them. "Not even a centimeter."

He saw Adi on the roof. Magus was using a repeating blaster, a powerful weapon that even a lightsaber had trouble deflecting. Qui-Gon raced toward the wall. Where was Gorm? Once again he wished for the Padawans.

He deployed his liquid cable and heard it whistle as it drew him at top speed up to the roof. Once there, Qui-Gon charged toward Magus, lightsaber swinging.

Magus surprised him. He didn't continue the attack. He ran.

Qui-Gon and Adi leaped, whirling in midair as Magus

changed course and dived off the roof. He landed on a roof several stories down and smashed through a skylight.

They had left the planetary leaders unprotected, and Gorm was still on the loose. But Magus was so close. What to do? Adi and Qui-Gon landed lightly on the roof and exchanged a quick glance.

"We've got him!"

Obi-Wan yelled the words from below as he appeared, streaking across the roof with Siri. They jumped into the broken skylight, lightsabers held aloft.

Without another word, Qui-Gon and Adi activated their launchers and slid down to the meeting room. The leaders had upended the table and were crouching behind it as flames roared in from the hallway. Gorm was using a flamethrower.

The heat was intense. Qui-Gon felt it scorch his skin. The table burst into flame and the leaders scrambled backward. Gorm flipped the flamethrower back in its holster and advanced, firing. Qui-Gon and Adi leaped in front of the smoldering table. Their lightsabers were a blur of light and movement. They drove Gorm back. Half-being, half-mechanical, he was more solid than most. Although his armor had blackened from the fire, nothing had slowed him down.

Qui-Gon wanted to end this. The beings behind him were terrified for their lives, and he intended both to protect them and to make this ordeal shorter. Jedi did not fight with anger, but bounty hunters always annoyed Qui-Gon. To kill was despicable. To kill for money was worse. He did not understand the mentality of a being who would hire himself out to hurt beings. Even ten-year-old boys.

He pressed forward. Gorm's disadvantage was his belief in his own invincibility. He thought he was a fortress. He thought he was unbeatable.

Until now, Qui-Gon told him silently. *Until now.*

Gorm's plated armor was formidable, but he hadn't yet met a lightsaber. Qui-Gon moved to one side. Gorm followed. He raised his arm to come down on Qui-Gon, believing, no doubt, that he would be faster and stronger. Qui-Gon ducked so that he received only a glancing blow. It was enough to turn his knees to water, but he'd expected that, planned for it. With an upward thrust, he aimed for Gorm's helmet.

His helmet was where his intelligence was. Where his targeting system spoke to his servomotors, where his motivator powered the blasters built into his hands.

Gorm shook his head. Smoke rose from one side of his helmet. He charged at Qui-Gon again. Sensing what Qui-Gon was up to, Adi moved to the other side. Together they delivered simultaneous blows to his helmet.

The helmet melted and fused to Gorm's neck.

For a moment, Gorm looked surprised. Then his eyes turned red with fury. With a scream, he flailed at Qui-Gon and tried to pummel Adi. But the lightsabers had done their work. Signals conflicted. Servomotors malfunctioned. Gorm toppled over.

Qui-Gon bent over him. He was not dead, but he was certainly incapacitated.

Qui-Gon looked up. Magus stood stock-still at the end of the hall. With one quick glance he took in the Jedi and the monster of a bounty hunter down on the floor. He looked right into Qui-Gon's eyes and shrugged, as if to say, *Oh, well, this didn't work out too well. Time to go.*

He leaped into the turbolift.

Obi-Wan and Siri rounded the corner, frustration on their faces. "We lost him."

"The roof," Qui-Gon said.

They used their cable launchers. When they jumped onto the roof, they saw that Pilot had landed a small cruiser. Magus started to run for it. They could see Taly in the front seat.

Magus stopped and pointed his blaster at Taly's head. The Jedi stopped.

The bounty hunter's eyes stayed amused.

"You want the boy, presumably," he said.

"You know we do," Qui-Gon replied.

"Pilot, bring him out," Magus said.

"He knows our names, our faces!" Pilot yelled.

"So do they, idiot. Do it."

Grumbling, Pilot picked up Taly, who was bound hand and foot.

"Pilot will throw him off the roof if you don't allow us to get away," Magus said calmly.

Pilot balanced on the front of the airspeeder. Taly looked out at them. He had been brave for so long. Now his terror touched Qui-Gon's heart.

"You can go," he said to Magus.

But instead of waiting for Pilot, Magus leaped into the speeder. He pushed the power. With a scream, Pilot went flying, dropping Taly. Siri took a leap straight off the roof and caught Taly with her legs. They bounced at the end of her cable launcher, which she had somehow managed to hook onto the roofline even as she fell.

Pilot fell off the roof. They heard his dying scream, and then a muffled thud.

And Magus flew off, free.

CHAPTER 19

Two planetary leaders had been badly wounded, but all of them survived. Raptor and Pilot were dead. Gorm and Lunasa were taken into custody. It was good to know that the galaxy would be rid of them for a good while.

Taly was being seen to by a medic droid. The boy had a few bruises but otherwise had not been harmed. Qui-Gon squatted next to him as the medic applied bacta to a scratch on his leg.

"How did you manage it?" the Jedi asked. "How did you stay alive?"

Taly grinned, then winced as the medic droid cleaned another scratch. "I told them I'd made another copy of the conversation I'd overheard. And I knew who had hired them, and it was on the recording rod, but it was hidden in a place where if anything happened to me it would be sent directly to the Senate. They were more afraid of the being who hired them, it turned out. Someone powerful who would ruin them, or maybe even hire other bounty hunters to track them down and kill them. They had too much else to do to try to make me tell them. I think they were going to deal with me after the attack. But I knew you Jedi would show up."

"And do you know who hired the bounty hunters?" Qui-Gon asked.

"I'm not sure. There were so many things said, I was confused."

"I don't think so. I think if you heard who hired them, you would remember it exactly."

Taly said nothing. Qui-Gon realized that Taly wouldn't tell him. He might not even tell the Senate. Too much of a burden was on this boy, but he had learned in a short time how to fight. He had been given a lesson in knowledge as power, and he could be holding the most important piece of the puzzle. He wouldn't give that up.

"I would tell the Senate, if I were you," Qui-Gon advised. "Knowledge is power, but it is also danger."

"I can handle the danger."

"You'll go far in life, Taly," Qui-Gon said. He stood with a sigh.

"When can we leave for Coruscant?"

"Soon. The hotel owner is sending his own cruiser to take us back. Should be pretty posh."

Taly brightened. "And my parents? Can we see if we can contact them?"

"Yes. We'll do that, too."

Qui-Gon turned. Obi-Wan and Siri were standing alone by the pool. An alarm sounded in him softly. Something was different.

They were looking at each other. They were not joking, or fussing with their utility belts. They were simply talking.

Qui-Gon felt a quiet dread. There was something between them. Something had happened. He saw Obi-Wan smile and reach up to touch Siri's lip where a small wound was. He had seen all of Obi-Wan's smiles, and he had never seen this one before.

"We have no proof," Adi said, coming up next to him.

Qui-Gon was confused for a moment. Had Adi seen what he had seen?

"Nothing on Passel Argente. He'll get away with this. The bounty hunters won't talk, of course. We can suspect the Corporate Alliance, but I don't think we'll be able to prove it." Adi sighed. She saw the same scene he did, two Padawans standing by a pool, but she didn't notice a thing. "So it's a small victory."

"Twenty beings are alive," Qui-Gon said. "Twenty worlds didn't lose their leaders. Twenty families didn't lose their loved ones. I wouldn't call that a small victory."

Adi lifted both eyebrows at him this time to indicate just how displeased she was. "I am not diminishing that, Qui-Gon. I am just saying . . . oh, I don't know," Adi burst out with uncharacteristic emotion. "It seems that these days, we complete a mission, and we are successful, yet there is always something we could not seem to do. We get the small thing, but not the big thing. Oh, I hate being imprecise!"

"I know," Qui-Gon said. "Many of us feel this. The Senate is becoming more fractured every day. Groups like the Corporate Alliance are becoming more bold in their trickery. I have visions of a day when we are no longer peacekeepers, but warriors."

Adi looked troubled. "Visions come and go."

"This one remains."

"I hope you are wrong."

"No more than I do." Qui-Gon's gaze rested on Obi-Wan and Siri. "No more than I do."

Taly's eyes grew huge as the Senate buildings came into view. "I knew it was supposed to be big. But this . . . it's beautiful. And how can you get anywhere in these space lanes? Everything is so crowded."

"You learn your way around," Obi-Wan said. "Here's the landing platform."

The pilot guided the cruiser to a smooth landing. Taly looked back with regret at the luxurious interior of the ship. "This is probably the most amazing ship I'll ever ride on."

"Somehow I doubt that," Qui-Gon said.

They personally escorted Taly to the meeting with the Senate committee. They watched him walk inside. He hid his nervousness well.

"I hope he tells everything he knows," Adi said.

With a glance at Obi-Wan, Qui-Gon said, "No one tells everything they know."

* * *

Back at the Temple, the Jedi split up to return to their quarters to rest. Qui-Gon beckoned to Obi-Wan.

"Let's take a walk," he said. He saw the puzzlement on Obi-Wan's face. A walk after a hard mission and no sleep for three days? Obi-Wan's exhaustion was evident, but he turned without a word and fell into step beside Qui-Gon.

Qui-Gon led him to the Room of the Thousand Fountains, the place where they had always had their most significant talks. The cooling spray revived them as they walked silently along the twisting paths.

"A hard mission for you," he said. "You must have thought the worst when you were aboard that ship."

"We did not expect to survive," Obi-Wan admitted.

"And how did that make you feel?"

Obi-Wan shook his head. "It made me feel many things. Fear, of course. And regret."

"Regret?"

"Regret for things not yet done," Obi-Wan said. "Regret for not recognizing earlier . . . not being able to have . . ." He struggled and fell silent.

"Siri," Qui-Gon said.

Obi-Wan stopped. "You know?"

"I saw it between you." Qui-Gon began to walk again, and Obi-Wan moved next to him. "It happens sometimes, between Padawans. Especially during extreme situations —"

Obi-Wan stopped again, and Qui-Gon saw that he was angry.

"Don't," the apprentice said. "I realize what I am about to hear from you. But don't diminish it."

He spoke like a man. *He* is *a man, you fool,* Qui-Gon told himself. *And he is right. Who are you to reduce his love?*

"I'm sorry, Obi-Wan," Qui-Gon said. "Come, let's keep walking. So, you know what I'm going to say, do you?"

"That attachment is forbidden. That I have chosen this path, and I must walk it. That there is no place for such personal commitment in the Jedi Order. That each of us must be free of personal attachment or we cannot do the work we are meant to do. That a Force connection is a gift that we must honor not only in our hearts, but in our choices."

"You say these things as if they have no meaning."

"Sometimes everything falls away when you realize that you love."

And what could Qui-Gon respond to that except to say *I know?*

"We have been together for many years, Padawan," Qui-Gon said instead. "I think we have earned each other's trust and respect. It wounds me that you don't want my advice on such an important matter."

There was a struggle on Obi-Wan's face. "I don't want your advice because it will break my heart not to follow it," he said finally.

"So you will not ask for it."

"Of course I want to hear what you think, Master,"

Obi-Wan said finally. "I don't want to wound you. Yet it seems inevitable that someone will get hurt."

"Ah," Qui-Gon said. "And there is your first lesson on why love is forbidden between the Jedi."

Obi-Wan said nothing. There was just the whisper of footsteps and the soft calming splash of the fountains.

"I advise you to give her up," Qui-Gon said as gently as he could. "This is based not so much on the rules of the Jedi, but from what I know of you. Of both of you. Obi-Wan, you are a gifted Jedi. The path is one that is ingrained on your heart. On your character. If you give it up, something in you would die. I feel the same about Siri."

"But I won't give up the Jedi," Obi-Wan insisted. "The Order could change its rules."

"Know this, Padawan," Qui-Gon said. "The Jedi Council will not change the rules."

"But —"

"They will not change the precepts. Not unless the whole galaxy changes, the whole Order changes, not unless an upheaval happens that changes everything. Then, perhaps, the rules will change. But with this Jedi Council? No. Make your choice. But do it with your eyes open."

"You are asking me to tear my heart in two."

"Yes," Qui-Gon said wearily. "I am. My advice is based on this — I feel that for both you and Siri, the heartbreak of losing each other will lessen over time. You will not forget it, it will be a part of you forever, but it will lessen.

Whereas if you leave the Jedi Order, that regret will never lessen. It will always be between you and part of you. Between the two, losing each other — something that seems so terrible, so painful — will be, in the end, easier to bear."

"I can't do it." Obi-Wan looked at Qui-Gon, his gaze tortured. "Don't make me do it."

"I can't make you do anything, my Padawan. You must choose. You must talk to Yoda."

Obi-Wan looked startled. "Yoda?"

"I contacted him about this. I had to. He will keep it to himself. He has always been, next to me, your closest advisor, Obi-Wan. He is seeing you, not as a member of the Council, but as your advisor and friend. And if you cannot face him," Qui-Gon added lightly, "then you are not ready to face the Council."

They turned a corner, and Yoda sat waiting, leaning on his stick, in the middle of the path.

At the sight of him something inside Obi-Wan seemed to break. Qui-Gon saw it. Yoda did not have to say a word. Yet within this small creature was all the nobility and wisdom that Obi-Wan aspired to. Here was the best that the Jedi path could lead to.

"Sacrifice, the Jedi Order demands," Yoda said. "No reward for you in it, either, Obi-Wan. Support you, we will. Change the rules for you, we will not."

Obi-Wan sank heavily down on a bench. He put his face in his hands. Qui-Gon saw his shoulders shake.

He did not think it was possible for his heart to break any more than it was broken already. Yet this must be it, the worst thing for him to have to bear. To give to the boy he loved like a son the same pain he felt. To hand it over, knowing what it would do to his heart.

It took a long time for Obi-Wan to regain mastery over himself. Qui-Gon and Yoda waited silently. At last Obi-Wan raised his face to them both. "What about you?" he said quietly to Qui-Gon.

Qui-Gon started. He knew, of course, what Obi-Wan was referring to. Tahl. He did not expect to be challenged about it. He did not expect to have to talk about it.

Yet, why not? Obi-Wan had every right to raise the question.

"You loved Tahl," Obi-Wan said. "You broke the rule. And now you're asking me to give up something that you took for yourself. What were you and Tahl thinking when you pledged your love?"

"Yes, Qui-Gon," Yoda said. "Interested I am in your answer as well."

Qui-Gon thought before he replied. He did not want to answer this question. It touched on the deepest part of him. If he spoke her name aloud, would he crack?

"It was a confused time," he said. "We barely had time to acknowledge what we felt before she was kidnapped."

"An answer, that is not," Yoda said.

"What were we thinking?" Qui-Gon passed a hand over his forehead. "That we would find a way. That we were

Jedi, and we would be apart much of the time. Yet we wouldn't deny the feeling."

"You would break the rule," Obi-Wan said. "You would have kept it secret."

Qui-Gon shook his head. "No, I don't think either of us wanted that. I think we felt that we would work something out somehow."

"The same way I feel now!" Obi-Wan cried.

Qui-Gon sat next to him on the bench. "Here is the difference between us. I did not get a chance to examine my decision. To see its pitfalls and its faults. I do not know what would have happened if Tahl had lived. We might have decided to put our great love aside. We might have left the Jedi Order. I do not know. I will never know. And I live with the heartbreak of losing her. But I am living, Obi-Wan. I am continuing to walk the Jedi path. What I'm saying to you is that once in a great while we have a chance to look at our lives and make a choice that will define us. You have that choice. It is ahead of you. Do not make it in haste. Use your head as well as your heart. Remember that you have chosen a life that includes personal sacrifice. This is the greatest sacrifice you can give."

"Add only this, I will," Yoda said. "Feel some of us do that great troubles lie ahead. We cannot see them or know them, but feel we do they are waiting. Need you, we do, Obi-Wan."

"And how will you feel," Qui-Gon said, "if the great troubles come, and you are not standing with us?"

"I don't know what's right." The words seemed torn from Obi-Wan. "I don't know what to do!"

Siri appeared at the top of the path. She ran toward them, her face stricken with sorrow.

"Magus has struck," she said. "Taly's parents have been killed."

CHAPTER 20

"Revenge," Qui-Gon said heavily. "It creates the greatest evil."

Yoda rose. "We must see what we can do for Taly."

"He gave information to the committee on the bounty hunters, but he did not reveal if he knew who had hired them," Siri told them.

"We'll never know the answer," Qui-Gon said.

"Increasing in power, the dark side is," Yoda said. He looked at Obi-Wan and Siri.

Qui-Gon and Yoda walked away. Siri stared after them.

"It's almost as if Yoda knows about us," she said.

"He does."

Obi-Wan drank in the sight of her. Her crisp beauty, the way she stood and moved and talked. The compassion in her eyes for Taly. He had come so close to having her in his life, to sharing things with her that she would not share with anyone else. So close to knowing her best. Loving her best.

"Don't look at me like that," Siri said, almost in a whisper. "You look as though you're saying good-bye."

Obi-Wan said nothing.

Her hand flew to her mouth. "What did they say to you?"

"They said to me what I already knew. What you already know. The rules will not change. And if we leave the Jedi together, we will never rest easy with that decision. We will regret it every day. And sooner or later that would lie between us and be greater than our love."

She turned away angrily. "I don't want to look that far ahead. I don't believe you can see what will happen. Anything can happen!"

"So what do you want to do?" He touched her shoulder. At first she jerked away, but then she relented. She leaned against him, her back against his chest. He slipped his arms around her waist. He couldn't help himself. *I will give you up, Siri. But not yet. Give me this last moment, Qui-Gon. Let me brush my mouth against her neck. Let me feel her shudder.*

"I didn't want to decide," Siri said. "Isn't that weak of me? I wanted you to decide. I was so afraid of what lay ahead that I wanted to let go of my own will." She shook her head, and he felt her hair swing against his cheek. "Is this what love is? Then maybe I'm not cut out for it after all."

He smiled at her rueful tone, even though his heart was breaking. He tried to turn her to face him, but she resisted.

"No. I can't look at you right now. Just . . . don't move." Her voice was a murmur now, and he could hear the tears behind it.

"I know we have to let each other go," she said slowly. "I can't imagine walking out of this room without being together, but I know it has to be done."

"You know that the Jedi need our service," Obi-Wan said.

Siri sighed. "Oh, Obi-Wan. Try not to be pompous." She twisted in his arms, ready to face him now, mischief in her eyes. "That is a trait I would tease out of you, given the chance."

"I'm sure you would. And I would tease your impatience with rules out of you."

"Yes, you were always better than me at the acceptance part."

Her words sank in, and the light left her eyes. "Even now," she said. "Even now you're teaching me acceptance, just at the moment I don't want to hear about it."

"Siri —"

"Wait." She pulled away from him and backed up. "Here is another thing you know about me — I don't like to drag things out. So let's make a pact. There's only one way this is going to work. We have to forget it ever happened."

"Forget?" Obi-Wan looked at her, incredulous. "I can't forget!"

"Well, you just have to," Siri insisted. "You have to push it down. You have to bury it. I'm not saying it's going to be easy. But I am going to do it. I am not going to think of you or wonder if we did the right thing. There will be no special looks exchanged when we see each other. You will never mention what happened between us again. We will be comrades when we meet. Comrades only. I am *not* going to look back, not once." She stamped her foot, as if stamping the memory into the ground. Obi-Wan started at the sound, wincing as though she had struck him. She was a warrior now, willing her body and mind and heart to obey her.

"And you will never remind me," she continued. "Not by a word or a look. Promise me."

"Siri, I —"

"Promise me!"

Obi-Wan swallowed. "I promise."

Her face softened for an instant. The last instant, he suddenly knew, he would see her look at him that way. "And I hope," she said, a catch in her voice, "that we don't meet for a long, long time."

Now that the moment was here, Obi-Wan saw more clearly what was ahead. A chasm of longing inside him that he would not be able to ever, ever fill up. A loss he could never acknowledge.

I can't do it, he thought, taking a step toward her. He had to touch her one more time. Maybe that would change everything.

"No." She backed up. "It starts now. May the Force be with you."

She turned and ran down the path. He reached out blindly for her. He felt the empty space where she'd stood. The waterfalls continued to mist the air, and he felt the spray on his cheeks. It tasted of salt, of tears.

Part Two

Twenty Years Later

21

"The problem is," Mace Windu told the Jedi Council, "that Count Dooku has had years to plan the Separatist uprising. We are still catching up. We gain small victories, but they grow stronger. What we need is to strike a big blow. Something that will turn the tide and get undecided worlds to join us."

"A battle?" Anakin Skywalker asked.

"No." Mace steepled his long fingers. "Something else." He turned to Obi-Wan. "Do you remember the name Talesan Fry?"

The truth was, the name was buried. He had piled mission upon mission on top of it. When the thought of the boy crossed his mind, he thought of something else. He forgot the name of the planet Taly was from, erased the memory of the ship rigged to explode, never thought of the cave he'd slept in for close to a week.

Yet even before the full name had left Mace's lips, he had remembered every detail.

"Of course."

"Kept track of young Taly, we have," Yoda said.

"Responsibility, we had, to protect him better than we had his parents."

Obi-Wan turned to his Padawan. "Taly had agreed to testify against some bounty hunters out to attack a meeting of planetary leaders. We foiled the attack, Taly testified, but one of the bounty hunters killed his parents in revenge."

"Who was behind the attack?" Anakin asked.

"Suspect we did that it was Passel Argente," Yoda said. "Prove it, we could not."

"Taly went underground," said Ki-Adi Mundi. "Took an assumed name. But then he popped up, under his own name again. He's an adult now, of course. He spent his years underground developing his knowledge of surveillance. He's fulfilled his early promise and become the foremost expert in the galaxy. He's a leading innovator of surveillance tactics and equipment. He built an empire. He's also a recluse."

"Who can blame him for that?" Obi-Wan muttered.

"He barricades himself behind the security he developed. All his workers have to agree to live in the complex. He has several trusted associates who deal with the necessary details of his business, visiting clients and such. He has no contact with the outside. He has no friends, no family, no allegiances. His only uncle died some time ago. He's managed to stay neutral in the Clone Wars."

That sounds like Taly, Obi-Wan thought.

"Now he has contacted us. While developing new

surveillance-blocking technology, he stumbled on a star-tling invention." Mace leaned forward. "A foolproof codebreaker."

"Nothing is foolproof," Anakin said.

"We've seen the tests," Mace continued. "This tech-nology could allow the Republic to break the code of the Separatists. And continue to break it no matter how many times they change it."

"Is Taly giving the codebreaker to us?" Obi-Wan asked.

Ki-Adi grimaced. "I wish it were that simple. Taly feels he owes the Jedi, because we saved his life. He's willing to offer us the technology first — if we come up with the right price. Taly has made it clear he's perfectly willing to turn around and offer it to the Separatists. What the Jedi must do is go to his compound and obtain the codebreaker, then bring it to the Azure spaceport. We've assembled a team of tech experts to study and deploy it. We know a Separatist attack is imminent. We need to discover where it will be."

"Who will go to Taly's compound?" Obi-Wan asked.

"You and Anakin," Mace said. "Taly asked for you, Obi-Wan. In consultation with Supreme Chancellor Palpatine, the Senate will send a representative as well, Senator Amidala from Naboo. She's proven to be an able negotia-tor for the Republic cause."

Obi-Wan noted Anakin's start. He knew Anakin and Padmé had forged a friendship. Although he liked Padmé and knew she'd be an asset on the mission, he wished the Chancellor had picked another Senator. It wouldn't do Anakin good to be around her too much.

"I have to object," Anakin said.

Mace raised his eyebrows. He was always surprised when someone disagreed with him. Beings rarely did.

"This mission could be dangerous," Anakin went on. "We already know that there have been attempts on Senator Amidala's life. We would be putting her in harm's way."

"It does not seem to me that the Senator turns away from danger if she sees a need to act," Mace said.

"And we could also be drawing the opposition. No doubt they are watching her every move."

"I have no doubt that we will be able to maintain secrecy," Mace said drily, "thank you though, Anakin, for the reminder."

"I just think there must be a better choice," Anakin said. Obi-Wan wanted to give him a hint to stop, but he didn't think it would have any effect. "Senator Bail Organa from Alderaan, for example —"

"This is the Chancellor's decision. Not the Jedi's. We cannot forbid her to go. Especially," Mace added sharply, "when we welcome her help."

If Anakin felt the sting of the rebuke, he gave no sign of it. There was no graciousness in his manner as he inclined his head, only a reluctant assent.

The passion in his Padawan's voice sounded an alarm in Obi-Wan. It stirred a memory. What had it felt like, to connect to a woman, to want to protect her?

He tamped down the memory as it rose.

I am not going to look back, not once.

The doors to the Council Room slid open, and Siri strode in. Since her Padawan, Ferus Olin, had left the Jedi Order years before, she had never taken another.

"I see that being at war hasn't helped your punctuality," Mace said severely.

"No," Siri admitted freely. "It's made my tardiness worse. There's so much more to do. But perhaps my excuses are improving."

Mace frowned. He didn't care for levity in the Council Room. "I have already briefed Obi-Wan and Anakin on the mission. It involves someone you may remember. Talesan Fry."

There was no reaction on Siri's face. No involuntary movement of her body. Her gaze stayed clear, her chin lifted. She did not look at Obi-Wan.

Ki-Adi Mundi went on to describe the mission. Siri listened impassively.

It was as though she had no memory of what had happened. As though she had wiped it clean.

She had buried her memories better than Obi-Wan had. He would follow her lead.

CHAPTER 22

Anakin strode along the walkway to the Senate. A speeder would have been faster, but he needed to feel the thud of his boots on the permacrete and hope the air would cool his temper. So far it grew with the pace of his walk.

He shouldn't have challenged Mace. He knew that. But he had been so stunned when Mace had told him Padmé would be on the mission that he had spoken without thinking. How could Padmé agree to this without telling him? Why would she agree at all?

Anakin thought he'd made some valid arguments, but Mace hadn't even listened, as if Anakin was still a youngling. Mace hadn't considered that he might be right, that putting a Senator in danger was a stupid idea. Their support in the Senate was crumbling by the day. Why should they risk losing such an important ally?

Of course, the reason he didn't want Padmé to go was more personal than that. She'd nearly been killed several times by an assassin. Why would she deliberately risk her safety? Anakin shook his head. He did not understand his wife. He only knew he loved her. Hungered for her. Needed her. And he could not let anything happen to her.

He had one last chance. Chancellor Palpatine had urged him to come share with any problem, no matter how small. Anakin knew that if Mace found out he'd gone around him, his momentary annoyance would change to anger, but he couldn't help himself. Palpatine was the only one who could order Padmé not to go.

The Blue Guards were standing at attention when he walked in. Sly Moore walked forward, her shadow robe moving with her gliding walk. She pressed a button on the wall. "You may go right in," she told Anakin.

Some Senators waited days or weeks until Palpatine could find a spot for them in his crammed schedule. But Palpatine had given a standing order to Sly Moore that when Anakin came, he would be seen immediately.

The Supreme Chancellor rose when Anakin hurried in.

"Something is wrong, my friend," he said, coming around the desk and approaching him with concern. "What can I do to help?"

"You know about this mission to Talesan Fry's headquarters?" Anakin asked.

"Of course. It could lead to the end of the Separatists. To peace. It is crucial."

"I understand you have picked Senator Amidala to accompany the Jedi," Anakin said. "I told Mace Windu my objections."

"Then tell them to me," Palpatine said. "I'm anxious to hear them. I always respect your opinion, Anakin. You know that. You have wisdom deeper than anyone I've ever known. You can see further than the Jedi Council."

Anakin felt uncomfortable when Palpatine said such things. But then again, there were times when he believed them himself.

"Whoever goes on this mission is in danger," he said. "Senator Amidala has survived several attempts on her life. But assassins could still be tracking her. We compromise our safety and hers if she goes. "

"All of this is true," Palpatine said. "I had not thought of those things." He clasped his hands together, his skin so pale that Anakin sometimes wondered if blood actually ran in his veins. "Anakin, I wish that I could help you. Especially in the light of your excellent argument. But I am not ordering Padmé to go. She chooses to go. How can I take back an order I did not give?"

Stopped in his tracks, Anakin didn't know what else to say. But Palpatine, as usual, had shown him the path. He needed to talk to Padmé directly. Palaptine couldn't order her not to go. But Anakin could.

Padmé's laughter bubbled, then died when she saw he was serious.

"You're *ordering* me?"

"Yes. I have a right. I have more experience than you

do; I'm a Jedi and I know what we could be in for. I'm also an officer in the Republic army."

"But I'm not." Padmé continued to fold a robe she was placing in a small bag at her feet. "So thanks but no thanks, *Commander*."

"It's dangerous and unnecessary for you to go, and I won't allow it."

Padmé turned. Her gaze was direct. Cool and composed. That always infuriated him.

"I think you know well enough how your attitude angers and upsets me. I don't respond to orders. I am a Senator. I have a duty to perform. So I am going."

"Padmé, please." He wanted to give in to her softness, but she stood before him, ramrod straight. She wasn't wearing her ceremonial robes, only a soft sheath down to her ankles, but she might as well be costumed in armor.

He collapsed on his back on the sleep couch. "I don't know why it's so hard to talk to you."

"That's because you're not talking to me. You're ordering me."

"I'm just trying to keep you safe."

"This is not the way to do it."

He looked up. She was smiling at him. She came and sat beside him.

"I know you worry about my safety," she said in the soft tone he loved. "I worry about yours. We live in perilous times, Anakin. We're in the middle of a war. I'm in danger no matter where I am. We've both been in some kind of danger since the moment you arrived to protect me."

"Agreed. But do you have to *volunteer* for it?"

She took his hand and laced her fingers through his. "I offered to go because I knew I would be safe. I knew the best Jedi in the Order would be there to protect me."

He groaned. "Now don't start flattering me."

She grinned at him. "I meant Obi-Wan."

He tossed a pillow at her, and she shrieked in surprise. She threw it back, and he held it suspended in the air with the Force.

"Are you still trying that same trick on me?"

"It's worked in the past."

She lay down beside him. They faced each other, almost nose to nose.

"I'll be careful," she said.

"I won't leave your side," he said.

"Don't," she said, drawing him close. "I don't want you to."

23

The planet Genian had so far managed to remain neutral in the Clone Wars. This feat had little to do with canny diplomacy, though the Genians were indeed noted for that particular skill, but more to do with the vast corporate holdings on the planet, the research laboratories, and the treasures locked in secure banks. One day, perhaps, Genian would fall, but it was not in a terribly strategic position and at this point in the war many Senators, both Separatist and Republic alike, found it useful to be able to slip in and out to sit with their wealth and make sure it was safe.

Taly was not the only one to take advantage of friendly laws and a large, educated workforce. Many businesses thrived on Genian, primarily in the technological and scientific sector. There were a number of large, prosperous cities, but Taly had chosen to site his complex in the vast desert that lay outside the city of Bruit. Mountain ranges ringed the desert, and the countryside was rugged enough that no towns or settlements were within hundreds of kilometers.

Taly provided for his workers by supplying them with a small city, with entertainment and leisure activities and luxurious dwellings that his workers would not be able to afford in the cities. The only thing he would not allow was families. Workers had to be single and childless. He said this was because personal connections interfered with work habits, but Obi-Wan had to wonder if there was a deeper reason.

The Jedi and Padmé had traveled on a fast Republic cruiser. The journey had taken less than a day. Anakin flew low over the desert, lower than Obi-Wan would have liked, skipping over the boulders and rocks, some of them fifty or a hundred meters tall, then zooming down to hug the ground again.

"This isn't a Podracer, Anakin," Obi-Wan said.

Siri grinned and Padmé smiled.

"He does this to me on purpose," Obi-Wan grumbled.

"I don't see the landing platform," Padmé said. "I don't even see the compound."

"It's behind a holographic portal," Anakin explained. The Jedi had been thoroughly briefed on Taly's security plan. "The hologram mimics the landscape. It's hard to see."

Padmé drew closer and leaned over Anakin's shoulder. "Can you see it?"

Obi-Wan watched them, her dark head against his shoulder. They had the ease of intimacy. Long friendship, he wondered, or attraction?

"When I use the Force, I can. See the shimmer over there, by that big rock?"

A craggy rock — at least a hundred meters tall — rose over the others.

"No," Padmé said, half-laughing as she shook her head. "I just see a big rock."

In answer, Anakin flew straight toward the rock. Padmé braced herself. Obi-Wan sat calmly. He wasn't about to admonish Anakin again. Let him have his fun.

Anakin did not slow his pace. The rock loomed, closer and closer. Just at the moment of impact, they passed through it, punching a hole through the image of rock, sand, and sky.

The landing platform lay ahead, a small, circular pad outside a larger hangar. Beyond it rose Taly's compound, a series of connected buildings made of stone that matched the desert tones of ocher and sand.

Anakin guided the ship to a featherweight landing. A male of middle years stood waiting. Obi-Wan recognized the violet-tinged skin of a native Genian. The visitors grabbed their kits and headed down the ramp.

Obi-Wan announced their names, and the Genian nodded. "You are expected," he said. "I am Dellard Tranc, head of security for the complex. Please follow me."

They followed him through the hangar. Anakin whistled softly when he saw the state-of-the-art cruisers lined up in the hangar bays.

"Very nice," he murmured to Obi-Wan. "He can get anywhere in a hurry, that's for sure."

The hangar door opened into a long corridor.

"We're now in the main building," Dellard Tranc said. "I'll escort you to the main business office."

The natural stone around them was like being in a cave. It was cool and dim. Obi-Wan was used to business complexes being built of durasteel and transparisteel, as if the corporations were trying to advertise their purity by using transparent materials in their buildings. He found the natural materials here refreshing.

They entered a large office suite, and Tranc left them with a bow. Two people stood in the center, waiting for them. A trim woman about Obi-Wan's age came toward them. Her skin was lavender-colored and her hair was white.

"Welcome," she said. "My name is Helina Dow. I'm Talesan Fry's executive in charge of production and distribution." She smiled briefly. "In other words, his second-in-command."

The male Genian at her side nodded at them. "And I'm Moro Y'Arano. Executive in charge of business outreach. Talesan asked me to be present at the meeting."

These were the trusted advisors Mace had spoken of, the ones who were Taly's connection to the outside. Obi-Wan introduced them all. Helina bowed. "It's an honor to meet such distinguished Jedi and officers in the

Republic army. Senator Amidala, your reputation precedes you. Thank you all for coming. Please follow us."

The double doors opened into Taly's office. In contrast to the neutral colors of the walls and floor, a table made out of a golden-tinged stone served as a desk. Two tall lamps behind the desk sent out a glow with an orange-yellow tint. On one side of the office, a seating area was set up, a long, cushioned sofa and a low table made out of the same gold-hued stone.

Taly sat behind the desk, his hands clasped in front of him. Obi-Wan was surprised at the man he'd become, but he couldn't say why. He recognized the same sharp intelligence in the eyes, the thin features, the rusty shock of hair. Taly had not grown very tall or broad. He was thin, and vibrated with an intensity Obi-Wan remembered well. But there was something missing. . . .

Ah, Obi-Wan thought. The eagerness in Taly's eyes. The wish to be liked. That was gone. But of course it was. Taly was a man now, not a boy. A vastly wealthy man. Obi-Wan could not imagine the amount of grit and guile it would take to amass such a fortune, to be such a success in the cutthroat business of surveillance.

"Obi-Wan Kenobi and Siri Tachi." Taly rose and came toward them. He stood in front of them, searching their features. "You look older."

"That seems inevitable," Siri said.

For a moment, Obi-Wan felt rocked on his feet. Seeing

Siri and Taly standing together had brought back a memory of a night in a cave, a thermal cape draped around two bodies, low voices, laughter. Of the cold, hard floor of a cargo hold, a coldness he did not feel.

Memories that, when they came, he always pushed down and buried.

He pushed, but the memories did not obey. They surfaced again, rising. Siri's smile. Her lips resting against his cheek.

Whatever happens, I'll remember this.

She met his eyes. He saw the memory there, reflected back. Or did he? A light went out, a shutter closed. She turned away.

"Please sit down," Helina said. Obviously, it was up to her to observe the polite rituals of meetings. "I'll ring for refreshments."

Taly led the way to the seating area. Within moments, food and drink arrived.

Taly leaned forward earnestly. "I don't pay attention to politics. I had my fill of Coruscant and the Senate a long time ago. But when I made this discovery, it was obvious how valuable it was. Politics has found me again, for the second time in my life. I am as unhappy now as I was the first time it did."

"Politics is another name for greed and corruption these days," Padmé said. "But we must not forget that it is also about compassion and justice."

Taly frowned at her for a moment as though she was speaking a language he didn't understand. "I had to choose between the two of you. The Republic and the Separatists. So I examined the two sides. The Separatists have much in their favor. They have the guilds and the trade associations. They have vast amounts of wealth and much power in the Senate. Most important, they have ruthlessness. There is nothing they won't do for power. But you — the Jedi — you tip the balance. Thousands of you are ready to fight for the Republic. I have seen what a handful of Jedi can do. I decided to bet on you. Because, believe me, I want to be on the winning side."

"Thanks," Obi-Wan said. "But we see this struggle as a noble cause, not a gamble to wager on."

Taly waved a hand. "Noble cause — sure, okay. The point is, I want you to know that if we can't come to an agreement, I'm ready to turn the codebreaker over to the Separatists. I'm giving you the first shot because I owe you, first of all, but also because I think you can win — *if* you have my device."

"We are authorized to make a deal," Padmé said. "What are your terms?"

Taly named a price. Obi-Wan sucked in his breath, but Padmé's face was impassive.

"That can be done," she said. "You would have to accept two installments, however. The first immediately, the second after the codebreaker is in our hands and has been proven to work. Do we have a deal?"

"Whoa, not so fast, Senator," Taly said. "I haven't finished. I also want an exclusive contract with the Republic. You only use Fry Industries surveillance and communication devices in the Republic army for the duration of the war."

"But that would mean abandoning systems that we already deploy and putting millions of credits into a system we don't need," Padmé said.

Taly shrugged.

Obi-Wan couldn't believe it. The brilliant, vulnerable boy he'd known had turned into a war profiteer.

"All right," Padmé said. "We will agree to this if you give us six months to make the transition. And, of course, if your system works. We have to do it gradually. I will not endanger our troops for your profit."

"Fine. I don't want anyone to get killed for me. I just want the business," Taly said. "We have a deal. Helina, can you get the contracts?"

Helina rose and departed.

"And Moro, can you bring me the model scenarios we developed for deployment of the codebreaker? We can surely share them with our new friends."

"Of course." Moro rose and left.

Obi-Wan noted how Taly watched until the door closed behind Moro and Helina. Then he activated a small device he had hidden in his palm.

"What —" Siri started, but Taly held up a finger.

He entered a code into the device, then waited for a green light.

"We have been under surveillance," he said. "Recently, I have discovered that there is a spy in my organization. Someone who wants to launch a takeover of the business. I have been able to intecept the surveillance device, but only for very short periods. I don't want him or her to know I'm onto them."

"Do you have a suspect?" Obi-Wan asked. "Is that why you sent Helina and Moro out of the room?"

"I don't suspect them any more than I do the rest of my top executives," Taly said. "Anyone who has access to my inner office. That is a handful of workers."

"Do you think the Separatists know about the code-breaker?" Padmé asked.

"All communication leaving the compound is moni-tored," Taly said. "That's what happens when you work for a surveillance company — I make it impossible for you to spy on me. I control all access to communication. I moni-tor all outgoing messages."

"Just like Quadrant Seven," Siri said.

"I learn from experience," Taly said. "So no, Senator, I don't think the information has been passed. Yet. But this brings me to my third condition for making a deal."

"We already made a deal," Padmé said.

"Not quite. You must find out who the spy is. And you must do it in the next twenty-four hours. Only then will I hand over the codebreaker."

Anakin's gaze was flinty. "The Jedi are not detectives."

Taly rose. "They are now. It is non-negotiable."

The Jedi and Padmé exchanged glances. Padmé turned back to Taly.

"We accept," she said.

"This is ridiculous," Anakin said as soon as they were left alone in their quarters. They had already done a sweep to ensure that they were not under surveillance of any kind. "He's holding us hostage, expecting us to solve his business problems."

"True," Obi-Wan agreed.

"We're wasting time," Siri said, sounding as impatient as Anakin. "I hate wasting time. He's taking advantage of us, and he knows it."

"The codebreaker could make the difference for the Republic," Padmé reminded them. "It's vital that we obtain it. Isn't that worth a little snooping?"

Siri threw down her survival pack with an irritable gesture. It thunked against the floor. Obi-Wan gave her a curious look. He had seen Siri be impatient before — many times, as a matter of fact — but there was an edge to her mood now that he couldn't identify.

"Well, we might as well start now," Anakin said. "Taly said he'd get us a list of the executives who have access to his private office. Until then, I'm going to take a look around, get a feel for the place."

"I'll join you," Padmé said. "Maybe we can come up with something to go on."

The door hissed behind them. Siri's survival pack had snagged on the leg of a table, and when she tugged at it, some of the contents spilled out onto the floor. She gave it a swift kick for its disobedience.

Obi-Wan leaned down and gently unwound the strap of the pack from the table leg. "Are you angry at the pack, or the table? Or me?"

Siri sat on the floor and looked up at him. "I didn't think we'd have to stay here."

"Only for a day."

"A day can feel too long, if it's long enough. What do I know about corporate intrigue?" Siri growled. "I'm not the right Jedi for this job."

"You're the right Jedi for any job." Obi-Wan sat next to her on the floor. "What is it?"

"I just told you."

"No, you didn't."

She looked at him, chin first. Defensive, challenged, annoyed. Then she let out a breath, and she shook her head ruefully.

"Do you remember," she said, "in the cave, when I wanted to help him escape?"

Obi-Wan felt his breath catch. They had not talked of this in almost twenty years. The subject of the mission with Taly was too close to the reality of what had happened between them.

He kept his voice light. "One of our many arguments."

"What good did it do to have him testify?" Siri asked. "A bounty hunter alliance was smashed. Some bounty hunters went to prison worlds. I haven't kept track, but I bet some of them are free now. His parents were killed, and now look at him. Look at what that boy has turned into. This unstable, suspicious, bitter man who only cares about wealth and power. But inside, the boy is there, I feel it, and he's still in pain. Did you notice his office? The desk, the lamps? What did they remind you of?"

Obi-Wan shook his head, baffled.

"The two orange lights," Siri said softly. "The golden desk."

Obi-Wan let out a breath. "Cirrus. The two suns, the golden sea."

"He hasn't forgotten what he lost. Not for a minute," Siri said. "What if we'd let him go? What if he'd been allowed to grow up in a loving family?"

"Jedi do not deal in ifs."

Siri shook her head, exasperated. "Obi-Wan, for star's sake, you can irritate me like nobody else. Jedi don't become Generals in galactic-wide wars, either. Jedi don't watch their fellow Jedi be blown apart in great battles. Things have changed. Have you noticed?"

"Yes," Obi-Wan said quietly. "I've noticed. But I still don't believe that looking back and questioning decisions you made twenty years ago is helpful or fair."

"Once, for me, there were no questions, only answers,"

Siri said. As her mood altered, her brilliant blue eyes shifted to navy. He had forgotten how that happened, how the color of her eyes could deepen with her feelings. "I've changed. Now I question everything. I've seen too much, I fear too much of what the galaxy is becoming, " She turned her direct gaze to him. "Don't you ever look back and question what you did about something? Wonder if there was something you could have done differently?"

"That is a dangerous place for a Jedi to be," Obi-Wan said. "We do what we do, as Qui-Gon used to say."

"Qui-Gon lived in a different time," Siri said. She leaned her head back against the wall. "When Ferus was still with me, we went on a mission to Quas Killam, out in the very edge of the Mid-Rim. We were to oversee peace talks between two government factions who were trying to form a coalition. One side was a cartel that controlled much of the planet's supply of trinium, a mineral used in the manufacturing of weapons systems. Very important, and it made many Killams very rich. We oversaw the talks, saw a coalition government formed. A very successful mission. But Ferus said to me, *Something isn't right here. The cartel made too many concessions. It's as though they know something we don't.* And I said, *What can we do? Our mission is done. Jedi do not interfere in planetary politics. And we have many places to go.* I'm sure you've said the same to Anakin." Siri stopped. She sighed. "At the start of the Clone Wars, the Trade Federation worked in alliance with the head of that cartel to take over the government of Quas Killam. Now they own all the factories, all the mines of trinium. The Killams who were not in the cartel — many of them were killed. Many of them were forced to work in the factories."

"I've heard this of Quas Killam," Obi-Wan said. "Are you saying you could have prevented it?"

"I don't know," Siri brooded. "But what if I had stayed? What if I had observed a little more closely, wondered a little more? We know the Separatists and Count Dooku plant seeds. They're willing to wait years for results. They were preparing for this, while we were going on peace missions. What if we had listened better and did more years ago, when it would have had an impact? "

Obi-Wan shook his head. "Siri, you are asking too much of yourself. Of us all."

"You didn't answer my question," Siri said.

"Question?"

"Do you look back?"

Did he look back? Of course he did, all the time. Mostly about Anakin. At a time they should be closest, they were further apart than ever. What could he have done differently? Had he turned his face away from what he did not want to see? Anakin was still his Padawan, but Obi-Wan was hardly his Master. Anakin had gone to a place where Obi-Wan could not reach him. He had the sense of a creature held in check by a harness that was long-worn. One of these days Anakin would break free . . . a thought that chilled Obi-Wan. But Obi-Wan chose to ignore those thoughts — out of friendship.

But he didn't want to tell Siri these things. What had she said, so many years ago? *We will be comrades.* Not best friends. She was not available for confidences. If he poured out his heart to her, where would he stop?

"I look back," he said, trying to find the words he wanted. "But I tell myself that the galaxy will be made safe with deeds, not regrets."

For some reason, his answer saddened her. He could see it in her eyes. "Yes," she said. "I hold onto duty. That's always saved me."

She jumped to her feet. In a flash, her mood had changed and she was back to the purposeful Jedi he knew best. "Speaking of which, we have twenty-four hours. We'd better get started."

With access to Taly's records and a quick tour of the complex, the Jedi soon reached the conclusion that it was not going to be easy to solve Taly's problem.

"All of his employees are well paid," Anakin said. "They even own shares in the company. It would make no sense to throw it into disarray."

"Not only that, without Taly the company will cease to be profitable," Padmé said. "Every breakthrough and discovery has been his. There's no other inventor on his level on staff."

"I agree — it makes no sense for someone to try a takeover," Obi-Wan said.

"So is Taly just paranoid?" Siri asked. "He thinks his employees are out to get him, but they're loyal."

Obi-Wan shook his head. "Taly may be paranoid, but he's still sharp. I doubt he would invent a plot. And his inner office *is* under surveillance, according to our devices as well. So he didn't invent that. But I don't think someone is attempting a takeover."

"But you just said he didn't invent a plot," Padmé said.

"There is no takeover plot," Obi-Wan explained. "But there *is* a spy. Someone is out to steal the codebreaker. And I think the Separatists are behind it."

"Taly said there's been no unobserved communication since the codebreaker was developed," Siri pointed out. "We've gone over the comm monitoring system, and it's solid."

"That's because we're thinking like Jedi," Obi-Wan said to Siri. "How do the Separatists think? Someone very wise once said to me that they plant seeds. They're willing to wait years for results." Obi-Wan pointed to the holofiles that filled the air around them. "All the employee records look perfect because they are meant to."

"One of them is a mole," Siri said slowly, revolving to stare at all the files. "Someone planted here, years ago, because someone in the Separatists knew that Taly was a brilliant innovator, and that someday there would be something to steal."

"So they don't want the company," Padmé said. "They want the codebreaker. Only they don't know it's a codebreaker. Not yet."

"It has to be someone in the inner circle. Someone he trusts." Anakin said. "Helina Dow? Moro Y'Arano? Dellard Tranc, the head of security?"

"I don't know," Obi-Wan said. "We don't have to know. All we have to do is set the trap."

*　　*　　*

They had something going for them. Because of Taly's expert foiling of the office surveillance, the mole didn't know that Taly was aware of the bug. So they could plant information and set the trap.

They explained their plan to Taly, and he agreed. Then they gathered in his office.

"I'm glad we were able to come to terms," Taly said. "I think given the sensitive nature of the codebreaker, it would be best to get it out of the complex as soon as possible."

"We can leave tonight," Obi-Wan said. "Can you arrange for security to be lifted?"

"I will handle the security myself," Taly said. "I'll tell my staff after you leave that the codebreaker is gone. This deal is on a need-to-know basis, and nobody needs to know but me that the codebreaker is leaving until it's gone. Here."

Taly handed the codebreaker to Obi-Wan. It was a black metal box the size of a small suitcase. He slipped it into a carrying case.

"When you open it, a holographic file will appear that will explain the procedure for deployment," Taly said.

"We'll leave at nightfall," Siri said.

Night fell, and the Jedi and Padmé started on their walk to the hangar. Obi-Wan carried the codebreaker. He felt confident, or at least as confident as he ever allowed himself to feel. There was every chance that the mole would not realize that the Jedi were waiting. And three Jedi against one attacker would surely prevail.

Padmé, too, had grown quite handy with a blaster. Obi-Wan was always happy to have her on his side in a battle. Funny, Obi-Wan thought, how he had dismissed her when they'd first met. She had been so young, and posing as the queen's attendant, of course. He had seen her as someone he had to protect, not the fierce, determined ally she eventually proved herself to be. It was Qui-Gon who had seen her strength. Obi-Wan missed Qui-Gon with an acuteness that hadn't diminished in the long years since his death. There was still so much he wanted to learn from his former Master.

Anakin held up a hand. They could hear footsteps approaching. Helina Dow suddenly appeared around the corner. She smiled as she came forward.

"Taly told me to make sure you were escorted to your ship. He wanted you to know that security has been cleared for you."

Was this true? Obi-Wan doubted it. Still, he was surprised that Helina had turned out to be the spy. She had been with Taly from the beginning. She had built the company with him. It seemed strange that she would abandon all that she had gained.

"Here we are." Helina stopped in front of the entrance to the hangar. She bowed. "Have a safe journey."

Surprised, Obi-Wan half-turned to watch her go down the corridor. He raised an eyebrow at Anakin, who shrugged — then tensed as the Jedi walked through the hangar door.

They found themselves not in the hangar, but a small, windowless room. The door clanged shut behind them.

"She tricked us," Siri said. "We just walked through a holographic portal."

Three lightsabers blazed to life. Within moments, they had cut a hole in the door. They rushed out into the corridor.

It was completely different. Instead of a set of double doors on one side and a corridor leading off to the right, there were doorways all the way down the corridor. Taly stood at the end of the corridor, smiling.

"What's going on?" Padmé shouted at him.

"It's a hologram," Anakin said, when Taly's image didn't answer.

"Helina Dow did this," Siri said. "There must be holograms all over this place. They use them for security."

"She wants to confuse us," Obi-Wan said. "But how does she expect to get the codebreaker?"

"Maybe she just wants to prevent us from leaving with it," Padmé said.

"Well, it doesn't matter. We know who the spy is. Let's tell Taly." Obi-Wan opened his comlink to contact Taly. There was no signal. "She must have blocked communication. This doesn't make sense. What is she hoping to accomplish?"

"Obi-Wan, maybe you should check the codebreaker," Padmé said.

A certain dread settled inside Obi-Wan as he flipped open the box. No holographic file appeared. He searched the database. No files were loaded.

"She switched it somehow," Siri said.

"Or Taly did," Anakin observed.

Siri and Obi-Wan exchanged a glance. They knew Taly hadn't switched the codebreaker. They believed in him, even after all these years. They remembered the boy who had run into a nest of pirates to save their lives. They knew that boy still lived in Taly.

"We've got to get to the hangar," Anakin said.

The low lighting made it harder to discern which of the doorways were holographic portals. It was impossible to navigate what they remembered as the route to the hangar. The Jedi charged down the hallway, Padmé trailing behind, letting them access the Force to discover which doors were holograms and which were real.

At last they found the doors to the hangar and charged through. Helina was ahead, racing to a cruiser, the codebreaker swinging with the motion of her run.

Obi-Wan and Anakin leaped at the same instant that Siri gave Helina a Force-push that sent her sprawling. The codebreaker slid away on the polished floor.

Obi-Wan and Anakin's boots thudded as they hit the ground near her head. She looked up at them, wide-eyed. "It's just business," she said. "Don't kill me."

"We're not going to kill you," Anakin said. "Who hired you?"

She shakily sat up, resting on her elbows. "Passel Argente hired me to get a job here five years ago. I was supposed to pass information along when I could to the Separatists. If something big came up, I was to steal it."

"Do they know about the codebreaker?"

"They know I'm bringing them something big. That's all. I can't send a communication, so I send out a code through one of Taly's business communications. It's to a supplier we've used for years, but Argente arranged to have someone there pass along the message to him."

Suddenly blaster fire lit the air and a smoke grenade exploded. Padmé dived to the floor, coughing. Anakin started toward her. Obi-Wan groped his way toward the codebreaker.

Someone else was here. Someone was firing, peppering the ground with blaster fire so fast it had to come from a repeating rifle.

The hangar bay doors were open, and the cool night air began to disperse the thick gray smoke. As it cleared, Obi-Wan saw the glint of a red-and-black starfighter. Someone was leaning out. He saw an arm sweep down and gather up the codebreaker.

He began to run, his eyes tearing from the smoke. The being wore an armorweave tunic and trousers as well as a full helmet with a breath mask, but Obi-Wan recognized him instantly.

It was Magus.

Taly suddenly ran into the hangar. Magus turned and saw him. Obi-Wan could not read his expression, but he sensed the satisfaction Magus felt as he aimed the repeating blaster even as he leaped back into his speeder.

Obi-Wan made a midair leap, his lightsaber swinging, as the intense fire ripped through the air. Behind him he felt Siri jump in front of Taly to protect him. Anakin blocked Padmé.

Magus turned and gave one more blast of fire. It hit Helina where she still lay stunned on the duracrete. She died instantly. Her usefulness to the Separatists was over, and she had become a liability.

Magus took off. Obi-Wan knew it was useless to go after him. By the time he got to a cruiser, Magus would be in the upper atmosphere.

He turned and walked toward Helina. He crouched next to her and allowed himself a moment to mourn the loss of a life.

"I can't believe it was Helina," Taly said, his voice hollow.

"Magus got the codebreaker," Siri said.

Taly shook his head. "Helina only thought she had it. We made two prototypes. She took one, but I put a bug in it. I'm the only one who knows where the real one is."

"Magus is no doubt taking it to the Separatists," Siri said.

"We have to get the codebreaker to the Republic

before the Separatists know the one they have is a fake," Obi-Wan said. "We have to monitor their broadcasts."

"Bring it to us," Padmé told Taly, sounding like the queen she had once been.

"I have it," Taly said, opening his tunic to reveal the codebreaker strapped across his chest. "And I'm coming with you. If Magus is after me again, I want your personal guarantee for my safety for the duration of the Clone Wars. That's a condition of your purchase of the codebreaker."

Padmé gave him a cool glance. "You never stop negotiating, do you?"

"I just want what I want."

"This is your last condition," she told him. "And you had better guarantee that this box is the real codebreaker."

Taly grinned, and the boy Obi-Wan had known was back. "It is."

27

They blasted off for the Azure Spaceport. The finest tech experts in the Republic army were already there, waiting to receive the codebreaking device.

Obi-Wan spoke to Anakin. "I suggest you get some rest on the journey. And Padmé looks exhausted. If you could persuade her that she needs rest, it would do her good."

Anakin's gaze was opaque.

I so rarely know what he is thinking anymore, Obi-Wan thought.

"Yes, Master," Anakin said.

He is still obedient, but it is as though he makes an effort to be so.

Obi-Wan watched as Anakin went over to speak quietly to Padmé. She nodded, and the two of them left the cockpit.

That left Siri and Taly and Obi-Wan. Siri kept her eyes on the instruments, even though Obi-Wan had plotted the course and there wasn't much for her to do. It all felt so familiar, the three of them in a cockpit, heading away from danger and most likely into more of it.

"Tell me something, Taly," Obi-Wan said, spinning around in his chair to face him. "Passel Argente placed Helina Dow in your employ. She bided her time, but Argente always meant to destroy you. Why are you still protecting him?"

"Protecting him?"

"He hired those bounty hunters and you never told the Senate."

"It was my last bargaining chip."

"But he hired Magus, and Magus killed your parents."

"Magus did that for revenge. I didn't blame Argente for their deaths. I blame Magus." Taly's face grew hard.

"So why didn't you tell?"

"I knew I would have to start over," Taly said. "I knew I needed a patron. I waited until I was older, and then I approached him when I was ready to take back my name and start my company. Who do you think gave me my first business loan?"

Obi-Wan shook his head ruefully. Qui-Gon had been right. Taly had known all along, and he had used that information. It must have taken an enormous amount of nerve to contact Passel Argente and demand hush money.

"I used Argente, but I never trusted him. He ended up coming at me in a way I didn't expect. But if I went to the Senate today and told some committee about a twenty-year-old plot, they'd laugh me out of the chambers. They have enough problems. Everything has changed, hasn't it? My best revenge on Argente now is to help you win the Clone Wars."

"Well, that's one thing we should be grateful for, at least," Siri said. She seemed more amused than irritated by Taly.

Taly approached her. "I have something for you." He held out his hand. Siri's old warming crystal lay in his palm, the cool deep blue of the crystal glowing slightly.

She took it wonderingly. "But how —"

"I went back to Settlement Five and bought it back from the same vendor you sold it to," he said. "I tracked him down. I always wanted to give it to you someday."

"Thank you, Taly," Siri said. She closed her fingers over it. A flush of pleasure lit her face.

"You think I don't remember," he said to both of them. "I remember how you fought for me. I remember everything."

He walked out of the cockpit. Obi-Wan gave a quick glance at Siri.

And you, Siri — do you remember everything?

She was keeping her face from him. They had buried this for so long. But how could they keep forgetting, when the reminders were so real?

"I promised you once never to remind you," Obi-Wan said.

"It's not you who is reminding me, though, is it?" A smile touched Siri's lips. "So much time has passed."

"And so little."

"And we've changed so much."

"Yes. You're more beautiful." The words left Obi-Wan before he could stop them. "And smarter, and stronger."

"And you," Siri said, "you've grown sadder."

"You can see that?"

"Forgive me if I still think I know you better than anybody else."

"You do."

"I don't regret our decision," Siri said. "I wouldn't want to go back and change it. Would you?"

"No," Obi-Wan said. "It was the right one. But . . ."

"Yes," Siri said. "It doesn't prevent you from regrets, does it? Regrets you can live with. It took me awhile, but I realized that Yoda and Qui-Gon were right. I would have regretted leaving the Jedi Order every day of my life. And that is not a life I would want to live. I've lived the life I wanted to live."

"I'm glad." Obi-Wan felt the same. But was it that simple for him? He wasn't sure. Somehow, on this trip, he was fully understanding, for the first time, how many regrets he did have. And secrets.

"What I regret," he said, "was not so much the decision we made, but what happened to us afterward. When we made the decision to part, it made our friendship become something else. Something that couldn't be quite as close as it should have been."

"Comrades, not best friends," Siri said.

He nodded. His other deep friendships — with Garen and Bant — were different. With them, he felt no barriers. With Siri, there was always a barrier. He did not think of it or speak of it, but it was always there. He wished it hadn't been. In some way he couldn't quite define, he felt like he had lost her twice.

"Well, it's not too late, is it?" Siri asked. "It took us almost twenty years to talk to each other about the past. Maybe now we can be the friends we were meant to be. I would like that. I'm tired of pushing away the past."

"Best friends, then."

Siri smiled, and the years fell away. Obi-Wan felt it then, the pain in his heart he had put away with his memories. It was as vivid as Siri's grin.

"Best friends," she agreed.

28

"You're going to tell me to live in the present moment," Padmé said to Anakin. "But I can't help it. We have the codebreaker. We have a chance now to end it all, a real chance."

They were in her stateroom, the one they had insisted on giving Padmé, the largest and most comfortable. She of course had tried to refuse. She could sleep in the cargo hold, or in a chair, she didn't care. They knew this was true, but something about Padmé made beings want to give to her.

He wanted to give her everything, but of course, she would not want it. Navigating his marriage with Padmé was like stumbling through a dark room sometimes, Anakin thought. He had believed on their wedding day that love would see them through any difficulty. What they felt was so huge that it would crash through every barrier.

He still believed that with all his heart. But he had not imagined, on the day of his wedding, that some of those barriers would lie within his wife herself. He did not think that he wouldn't be able to talk her out of putting herself in danger. He had secretly hoped that, in time, she would resign her Senate seat. As the wars went on, she would see how ridiculous it was to try to talk planets out of something that would bring them more power or more wealth.

Now he saw how naïve he'd been. She would never quit the Senate. She would keep talking about justice with the last breath in her body. She believed that words mattered.

He accepted that. He was even proud of her reputation as a sharp-tongued orator. In the Senate, held together somehow by the strength of Palpatine, she had made enemies. He feared for her. It was a nameless dread that sometimes could clutch him by the throat and drive the air from his lungs.

"We're not at Azure yet," he said. "And it won't be long before the Separatists come after us. Did you see how Magus targeted Taly? Now they know that Taly has contacted us, and that means he cannot be allowed to live. If he throws his knowledge on the side of the Republic, they'll do anything to stop him. His life is not safe until the Clone Wars are over."

"I didn't think of that," Padmé said. "Of course that is true."

"The Jedi must remain on Azure to ensure that the Republic experts can deploy the codebreaker. Then we must accompany the experts to another safe location. At least in the beginning, we're going to have to keep moving. That's why you must return immediately to Coruscant with Taly."

Her expression turned flinty. "That sounds like another order."

"No. It is a necessary step to protect you and Taly, and you know it. And it is a request," he said, softening his voice. He was relieved when he saw her slowly nod.

"All right."

"Padmé." He reached out for her hand. He needed the reassurance he felt when he touched her. "Your job lies in the Senate. My job lies is in the field. Until these wars are over, that is the way it must be."

"I hate these separations."

"No more than I."

"We chose this life," she said. "But it's so hard to live it."

"It's worth it, to know that you're mine. But if anything happened to you, I don't know how I could survive it. I can't . . . I can't lose you."

"I feel the same."

She stood, her cool fingers sliding out from between his. She began to pace. "But the secrecy is tearing me apart. I'm always afraid I'll betray us with a look or a word. Sometimes I wonder . . ."

"What?" he asked. If she hadn't been so agitated, she would have recognized the tone in his voice, a warning.

She whirled to face him. "Did we do the right thing? Not in loving each other — we couldn't help that — but in marrying? I've put a wedge between you and the Jedi."

"No, you haven't."

"But your first loyalty is to me," Padmé said. "That makes your path confused. I know enough about the Jedi to know how wrong that is."

"It is *they* who are wrong." Anakin insisted. "I am strong enough to do both, and they can't see it."

The comm unit crackled, and they sprang apart instinctively. They heard Obi-Wan's voice. "Anakin, are you there? Come to the cockpit immediately."

They hurried down the corridor into the cockpit. Taly was standing with the codebreaker. There was a mixture of awe and trepidation on Obi-Wan's face.

"It works," Obi-Wan said. "We've been listening to coded Separatist communications. It really works."

"There's too much space interference here," Taly said. "We have to get to the spaceport. Clearing devices can be used with it But we were able to hear something."

"What did you hear?" Anakin asked.

"They are moving ships and troops," Obi-Wan said. "A massive battle is planned. But we can't seem to pinpoint the location. Originally, it seemed to be planned for Nativum, which we suspected. But that changed to a new target recently."

"If we find out in time, we could score a great victory," Padmé said.

Obi-Wan nodded. "We could destroy most of their fleet."

Padmé gripped the console. "If General Grievous is with it, we could win the war," she said.

29

Azure was a tiny planet with no strategic importance. It was a blue dot in a vast expanse of space. It stood alone, not part of a system, and had no satellites. It boasted a spaceport that took up a good portion of its land. A convenient waystation for those traveling through the Mid-Rim, but not a draw in itself. It had no industry, no minerals, and no great wealth.

In other words, it had no reason to exist in the minds of the Separatists, and made a perfect secret base for the Republic, one of many in the galaxy.

They landed without incident. It seemed impossible that they had come so far, had made the journey without trouble. The crucial piece of equipment that could turn the tide of the war was now in Republic hands.

Taly handed it over to the tech experts with regret on his face. "It is my greatest invention," he said. "Now I must lead the life of a fugitive."

The cluster of tech experts hurriedly transported the codebreaker off to the command post. They were followed closely by General Solomahal. Recently promoted to the post, the Lutrillian could hardly contain his satisfaction at having the codebreaker arrive at his base. He had assured the Jedi that the name of Azure would live on in the chronicles of the war.

"This is the day the war will be won," he said, the large furrows in his head deepening.

Anakin didn't approve of such talk. The war had not been won yet. Even if they found out where the Separatist fleet was heading, it remained to be seen whether they could get enough Republic ships organized for a surprise attack.

Still, it was hard to concentrate on the matters at hand when Padmé was leaving. He had tried to contrive a way to say good-bye to her alone, but it would attract too much suspicion. They would have to bid farewell to each other in public. He hated that. She told him with her eyes that she hated it, too.

"Good-bye, Senator Amidala," Obi-Wan said, bowing. "Have a safe journey, and may the Force be with you."

He stood there, not moving, waiting for Anakin to say good-bye. Anakin swallowed his resentment. It wasn't his Master's fault that he did not give him privacy.

Anakin bowed. When he lifted his head, he told her with his gaze how much he would miss her. "Safe journey, Senator. I'm sure we'll meet again soon."

"I'm sure we shall." *Soon,* she mouthed to him.

"Taly, you have done a great service to the galaxy," Obi-Wan said.

"We are grateful," Siri said.

"I hope the war ends quickly," Taly said. "Even though it's good for business."

His eyes twinkled when he said it. Was he really as cynical as he appeared? Anakin didn't think so.

Under the cover of her robes, Padmé placed her hand in Anakin's, squeezed it for a moment, then dropped it. The touch was so quick that he barely had time to register it.

She had mentioned regrets. He had never had a chance to ask her what she meant. Now she was going and he didn't know when he'd see her again.

Padmé walked up the ramp of the cruiser. General Solomahal could not spare a pilot so Padmé would guide the ship to Coruscant, with a few clone troopers accompanying her for protection. She sat close to the windscreen so that she could see Anakin. She didn't lift a hand or smile but she kept her gaze on his as she fired the engines. Then the silver ship lifted and streaked into the sky.

Anakin kept his eyes on it. Was this his fate, he wondered, to know that something was his, but yet never be able to truly possess it?

He heard the stamp of boots behind him, but he didn't turn. He wanted to watch the silver ship.

"We have a problem," General Solomahal's voice boomed out.

Anakin turned reluctantly.

"There was a tracer imbedded in the codebreaker," General Solomahal said.

"Helina Dow," Siri said. "She must have put them in both prototypes."

"So the Separtists might know it's here on Azure," Obi-Wan said.

"I think that's a fair assumption," General Solomahal said. "The reason you could not pinpoint the site of the Separatist attack was because there was not yet a target. Not then. They were waiting to see where the codebreaker would end up." The General paused. "The target is here. The Separatist fleet is heading to Azure spaceport."

30

The Jedi rushed to the command center. Countermeasures had already been ordered. Every available ship in the Republic fleet was streaming toward Azure.

But they were hours away.

"How many battle cruisers do you have in the spaceport?" Anakin asked the general.

"Not enough," he said grimly. "A small fleet. Here." He called up the list on the datascreen. Anakin leaned over to study the specifications.

"Let's divide the fleet into two divisions," Anakin decided crisply. "Hold off the second for spaceport defense. I'll lead the first to try to draw off some of the Separatist fleet. Our strongest chance is to keep them busy until the bulk of the Republic ships arrive. I'll need your best pilots."

The general blinked his heavy-lidded eyes at Anakin, as if he needed time to process that a commander was giving orders to the general in charge. Luckily, General Solomahal was a practical sort, a soldier who did not care where the best tactical ideas came from, as long as they came.

"Lieutenant Banno," General Solomahal said, turning to a tall Bothan at his side. "Take Jedi Commander Skywalker to the fleet. He'll be in charge."

The lieutenant nodded. Anakin started away, but Obi-Wan put a hand on his arm. "Anakin, take care. May the Force be with you."

Anakin nodded, but Obi-Wan could see that his mind was already moving on to the battle ahead. They could have no better air commander than Anakin for this battle.

The lieutenant and Anakin hurried off. Obi-Wan and Siri turned to the large, circular monitor in the center of the command room. The Separatist fleet was close enough now to be tracked.

Obi-Wan could see instantly by the size of the fleet that the spaceport was extremely vulnerable. Siri frowned at the monitor.

"Here," she said, grabbing a laser pointer. "And here. That's where they are vulnerable. If Anakin can get to the rear —"

Obi-Wan nodded. "We don't have to defeat them. We just have to slow them down."

"They don't know that we have the codebreaker working, so it's possible they're expecting to launch a surprise attack," Siri said. "That could be an advantage for us. Do you see this small cloud nebula? If Anakin could get his ships to lurk there until the last possible second, when the fleet has already passed him . . ."

Obi-Wan was already pushing the comm button. He quickly gave Anakin the coordinates of the nebula. "Do you see it?"

"I've got it. There's quite a bit of atmospheric disturbance within it," Anakin said. "I might lose communication capability temporarily."

"We'll have to risk it. Then if you could manage to sneak down the side flank to the rear — that's where the big gunners are."

"Got it."

They watched as the blip that was Anakin's ship peel off, followed by the rest of the small fleet.

Obi-Wan turned to General Solomahal. "You'll have to time the countermeasure artillery attack to when Anakin attacks the rear. There will be confusion then. I'd try to hit the lead ship."

He nodded. His face was grim. "We will do our best, Commander."

"They are approaching the outer atmosphere of Azure airspace," Siri said. "There are some civilian ships heading into deep space . . ." Suddenly one blip flared and disappeared. "They're firing on civilian ships!"

A sinking feeling hit Obi-Wan. "Where are Padmé and Taly? Are they out of range?"

Siri went pale. "They're on the fleet's right flank."

Obi-Wan reached for his comlink, but suddenly Padmé's voice filled the air. "Come in, General. They're firing on us. . . . We can't hold the ship. . . ."

"Evacuate!" Obi-Wan shouted at her.

"Anakin!" Padmé shouted.

The blip that was Padmé's ship flared and disappeared.

"It's gone," Siri said. "Padmé's gone."

CHAPTER 31

"No," Obi-Wan said. "They got to an escape pod. Look." He pointed to the monitor. A tiny pulse was moving. It could have been space debris, but Obi-Wan knew it was Padmé. He could feel it.

"She's going to land outside the spaceport. We have to help them," Siri said.

"There are starfighters fueled and waiting in the hangar," the general said. "We still have the codebreaker working on communications. Keep your comm open and I'll feed you information."

They ran to the hangar and leaped into the two starfighters at the head of the line. Nearby pilots were rushing to their ships. Anakin had burst out of the nebula and hit the fleet in the rear with his small squadron. The battle had begun.

Obi-Wan and Siri took off, flying in formation.

"I've received a distress call from the planet's surface," General Solomahal said, giving them the coordinates. "It's out where the survival systems for the planet are based — the water conduits, the fuel tanks, the fusion generators. Watch your flank — the fleet is planning to turn at eighty degrees."

Obi-Wan and Siri executed a diving turn to avoid the fleet. Obi-Wan could hear the chatter of the pilots on the comm. Anakin was flying brilliantly, taking chances that the pilots could not quite believe and inspiring them to try similar feats.

By the end of the Clone Wars, he'll be a legend, Obi-Wan thought.

The air around the ship suddenly lit up. Obi-Wan felt the thud of cannonfire.

"On your left!" Siri shouted.

He turned and went into a screaming dive. Siri followed.

"Two starfighters have been ordered to break off and follow you," General Solomahal barked. "They are ordered to shoot you down." He quickly told Obi-Wan and Siri the angle of attack.

They were able to turn at the last minute and surprise their attackers. Laser cannonfire boomed, and the ships went into spiraling, smoking ruin.

Obi-Wan and Siri peeled off and continued toward their goal. From this angle, they were far enough away to get a clear look at the battle.

His heart sank. He believed in Anakin. He believed in the strength and will of the Republic pilots. But he knew the exact time it would take for the rest of the Republic fleet to arrive. The battle was already lost.

His heart heavy, he contacted General Solomahal. "General, I suggest you give the codebreaker to your best pilot and get it off the spaceport now. We have to risk it. We can't have the codebreaker fall into Separatist hands."

"Are you insane, General Kenobi?" The general's voice boomed out. "That's our only hedge against disaster!"

"I agree with Commander Kenobi," Siri said. "It's vital that the codebreaker remain safe. We can see clearly from up here. Ultimately, we cannot win this battle. I also suggest that you stand by to evacuate the base. We need to save as many Republic soldiers and ships as we can."

"It's a little early for surrender."

"I agree. There are still blows that can be struck. But it's inevitable," Obi-Wan said. "We need to cut our losses."

"You are too cautious, Commander Kenobi. I think we can win this."

"Commander, we can see things better up here," Siri said.

"I have a monitor here, too, Commander Tachi. And I don't have time for this argument. Save your Senator and your scientist and come back to fight."

Cannonfire blasted, and the controls shook in Obi-Wan's hands. He and Siri had blundered into the center of a battle between Republic starships and an attack ship they were peppering with fire and trying to disable. Obi-Wan saw cannonfire rip into his hull. Smoke poured from

Siri's fighter. Quickly, they zoomed up and around the battle. When they were through the worst of the fire, they returned to their course and dived down to the planet's surface. Obi-Wan heard his comm unit crackling. He must have sustained some damage to the circuitry when the ship was hit.

They saw the escape pod resting in an industrial area. Padmé had guided it to a safe landing between gigantic fuel tanks. Obi-Wan let out a low whistle as he landed gingerly next to her. It must have taken nerves of steel to navigate between those tanks. Escape pods weren't known for their maneuverability.

Siri landed close by and they hurried over to Padmé, who was holding a blaster rifle casually at her side. Her clone trooper escort must have landed elsewhere, but the pod had had enough room for Taly to join her.

"Happy to see you," she said, though her face betrayed her. She was disappointed, too. She'd been hoping for something, Obi-Wan thought. The answer sprang instantly to mind. *Anakin.*

"Anakin is in command of the air battle at the moment," he told her.

She smiled briefly. "How close is the Republic fleet?"

"Still hours away," Siri said.

"Even a codebreaker can't save this battle, can it?" Taly guessed shrewdly.

Obi-Wan decided not to answer the question. No matter what his doubts, he wouldn't want to voice them except to the commanding general.

But Padmé, too, was too shrewd not to see. She glanced up at the sky. "We should get the codebreaker off planet."

"Let's escort you and Taly to safety first," Siri said. "I think one of us should pilot you out of here."

"We can return to the command post," Padmé suggested.

Obi-Wan shook his head. "Not safe. We'll have to get you through enemy lines and to the nearest safe port." But which of them would do it? He looked over at Siri. They both wanted to stay to fight the battle, but she knew that it would be harder for him to leave his Padawan.

He felt the dark side surge then, a warning so clear he heard it like a shout. A starfighter was streaking toward them. Obi-Wan recognized the red-and-silver starfighter of Magus. He was surrounded by five droid tri-fighters.

"Take cover!" Obi-Wan yelled.

The laser cannons tore up the ground as they scattered.

"We can't hide behind fuel tanks," Siri said. "That's madness. We'll get blown up."

Magus came in for another assault. The fire hit the fuel tank, and it exploded in a whoosh that sent them flying through the air. The air was like a flaming wall that hit

Obi-Wan like an obstacle. He felt himself falling, and it was like falling through pure fire.

They landed, bruised and shaken, but unhurt. Magus and the tri-fighters zoomed out and turned, heading for another strike.

"I think it's time we got out of here," Obi-Wan said.

CHAPTER 32

Siri and Padmé were closest to Siri's ship. They began to run through the thick black smoke and burning fires. Obi-Wan grabbed Taly and hustled him toward his own ship.

This time Magus bypassed Siri and Padmé, coming straight for Taly.

Obi-Wan noticed that a worker had left his servotool kit close by. He reached out a hand — a fusioncutter flew through the air toward him. It was a large one with a big tank, built for special jobs. He grabbed it and timed his response. At the last possible second, he activated the fusioncutter and flung it directly into the spilled fuel. The fuel ignited and the flame shot up just as Magus dived to strafe them again.

Magus had to climb to avoid the fire, and the smoke was good cover. Obi-Wan and Taly leaped into the ARC 170 starfighter and took off after Siri.

"He's after you," Obi-Wan said.

"No kidding," Taly answered.

Siri flew closer and made a gesture, her hand at her throat. Obi-Wan did the same.

"What does that mean?"

"Our comm units are out," Obi-Wan said. "They were damaged. We're on our own."

"More good news."

Siri signaled. Obi-Wan nodded.

"You two speak the same language without even talking," Taly said. "Not much has changed. What's the plan?"

"We're going to try to get the two of you out of harm's way, then return for the end of the battle," Obi-Wan said.

"The end of the battle? Considering that you're going to lose, that doesn't sound like such a wise idea."

"I can't leave my Padawan. Hang on."

They zoomed upward. But Magus was on their tail with his five fighters, keeping up a steady barrage of firepower. The starship shook. Siri dived under Magus and shot, clipping him just a fraction. He zoomed off.

They played cat-and-mouse games. Every time they got ahead, he found them. Siri destroyed one of the trifighters, and Obi-Wan scored a direct hit on another. Then, working in tandem, they squeezed two between them and blasted them into space debris.

Magus must have contacted the Separatist fleet for help, for two large attack missiles suddenly peeled off from the battle above and began to descend.

"This doesn't look good," Taly said.

No. It wasn't good.

Obi-Wan raced his craft toward Siri. When he was in

her sightline, he indicated with his chin what he thought they should do. She nodded. He felt the connection surge between them. This was more than the Force. It was part of the Force, but it was part of them, part of the understanding that flashed between them so freely now. All barriers down, they had locked onto each other's every thought now.

They were over the deep trenches of the electrical conduits, where power flowed from the two gigantic fusion furnaces that supplied the energy to the spaceport. Siri dipped into the trench, and Obi-Wan followed. At least they were in a place where the large attack missiles could not follow. And if they were lucky, they could escape Magus in the maze.

The battle was lost. Anakin could see that. As much as he believed in his abilities, as much as he believed in the pilots around him, he could see that they were meeting an overwhelming force, and according to General Solomahal, Republic reenforcements were still an hour away.

At first he'd felt hopeful. The information the general was able to give the pilots gave them an edge they were able to exploit. They had taken down one starfighter after another and had managed to cripple a landing ship. But they could not fight this huge fleet.

He had lost track of Obi-Wan and Siri. But at least Padmé was safe.

"... status report," came over the comm. "Report in, Leader One."

His comm unit sounded fuzzy. Another thing going wrong. "Five more starfighters down, "Anakin said. "I'm trying to slow down the second landing ship. None of our ships lost on this end."

"Two of our defense starfighters down, plus the three civilian ships and the Republic cruiser . . ."

The interference made the words come in and out. "What?" Anakin barked. "What Republic cruiser?"

"Senator Amidala . . . Under fire . . . Distress . . ."

"Repeat," Anakin said desperately. "Repeat. Survivors?"

"No survivors . . ."

Anakin felt the galaxy collapse. He could not see or think or feel.

"Jedi went in search . . . Possible . . . escape pod sighting . . ."

Anakin went into a dive that nearly plastered him to the ceiling. He would find her. She would be alive. She had to be.

Obi-Wan wished that Anakin were flying this ship. He needed Anakin's nerves, his split-second timing, his instinctive knowledge of exactly how far to push a craft.

The attack ships hovered overhead. The last of the droid tri-fighters had crashed into a wall and flamed out.

But Magus was on their tails, keeping up steady fire. The trench was narrow, and opened wider and narrowed again. Huge pipes and conduits presented barriers that had to be snaked around or dived under.

Up ahead, Siri suddenly slowed her speed. He shot ahead but she didn't follow. She flew up, almost to the edge of the trench.

Siri, what are you doing? Whatever it is, Obi-Wan thought with a sudden, sharp pain, *don't do it!*

"Siri, don't do it," Padmé said. "There's still a chance —"

"*This* is our chance. Can you hold it steady?"

Padmé nodded.

"When I tell you to cut back, cut back."

"You'll fall —"

Siri grinned. "No, I won't. I'll jump."

"No —"

But Siri was already opening the hatch and climbing out. This was a model that had room for an astromech droid, if the pilot wanted. The space was empty. She felt the wind whip through her hair. She saw Obi-Wan's ship in the near distance. No doubt he was wondering what she was up to.

She knew this was crazy, but it just might work.

Magus dove through the last of a series of pipes. She could see the exact moment when he realized she'd cut her speed. He cut his, too, to avoid running into her. He didn't want to get ahead of her. That would make him vulnerable to her fire.

"Cut your speed!" Siri yelled, and she felt the ship slow and come close to stopping.

Magus shot underneath and slowed again, not wanting to get ahead of the Jedi ship. Summoning the Force, Siri leaped.

The starfighters had slowed, but they were still moving. Jumping from one to another was not easy. To say the least. Siri used the Force to slow her perception of time. She had never felt so in tune with it. She felt her body turning, but it was turning just as she wanted it to, not propelled by the speed of her descent or the turbulent air, but moving exactly so.

She hit the ship. Her knees buckled and her hands slapped against the top of the hull. The fall had knocked the wind out of her and for a moment all she could do was try to hold on. She clamped a cable from her belt to the ship.

He still didn't know she was there. She was light enough and he was moving fast enough, firing at Padmé now, who had immediately increased speed. He did not hear or feel her.

Time to let him know he had an extra passenger.

She activated her lightsaber and began to cut through the top of the starfighter.

It lurched violently to the left.

Siri grimaced as she held on with one hand.

Magus knew she was here.

Obi-Wan realized too late that this trench was a dead end. He should have taken one of the branches, but he was distracted at the sight of Siri on top of a starfighter. She had to be crazy. What she was doing was impossible. But she was doing it.

He would have to pull up in a few short minutes. The attack cruisers were waiting to blow him out of the sky. He would have to double back somehow. There was barely enough room to maneuver, let alone turn around.

Behind him, Magus was flying erratically, zooming from one edge of the trench to the other, trying to knock Siri off. Obi-Wan couldn't believe how she was managing to continue to cut through the ship's shell as she was slammed repeatedly against the metal.

He had to do something.

"Any ideas?" Taly asked.

"Yes. Hang on," Obi-Wan said as he flipped the ship upside down.

It was a maneuver he'd seen Anakin do, fly backward and upside down. *Though I wouldn't recommend it,* Anakin had said with a grin.

Obi-Wan headed straight for Magus. Padmé zoomed out of his way, then up out of the trench for a moment.

Evading fire, she managed to zoom past Magus and start back along the trench, marking time. *Good move, Padmé.*

Obi-Wan did some quick calculations. His fingers flew on the weapons-system control board. It was hard to fly at the same time.

"What are you doing?" Taly asked.

"Disarming a concussion missile by half."

"Let me do it." Taly worked over the keyboard, fingers flying. "Done."

Obi-Wan slowed his speed. He didn't want to get too close — he had to be far enough away, past the top end of the missile's range, so that he didn't severely damage the ship. All he needed was shock waves. That, and Siri's command of the Force to know what was coming before Magus did.

He fired. The concussion missile flew and exploded.

The shock wave jolted Siri, but she recovered quickly.

Magus went flying. Obi-Wan saw him bounce out of the seat. At that instant, Siri dropped through the hole she had created.

The ship was careening crazily now. Siri was fighting for control. Obi-Wan reversed again. He thought he saw a dark shape move across the cockpit.

"They're fighting," Taly said.

The ship listed to one side. It spun out of control and clipped a gigantic pipe. Smoke began to pour out of the exhausts.

"The hydraulics are failing," Taly said anxiously.

Obi-Wan began to follow the route of the dying ship. He pushed the engines, but he watched in horror as the ship crashed into the trench. Sparks as big as fireballs flew in the air as it bounced against one wall, then another, then smashed into the side and stopped. Something flew out of the hole on the top, bounced and lay still. Magus.

Obi-Wan screamed down to the trench bottom. He activated the cockpit cover and leaped out. Magus was unmoving but he wasn't dead. Obi-Wan scrambled on top of the cruiser and dropped inside.

Was it now, or was it twenty years ago?

She lay on the floor of the cockpit in a crashed ship. Her blond head was pillowed in her arms.

He landed on his knees by her side.

He touched her hair. He could not bear to touch the pulse on her neck. He could not bear not to feel life there.

"Siri."

"Blasterfire." She groaned as she turned slightly so she could look up at him. "Magus."

Obi-Wan glanced out of the cockpit window where Padmé now stood, holding the rifle at the unconscious Magus. She was taking no chances. Taly stood next to her, a blaster in his hand, also pointed at Magus. Obi-Wan could see something working in Taly's face, a temptation to fire. He had, at his feet, the being who had killed his parents.

Above, in the sky, he saw Anakin diving around the attack cruisers, pummeling them with fire.

"Padmé has him covered. We're safe for the moment."

"Everything is so gray."

"That was such a risky move," Obi-Wan said.

"It worked, didn't it?"

His relief at her sharp tone was erased when she winced, and he saw she was in great pain.

"I'll get the bacta . . ."

"Don't leave me." Siri's hand dropped on his. "I wanted to say —"

"Siri, I must get the med kit —"

"For star's sake, Obi-Wan, I'm dying. Do you have to interrupt me now?"

Tears sprang to his eyes. "You're not dying."

Her fingers plucked at her belt. "I can't . . . Get it for me."

Get what? he almost asked, but then he knew. He slipped her crystal out of her belt and pressed it into her hand.

"No . . . yours." She let it fall into his palm. "Now I will never leave you."

"You will never leave me," he repeated.

She touched his cheek, and her hand fell. "Don't worry so much," she said.

Her eyes closed, and she was gone.

He lay his head on the cockpit floor and held her hand. He did not know, at that moment, what living was for, if he had to carry this pain.

* * *

Anakin had been out of his mind with the frenzy to find her. He had attacked the ships again and again, determined to slip through.

When he saw that a ship had crashed, he had thought Padmé was dead, and his heart had become a fist.

Revenge was all he wanted.

And then as he swooped down he had seen her, blaster rifle in her hand, her face turned up toward him.

He held her to him only seconds later.

"I'm afraid for Siri," she whispered.

Obi-Wan climbed out of the ruined ship. He came toward them. Something in his face, his walk was different.

"She has joined the Force." He spoke the words to them, but he was looking down at Magus. The bounty hunter was beginning to stir. Taly gripped the blaster tighter. Anakin saw strain and anguish in his face.

He wants to shoot, Anakin thought.

For the first time since he'd known Obi-Wan Kenobi, Anakin was afraid for his Master. He saw the way he looked at Magus. His eyes were dead, as if now there was nothing at his feet, not a living being, just clothes and hair and skin.

Obi-Wan activated his lightsaber.

Padmé looked at Anakin, her eyes wide. *Say something,* her face pleaded. *Stop him.*

Anakin recognized that there was something here he could not stop.

Taly's breath caught. He did not take his eyes off Obi-Wan.

Obi-Wan crouched down and held the glowing light-saber to Magus's neck. He locked eyes with Magus. Anakin saw the flare of fear in the bounty hunter's eyes.

"You kill without thought or feeling," Obi-Wan said. "But I am not you."

He stood.

"Take him aboard," Obi-Wan said. "He is now a prisoner of war."

CHAPTER 33

The codebreaker was lost in the Battle of Azure Spaceport. The fusion furnace blew, an explosion that came close to leveling the spaceport itself. The smoke that rose served as cover for the evacuation of Republic ships. General Solomahal was captured with the codebreaker as he attempted to escape with it. He blew it up instead of handing it over. Two days later, he managed to escape and was given another command.

The Separatist forces bombed Taly's laboratory. All his notes and documents were lost. It could take him years to reinvent what he had discovered . . . if he could reproduce it at all. In the meantime, he was taken in secrecy and transported to a Republic outpost.

On Coruscant, Anakin and Padmé met before dawn in her apartment on her veranda. It was their favorite time to meet, under cover of darkness, but with the beginnings of morning freshness in the air. Even in the darkest of times, it made them feel hopeful.

"I am being sent away again," he told her. "Obi-Wan and I leave this morning."

"There is a vote I must attend this morning," Padmé said. "So we must say good-bye here."

"A vote is so important?"

"They are all important now. Senator Organa needs my support."

Anakin made an impatient gesture, but he did not want to fight. He was still struck with the horror of almost losing her. But he did not understand these Senate votes, useless during a time of war when only battles won mattered.

"I will wait for you to return," Padmé said. "I will wait as long as I must."

Anakin's eyes lifted to the Jedi Temple. What did they know, Yoda and Obi-Wan and Mace, of this? Of this moment of agony, being torn from his wife. He fought for them and alongside them, but they no longer had his heart. They no longer understood him.

He had thought for a moment on Azure that Obi-Wan had loved Siri. He thought he'd seen it in his Master's eyes after she had died. But Obi-Wan had stood over the man who had killed her and spared him. If he had loved Siri, could he have done that? Of course, it was what a Jedi should do. But the way Obi-Wan had spoken had been so measured. With a temperament like that, it was impossible to love, Anakin was sure.

With Padmé, he had passion, and he was whole. The stars began to disappear above, and a thin line of orange indicated the sun was beginning to rise. They would lose the cover of darkness. They would once again be Jedi and Senator.

He would once again be split in two.

For several nights now, Obi-Wan had not been able to sleep. He lay on his sleep couch. He closed his eyes. He hoped to dream. He could not.

So he walked. Through the Temple, the glow lights a faint blue. He did not seek the places that reminded him of Siri. He couldn't do that, not yet.

Oddly, he thought of Qui-Gon on these walks. He remembered, as he had not remembered in years, how he had known that Qui-Gon had walked the Temple halls at night. He had taken him *sapir* tea, he remembered. He had tried to comfort him, even though he knew there was no comfort for him.

If Anakin knew of his grief, he didn't mention it. He, too, had risen early — Obi-Wan had seen him heading toward the exit. Anakin had always been restless, had always needed to escape the Temple to think. Something was between him and Padmé. Obi-Wan would not ask. In some ways, he envied it. Let Anakin make his own decisions.

He found it extraordinary that at the time of this grief, when he had lost Siri forever, he did not question that their parting twenty years ago had been the right thing. He saw that clearly now, more clearly than he had ever seen it. Love was different from possession. He had loved her. That was enough.

. . . I live with the heartbreak of losing her. But I am living, Obi-Wan. I am continuing to walk the Jedi path.

This was what he had learned — the Jedi had kept him from her. But the Jedi had taught him how to live with losing her.

Obi-Wan stood by the window. The blues and grays outside were changing, warming to pink. Orange streaks lit the sky. The space lanes were beginning to fill up with flashes of silver. Another day. Another mission.

He was ready. He had learned something else, something important. Once he'd thought he had to lock away memories of love. Now he was no longer afraid of them. He could live with them. He could breathe in his sadness and remember his joy.

At last he had learned the secret that Qui-Gon had always tried to teach him. It had taken him years of loss to learn it. It had taken a death that had sent him to his knees. But he had finally learned it. He had learned to live with an open heart.

The Jedi legacy continues in an exclusive new story from
Jude Watson . . .

The Last One Standing

Sometimes he talked to him in his head. Arguments more furious than the ones they'd had. Talks in which he explained, Master to Padawan, why he'd done what he'd done. Simple words that managed to say everything he'd meant to say, only more clearly than he'd ever been able to say it. In these talks, Anakin listened and understood.

Of course, he was talking to a ghost. Anakin Skywalker was dead.

Obi-Wan Kenobi shut the door of his dwelling on Tatooine and drew his cloak up over his nose and mouth to block the blowing sand. He headed off across the empty dunes. The suns were just rising, but the air still held the night chill.

The galaxy was in the hands of a Sith. The Jedi had been completely destroyed. He would tell himself these things, but there were moments when it all still seemed impossible, even though he'd been in the middle of it. He had seen events firsthand and learned of others as if they were body blows.

Anakin was still alive in Obi-Wan's mind. Obi-Wan was engaged with him so intensely that he expected his apprentice to walk over one of those shifting sand dunes and grin at him again. Or scowl. He'd take anything. Any mood, any defiance. Just to see him again.

Every day and every night he violated every principle the Jedi had taught him about staying in the present moment, about acceptance. Going over every argument, every talk, to find the key that he should have turned in order to unlock the secrets of Anakin's heart.

Why had he turned to the dark side? When did it happen? The Anakin he knew and loved couldn't have done it. Something had twisted in him, and Palpatine had exploited it somehow. Obi-Wan knew it wouldn't change anything to know, but he couldn't help going over the same events, again and again. The chances he'd missed, the things he'd seen, the things he hadn't.

Obi-Wan reached the top of the dunes and began the hike down to the salt flats. He had grown used to land that constantly shifted under his feet. He had learned how to move forward even while the very ground he walked on fought his progress.

Anakin had always hated sand. It was one of the many things about his Padawan that Obi-Wan understood better now that Anakin was dead. That was the horror of losing someone: Understanding came too late.

As a boy, Anakin could walk through a storm of ice pellets so sharp they cut his skin. He could hike kilometer after kilometer in the blaze of three suns. He could plunge into a lake dotted with ice floes . . . but he would complain bitterly if he got sand in his boots.

Obi-Wan didn't like the sand, either, but he was grateful for the absence of color. He didn't find the planet beautiful, so at least he felt no loss when he traveled across the landscape. Once he had loved the vivid greens of forests, the deep blues of lakes and seas. Now everything blended into everything else, mesa, cliff, hill, road. There was no vegetation to refresh the eye, no sudden explosions of flowers to startle you into a fresh appreciation of living. He didn't want to appreciate anything. He wanted a place of no color, flat light, dark shadow. It suited him now.

Every sunrise and every dusk he went to the Lars homestead. They did not see him, or, if they did, they did not acknowledge him. He traveled the perimeter, making sure that all was well.

He had only one purpose now.

Luke was a baby in a straw bassinet, who laughed as Beru went about her chores with him strapped to her, nestled in a sling. It was hard to picture that happy baby growing up to be the new hope of the galaxy, but Obi-Wan knew he must trust Yoda.

He waited for Qui-Gon. Yoda had told him that his former Master had been as powerful, as attuned to the Force, as any they had known. Only more so. Qui-Gon now had the ability to transcend death. He had trained with the ancient Whills, and would train Obi-Wan.

But Qui-Gon hadn't spoken to him. There was only the sound of the wind.

Obi-Wan reached out to the Force to find him, but met only the thin stirring of a barren world. It was strange to live in a galaxy now that had no Jedi in it. He hadn't realized that he had once felt a humming presence, alive with the Force-ability of his fellow Jedi. It had fed him, and he hadn't even known it.

Obi-Wan climbed a cliff overlooking the Lars homestead. He knew the routine of Owen Lars, who would wait for first light to check the vaporators. Owen and Beru — Luke slung securely at her side — went out together, he to check the perimeter, she to gather the mushrooms that clung to the moisture that beaded on their exteriors. There was little fresh food on Tatooine, and mushrooms were highly prized.

Beru, of course, was perfectly capable of getting the mushrooms on her own, but Obi-Wan knew why Owen insisted on going with her. It had been on an early-morning mushroom hunt that Anakin's mother, Shmi Skywalker, had been taken by a band of Tusken Raiders. Taken and tortured, for a month. She had died in Anakin's arms. That was all he knew.

Obi-Wan lay flat, far enough away that even Owen's sharp eyes couldn't pick him out, but close enough that he could reach the family should a raiding party appear.

Despite the presence of a blaster rifle on Owen's shoulder, Obi-Wan took no chances with Tusken Raiders. They were tribes without mercy or scruples, who stole what they needed to survive and took pleasure in their brutality.

Obi-Wan sensed something was wrong before Owen did. He reached for the electrobinoculars hanging on his utility belt and raised them to his eyes. He scanned the expanse of sand and salt flats. Something was missing . . .

The vaporators. The electrobinoculars jerked as Obi-Wan searched, moving from one position to another and seeing only clots of sand and a set of snaking bantha tracks. The Tusken Raiders traveled in single file in order to confuse their trackers.

Owen and Beru stood, shoulder to shoulder, looking at the places where their vaporators should have been. The devices were what gave them water, enough to run the farm and enough to sell to keep on going. The loss was a huge blow.

Forsaking his promise not to interfere, Obi-Wan Force-leaped down from the bluff and trudged the last few meters to where Owen and Beru were standing.

He noted how Beru moved a bit closer to Owen and turned slightly, shielding the baby from Obi-Wan. It wasn't that she didn't trust him, exactly. He had delivered Luke to her, placed the baby in her arms. But perhaps the preciousness of that gift made it all the more likely to be taken away, in her mind.

"They're back again," Owen said. "It's them."

He would not speak their name, but Obi-Wan knew he meant the Sand People.

"How many vaporators did you lose?" Obi-Wan asked. His voice cracked like a dry riverbed. He hadn't spoken to anyone in months.

"Maybe twenty," Owen replied.

"Oh, Owen," Beru breathed. "What are we going to do?"

Owen squinted out into the distance. "Get them back."

"No," Beru said. "We'll let them go."

"We can't survive the year without them," Owen said. "Do you want us to starve?"

"We'll find a way," Beru said. "How can you think of going after Sand People, after what they did to your step-mother and your father? I can't lose you, too!"

Cliegg Lars had lost a leg in the attack meant to rescue Shmi. Obi-Wan knew that he had eventually died of his injuries, later, during the Clone Wars.

"What would you have me do, then?" Owen burst out. His frustration and anger rang in his voice, and Obi-Wan could hear the undertone of panic.

Beru hung on to his arm. "Just let it go," she pleaded. "They've probably already broken them down and sold the parts for scrap to the Jawas."

"And now I'm to buy back my own vaporators?" Owen's mouth was a thin line of determination. "I'll talk to the other farmers. They know that if one of us is hit, we are all in danger. I'll visit every farm today. We'll be off by first light tomorrow."

"You'll start a war."

"A war they began."

Obi-Wan saw the anguish on Beru's face. Despite his courage and resourcefulness, Owen was no match for the Raiders, and she knew it. The lessons Obi-Wan had learned from Qui-Gon flooded into him: how to connect to the Living Force, how to read what someone is feeling.

Look at their eyes, their hands, the way they stand. Listen to what they will not say. Feel the vibration in the Force and read it.

They were desperate and afraid. Young and untried. Cliegg was dead, and he had been the bulwark between them and the harshness of this life. They had not yet found their rhythm here without him. Beru came from three generations of moisture farmers. She knew this life and loved it. Owen had to be strong for her. He could not risk losing the farm. In his fury and resolve he would go too far.

"I can help you," Obi-Wan said.

"Meaning no disrespect, Ben," Owen said, "but I can take care of my own."

Beru slipped her hand into Owen's, and they walked off back toward the homestead.

And if Owen lost his life, Obi-Wan wondered, *what would happen to the baby?*

Yoda had given him no parameters. Just to protect the child. Make sure he grew to adulthood.

The Tusken Raiders couldn't have gone far. He had a day to act.

He would retrieve the vaporators himself.

Sand People were not easy to track. They moved in single file and used switchbacks, false turns, and seeming dead-ends to confuse any trackers. Even though he knew their tricks, Obi-Wan still had trouble following the trail. He kept losing it and having to double back.

It is not the Tusken Raiders that are preventing you. It is your own concentration.

That was what Qui-Gon would tell him, and he would be right.

Obi-Wan came to a canyon that was scored with a series of twisting dry riverbeds. While his eyes searched the ground for every sign of disturbed pebble or partially obliterated bantha hoof-print, part of his mind drifted to the past.

Anakin had done exactly this. He had successfully tracked the band of Raiders who had kidnapped his mother, even though Shmi had been held for so long. He had found her, but too late. He had brought her dead body back to the Lars homestead.

What else had he done there? Obi-Wan didn't know. He knew only from that day on, a shadow began to engulf

Anakin, something Obi-Wan couldn't penetrate. He had tried to talk to Anakin about it, but his Padawan had brushed off his questions. He realized now that Anakin had begun to confide in Padmé instead. They had married in secret, and the marriage had been part of the reason Obi-Wan had felt a divide between him and his Padawan. If Anakin had told him of the marriage, he would have understood. Not approved, but understood.

He had been tempted once, too. He had loved, too. If only Anakin had confided in him.

If only . . .

And why hadn't he? Because Obi-Wan had failed him. If he'd been a better Master, if he'd had more of Qui-Gon's kindness and wisdom . . . Anakin might have approached him, have felt free to say whatever he was thinking or feeling . . .

If . . .

They had flown together, wingtip to wingtip. They had relied on each other. He was more daring when Anakin was with him. Anakin had taught him how to take risks.

But in the end he had lost everything.

I hate you! Anakin had screamed at him on the volcanic slope. Writhing in pain on the black sand while the lava river burned behind them.

That was where Obi-Wan kept returning. That vision of hatred. Because no matter how Palpatine had corrupted Anakin, no matter how the dark side had taken him over, no matter what decisions he'd made in his heat and his fury, he was Obi-Wan's apprentice and he ended by hating his Master. And that was a Master's failing.

The landscape faded and Obi-Wan saw the black ash of Mustafar. He tasted ash in his mouth and fire in his lungs.

He had never expected, in all his missions, in all his wanderings, to taste the depth of this kind of failure, the agony of this grief.

He could see the moons rising. He knew he was close, but now it would be too dark to track. Obi-Wan stopped and looked up in frustration at the first star overhead. It was then that he heard it . . . a soft sound, a high sound . . . children calling.

He dropped to his knees and took shelter behind a rock. He could hear the children of the Sand People, called Uli-ah, running, sticks in their hands. They pretended the sticks were gaderffi, the poles the Tuskens used as weapons. One end a deadly spike dipped in venom, the other a spiked club. With guttural cries, the children used the rock he crouched behind as target practice. He could feel the shudder of the blows through the solid rock. He understood why the Sand People were such fierce fighters. They trained, from the time they could walk, how to kill.

Obi-Wan followed the Uli-ah at a distance and, after scrambling over a dune, he saw the camp. The urtya tents, made of animal skins and sticks, formed a circle. Off to one side, banthas were tethered to poles fashioned of scrap metal.

The Raiders were noted for their skills as sentries. They knew when someone was approaching their camp. No one knew whether it was their sense of smell, or their sight, or an ability to divine changes in the air currents, or some extrasensory ability. But a Jedi knew how to walk the world lightly, to move through air and on ground without leaving a trace. Obi-Wan was just another shadow in the dusk.

The smells and sounds of the preparation of the evening meal came to him. Good. They would be distracted. The Sand People weren't sociable, even amongst themselves. Each family retreated to their own tent. There they ate their meal and then retired.

He had learned about the Sand People shortly after he'd arrived. The men fought. The women kept the camp. They did not invite each other into family tents. Their need for concealment was close to a mania. If skin were exposed on a Tusken Raider, he would be banished or killed. So at this time they wouldn't be wandering. Families would be secluded.

Obi-Wan moved from shelter to shelter, treading lightly. If the vaporators were still intact, he hoped he would be lucky and they would be out in the open and unguarded.

But he was not lucky. He spied a sentry in front of one of the tents.

He pressed himself against the skin of the tent and

activated his lightsaber. He felt the hum in his hand, the familiar heft. He sliced through the back and stepped through.

Spoils from raids littered the tent, bundles of cloth, metal, a droid half-dismantled for parts. The vaporators were stacked in the middle of the tent. Obi-Wan let out a slow breath. They hadn't been dismantled. He was in luck.

He didn't want to fight a battle. He wanted only to get the vaporators out of here. But he needed a bantha to carry them. The thing about banthas was, you couldn't count on them to keep their mouths shut.

He'd have to take the chance.

The banthas were tethered twenty meters away. Slipping through the shadows, he approached them. He watched them for a moment, letting the Force work. He picked out a bantha and put a hand on its flank. He felt it shudder, then relax. He dipped into his pocket for the lichen he had picked on the way and fed the beast.

Then he led it back, closer to the tent. He should be able to load all the vaporators on one beast. Luckily banthas were capable of carrying heavy burdens.

Boldness. That's what Anakin would encourage.

Moving swiftly, Obi-Wan transported the vaporators, four at a time, into the satchels that were slung over the bantha's back. He did not make a sound. The bantha stayed quiet as he fed him more bits of lichen from his pocket.

He was almost done when the Force warned him,

surging an alarm. Behind him the gaderffi moved, the spiked club end headed for his skull. Obi-Wan leaped to one side, his lightsaber activated and in his hand. He struck the gaffi stick and turned it into splinters of smoking horn and metal. The Tusken Raider let out a howl of fury and challenge.

The cry was picked up by others.

The men ran out of their tents. Obi-Wan spun in a slow circle. They raised their gaderffi above their heads, crying the terrible howl that could freeze the blood in anyone unlucky enough to be within its hearing.

He could read their confidence in their identical stances. They didn't need to hurry. It was one lone figure against many. They had him. They would enjoy this.

Then with astonishing speed, they came at him. The gaffi sticks whirled. He jumped and twisted, his lightsaber coming down again and again, whirling in an arc of light. He flipped, his boots connecting with a Raider, who went over with a strangled cry of rage. As he went down, Obi-Wan grabbed the gaffi stick.

He was more than they had bargained for, but they weren't daunted. He could smell their bloodlust. He was only enraging them.

Obi-Wan's fighting style had always been about evasion and disguise. His most successful battles were based on his ability to deflect attack and surprise his opponent. He rarely depended on brute strength to achieve victory.

Anakin had taught him about aggression.

He knew this was what the Tusken Raiders would understand. They understood necessity; they lived by it. They did not farm or make things or buy things. They attacked and they stole, and they survived.

Time slowed down. He looked into their faces, obscured by their intentionally terrifying headgear. Round dark holes for eyes, mouths composed of metal shards around a gaping gash. Not a speck of skin or flesh to be seen. That would soften them too much, make them look like living beings, connect them, somehow, to the life-forms around them. They wanted to be distinct. They wanted to look like walking death.

Loathing choked him. The Sand People made nothing and gave back nothing. They merely preyed on the weak. The moisture farmers, who worked backbreaking days, were attacked on raids that often resulted in death and complete destruction. Stealing the vaporators from Owen and Beru's farm would bring on terrible hardship.

They had tortured Anakin's mother for a month. Just to test her resolve. Was it any wonder that Anakin had been left with such a deep, festering wound?

He could do this for Anakin. His Padawan was dead, his brother, his son, his friend. He could give him this. A fearsome anger unleashed. Vengeance. Vengeance against the beings in the world with so much darkness inside them that life meant nothing to them. They swallowed life and hope. That was what the Sith counted on, beings like these.

They had taken over the galaxy. They had won.

But not here. Not today.

He stopped. His stillness intrigued them. He held his lightsaber in a way that any Jedi would recognize as the beginning of aggression. He had no hesitation, no doubt that he could vanquish them all, destroy this camp and destroy every breath of life in it.

He felt his anger rise, and he took pleasure in it. It was growing inside him and obliterating everything else. He wanted to be overtaken. He didn't want to be careful. He wanted only the white heat of satisfaction.

Do not become your enemy.

Qui-Gon was like static in his brain. He didn't want to hear it. He didn't want to remember him right now.

But the memory was too strong.

Qui-Gon's compassion had been infinite. His Master had been impatient, to be sure. He could be brusque. But his connection to the Living Force had never faltered. He did not take away life if there was an alternative.

The alternative.

What had Qui-Gon always said? *If you know their weakness, you can defeat your enemy. Expose them for what they are.*

The anger was still there, but he turned his face away from it. He reached out for what he knew and treasured — the Force. It was here, even in this place of darkness, of grasping evil. He soared above the heads of the Tusken

Raiders, enraging them. They swiped at him with their gaderffi, missing him by a centimeter of grace.

He called on the Force and it moved around him, propelling him over the tents. As he flew over their tops, he slashed down with his lightsaber, one, two, three times, then landed and leaped again. The tents collapsed in a gust and a clatter of sticks.

Women and children blinked. Some of the women weren't wearing their face masks or their gloves. They shrieked and clawed at the sand, trying to bury themselves. Some threw tarps over their children. They moaned and howled with the shame of their unmasking.

Obi-Wan landed. He took advantage of the stunned reaction of the men. Using the gaderffi stick he'd pried from the hands of a Tusken Raider, he charged forward, slashing at utility belts and face masks. In his hands the stick became as elegantly precise as a med droid's scalpel. Sandshrouds peeled back, skulls were exposed, fingers, limbs.

They couldn't fight now. Their centuries of rules and rituals defeated their need to strike. Exposure meant death. The men ran to their tents to protect their women, to find cover.

Obi-Wan knew he was now more than an opponent who dared to invade the camp. He'd become something supernatural, a wraith that had blown away the concealment they prized, fiercer than any wind. He had no doubt the news of this would spread among the tribes. Perhaps it would buy him a mystique that would offer him a degree of protection. They'd be wary of him now.

He leaped onto the bantha and urged it into a gallop, the cries of the exposed echoing in his ears.

He brought Lars and Beru the vaporators that night.

He wasn't expecting anything, but the coolness of Owen's response did surprise him. His face was stony as he looked at the vaporators. Beru hung back. He could see the battle of emotions on her face from the light of the open homestead door. She was relieved that Owen would not have to fight, but she didn't want to owe Ben Kenobi a favor.

"I told you to stay out of it," Owen said.

"It was something I could do," Obi-Wan answered.

"It's not that we're not grateful," Beru said. "It's that . . ."

"We can take care of our own farm," Lars completed. "We're a family here."

They stood close together, Luke between them, nestled against Beru's body. Obi-Wan saw with sudden clarity the baby's fingers, small and perfect. His mouth opened and he gave a baby sound, something like a whimper, a sound Obi-Wan didn't know how to interpret. The Living Force was one thing. Babies were quite another.

Beru extended a finger, and Luke grasped it, making, this time, a sound Obi-Wan recognized as contentment.

"I'll be going," Obi-Wan said.

Stiffly, Owen Lars inclined his head. "Thank you," he said gruffly.

Obi-Wan turned his back on the open door. He climbed out of the homestead and trudged away. The sand sucked at his boots. He felt the wind pick up in the sudden way he'd become accustomed to on Tatooine.

Sand pelted his cheeks. This was his life now. To protect a baby who didn't know him, might never know him. To have no one by his side, ever again. To be Master to none, to have his life linked to no one.

To coexist with memories that he could not live with. To have the memory of Anakin be like living fire in his gut.

To get up every day, to stand, to watch, to live, when so many had died.

And keep on walking.

Between the End and the Beginning
There Is an Untold Epic

STAR WARS
THE LAST OF THE JEDI

After the events of Episode III, Obi-Wan Kenobi is alone in the galaxy, concealed from the Empire—and he must protect the Skywalker twins at all costs. Follow the Jedi adventure you won't read or see anywhere else!

The *New York Times* Bestselling Author **JUDE WATSON**

IN STORES NOW!

Coming December 2005!
Star Wars: The Last of the Jedi #3: Underworld

SCHOLASTIC

www.starwars.com

LUCAS BOOKS

Michael Deno